FIRST AMERICAN EDITION

FIRST PUBLISHED IN 1985. ORIGINATED BY J. M. DENT AND SONS LTD,
LONDON.

LIBRARY OF CONGRESS CATALOG CARD NUMBER 85-071645

ISBN 0-87113-048-3

PRINTED IN PORTUGAL

JAM

A TRUE STORY

MARGARET MAHY

ILLUSTRATED BY HELEN CRAIG

The Atlantic Monthly Press
Boston   New York

Mr. and Mrs. Castle lived in a white house with a big, green lawn. Their three children were called Clement, Clarissa, and Carlo.

"Three little Castles," said Mr. Castle, "but very small ones—more like Cottages, really."

Mrs. Castle was studying to be an atomic scientist.

"What a clever one *she* is," said Mr. Castle. "If she decided to go to the moon I don't think she'd even need a rocket to get there."

One day Mrs. Castle announced that she had
found herself a job. Important scientists were devel-
oping an electronic medicine to cure sunspots, and
they had sent for Mrs. Castle.

"But who is going to look after us?" asked Clement.

"Isn't anyone going to be here when we come home from school?" asked Clarissa. Carlo was too young to say anything, but he looked worried.

"*I* shall be here, my dear little Cottages," Mr. Castle cried. "You have no reason to be anxious."

He washed and dried
the dishes.

He swept the house from top
to bottom.

He vacuumed the carpets, put the
dough to rise in a warm place

wiped down the counter, had
a quick cup of tea.

planted a row of cabbages,
folded the wash, baked
the bread *and* a cake…

put Carlo down for his
afternoon sleep…

had another cup of tea...

cleaned the bath...

prepared dinner...

read the paper...

kissed the children when they came home from school—and
Mrs. Castle when she came home from work—and asked them
all what sort of day they had had.

Then he gave Mrs. Castle something to drink, handed her the paper, and took the children out for a game on the big, green lawn. He was an excellent housefather.

Indeed, he was so good that one day he actually ran out of work. While he tried to think of just what to do next, there came a soft thud on the roof, and then another one.

"Sunspots!" cried Mr. Castle, and ran outside. It was not the sound of falling sunspots he had heard, but ripe plums tumbling off the old plum tree that grew behind the house.

Mr. Castle was delighted. Gathering up the fallen plums he made three pots of plum jam.

"Jam! What a treat!" the children cried.

The next day many more plums fell from the tree and Mr. Castle made twenty pots of plum jam.

The following day the ground under the tree was
covered with big, purple plums. That day Mr. Castle
had enough plums to make thirty pots of jam.

But the day after that there were even more plums. Mr. Castle had run out of jam jars.

"What a challenge!" he cried. "Not a single plum must be wasted."

He filled all the vases in the house with jam. He filled all the glasses, too. Even Carlo's rabbit mug and the teapot were filled with jam.

"The whole house is like a jam factory," said Clement.

"It's like a school for jam pots," said Clarissa.

"Your father is a born artist," said Mrs. Castle. "He is the Picasso of jam makers."

"Now all the work is done," said Mr. Castle, looking pleased. "We can look forward to eating this delicious jam all year long."

They began with jam sandwiches. Mrs. Castle, Clement, and Clarissa had jam sandwiches in the lunches Mr. Castle prepared for them every morning. Carlo, who was cutting new teeth, had jam on his crusts.

"Hooray!" called Mr. Castle. "We've emptied the teapot already. We'll be able to have tea with our cakes, cookies, and tarts."

That winter the roof leaked a little. Mr. Castle's
jam proved very useful, for as well as being delicious, it stopped leaks. When the tiles came off the
bathroom floor, Mr. Castle stuck them down again
with jam. After weeks of devoted jam eating they
could put flowers in the vases again, and drink from
glasses instead of from eggcups.

"I wouldn't really care if I never saw another pot
of jam in my life," Clarissa whispered to Clement.
"But don't tell Daddy I said so."

In the meantime they had jam with everything, and on everything, and under everything. Their dreams became haunted with jam. Clement dreamed that the sky opened and jam rained down on him. Clarissa dreamed of fat, shadowy jam pots marching through the night, crying out a terrible war cry of "Jam! Jam! Jam!"

Mrs. Castle dreamed that it was proved that sunspots were caused by too much jam, and Carlo dreamed great jammy dreams as well. Their days were full of jam eating, and their nights of dreams all dripping with jam.

Finally, one morning Mr. Castle went to the cupboard to get down the next pot of jam only to find it was empty. There was not a single potful left.

"Let's have egg sandwiches for lunch," said Mrs. Castle.

"Let's have fish and chips," suggested Clement.

"Spaghetti and salad," cried Clarissa.

!

"But first let's have a game on the lawn," said Mr. Castle. "We've eaten so much jam that we look like jam pots ourselves. We shall have to get back in shape."

While they were playing on the lawn, Mr. Castle heard a soft thud on the roof.

The plums were ripe again.

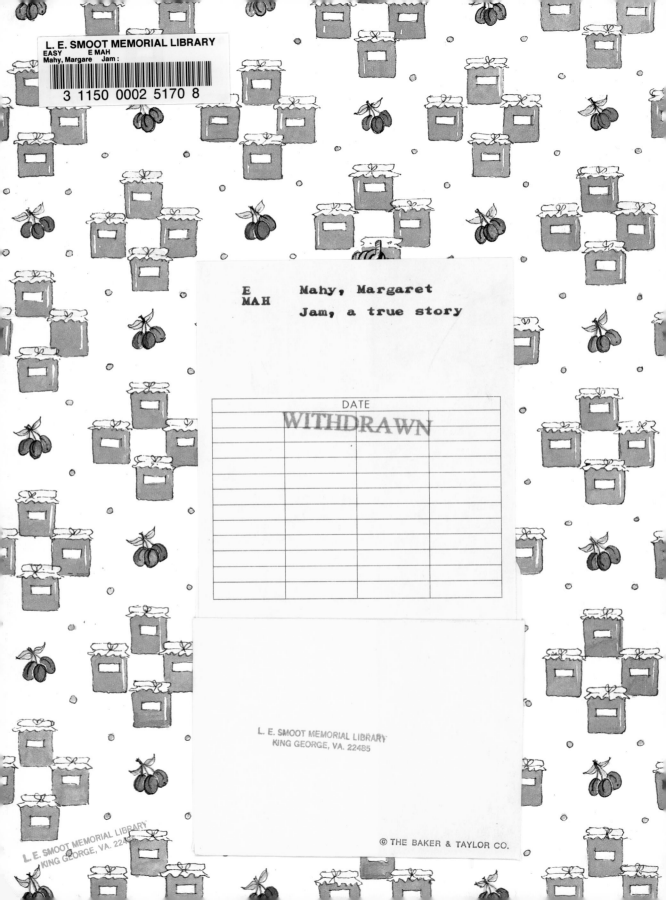

E
MAH

Mahy, Margaret

Jam, a true story

DATE

WITHDRAWN

© THE BAKER & TAYLOR CO.

South Wind Come

Also by Tina Juárez

Call No Man Master

South Wind Come

Tina Juárez

Arte Público Press
Houston, Texas
1998

This volume is made possible through grants from the National Endowment for the Arts (a federal agency), Andrew W. Mellon Foundation, and the City of Houston through The Cultural Arts Council of Houston, Harris County.

Recovering the past, creating the future

Arte Público Press
University of Houston
Houston, Texas 77204-2174

Cover design by James F. Brisson
Cover art: Detail from *Valley of Mexico, 1875*,
by Jose María Velasco

Juárez, Tina.
    South wind come / by Tina Juárez.
    p.   cm.

    ISBN 1-55885-231-X (alk. paper)
    1. United States— History — Civil War, 1861-1865—Fiction.
2. Mexico — History — European intervention, 1861-1867 — Fiction.
I. Title.
PS3560.U25S68   1998
813'.54—dc21   98-10312
                                                                      CIP

♾ The paper used in this publication meets the requirements of the American National Standard for Information Sciences—Permanence of Paper for Printed Library Materials, ANSI Z39.48-1984.

8 9 0 1 2 3 4 5 6 7   10 9 8 7 6 5 4 3 2 1

To Margarita and Louise

I

My mother's anger could have been avoided if I had told her of our plans before the president lowered Esteban and me into the cold and murky waters of the Buffalo Bayou. I could have explained to her that Sam Houston, the first President of the Republic of Texas, was going to initiate my little brother and me into the Exalted Order of the River Styx by immersing us in the bayou. I could have tried to make her understand there was no cause for alarm. The ceremony would be early in the morning before President Houston had had an opportunity to drink very many spirits. He would not let us drown. Moreover, as a precaution, Esau and Tom Blue, the president's slaves, were to be present to keep a lookout for alligators and cottonmouth water moccasins.

I could have told my mother all these things, but I did not. It would have only added to her worry. Though it had been over a year since my father had died of yellow jack in the epidemic that swept Houston Town and Galveston during the summer of 1836, my mother was still in mourning. She had never stopped grieving and usually did not come out of her room except late at night after everyone had gone to sleep. There were days when Esteban and I did not even see our mother or hear her voice except for the soft weeping behind the closed door in our grandparents' house. Nevertheless, we should have told her what we were planning. I should have told her. Even though I was only seven years old at the time, I was two year's older than Esteban and was responsible for his safety. My mother had impressed the obligation on me time and again since we had come to Texas.

"Teresa," she said, "you must guard your brother's life as though it were your own. No harm must ever come to Esteban in this godless place. Do you understand?"

I would never allow anything that would cause harm to Esteban, but I knew very well my mother did not share my trust for the man who had defeated General Antonio Lopez de Santa Anna at San Jacinto and made possible the existence of Texas as a nation independent of the land of our birth. If I had disclosed to my mother what we were doing, she would not have allowed it; which, if truth be told, is the real reason I did not tell her about the Exalted Order of the River Styx.

From the perspective of the many years that have passed since that day, I can understand how my mother must have felt when, unexpectedly, she appeared on the rise above where we were conducting our ceremony on the west bank of the bayou. I can only imagine what she thought when she witnessed that long-legged giant of a man, his auburn hair whipping in the wind, grasp her naked babies by the ankles and lower them headfirst into what was to her a dirty, mosquito-infested swamp filled with alligators, gars, snakes, eels and all sorts of dangerous creatures.

Whatever my mother saw, or thought she saw, was a far different thing from what I imagined was happening, which was nothing less than a solemn and sacred ceremony that would make my brother and me forever unconquerable by mere mortal beings. It would make us exactly like the man whose big and powerful hands, hands that had ended the life of more than one evil-doer, held our small ankles firmly but with tenderness and affection.

Since the day Sam Houston had first read to us from his whiskey-stained copy of Alexander Pope's translation of *The Iliad,* I had been unable to think of little else than the account of how the mighty Greek warrior Achilles could not so much as be scratched by an opponent because his goddess mother, Thetis, had dipped him as an infant into the River Styx in order to render his body invincible to any blows directed at him by the weapons of men. I wanted to be the same as Achilles and so did Esteban. My brother usually wanted what I wanted. Even as a baby, Esteban had always been extremely intelligent.

"We must go and swim in this River Styx," I had announced upon hearing the story of Thetis and Achilles. "We must go there at once, Kalanu!"

Sam Houston had acquired many titles and names in his forty-three years of life, and he liked to be called by different ones, depending on the occasion and his mood. I always called him "Kalanu," because he said it was the war title his Cherokee brothers had given him when he lived with them as a boy. It had been a happy time in his life, and I knew the name gave him good memories and caused him not to want to drink quite so many spirits. Vice President Lamar, who hated the president, said Kalanu was Cherokee for "drunken turkey buzzard," but it was not. Kalanu meant "Raven" and was the name given to Sam Houston by the Cherokees because a raven is a bird of wisdom and courage.

In answer to my suggestion we swim in the River Styx, Kalanu had explained: "It was Achilles' mama who dipped him down into that river, Teresita. Thetis was a goddess. It might just take one of them goddesses to make it work the way it's supposed to. I expect it's all a right tricky thing."

My response had been automatic: "You can do it, Kalanu! You're like a goddess. You're invincible!"

And why would I not have made such a proclamation? Samuel Pablo Houston, the name he had used upon swearing his undying allegiance to the Republic of Mexico and the Roman Catholic faith not so many years before, was invincible. At the Battle of Horseshoe Bend in 1813 he had saved the day by personally leading General Jackson's army up a hill to take on the entire Creek Nation. Andrew Jackson himself had said that all would have been lost if Sam Houston, out front and in the center, had not led the men straight into the heart of the main body of Creek warriors who had let loose at the approaching army with every arrow, lance, knife and tomahawk they had.

Though his magnificent body was shot full of arrows and he was bathed in his own blood, Sam Houston remained on his feet, turned the tide of battle and made possible General Jackson's victory over the Creeks and later the British at New Orleans. Andrew Jackson probably would not be President of the United States and live in the big White House in Washington City at that very moment if Sam Houston had not laughed at death and led the army to victory. I knew for a fact all this was true, because I had heard it from Kalanu's own mouth many times.

Sam Houston had smiled when I told him I knew he could do for Esteban and me what Thetis had done for Achilles. I knew from the sparkle in his mischievous grey eyes he appreciated the observation, even as he pointed out that Thetis was a woman and he was a man. It was not long before he had invented the wonderful idea for the Exalted Order of the River Styx. We would have our own exclusive society, complete with secret rituals and ceremonies. It would be great fun, and no one enjoyed great fun more than Sam Houston.

And so, after much planning and preparation, we had made our way to the bayou on the day of the initiation. We had selected a quiet spot down a piece from Houston Town, because we wanted our rites to be conducted without the interruptions of the many people who might be looking for the president in the government offices or saloons. The

Republic's capital, named after and with the approval of its first elected president, was less than two years old; but with each passing day, it was becoming a more bustling place because thousands of people were coming to Texas to secure cheap land and make their fortune. The noise from axes, saws and hammers was non-stop, from dawn to dusk, as wood-frame buildings went up to replace the rows of tents lining both sides of the mud-clogged streets.

After Esteban and I removed our sandals and stripped off our white cotton pants and shirts, Kalanu held us by our ankles over the water and intoned: "I, Sam Houston, President of the Republic of Texas, do induct Teresa Maria de Jesus Sestos y Abrantes and her gigglin' and squirmin' little brother, Esteban Cristobal Sestos y Abrantes, into the Grand and Exalted Order of the River Styx. Close your eyes and hold your noses, chil'run!"

Down we went into the dark currents where I opened my eyes thinking I might catch a glimpse of mighty Poseidon, come to welcome us into the realm of immortality. We were quickly lifted out of the water where I saw that Esau and Tom Blue had entered the bayou and stood waist-deep beneath the bank where Kalanu had bent down to dunk us. The two slaves were there to make sure that if we were dropped, they would snatch us up before an undertow might sweep us out into Galveston Bay and perhaps even into the Gulf of Mexico.

But we were not dropped. Sam Houston got to his feet and lifted our gleaming bodies, dripping with water, to the sky, as if presenting us for the gods' approval. Grinning broadly, he stood there in his black velvet suit, the crimson of his satin vest matching in color the bands around the top of his knee-high black boots. It was what I had requested he wear on this occasion, my favorite outfit from among the dozens of costumes that filled one whole room of the log cabin that served as the Republic's Presidential Mansion. Tom Blue, whose principal duty was "Keeper of the President's Wardrobe," had done a splendid job in cleaning off all the mud and liquor stains that always seemed to befoul Sam Houston's magnificent clothes.

It was at this exact moment I heard my mother's ear-piercing cry: "My babies! What is he doing to my babies?"

As she came running down the hill while shouting in Spanish for someone to help her save her babies, Sam Houston, dumbfounded, unable to fathom why my mother was so distraught, continued to hold us aloft even as I whispered, "Kalanu, put us down. Hurry, put us down!"

Finally, he lowered us into the waiting arms of Esau and Tom Blue who wrapped us each in brightly colored blankets that had been given to the president by Chief Bowles upon the signing of the treaty that had established the eternal territorial rights of the Cherokee Nation within the boundaries of Texas. I had requested the blankets be used as our ceremonial robes in the induction. Esau and Tom Blue proceeded to vigorously rub our heads and, because we both wore our hair cut short, we were almost dry by the time my mother reached us, sank to her knees and clasped us to her bosom.

"Cata Valeria," the president asked, "what's wrong?"

In the confusion, Kalanu had apparently forgotten my mother spoke no English; and she did not remember his Spanish was very limited because she shouted, "Why are you trying to kill my babies? Have you not killed enough Mexicans? Now you must drown our children?"

Though I was being held very tightly, I managed to look into my mother's face and see the tears flowing from her eyes. My mother had blue eyes and golden red hair, the same as Esteban's. I had my father's dark hair and dark eyes, and there were times I wished I had blue eyes and golden hair because everyone made such a fuss about my mother's beauty.

The president looked at me and pleaded, "Teresa, what is she saying? Why is your mama so angry?"

What had happened was about the worst thing that could have happened; and I was embarrassed, especially when I noticed people were running from the edge of town to see what all the shouting was about. We were not far from the Round Tent, one of the more than fifty saloons in Houston Town; and the gamblers and professional loafers were coming outside to investigate. When they saw the commotion involved Sam Houston, they shouted for everyone to come have a look-see at what The General was up to now. Most men called Sam Houston "The General" because he had been the General-in-Chief of Texas' Regular Army during the revolution.

"Teresita," Kalanu asked, "didn't you tell your mama what we were going to do? You didn't tell her about the Exalted Order of the River Styx?"

I could not lie to Sam Houston. Everyone, friend and foe alike, acknowledged the President of the Republic of Texas was without peer in the art of lying; and he would surely catch me if I tried to take advantage of the fact he and my mother did not understand what the other was saying. I confessed, "I did not tell her, Kalanu."

"I did not tell her either, Old Chief!" Esteban volunteered, using his favorite name for Sam Houston. A big grin on his cherubic face, Esteban was enjoying the whole show and did not mind a bit the blanket had slipped from his shoulders and he was standing naked in front of a growing crowd of onlookers, which now included Mrs. Foley and the students she taught in her Latin Grammar School.

"Oh, Teresita," Kalanu groaned. "Poor Cata Valeria. What must she think of me?"

Between sobs, my mother continued to voice exceedingly harsh words about Kalanu. She used words I had never heard, and I took pride in my fluency in both Spanish and English, something none of Mrs. Foley's students could boast.

While my mother continued to say bad things, Esau brought our clothes and helped us slip into them. Esau's kind expression never changed. Nothing Sam Houston did surprised him, because he had been the slave of the man he called "The Governor" since Kalanu had served as the Chief Magistrate of Tennessee. The fringe of grey around Esau's balding dome contrasted with his dark complexion. Esau looked quite distinguished, as he should, for he occupied the most important position in the Mansion: "Keeper of the President's Libations."

After I had pulled on my pants, I looked toward the ever increasing crowd of people who had gathered around us and I could see Mrs. Foley's disapproving frown. She never tired of saying that Tejanos were immoral, and she seemed to think this opinion was confirmed by the fact my family, as did most Tejano families, regularly bathed nude in the river. I never saw her at the river or take a bath of any kind, with or without clothes; and we were the ones she would call "dirty Mexicans."

In a way, it had been Mrs. Foley who was responsible for our induction ceremony in the first place. When she had advertised she was going to open a Latin Grammar School, my grandmother had gone to her with the intention of enrolling me. Mrs. Foley refused, saying, "I'll allow no idol-worshippin' papists in my school! I would sooner teach niggers!"

The last thing in the world I wanted was to be in a school run by the wife of Judge Foley, the closest friend and advisor to Vice President Lamar. I had no need to go to her school or any school at all for that matter. But when Sam Houston heard about what had happened, he announced, "I'll open a school! And I'll teach all the chil'run. All of 'em!"

Of course, he could not teach all the children, because among the first laws passed by the congress of the new republic was one forbidding the teaching of reading or writing to negroes, free or slave. The President had opposed this law, but it was part of a compromise which made it possible for free negroes to continue living in Texas. Vice President Lamar and Judge Foley had wanted to enslave all free negroes, even those who had fought in the revolution such as Lebe Seru, the partner of my grandfather and the Montemayors in their freight-hauling business.

Kalanu said the first job for which he received money in Tennessee had been as a schoolmaster; but after becoming a lawyer, he had gone downhill from there, especially when he served in the United States Congress and then as governor of the state. He had saved all the books he loved as a boy, such as *Robinson Crusoe* and *The Iliad*; and we learned to read from those books a lot faster than Mrs. Foley's pupils, because our teacher not only read to us, he acted out the stories and even had Tom Blue make us costumes so we could act right along with him.

Now fully dressed, I managed to wiggle free of my mother's grasp and step back. I suppose my mother might have shouted all morning if Juan Seguin, the senator from San Antonio, had not come forward to console her and try to explain what had happened. Senator Seguin was one of the president's best friends. Many times, Sam Houston said he would never have been able to defeat General Santa Anna without Juan Seguin and his gallant Tejanos, who fought like wildcats.

My grandmother said the Tejanos had fought so well because they had been battling Santa Anna a lot longer than the Texians, which is what the people who had come from the United States in recent years to live in Texas were called. My grandmother had herself been a soldier many years ago when the Tejanos battled Spanish armies which were trying to prevent Mexico from gaining its independence.

While waiting for Senator Sequin's gentle words to calm my mother, I noticed Kalanu was staring into the crowd of people around us. When I saw that the president's face had hardened into his Old Chief expression, I knew even before I looked who I would see. Tracing the gaze of those smoldering eyes, I spotted Vice President Lamar and Judge Foley.

The expression the president had fixed on the vice president was one he had learned from Andrew Jackson. Kalanu said President Jackson had used the expression on Senator John C. Calhoun, who was Mirabeau Lamar's mentor, when he had threatened to lead South Carolina out of the Union. One look from Andrew Jackson's stern eye, Sam Houston said, would exterminate a man where he stood and leave not a smudge to mark the spot.

Kalanu understood I knew what he was doing because when I again looked at him, he made a little wink with his left eye. With that wink, he was saying in silence what he had said out loud many times before: "Watch me make that little toadfrog run to the privy house and drop his pants." He used to use a word other than toadfrog to describe Mirabeau Lamar until my grandmother told him I was too young to hear that kind of language. And she also told him it was unkind to make fun of the fact the vice president suffered from an intestinal disorder. She agreed Lamar was a toadfrog, but she did not think we should make fun of him and the president should not try to make him so nervous he had to run to the privy house.

We both knew why Lamar had come down from the Hall of Congress to join the crowd of people gawking at us. Lamar, along with Judge Foley, was always trying to discover new things to tell people that would make them think the President was unstable. They never tired of telling stories of Sam Houston's past such as the time Congressman Houston shot a man in a duel; or the time in Washington City he beat up another congressman so badly with his cane the House of Representatives had him arrested and brought before them for a trial, something that had never happened before or since.

These stories were supposed to make the President of Texas seem to be of unsavory character, but most folks would laugh when Sam Houston responded to queries about these events by saying something like: "I still got my duelin' pistols, and I still got my cane; and I sure as hell ain't fergitted how Old Hickory taught me how to use 'em, 'pecially on a damn fool nullifier like John Cur Calhoun who thinks he's gonna defy Andy Jackson and break up our glorious Union!" The people of Texas loved it when Sam Houston talked funny.

Lamar and his followers did not want Texas to join the United States, something Sam Houston was working very hard to accomplish. Men like Lamar wanted to take more of Mexico's territory and build an empire which could be joined by southern states after they seceded from the United States, which now prohibited the trade in African slaves.

Sam Houston made certain the trade of slaves from Africa was forbidden by law in Texas. Even though most Texians had great respect for their president, more and more were listening to Lamar because owning slaves was the quickest way of building a great fortune in cotton farming. Reopening the trade in African slaves would make slaves affordable to Texians, most of whom did not have a lot of money.

More men were also listening to Lamar when he criticized the president for his treaties that set aside territories in the Texas Republic for Indian Nations, such as the Cherokees. Some of the territories were as large as states in the United States, and Lamar said the land should be sold to men of the Anglo-Saxon race to be used as farms and plantations. He said Sam Houston turned against his own people because he had lived with the Cherokees and one of his former wives had been a Cherokee whom he had married even before he had been divorced from his first wife.

Lamar and Foley spread bad stories about Sam Houston in hopes the people of Texas would elect Lamar President of the Republic in the next election. Therefore, Kalanu and I both understood why Lamar and Foley had joined the many people who had come down to the west bank of the bayou. Lamar stood slightly behind Foley as if trying to hide from the president's steady gaze. He and Foley both wore short-tailed frock coats and the strapped-pantaloons that the wealthy men wore even in the sultry summers of the Texas gulf coast.

Senator Seguin had almost convinced my mother to stop crying when, suddenly, Mrs. Foley shouted, "This is a disgrace! The President of the Republic of Texas dippin' two naked Mexican children in the water. Inebriation is no excuse this time. Something must be done! It is a disgrace to the Republic!"

Both the vice president and the judge nodded their heads in agreement with Mrs. Foley's words, but neither man would look directly at the president, who continued to contort his face into the meanest Old Chief expression I'd ever seen.

No longer crying, my mother stared at Mrs. Foley. Though she did not understand the meaning of the words spoken by the school mistress, she understood the hostility this woman had for our family. It made no difference to Mrs. Foley that my mother's father was an Anglo. It did not matter that my grandfather had fought Santa Anna.

Gathering my brother into her arms, my mother got to her feet. If it were my mother's intention to return to my grandparent's house at that moment, I do not think she could have gotten through the crowd which now surrounded us and stood quietly waiting to hear what was going to be said next. Most were men, rough men wearing coats made from blankets or animal skins; but there were also a number of ladies dressed in ankle-length calico dresses and carrying parasols to ward off the sun.

Judge Foley stepped apart from the crowd and said, "Is it not peculiar that we so frequently find Houston with this woman and her children? This woman was the wife of one of Santa Anna's officers. Is this why we do nothing while Mexican armies approach our borders and Mexican warships prey on our merchant vessels?"

What Judge Foley was saying was true as far as it went. My father had been an officer in Santa Anna's army; but after my mother had come to Texas and discovered her parents, from whom she had been separated since birth, my father left Santa Anna's army and made our home in Texas.

The truth about my father was of no interest to Foley who, seeing he had the attention of the crowd, continued, "Maybe this woman is the reason Sam Houston refused to go to the assistance of our brave men at the Alamo who were slaughtered by the Mexicans. We defeated the Mexicans at San Jacinto and yet they still live among us. Why do—"

"Señor Foley," Senator Seguin interrupted. "Forgive me, Señor Foley, but what you are saying is not accurate. We did not defeat the Mexicans, as you say. We defeated Antonio Lopez de Santa Anna because he had illegally seized the government of Mexico and annulled the Constitution of 1824."

For a moment, no one said anything and the only sounds were the hissing noises of the steamers plowing their way down the bayou toward the port of Galveston. A short distance upstream were the wharfs where the steamers were loaded. I knew that was where my grandfather and Lebe Seru would be with our wagons, waiting to unload bales of cotton onto the steamers. I was beginning to wish they were where we were. Some of the men in the crowd did not look friendly. Many did little all day except drink spirits and talk about how Sam Houston was making it difficult for them to get free land and slaves.

Judge Foley said, "Santa Anna and his men killed our men at the Alamo. He killed them all, even the prisoners! Do you deny that, Seguin?"

"I do not deny it, Señor Foley. I know it all too well, because many of the men killed at the Alamo were friends of mine that I had known since I was a boy, and some were my relatives."

Suddenly, the president stepped toward Lamar, and I thought he was going to speak in support of what Juan Seguin had said; but apparently, he had not been listening to what anyone had been saying, because he drew himself up to his full height to tower over the vice president, and shouted, "Good morning to you, Excellency! By God, good morning to you, sir!"

Lamar seemed to shrink in size. With great effort he managed to tear his gaze from the ground and glance up at the president. He growled, "I do not say good morning to scoundrels, sir!"

Grinning, Sam Houston raised his head, looked at the crowd and yelled, "I do!"

Immediately, there was an eruption of laughter from the crowd of men around us. The president, roaring with laughter, almost fell over when he brought his left knee up and slapped it hard with the palm of his right hand. More peals of laughter merged into the general uproar as the slower thinkers finally caught on to what a good one their president had put over on the pompous vice president. Texians loved to see the high-and-mighty brought down a notch. Suddenly, the vice president clutched his hand to his lower abdomen and began to shove his way through the crowd, many of whom were doubled over in laughter.

"Make way!" the President of the Republic intoned. "Make way for His Diminutive Excellency, Mirabeau Buonaparte Lamar, Vice President of the Republic of Texas, who must needs get to the Privy Chambers! Make way, make way!"

I thought everything that had happened was grand and was surprised when Senator Seguin did not seem to share mine and my brother's merriment. He took my mother's arm and escorted her in the direction of the road leading to my grandparents' house. My mother, too, had failed to see the humor in what the president had done. Clasping Esteban in her arms, she was about halfway up the rise overlooking the bayou when she remembered to look back and call, "Come, Teresa."

"Yes, Mama," I replied but held back until she and the senator disappeared over the hill.

A crowd of men pushed as close as they could to Sam Houston, patting him on the back and trying to outdo each other in telling how The

General had once again made Mirabeau Buonaparte Lamar look like a jackass.

While waiting for the commotion to die down, I looked up at Esau who smiled at me and felt to see if my hair was dry. Tom Blue, holding the president's blue velvet cape and his dueling pistols and gold-headed cane, gazed out across the bayou at the steady line of steamers making their way toward Galveston with their heavy cargoes of cotton.

After promising to join the men later for a celebration at the Round Tent, Sam Houston stepped to where we were standing and extended his hand. I grasped the long fingers and held on as he swung me up to a perch on his shoulder.

"I'm hungry!" the president announced. "Let's let Esau go cook us up a big batch of hoecakes for breakfast, Teresita. Would you like that?"

"Hoecakes and cottonseed honey! Do we have plenty of cottonseed honey?"

"We gots lotsa cottonseed, honey! C'mon, Esau and Tom Blue. Make haste! The newest member of the Exhausted Order of the River Styx is one hungry chile!"

That day, as I rode on my perch, seven feet off the ground, I knew we had been playacting and having fun when my brother and I were inducted into the Exalted Order of the River Styx. Still, I had no doubt that I was now exactly like the mighty Achilles. Sam Houston was not a goddess, but he was my Thetis. He would never allow anyone to harm me. I knew that as long as we were together, I would be protected.

II

When I look back to those early years of the Republic of Texas, it is sometimes hard to distinguish if the events I recall are my memories or if they are the memories of my grandmother, Carmen Owens. Esteban was only a baby in my mother's arms when we accompanied my father to the cabin where General Santa Anna was held prisoner after the battle of San Jacinto. As a favor to my grandparents, Sam Houston personally escorted the defeated leader to a place near a giant oak tree to hear my father's petition that he and his family be allowed to return to Mexico. I stood next to my grandmother as she translated Sam Houston's directives to Santa Anna and then related a request the General wanted to make of his captors.

At that time, I was only beginning to learn my first words in either Spanish or English, and so it is unlikely that my knowledge of what was spoken at that meeting is the result of my memory. However, because my grandmother in later years told me what was said on that day, I can relate what transpired and who said what to whom. I know that Santa Anna's request was for opium pills to settle his nerves. Most Texians were clamoring to hang the man who had ordered the execution of all prisoners taken at the Alamo and at Goliad. Many Tejanos agreed with this punishment not only because of what he had done in Texas, but because Santa Anna had ordered the execution of prisoners in Yucatan, Sonora, Zacatecas and many other places where the citizens of Mexico had been unsuccessful in their defense of the Constitution of 1824.

I do not remember Santa Anna's asking for the opium pills or, for that matter, anything he said; but I do recall that Sam Houston wrapped one of his own Cherokee blankets around the Mexican President when he shook from the cold and, probably, his fear that he was going to be hung by the neck. Santa Anna had large expressive eyes, and I remember the enormous relief in those eyes when my grandmother translated to him Sam Houston's decision to send him to Washington City where President Jackson had agreed to negotiate the terms for Mexico's recognition of Texas as an independent nation.

The fact is it would have been much better for my family, and for all Tejanos, if the Texians' demand that Santa Anna be executed had been carried out. In Washington City Santa Anna told Andrew Jackson he accepted the independence of Texas; but as soon as he returned to Mexico, he repudiated all promises and agreements he had made with both Andrew Jackson and Sam Houston. He issued an order that any Tejano who had fought against him was to be considered a traitor and would be executed if caught. Therefore, my family could not return to Mexico; and Tejanos were no longer able to travel to the land which continued to claim Texas as part of its territory.

The details and significance of all of these events were explained to me by my grandmother. Even as a little girl, it was difficult for me to think of Carmen Owens as my grandmother, my abuela. She was, of course, my mother's mother and, therefore, she was my grandmother; but she did not look like a grandmother. The grandmothers of other children my age had white hair, and they did not move about very quickly. Perhaps it was because she had been but sixteen years old when my mother was born that Carmen seemed young to me. Her face was wind-burnt but unwrinkled, and her hair was as dark as the night, the same as mine; she always wore riding boots, leather breeches and unbleached cotton shirts. Few grandmothers I knew dressed this way or could fire a Pennsylvania long-rifle with the authority of Carmen Owens.

My inability to think of Carmen as a grandmother was also due to the stories she told Esteban and me of when she was young. My grandmother had been a soldier and had fought in battles when she and my grandfather were a part of the army that followed Father Miguel Hidalgo after he had proclaimed against the corrupt government of the Spanish Viceroy in 1810. I never tired of hearing of the stories of those days and how Carmen had met my grandfather, Coalter Owens, when he had traveled to New Spain to seek permission to establish a colony of norteamericanos in Texas. They had fallen in love only to be parted in battle, each going their separate way while thinking the other had been killed, and Coalter never knowing that Carmen was pregnant.

Shortly after my mother's birth, Carmen had been forced to leave her baby with her father in Guanajuato and flee to Texas where she joined the Tejanos who were fighting the Spanish and, after independence, the Mexican generals who did not believe in liberty and equality. It was in Texas that Carmen discovered Coalter was not dead; and when Santa Anna invaded Texas, my grandparents were surprised to encounter their daughter and to learn they had a granddaughter and a grandson.

After hearing the story of Carmen's youth, I could not think of her as a grandmother. She was a warrior goddess like Athena, who sprang from Zeus's head fully armed and ready for battle. It was not long after my initiation into the Exalted Order of the River Styx that I explained to Carmen why I had decided that from now on I would call her "Athena" rather than "Abuela."

She looked at me in the peculiar way she sometimes did, and her gaze drifted to the jade pendant suspended around my neck by a leather cord. The stone had been carved to depict the head of the Mexican goddess, Chimalma, and had once belonged to Carmen's mother.

Finally, she said, "Your mother is right, Teresa. You are spending much too much time with Houston and his books."

It was never clear to me whether Carmen liked Sam Houston or not. Kalanu was often at my grandparents' house. He and my grandfather and Lebe Seru were friends; but I do not recall my grandmother's ever referring to the president by anything except his last name, which I thought was disrespectful. After all, he was the President of Texas.

"You said that Esteban and I could learn many good things in Kalanu's books," I reminded her. "We are learning to read and to write. Kalanu will teach us many things, Athena."

"If he does not kill you first." She glanced toward the closed door of my mother's room. "Cata Valeria was very upset with what happened at the bayou. She does not want for you and Esteban to visit Houston ever again."

"Nothing bad happened, Athena. I explained to you what occurred at the bayou."

"Nevertheless, Houston should be more careful. You and Esteban are very young and—"

"You should not call him 'Houston,'" I interrupted. "It is disrespectful, Athena."

"It is his name, Teresa. What else should I call him?"

"You could call him 'Kalanu.' That is what I call him."

"Is that not the Cherokee word for 'Big Drunk?'"

It was hard to always know what Carmen was thinking since she did not often change her expression. She seldom laughed and never cried, but I had begun to realize she derived pleasure from making me a little angry.

"Kalanu does not mean 'Big Drunk.' As you well know, Athena, Kalanu is the Cherokee word for 'raven.' It would be a good name for you to call him, and he would like it."

Carmen pretended to think very hard. "Why don't I call him De Dos Caras?"

"De Dos Caras?" I asked, suspecting a trick. "Why would you call him Two Faces?"

"Because Houston finds it easy to say one thing to one group of people and a different thing to another group." She tilted her head at my puzzlement. "For instance, when he was campaigning for the office of president of the republic, he told the Texians he was able to defeat Santa Anna because Mexicans are a cowardly people. A few weeks later, he told voters in San Antonio he would never have defeated Santa Anna without the brave Tejanos. De Dos Caras. It is a good name. That is what I shall call Houston."

"Abuela," I said, "please do not prevent Esteban and me from going to visit Kalanu."

"I am no longer Athena?" she asked as I put my arms around her thin waist. "I become Abuela when you want something. We shall see about Houston, Teresa. Let's wait a few days until your mother is not so angry, and then we shall see."

More than a few days passed without my seeing Sam Houston. My mother instructed me each morning not to take Esteban to see him, even though my brother begged her exactly as I had coached him. However, it was not my mother who was the main reason I did not visit the President. I could always contrive a way to get my grandfather to take me along with him when he went to the wharfs to receive goods he and his partners imported to sell in San Antonio. Sam Houston spent a lot of time at the wharfs because he enjoyed seeing what new products were coming into Texas each day. I would often go with my grandfather and sit with the president as he whittled sticks and greeted the many new people from all over the world who had come to do business in his Republic.

And so although we could have gone to see Kalanu, we did not because I knew he was busy trying to arrange for the annexation of Texas to the United States. His minister to the United States, William Wharton, was in Houston Town; and he had to be instructed what to do since the United States Congress had voted against annexing Texas. This had been a disappointment to both President Houston and President Jackson. Many

Congressmen in the United States said they did not want Texas in the Union because Texas allowed slavery and also because annexation would mean war between the United States and Mexico.

It had been many weeks since I had seen Kalanu when Tom Blue came to our house one night after we had gone to bed and pounded on the door. As soon as my grandfather raised a beeswax candle to light Tom Blue's anxious face, I knew something terrible had happened to the president.

Tom Blue was out of breath from running. "Esau says for you all to come as fast as you can!" he gasped. "He says bring blankets, a long rope and a mule."

"What's happened, Tom Blue?" I asked before either of my grandparents or Lebe Seru could say a word. We were the only ones home, except for my mother and Esteban. Lebe Seru's son, Binu Seru, and his granddaughter, Alma, had gone to San Antonio with a train of wagons filled with products for the Montemayors. "Is Kalanu hurt? Did he fall in a hole again? Did he—"

"Teresita," my grandfather interrupted, "calm yourself, little one. Let Tom Blue speak."

Tom Blue explained that Esau had sent him because the president was stranded on a sandbar that was submerging under the incoming tide. He said Esau asked that we not tell anyone in town because this was another one of the kind of incidents Sam Houston would not want people to know about.

We followed Tom Blue to the shoreline a considerable distance from town, where Esau was waiting beside a bonfire he had built to provide light to see across the thirty yard channel to the sandbar which was now under the choppy water. Only after our eyes adjusted to the orange glow of the firelight could we see the president hip-deep in the still surging tide.

"What's he doing out there, Esau?" Coalter yelled in order to be heard above the roar of the surf. "How did he get out there?"

"The governor received some bad news tonight, Coalter. He came out here, took off his clothes and swam out to that sandbar. He said he wanted to die at sea. He's very drunk."

My grandfather's dark hair, which normally hung to his shoulders, was whipped in all directions by the stout wind. He cupped his hands to shield his eyes from the gusts that carried bits of fine sand. "We've got to do something fast. When the tide gets just a little higher, it's going to take him off that bar and the current will carry him into the bay. There are strong undertows around the sandbars when the tide's coming in."

Esau shouted, "That's why Tom Blue and I couldn't swim out there. We're going to have to try to throw him a rope and pull him across with your mule."

Coalter turned his ear toward the bay. "Is that him yelling? What's he saying?"

We all strained to listen to the faint voice over the churning waves.

"He's calling for Talahina!" Tom Blue yelled.

"Talahina?" Carmen asked, holding Coalter's arm for support against the wind. "That's his second wife's name, isn't it?"

"Yes," Esau answered. "Talahina is dead. That's the news he received tonight. A messenger from the Cherokee Nation was sent to tell him. She died of malaria."

My heart ached for poor Kalanu as I watched him bobble up and down in the water like a cork. He had never spoken with anything but kindness for the Cherokee woman he had left behind in the Arkansas territory when he came to Texas. I knew he loved her. He told me he did.

Lebe Seru waded as far out in the current as he dared with the rope he had attached at one end with a short length of plank. If anyone could fling a rope to Kalanu it would be this tall and dignified man, who had been taken as a child from his home in Africa by slavers. Though old enough to be my grandparent's father, Lebe Seru was still very strong.

After several unsuccessful tries, Lebe Seru did get the plank to land near the president, but Kalanu made no attempt to grab it before it and the rope were rapidly swept away by the current. He did nothing except call out his dead wife's name in a mournful tone.

"Grab the rope, Governor!" Esau pleaded as he paced back and forth over the frothy seaweed at the shoreline. "Grab it and tie it around you!"

"It won't work," Lebe Seru concluded. "Even if he were to take the rope, I don't think he is in any condition to hold on when we pull him to us. If he goes under where the water is deep, the undertow will take him."

"I could swim out to him and tie the rope around him," my grandfather suggested.

"No, Coalter," Carmen said. "The current is too strong!"

We convinced my grandmother that it was the only way to save Sam Houston's life. After going up the shoreline some fifty yards, Coalter waded out until he was chest deep and then plunged into the current which swept him along as he swam toward the sandbar. Grasping the rope, Lebe Seru and Esau waded out as far as they could while Tom Blue and I helped Carmen steady the mule.

Coalter was a strong man and a good swimmer, which enabled him to navigate across the channel before the current pushed him beyond the sandbar. We all watched as he found his feet and approached Kalanu, who continued to shout Talahina's name. My grandfather attempted to secure the rope around the president, who flailed his arms wildly.

"Governor!" Esau yelled. "Don't fight him!"

Finally, Coalter gave the signal for us to pull, and he wrapped himself around Kalanu to secure him to the rope.

Gripping the bit, Tom Blue urged the mule on, and we watched as both men disappeared under the water.

"Oh, no!" Carmen screamed. "The undertow's got them. Coalter!"

"Pull!" Lebe Seru commanded. "Hurry!"

It seemed an eternity before we began to make some headway against the powerful force of the undertow. Finally, we pulled them free of the current. I raced to the shallows and tried to lend a hand as Lebe Seru and Esau helped Coalter drag Kalanu to the sand and lay him down next to the fire.

Kneeling over the president, Esau shouted, "He's not breathing!"

On his hands and knees, wheezing for breath, Coalter looked up. "He must have gotten water in his lungs. I told him to hold his breath."

Quickly, Lebe Seru rolled Kalanu over onto his stomach, straddled the huge frame and used his hands to push down on the president's back. He let up and pushed down again, repeating this action until, finally, Kalanu coughed and gasped for breath. He then heaved the salt water he had swallowed.

"Sit him up!" Esau said.

It took all three men to raise Kalanu to a sitting position while I stood with Carmen and Tom Blue. In the light of the fire I could see the powerful body, and I was astounded. It was not that I had never seen a naked man before; but I had never seen Sam Houston's body, and it was marked with scars where he had been wounded in battle. In the glow of the firelight, I could see the ugly purple ridges where hot lead had entered his flesh and physicians had made cuts to dig it out. These ridges were all over his body.

I stepped to Kalanu and tried to push back the strands of his hair that had matted over his face. He turned his head to look at me, but I could tell from his unfocused eyes he did not recognize who I was. Slowly, he raised his right hand and gently took my hand in his.

"Talahina," he whispered hoarsely. "I'm sorry, Talahina. Please forgive me. I am sorry."

Esau looked up at my grandmother. "I don't think I'll be able to manage him at the mansion. He's got too much whiskey stored away there."

Carmen sighed. "Bring him to our house."

It was two days before Kalanu was able to take food. I, of course, was as delighted as my mother was appalled that the President of the Republic of Texas was now sleeping in the upstairs bedroom next to mine. I had often suggested he live at our house all the time. It was far superior to the Presidential Mansion, which had clarified rawhide over the windows in place of glass and leaked water when it rained.

Ours was the biggest house in all of Houston Town. It had been built under Lebe Seru's supervision. With little more than an axe and an awl, he had fashioned perfect plankwood from the pine logs we had hauled from the forests northeast of town. We had walnut wood floors and a roof made from cypress shingles the Montemayors had sent from the hill country north of San Antonio.

Coalter wanted us to remember the house was as much Lebe Seru and his son and granddaughter's house as ours, even though the house and the land had to be registered in my grandfather's name since free negroes had no more right to own property than slaves. I was proud of our house. Most houses in Houston Town were usually two cabins separated by a dog trot and had packed earth floors and canvas roofs. We had an upstairs balcony where we could get up high in the sea breezes that cooled us and blew away the mosquitoes. As far as I was concerned, Kalanu could run the government from our house.

It was soon evident, however, that Sam Houston was in no mood to run the government of the Republic of Texas from our house or from any other place. His attorney general, Peter Grayson, came by several times with urgent papers; but the president had Esau turn him away. Though Mr. Grayson told Esau to explain that Vice President Lamar might try to take control of the government, Kalanu did not seem to care. He had lost the will to live since learning of the death of Talahina.

Kalanu did not even dress himself in the clothes Tom Blue brought from the Mansion but continued to wrap himself in Cherokee blankets even when he went down to sit in the flower garden and talk with Carmen. One afternoon, he was in a very dark mood, and my grandmother sent me away; but I lingered nearby and pretended to work in the vegetable garden so I could hear what they were saying.

"You have got to stop drinking spirits," Carmen said. "Look at you, Houston. Your hands are trembling and your legs wobble when you walk."

"That's because I haven't had any spirits in four days," Kalanu said. He was squatting on the ground, his bare legs crossed, Indian style. "If I had a little whiskey, I'd be all right. Just a bottle. A little bottle."

"If you don't stop drinking whiskey, Houston, you are going to die."

In order to hear a little better, I moved from the carrot patch to where the bean vines were strung. It was Alma's garden, and I had promised to take care of it while she was in San Antonio with her father. Lebe Seru's only grandchild had planted yellow squashes, tomatoes, turnips, a half dozen different kinds of greens, potatoes and yams. Alma was three years older than me. She said she loved me like a sister, except when I let the chickens and goats, which were my responsibility, get into her garden and eat her plants.

"I don't care if I die," Kalanu said. "I deserve to die."

"Why, Houston?" my grandmother asked. "Why do you deserve to die?"

"Because I ran off and left Talahina in Arkansas. I abandoned her. I should have brought her with me to Texas. Better yet, I should have stayed with her. I was happy with Talahina, and I loved her. I should have stayed with her, but I couldn't do that. I had to come do what they wanted me to do here in Texas. I had to do it. That was more important than Talahina."

"What they wanted you to do? Who is they? What are you talking about, Houston?"

"Taking Texas away from Santa Anna. President Jackson wanted me to do it. He said I was the only one who could do it." His eyes narrowed. "And by God, I did it. I took Texas away from Santa Anna. I did what the Old Chief asked me to do."

Carmen put her hands on her hips. "Well, you didn't do it by yourself! Many of us were fighting Santa Anna long before you came to Texas, Houston. We fought him here in Texas, and we fought him in Mexico.

There are many who are still fighting Santa Anna. Santiago Montemayor's son is in Yucatan fighting today. What happened in Texas was only a part of a much larger struggle that Miguel Hidalgo began over thirty years ago in Dolores."

"I know that, Carmen."

"Do you?"

"Yes."

"Well, maybe you need to tell the Texians. Since San Jacinto, many of the people coming from the United States think that what happened in Texas was a matter of the Anglos defeating Mexicans. That's what Lamar tells them. You need to speak up and tell them the truth, Houston. Men like Juan Seguin are being called traitors to Texas simply because he is a Tejano. Nobody fought Santa Anna harder than Juan Seguin. Not Sam Houston. Not anyone!"

"I know, Carmen. I've said it."

My grandmother was very angry now. "And I can tell you what else you need to tell the people coming from the United States. You need to tell them we did not fight Santa Anna to make Texas a slave state. You tell them that, Houston. We did not fight Santa Anna to make Texas a slave state in the United States!"

I had always been proud that my grandmother had been a soldier; but now, for the first time, I think I began to understand why she had been a soldier. There were certain things that she believed, and she was willing to fight for these things.

Carmen stalked back to the house. The president looked so forlorn sitting on the ground all alone. I walked over to him and considered what I might say to make him feel better.

"Kalanu," I said. "Some people came to town last night. Mrs. Foley's sister and her husband came in a wagon, and there were two men with them. I saw them arrive just before sundown."

"It doesn't matter, Teresita. Nothing matters. I've lost everything that was important to me. I don't care who comes to Texas. The devil can come for all I care."

"These new people are from South Carolina, Kalanu. I listened from my hiding place behind the Foleys' groggery. They were talking about Lamar. Judge Foley said Lamar would come visit them today and tell them what he wants them to do."

His right eyebrow arched. "South Carolina?"

"John Cur Calhoun's state," I reminded him. "I could go over there and listen when Lamar comes to see them. I could find out what they're planning."

He slapped at mosquitoes swarming around his bare legs. "It would be too dangerous, Teresita. They might see you."

"They never have, Kalanu. You taught me how to hide without being seen."

The president studied the situation. "Well, I guess you could slope on over and have a listen just to find out what that miserable little . . . toad-frog might be planning. But be careful, Teresita. I don't know what I'd do if anything happened to you. You hear me? You be careful."

My hiding place in a thick island of mesquite bushes was just a short distance from the timber benches in the beergarden behind the Foley's groggery. Adjacent to a huge stone barbecue pit that belched great plumes of smoke, the beergarden was a regular meeting place for Vice President Lamar and his supporters to assemble just up the street from the Hall of Congress. I always approached it with great caution and a long stick because once I discovered a diamondback near some prickly pears that bordered the mesquites. The Foleys did not know enough to keep hogs around their place. You never find snakes around where hogs live, because hogs kill snakes and eat them.

Fortunately, I made it to my hiding place and made certain there were no snakes around just before Lamar arrived at the tables and Judge Foley came outside, followed by the three men I had seen arrive the previous evening.

"Excellency," the Judge said, "I would like to introduce my brother-in-law, Chandler Watts. Chandler, this is our esteemed vice president, the honorable Mirabeau B. Lamar."

Chandler Watts was a lean, gaunt-faced man. He was wearing the same kind of expensive clothing that Lamar and Foley favored. His grey, short-tailed frock coat and his mustard-colored vest were those of a gentleman of high station. He gripped a coiled black-leather whip in his gloved hands. I could see in his dour expression a family resemblance to his sister, Mrs. Foley.

After bowing, Watts introduced the men with him as Bob King and Possum Lanfer. Both of these men were dressed in yellow buckskin marked with a good many bloodstains. They wore beards, and the one called Possum had a bulge in his cheek and tobacco juice seeped from the corner of his mouth. Both gripped Pennsylvania long-rifles even after they had accepted Judge Foley's invitation to sit down at one of the heavy, butcherblock tables. Fastened to leather belts around their waists were long-blade hunting knives.

After a brief discussion of his guests' journey from South Carolina, Judge Foley turned to call for his wife to bring them beer.

"No need to trouble Janelle," Watts said. "Lightnin'?"

Very quickly, a small negro man came racing out the back door of the groggery. The sleeves of his unbleached cotton shirt were rolled up, and he was drying his arms. "Yes suh, Mr. Watts. I's heah, suh."

Watts appeared to study the little man who had come to stand before him in a hunched over stance not unlike that of a scolded dog. "What are you doing in there, boy? Have you been in there sleeping? Don't lie to me."

Never taking his eyes from his worn brogan boots, the negro said, "I's washin' da massa's clothes, suh. Lightnin's doin' what you tole 'im, suh."

Watts looked at Lamar. "This is the slowest, laziest damn nigger you have ever seen in your life. That's why I call him Lightnin'."

The vice president seemed to find the remark quite amusing and laughed with the other men.

Narrowing his eyes, Watts looked again at his slave, who somehow managed to hang his head ever lower. "Lightnin', you get yourself in that house and tell Mrs. Foley you been sent to fetch our beer."

"Yassa, Mr. Watts."

"And don't you fool around in there. If you're not out here in about two minutes, you know what will happen." He raised the coiled whip still in his hand. "Understand, Lightnin'?"

"I understands, suh! Lightnin' gonna go gets that beer rights now, suh. C'mon feets, move ol' Lightnin' in that house!"

The men had another good laugh after the negro had scampered up the steps and entered the house. They then proceeded to talk about how the price of slaves had climbed to levels making their ownership prohibitive to any but wealthy men.

"It's Houston's doing," Vice President Lamar said. "He engineered the passage of the law against allowing the import of slaves from Africa. Thousands of darkies have been brought from Africa to Havana, but we can't bring a one to Texas."

Watts asked, "How does Houston get away with it?"

"It's the Mexicans. They didn't allow slavery before the revolution. Houston got the law against importing slaves from Africa passed to please the Mexicans and get their votes."

"I thought you whipped the Mexicans. Why the hell should you care what the Mexicans think? Why should you even let them have the vote?"

Judge Foley made an attempt to explain how many Tejanos fought against Santa Anna and that men like Juan Seguin and Jose Navarro served in the republic's congress. While he was talking, the man called Possum got up and walked slowly toward where I was hiding in the mesquites.

"Where you going, Possum?" Watts called.

"Whar you think I'm goin'?" Possum growled and spat tobacco juice.

"Go use the privy house," Watts ordered. "You can't just go out here behind the house where people eat. Damn, Possum."

I breathed a sigh of relief as I watched Possum amble toward the privy house some twenty yards on down from the groggery. He had come close enough that I could see scars on his face that looked to have been made by a knife. I was getting a little uneasy about my mission and thought it might be wise to try to beat a retreat as soon as possible.

Before I could move, the back door opened and a woman in a yellow and red striped calico dress stepped down the stairs. She smiled when the vice president quickly got to his feet and removed his palmetto straw-hat.

"Don't come out here!" Watts yelled. "We're still talking. I told you not to come out here until we get through talking."

The woman's smile quickly faded and she started to turn back to the house, but her way was blocked by Mrs. Foley who was stepping from the porch while balancing a tray of mugs.

"Oh, Chandler," Mrs. Foley said and laughed. "Don't be like that! We're not going to bother you men. We just wanted to bring your beer. Don't get all in a tizzy, brother."

"I told Lightnin' to bring the beer. That lazy nigger! How come—"

"There, there," Mrs. Foley interrupted and placed the tray on the table around which the men were sitting. "I told the boy to go back to washing the clothes. I can bring a tray outside. I'm not helpless." She looked at Lamar. "Have you met my sister-in-law, Excellency? Please allow me to introduce Mrs. Constance Watts. Constance, this is Mr. Mirabeau Buonaparte Lamar, who will be the next President of the Republic of Texas."

"It is indeed an honor, dear lady," Lamar said and kissed the woman's hand.

After the men had each taken a mug, Mrs. Foley stepped back and said, "I suppose you gentlemen have been discussing Sam Houston's latest debauchery."

Judge Foley said. "If this latest incident doesn't turn every decent citizen against that lunatic, I don't know what will."

"What happened?" Watts asked.

"Houston's off on another one of his wild drinking binges. A few days ago he got word that some Indian squaw he'd lived with up in the Arkansas died. Since then, he's been over at Coalter Owens' place carrying on like a crazy man. Abandoned all his duties, he has. If it weren't for Vice President Lamar here, the government would have collapsed. No one's seen him in almost a week."

"Who is Coalter Owens?"

"A friend of Houston's," Lamar said. "He's married to a Mexican woman and owns what is probably the largest freight hauling business in the Republic. He's in partnership with a free negro and a Tejano in San Antonio. They've managed to buy some of the choicest farm land along the Brazos. They've hired free negroes to work it."

The man called Bob King said, "You people in Texas let the niggers run free and every slave in the south will do everthing he can to come here. We've got enough trouble with those damn abolitionists up north stirrin' up the niggers."

"Bob's right," Watts said. "And I tell you something else. You let Texas get annexed to the United States and the African slave trade will never be reopened. The states in the north have a much larger population than we have, and someday they're going to abolish slavery."

"Texas," Lamar said, "is not going to be annexed to the United States. We're going to cross the Rio Grande and finish what we started at San Jacinto. We should never have stopped until we took all of Mexico clear to the Pacific. And when we do, there won't be anything to keep the southern states from leaving the Union and joining us. The northern states will have no say in whether or not we establish a commerce in African slaves."

Watts said, "Well, that sounds very good, but it appears to me that you've got a problem standing in your way. You've got a very big problem by the name of President Sam Houston."

"He's not going to be president long," Mrs. Foley said. "The president of Texas cannot succeed himself. Mr. Lamar will be our next president. That's why we need to bring more of our people to Texas, Chandler. If Houston gets his man elected, he will still run the republic from behind the scenes. We've got to get more of our people into Texas before the election."

It was difficult to hear all that was being said, and I wanted to be able to tell Kalanu every detail of what was being discussed. Crawling on my belly, I inched forward to almost the cactus patch until, suddenly, I felt something grab my arm and I was lifted up into the air.

"Looky what I found!" Possum Lanfer shouted.

"Put me down!" I yelled.

Everyone got to their feet and stared as the big man, who smelled as if he had never taken a bath in his life, carried me dangling by the arm to the beergarden.

Mrs. Foley shouted, "It's that sassy little meskin girl who's always with Houston."

Lanfer said, "I seen her out thar a lookin' at us. She been watchin' us fer a spell."

"Please," Mrs. Watts said. "Put her down, Possum. You'll hurt her arm. She's just a little girl."

The big man lowered me to the ground but continued to grip my arm tightly. I looked at Mrs. Watts and saw that hers was the only kind expression. Very quickly, my attention shifted to her husband, because he had begun to uncoil his whip.

"She's Coalter Owens' granddaughter," Judge Foley said. "Her daddy was an officer in Santa Anna's army. She is a sassy little thing. She's always hanging around Sam Houston."

"She has a face like an angel," Mrs. Watts said softly.

"Like a devil!" Mrs. Foley huffed. "Meskins are the children of the devil, Constance! And they are all natural-born thieves. That's probably what she was doing out there. She was watching to see what she could steal!"

"So she's a little thief," Watts said, a cruel smile twisting across his lips. "Maybe I should show her what we do to thieves in Carolina. What do you think, Possum? Should I show her how we deal with thieves back home?"

Tobacco juice drooled from Lanfer's mouth as he laughed. Despite my every effort, he continued to hold my arm tightly, and it was beginning to feel numb.

"No, Chandler," Mrs. Watts said. "Please. Let her go. She's just a little girl. Let her go."

Watts prepared to draw the whip back.

Lamar said, "It might be advisable to release her, Mr. Watts. Houston has taken quite a fancy to this girl. He would view with disfavor anyone who struck her."

"I'm not afraid of Sam Houston. It seems to me that's the problem here in Texas. Everyone's afraid of Sam Houston. Well, Chandler Watts is not afraid of Mr. Sam Big Drunk Houston."

Judge Foley glanced nervously at Lamar and then to his brother-in-law. "It might be best to let her go, Chandler."

For a moment it appeared that Watts was going to swing the whip at me, and then he relaxed. "You say Houston is staying at this Coalter Owens' house, and this is his granddaughter?" He waited for Foley to nod. "Let her go, Possum."

The big man released me, and I took a few steps back. It occurred to me that they would enjoy seeing me run, which was my initial impulse; but I did not wish to give them any pleasure. I glared at each of them, except for Mrs. Watts, with as much defiance as I could muster.

"Go home!" Watts ordered. "Run!"

I did not move until Watts flicked the whip in my direction. Certainly, I did not want to give him the satisfaction of making me run; however, I also did not want to be struck with that whip, so I backed away and started toward the trail to our house. I accelerated my pace until I heard the sound of footsteps behind me. Watts was following, and he still held the whip.

"Chandler," Mrs. Foley asked, "where are you going?"

"I thought I might just see that our little thief gets home safely. We wouldn't want her to encounter any troublemakers on the way home, would we? You and Constance stay here."

Walking ahead a piece before turning to walk backwards so I could see, I watched King and Lanfer, rifles in hand, fall in behind Watts. Lamar and Foley lagged behind a few paces behind them. Seeing the Vice President of the Republic of Texas trailing a man with a whip, some men outside the Round Tent Saloon shouted to their friends inside that something was happening. Before long, several dozen men had joined what was becoming a procession to my grandparents' house.

Before arriving at the front gate, I considered whether it might not be best for me to detour away from the house. It was early afternoon, and I knew my grandparents and Lebe Seru would be at the wharfs to load the wagons with freight from the steamers arriving from Galveston. I did not know the intentions of this man with the whip. The only thing I could think was that I needed my grandfather and Lebe Seru.

However, just as I was about to bolt down the trail that would lead to the bayou, my mother came running out the front door, down the gravel pathway and out the gate. "Teresa!" she said. "What is happening? Who are these men?"

Quickening his pace, Watts hurried to the gate to position himself between us and the house. "Well, well," he said, looking at my mother. "What do we have here?"

Cata Valeria held me to her. "Who are you, Señor?" she asked in Spanish. "What do you want?"

By now, King and Lanfer had entered our yard to reinforce Watts' blocking our path back to the house. Lamar and Foley remained some distance away with the crowd of men that had gathered to witness what was happening.

"Esteban!" my mother shouted when my little brother came rushing from the house. "Go back inside!"

Esteban quickly obeyed; but when my mother attempted to shepherd me in the same direction, Watts stepped in front of her.

"Good afternoon, ma'am," he said, touching the brim of his hat. "My name is Chandler Watts, and I brought your little girl home to you."

Cata Valeria shook her head that she did not understand and looked down at me. "What is he saying? What have you done now, Teresa? Why are all these men here?"

Judge Foley inched forward to the gate and said, "Chandler, I think we had better go."

Watts said, "This is a fine looking woman, Delford. You never told me Mexican women could look so good."

When Cata Valeria again asked for an explanation as to why the men had followed me home, I was not at all certain as to what to say. Finally, I blurted, "These are evil men. They are enemies of President Houston and—"

"Houston," she said, raising her eyes to the sky. "I should have known this had something to do with that man!"

Grinning, Watts said, "How do these people understand what they are saying to each other, Delford? Spanish sounds like just a lot of noise to me."

Judge Foley did not answer because he was staring at the front door of our house.

My heart raced when I saw what had captured his attention.

"Kalanu," I whispered as Sam Houston closed the door behind him and reached for one of the poles supporting the porch.

Chandler Watts, too, turned his head to see what all of us, including the people in the large group outside our gate, were watching. President Houston was coming to my rescue. I would be safe from this man's whip.

But something was wrong. Kalanu held tightly to the pole. His legs were limber. He was having difficulty standing. He was still in his bare feet and was wearing only pants and a shirt that had been buttoned wrong.

"Well, well," Watts said, stepping a few paces toward the porch. "Who is this fellow? Could this be the great Sam Houston? Is this President Sam Houston, the Hero of Horseshoe Bend and Conqueror of Santa Anna?"

Kalanu managed to negotiate one of the porchsteps but was reluctant to let go of the pole. When he finally let go, he almost fell before he grabbed the bannister and steadied himself.

In a low voice, Judge Foley said, "Be careful, Chandler. He's dangerous."

"Dangerous?" Watts shouted and joined in the laughter of King and Lanfer. He looked toward the crowd of men behind us, none of whom had added their voices to the merriment of the three strangers who faced the President of the Republic of Texas. "This is not a dangerous man. This is a drunken fool. This is a lying, drunken fool who is afraid to fight the Mexicans and turns the best land in the Republic over to savage Indians. This coward, who can't even stand up straight, tells you that you can't import darkies from Africa at a fair price to work your land."

Some of the men behind us murmured approval of what they were hearing.

The way Kalanu looked was sad. He could not seem to walk and his entire body was trembling. He wanted to come down to where we were. He wanted to help me, but I could see that he was unable to move.

Watts continued, "This man has lied to you. He's no hero. I've known men who were at Horseshoe Bend, and they say Sam Houston was drunk during the battle and wouldn't fight, the same as here in Texas. He was drunk during San Jacinto and tried to run from the field of battle and hide."

My mother made an attempt to move me around this man and walk to the house, but Watts raised his hand with the whip and stopped her. His ugly leer returned as he looked at her. "Why is Houston coming half-naked out of this woman's house? Is this why he doesn't go across the Rio Grande and whip the Mexicans once and for all? Could it be Houston's taken a fancy to this Mexican woman and—"

"Shut your mouth!" Kalanu yelled. He had moved to the bottom of the stairs and was looking about for something to hold that might steady him. There was nothing else. He fastened stern eyes on this man who was taunting him. "Who are you?"

Watts took another few steps toward the president. King and Lanfer, apparently satisfied there was no threat from an unarmed man who could not walk, had lowered their rifles. "My name is Chandler Watts. I am from South Carolina, home of the great patriot John Calhoun, who is going to take our state out of the Union run by that back-shooting coward, Andy Jackson."

Despite a great effort, Kalanu still could not move since there was nothing for him to grab and hold. He began coughing and sank to one knee.

Watts uncoiled his whip. "I think its time to do what I came here for. We caught this girl preparing to steal some things at my brother-in-law's house. I'm going to teach her a lesson. She won't think about stealing for a long time."

When he drew back the whip, I tried to pull away from my mother because I did not want her to get lashed. She struggled to hold me as I prepared to feel the sting I knew was coming.

But the blow did not come. Instead I heard my grandfather say, "Put that whip down, mister."

Looking around, I saw King and Lanfer standing with their hands raised and their rifles at their feet. Behind them were Carmen, Lebe Seru and Esau, each aiming long-rifles at the men's heads. Esau had gone for my grandparents and Lebe Seru at the wharfs.

Watts must have thought he had an opportunity to get the jump on my grandfather, because he suddenly brought the whip around to strike him. But Coalter caught Watt's wrist, twisted his arm behind him and jerked it very hard, causing it to make a loud popping noise.

"My arm!" Watts screamed and grabbed his right arm with his left hand. "My arm is broken!"

Looking at Lanfer and King, Coalter said, "Get him out of here. And if you ever threaten my granddaughter again, if you ever even come around her, I will kill you."

After the two men escorted Watts away, Carmen rushed to where I stood and kneeled. "Are you all right, Teresa?" She looked up at my mother. "Has she been hurt?"

Cata Valeria ran to the house without answering her mother. She paused briefly to glare at Sam Houston before going inside.

I assured my grandmother I was unhurt and rushed to the president, who was being helped by Esau to the steps.

"Kalanu?" I said.

He looked down at me through swollen eyes. "Teresa," he whispered. "I promise you. I solemnly promise you I will never be like this again. Never again. I will always be able to protect you. I promise you, Teresa. I promise."

Slowly and with great care, Esau labored to prevent the President of the Republic of Texas from falling as he climbed up the stairs and went into our house.

III

Chandler Watts and his friends stayed far from our house in the weeks following his threat to use his whip on me. When in Houston Town, they spent most of their time at the Foleys' beergarden. I did not fear them, but I was relieved when Binu Seru returned from the trip to San Antonio. Most of the men and women who worked as Binu Seru's teamsters were former slaves who had run away to become freemen in Texas during the years prior to the revolution. With so many people at our house or at our farm on the Brazos, I felt safe even after we learned that more men from South Carolina had arrived to join Chandler Watts at a ranch Judge Foley owned north of town.

Binu Seru was known for his skill in driving oxen. We used oxen to pull the wagons to San Antonio because the roads west of Houston Town were often little more than rivers of mud. The broad-hoofed oxen could negotiate this kind of terrain better than horses or mules. The Montemayors used mules on the dry and hard ground south of San Antonio when they hauled freight to the towns on the Rio Grande. Mules would take a bit and could be driven with reins, but oxen needed to be led and prodded. Binu Seru trained our oxen to obey voice commands and, regardless of the weather, he always got our wagons to San Antonio and back to Houston Town without losses.

Besides the security of their numbers, I was glad Binu Seru and his teamsters were home because I had missed Alma. The same epidemic of yellow jack that took my father killed both Alma's mother and her grandmother, Lebe Seru's wife. She was the sister I did not have; and though we would squabble over such things as her garden and my chickens and goats, I depended on her for many things and she on me. After Alma's mother died, my grandmother treated her like a daughter. Carmen did not like to cook any more than I did, but Alma enjoyed it. She became very good at making gumbo out of okra, red peppers and the blue-claw crabs Lebe Seru would catch in Galveston Bay.

On the day the teamsters arrived from San Antonio, the first thing Alma did was inspect her garden. I thought she might be displeased since I had forgotten to turn the melons, and I had let the okra pods grow long and spiny. In her soft voice Alma said, "I'm just happy there is anything left at all."

I did not know whether to interpret her remark as a compliment or sarcasm; but when she smiled, I knew Alma had meant nothing mean. She had a beautiful smile, one that made dimples in her cheeks and caused everyone else to want to smile when they saw it. Her eyes, even darker than mine, would sparkle like diamonds when she smiled.

"Oh," she said, raising a package in her hand. "This is for you, Teresa. I almost forgot."

I removed the wrapping despite the fact Esteban had come up to poke his nose where it was not wanted. It was a bright metal object with thin teeth.

"What is it, Alma? A curry comb?"

"No, silly," Alma replied and laughed. "It's a silver comb to wear in your hair."

There were fancy carvings on the metal, but it looked for all the world to me like a curry comb for horses, which is something I could have used. Trying to conceal my disappointment, I said, "Thank you, Alma. It's very nice."

"It's not from me, Teresita. Jorge sent it. He bought it for you on the last trip his family made to Matamoros."

"Jorge?"

"Señor and Señora Montemayor's grandson. You remember him."

Only too well did I remember Jorge. On the last trip I had made to San Antonio, I had been forced to hit Jorge in the nose because he would not stop pulling my hair. Each time I went to San Antonio, the little green-eyed, red-headed rooster we called Gallito Rojo would make my life miserable. But I knew how to take the smile off his pudgy baby face.

"Why would Jorge send me this?"

Esteban shouted, "Teresita's got a sweetheart!"

"I think it's very sweet of Jorge to give you the comb," Alma said, smiling. "He had to save his money to buy it, and he works hard for his money. He delivers water door to door in San Antonio."

It was a mystery to me why Jorge would want to send me a comb that served no useful purpose.

When we went into the house to put away Alma's things, I knew Binu Seru had brought important news to his father and my grandparents because he stopped talking when he saw us. There were certain things that were not discussed in front of Alma or me or Esteban.

Finally, after a long silence in which no one said anything, Carmen asked Binu Seru about Santiago and Pilar Montemayor's sons and their daughter who had gone to Mexico to help those who were continuing to fight Santa Anna.

"Josefa and Miguel have gone to Oaxaca," Binu Seru said, referring to Jorge's aunt and uncle.

"Oaxaca? Is there any news of Benito Juarez? Is he still under arrest?"

"Benito Juarez was released but has not been allowed to take his place as a deputy in the state legislature. Miguel writes that Señor Juarez is teaching at the Institute of Sciences and Arts in Oaxaca." Binu Seru looked down at Alma and me and smiled. "This would be a good school for you girls when you are a little older. Josefa says the Institute of Sciences and Arts in Oaxaca teaches both young men and young women. She wants Jorge to go there someday."

After we left the room, I lingered for a moment in the hallway to listen to what was being said. I was unable to satisfy my curiosity because Alma insisted it was not polite to eavesdrop. We hurried to our room and while she unpacked, I told her about how she had missed the initiation into the Exalted Order of the River Styx and all the other fun we had had with Kalanu while she was in San Antonio.

With Binu Seru and the teamsters back home, I went often to the wharfs because the cotton on our farm on the Brazos was hauled to town each day to be placed on the steamers bound for Galveston. Our cotton was top grade, and my grandfather had arranged to sell it to a French merchant who said the textile manufacturers in his country needed all the cotton they could get to meet the growing demand. One day, the merchant asked my grandfather what he was going to do with all the money he made selling our cotton.

Without hesitation Coalter said, "Buy more land."

On the way back home, I asked my grandfather why we needed more land. We already owned many thousands of acres of land along both banks of the Brazos River.

"Because we will need much land to farm, Teresa. We will raise vegetables and grains someday. We will have fruit trees and grape orchards."

"But we do not have enough people to do that," I said, remembering the many times I had listened to my grandfather talk about how many people it took to do the kind of farming he wanted to do. "Are you going to buy slaves, Abuelo?"

"No, Teresa. Slavery is wrong. You know that."

"Then from where will the people come to farm the land you are buy-ing?"

"Someday there will no longer be slavery, Teresa, and the people who were slaves will come to farm this land we are buying. We will sell the land to them."

"Slaves are not allowed to have money, Abuelo. How can they buy land if they do not have money?"

"They will purchase the land with the money they will earn from sell-ing crops they grow on the land. In the meantime we must have it ready, or they might find it difficult to find land they can buy after slavery has ended."

Almost every day my brother and I went to the wharfs to watch Binu Seru and his teamsters load our cotton on the steamers. Though at first reluctant, Alma finally agreed to come with us, which I liked because she helped me watch Esteban who was always trying to sneak away and get on the boats. I wanted Alma to come along not only because she helped with Esteban, but because she could share the fun of seeing the hundreds of people arriving each day from strange and exotic places all around the world.

Alma enjoyed all the many sights and festivities until the day we hap-pened to be present when a steamer unloaded a cargo of negroes who were to be sold at an auction on the south wharf. Some fifty men, women and children were herded off the boat like cattle. Clutching what few pos-sessions they had in ragged bundles, the people huddled in groups and stared at the ground, not looking up even when the brokers yelled at them or struck them. Children, some little more than babies, cried because their mothers had been sold to someone who did not want them.

Because I had seen slave auctions before, I tried to get Alma to leave. It did not take much to make Alma cry. But she had never seen an auc-tion and was curious. When Lebe Seru and Coalter came to where we were, I told Lebe Seru I did not think Alma should see what was hap-pening.

Lebe Seru looked up at the platform where some of the slaves were being inspected by buyers. A large crowd, both men and women, was assembling below.

"No, Teresa," Lebe Seru said, "I think Alma should see what happens here."

On the block, several well-dressed men gathered around one of the young slave women who had been made to unbutton her dress. She was very pretty.

The broker, who carried a thick baton, stopped where the men were standing and said, "An octaroon from New Orleans, Gentlemen. The bidding on her will start at five hundred."

"Five hundred?" one of the men said. "I can get a good field nigger for three hundred."

"Your field is not where you will want this one to be working, sir," the broker said. "And that's five hundred in U. S. currency. I don't take Lone Star Redbacks even if they do have Sam Houston's pretty face on them."

The men laughed and, at the broker's invitation, proceeded to place their hands inside the young woman's dress. She did not change expressions even when her eyes drifted down to the crowd below and met mine.

Suddenly, there was a disturbance on the gangplank leading from the steamer to the wharf. A young negro man in chains was being forced by three white men to take his place on the block, and he was resisting. When they got him to the block and tried to force him to his knees, he jerked away and brushed up against the chief broker.

The broker cursed when he looked down at the blood that had smudged his white linen jacket. Gripping the baton tightly, he swung it into the head of the slave, who had now been subdued and made to kneel. Several times, he repeated the blow, bringing the baton down again and again against the slave's head.

One of the men holding the negro said, "You'd better stop. His ear's a comin' off."

What the man said was true. The slave's ear was hanging by only a piece of flesh.

The broker backed away and wiped at his jacket with a cloth he snatched from one of the slaves. He looked out over the crowd and announced, "I'll sell this one real cheap!"

The people in the assemblage laughed.

A man with whiskers down to his chest shouted, "I'll take him. I'm drainin' a swamp on my place, and I don't wanna lose any of my good niggers to the yellow jack."

Another man in the crowd said, "You ain't gettin' no work out of this one. Look at his back."

From his neck to his waist, the young slave's back was thick with welts.

"Oh, he'll work," the bewhiskered man said. "I've got six blue healers that'll have 'im fer supper ifen he don't. Ain't never seen a nigger yet what won't do what a pack of blue healers tell 'im to do."

The slave was sold to the man for three dollars.

When the broker offered to give the buyer the key to the lock on the chains, the man laughed and said, "Won't need it. Don't need this neither." He grabbed the slave's dangling ear, snapped it loose and tossed it in the water by the pier. "Let's go, boy!"

That night Alma sobbed and cried despite everything anyone said to her. I kept trying to get her to eat, since she had gone straight to her room after we returned from the auction and had not come down for supper. My grandmother would come in Alma's room from time to time, hold her and stroke her hair. She told me not to worry about the food and that it was best I not keep telling Alma not to think about what had happened on the wharf. Downstairs, Carmen asked Coalter and Lebe Seru why they had let Alma see the auction. Lebe Seru said that unless someone saw an evil with their own eyes, it was not possible for them to understand why it must be opposed.

A few days after the slave auction, I went with Coalter to an election rally held south of town. There was to be a debate between Mirabeau B. Lamar, who had announced for the presidency of the Republic, and Attorney General Peter Grayson, who had agreed to run for the office since Sam Houston could not succeed himself as president of Texas. Speechifying was something the Texians enjoyed, especially when it was combined with gambling on horse races.

We arrived just as a horse race had ended and the men were collecting their winnings. Great sums of money exchanged hands at these races as well as possessions, including livestock and slaves. Sometimes, men would bet their entire farms on the outcome of a race between horses that were valued as much as ten thousand dollars apiece. The tracks were laid out in straight lines for as much as a mile or more, and it was not unknown for the losing jockeys to just keep on going rather than return to face the anger of men who had lost everything they owned in the world.

What helped to make the losing riders wary of facing those who had bet on them was the large quantities of spirits that were consumed at these events. Kegs of whiskey were everywhere, usually situated near cast-iron kettles in which were frying all kinds of meats including pork, beef, fish, venison, wild turkey and rattlesnake. Nobody had to pay for anything since the candidates provided food and spirits as an inducement to favorable consideration on election day.

I was surprised that Kalanu was nowhere to be seen as Judge Foley mounted a platform that had been erected for the debate and announced that the speeches were about to begin. Even though the president was not a candidate, everyone knew Attorney General Grayson was Sam Houston's man and would only be a figurehead when elected. Kalanu loved speechifying and never missed an opportunity to address a crowd or bet on the horses.

Mr. Grayson appeared nervous as Vice President Lamar approached the podium and waited for his supporters to cease their cheering. The attorney general did not share his mentor's enthusiasm for campaigning.

Finally, after the shouting stopped, Lamar, barely able to see over the tall podium which was usually in the Hall of Congress and had been made especially for the president, gathered himself up on his tiptoes and said, "For the past two years, the entire world has watched as the Chief Magistrate of the Republic of Texas has sat reeling in the chair of state with his robes of office dappled in the vomit of his intoxication!"

Half the men in the crowd cheered, and the other half booed.

Lamar raised his hands for silence. "The brain of Sam Houston is, in spite of long habitual inebriation, still prolific in low devices and foul machinations to injure others, and cunning contrivances to benefit himself!"

There was more cheering and booing. When it subsided, a man in the crowd called out: "General Houston ain't the one running for office, Lamar!"

Ignoring the man's observation, the vice president continued to voice insults and lies about Sam Houston for more than an hour. He then spoke of how he would, if elected president of the Republic, run the Mexicans out of New Mexico, which, he said, belonged to Texas, and force all Indians to leave Texas or face extermination. He promised to reopen the trade in slaves from Africa and keep Texas an independent nation with borders that would eventually be expanded to the Pacific Ocean.

When it was his turn to speak, Peter Grayson walked slowly to the podium and stared at the paper on which he had written his speech until someone in the crowd shouted for him to speak up. He mumbled a few words which no one heard and returned to his seat without once looking at the crowd. A lot of the men laughed, and one of those laughing the loudest was Chandler Watts who stood between Bob King and Possum Lanfer. They were in the company of about three dozen other men, each cradling a long-rifle.

Obviously pleased with how the debate was going, Vice President Lamar strode to the podium and started to speak; but when he looked up from his papers, nothing came from his open mouth as he gazed over the heads of the assembly.

We all turned to see what had caught his eye. What he saw was President Sam Houston mounted on the back of his magnificent dapple grey, Proclamation, riding slowly toward where we were gathered. Kalanu was wearing a buckskin jacket, adorned with colorful beads, and on his head was wrapped a scarlet Cherokee turban. On his feet were moccasins, also decorated in beads. His supporters began cheering.

Reaching the platform, the president slowly dismounted and climbed the steps. Grinning broadly, he acknowledged the cheers by drawing his sword and waving it above his head. He glanced down at me and winked before sheathing the sword and walking slowly toward the podium which Lamar quickly vacated.

Judge Foley approached the president. "What are you doing here, Houston? This is a debate between the men running for president. You're not a candidate."

President Houston unbuttoned his jacket revealing the red and green Cherokee hunting shirt he was wearing as well as the ivory handles of two dueling pistols tucked inside the blue silk sash around his waist. Jewel-encrusted gold rings adorned each finger of both of his hands.

"I did not come here to debate, Judge," Kalanu said. "I just thought I'd come over and welcome all these here folks that are new to Texas. Lots of new folks here that don't know much 'bout Texas 'cept what this . . ." – he pointed to Lamar who had returned to his chair– ". . . this little caterpillar of calumny has been saying!"

There was a wild chorus of cheers, and an equally loud round of hisses and boos.

"So," Kalanu continued, "I thought I'd stop by and point out to all you folks that don't know much about Texas that this here man, Mirabeau Buonaparte Lamar, has all the attributes of a dog except one: fidelity!"

The vice president jumped to his feet, but whatever he shouted was drowned out by howls of laughter and more jeers.

"This man here," the president said, again pointing to Lamar, "believes we oughta take an army down to Mexico and whup Santa Anna. Well, that sounds just grand 'til you consider that we here in Texas have got a population of 65,000 and Mexico has a population of eight million.

"Shore, I whupped ol' Santa Anna real good over here at San Jacinto a few years back, but that was because I drew him up where I wanted him and whupped him in my back yard. You go off down to Mexico, and it is going to be a different story."

The crowd was by now in a considerable uproar, and some of the men were on the verge of trading blows.

Raising his hands for silence, the president said, "Now if all you mamas that brung your boys here to Texas wants 'em to go off and get killed in Mexico, I guess you oughta get your menfolks to vote for Mirabeau Buonaparte Lamar here. But remember this, the last time a little feller named Bonaparte took a bunch of boys out to invade another country, about half of 'em didn't come home. Not alive anyways."

Again on his feet, the vice president shouted, "Houston doesn't want to fight the Mexicans! The Mexicans are his friends. He's big friends with traitors like Seguin and Navarro. It's the Mexicans right here in Texas that are encouraging our darkies to run away to Mexico. And—"

Suddenly, gripping his stomach with both hands, Lamar bent forward. It appeared his intestinal disorder was acting up again. He walked quickly to the steps leading off the platform.

Victorious, Sam Houston drew his sword and, grinning broadly, waved it over his head to lusty cheers. He then dismissed the assembly and ordered all Texians to adjourn to the kegs to commence serious drinking.

At home that night, I was finally successful in getting Alma to take a little food. I tried to cheer her with an account of how the president had bested Lamar in the debate that afternoon.

Just before I was about to set up the mosquito netting for bedtime, Carmen came to the room and said for both Alma and me to come out-side with her. She escorted us out the back door, down the pathway past the stable, and to the barn. It was dark and when I started to ask why we did not have a lamp, my grandmother touched her fingers to her lips as a sign to be quiet.

Once inside the barn, Carmen secured the door behind us with a plank. My eyes adjusted to the faint glow of a bear-oil lantern, which I saw was held by Binu Seru. Looking beyond him, I saw Coalter and Lebe Seru. They were standing over someone sitting on a barrel.

Alma gasped because she recognized before I did that the person on the barrel was the young slave we had seen a few days before on the wharf, the one who had been sold at the auction for three dollars. We drew clos-er, and my grandfather put his hand on my shoulder and smiled.

"Teresa and Alma," Lebe Seru said. "We would like for you to meet Ralph."

The young man watched Alma and me very closely. I saw that a ban-dage had been wrapped around his head and covered where his ear had been torn off. There were also towsacks secured to each of his feet.

"Ralph," Coalter said. "This is Lebe Seru's granddaughter, Alma. This is my granddaughter, Teresa."

Ralph nodded his head and for an instant, a smile played at the cor-ner of his lips until he winced with pain. His face was covered with bruises, and one eye was almost swollen shut. He was now wearing a shirt, and so the big welts on his back were not visible.

"I don't understand," I said, looking at my grandfather. "I thought he had been sold to that man. Did you buy him, Abuelo? Did you buy a slave?"

"No, Teresa," Coalter said. "We did not buy Ralph. We" —he looked at Lebe Seru and Carmen and Binu Seru— "helped Ralph to run away from the man who bought him. And we are going to help Ralph get to Mexico, where he will join others like him that we have also helped to run away."

"Girls," Carmen said, "you are old enough to know what is right and what is wrong. Slavery is wrong. The day will come when there will no longer be slavery; but until that time, we must find ways to hasten its end. What we are doing here is right, but it is against the law. What we are doing is very dangerous. If the wrong people find out what we are doing, our lives will be in jeopardy. Do you understand what I am saying?"

Alma and I both nodded.

"You must tell no one what we are doing. No one, Teresa. And you know who that must include?"

I looked into Carmen's dark eyes. "I cannot tell Kalanu?"

"No, Teresa. You cannot tell Houston."

"Kalanu would do nothing to hurt us, Abuela."

"I do not believe he would, Teresa, but he is the President of the Republic of Texas. He is sworn to uphold the laws of Texas, and what we are doing is against those laws."

Looking at Ralph, seeing the relief on his face that he was no longer going to be someone's slave and be beaten and hurt, I knew that the laws upholding slavery were wrong. Even if Sam Houston was sworn to uphold those laws, they were wrong; and I must oppose them. Slavery was wrong. It was very wrong.

Coalter knelt before me. "Teresa, you must not even tell your mother or your brother."

"My mother does not know what you are doing, Abuelo?"

"She does not. Since your father's death, your mother is not herself. Someday, we will tell her."

Lebe Seru and Coalter secured the tow sacks to Ralph's feet with leather cords. Inside the tow sacks was ox dung which, my grandfather explained, would keep dogs from following his trail as Ralph traveled to a place south of the Nueces River, where he would be met by other runaways. Alma and I helped in the preparations for Ralph's escape. We were now both in violation of the laws of Texas. It was far from the last time we would violate those laws.

One month before the presidential election, Attorney General Peter Grayson put a pistol to his head and pulled the trigger. President Houston put forward another candidate, James Collinsworth, the Chief Justice of the Supreme Court of Texas; but a week before the election, Mr. Collinsworth jumped off a steamer and drowned himself in Galveston Bay. The man who finally agreed to run said he was too busy making his fortune to be president of Texas. As it turned out, this man, whose name I cannot recall, did not have to be bothered, because Mirabeau B. Lamar was overwhelmingly elected to serve as the second president of the Republic of Texas.

Immediately upon the convening of the new Congress, President Lamar demanded that the capital of the Republic be moved. He did not want to serve as the nation's chief executive in a town named after a man he despised. The majority of the new lawmakers were his supporters, and they quickly approved the establishment of the capital at a place favored by the president on the Colorado River. The new capital was to be named after the late Stephen F. Austin, who had been Sam Houston's Secretary of State. The city of Austin would rise on the site of an already existing village called Waterloo. Sam Houston said it was inauspicious that a government headed by a man named Mirabeau Buonaparte Lamar would have its capital at a place called Waterloo.

It did not bother me in the least that President Lamar and his government packed their bags and headed for Austin. I was especially delighted that Chandler Watts and his men elected to follow their leader, though Judge Foley and his wife stayed in Houston Town. We would no longer have the excitement of fisticuffs and gunfights in the Hall of Congress, which was quickly converted into yet another saloon and gentleman's parlor; but I did not mind. It would mean, or so I hoped, I would have more of my teacher's time, since he was now a private citizen like the rest of us.

My hopes were unexpectedly brought to an abrupt end when the now former president rode up to our gate one morning on Proclamation. Behind him, Esau and Tom Blue were on the deck of a mule-drawn wagon piled high with trunks, furniture and a gold-framed portrait of George Washington. It was obvious what was happening, and I knew something very special was coming to an end.

When he dismounted and knelt before me at the gate, I said quietly, "Kalanu. You're leaving."

At that moment, Esteban came running out the front door and to the gate. My brother would always be younger than me, but he was beginning to catch up in size; and I was getting taller each day.

"Old Chief," Esteban yelled, "where are you going?"

Esau and Tom Blue climbed down when my grandparents and Lebe Seru came outside and walked to the gate. Binu Seru and Alma were at the farm on the Brazos.

"I'm going to Nacogdoches, Esteban," Kalanu said and, seeing Carmen, removed his hat. He stood up. "Mornin', folks. Thought I'd come by and wave at you all on the way out."

Esteban shouted, "I don't want you to go!"

"I'll be back real often, Esteban. A man's got to keep an eye on a town named after him." He grinned at my grandmother. "I don't want the folks here to go and do something that might tarnish my reputation."

Lebe Seru asked, "What are you going to do in Nacogdoches, General?"

"Thought I might try my hand at lawyering again." He reached into the pocket of his leopard-skin vest, pulled out several cards and gave one to each of us. "Had these printed up. What do you think?"

The card read: "Sam Houston. Attorney-at-Law. You will find him where he ought to be."

After saying his good-byes, Kalanu got on Proclamation and reined him to the trail.

My grandmother stepped to Esau and said, "Take care of him, Esau."

"I'll do my best."

Esau and Tom Blue gave us each a hug before climbing to the deck of the wagon and following the man who no longer governed the Republic of Texas.

The weeks following Sam Houston's departure turned into months, but they seemed like years because each day was an eternity to me without my teacher. Carmen did her best to help Esteban and Alma and me read books and do our lessons in writing and arithmetic. However much my grandmother tried to teach us, it was not the same as with Kalanu. For one thing, Carmen did not have much free time. She worked hard each day, and at night she frequently was in the barn tending the wounds of the runaways that came to our house before starting out on the long and dangerous trip to the Nueces.

Alma and I would haul hot water to the barn to be used in cleaning cuts; and we would gather the ox dung to put in the tow sacks tied around the runaways' feet. Sometimes, we would get very sleepy if we worked late into the night; and Lebe Seru and Coalter would carry us upstairs to our room, after which they would return to work through the night to get the fugitives safely on their way south.

When I asked exactly where the runaways would go, my grandfather said, "They go to a place about a hundred miles south of the Nueces River, Teresa. Not many people go there because it is a very harsh land. Few people want to live there. It is hot and dry and difficult to farm, and so the runaways will be safe there until slavery ends."

Alma asked. "Do you ever hear from the runaways again?"

"Oh, yes. We hear from them often because they come north to the Nueces River to guide those we send."

"Did the one called Ralph get to this place safely?"

"Yes, Alma. Ralph arrived safely, and he is doing very well. He has become one of our best guides."

One of the many things I missed about Kalanu was his habit of reading the newspapers to us. Each day, he had been the first to meet the steamers that carried the latest editions of papers from New Orleans, Washington City and New York. He would read the stories in these papers to us and explain why this or that person was doing the wrong thing or the right thing. The right thing was usually something he and Andrew Jackson said was right, while the wrong thing was most often something John Calhoun or others who threatened the Union advocated.

When I told Coalter about how I missed the newspapers, he began bringing home some for us to read. By reading the Austin newspaper we began to learn of the things being done by President Lamar. One of the first actions taken by Lamar was to have declared null and void all treaties Sam Houston had made with the Indian nations in Texas. His Congress passed laws ordering all Indians to leave Texas; and when many did not comply, the president dispatched Ranging Companies, or Rangers, to force their expulsion. A series of battles followed, which resulted in the deaths of many Indians—men, women and children. Chief Bowles, the eighty-seven year-old leader of the Cherokees in Texas, was killed. The sword Sam Houston had given him to commemorate the Cherokees' treaty with Texas was taken to Austin as a trophy of war.

According to the reports we read in the newspapers, Lamar spent large sums of money to expand the Texas Navy and sent his ships to prey on Mexican merchant vessels. Two of his warships were captured and the crews imprisoned in Mexico. The president ordered several invasion forces across the Rio Grande, but they were unsuccessful; and many of the men were captured, imprisoned or executed. In retaliation, Mexico sent armies into Texas and briefly held several Texas towns before retreating back across the border. The Mexican show of force was pointed to by those in the United States who did not want to annex Texas because of the fear it would lead to war with Mexico.

Undeterred by his military failures, President Lamar dispatched an expedition to capture Santa Fe and incorporate New Mexico within the borders of Texas as a first step in expanding the boundaries of Texas to the Pacific Ocean. Instead of taking Santa Fe, the expedition was itself captured and its members force-marched to Mexico City where many of them were executed and others placed in prison. The disaster alarmed European investors to the point that English and French warships appeared off Galveston as a warning to the government of Texas not to seize assets of their citizens to finance further military adventures. There were even rumors in Houston Town that England or France might land soldiers to take over the Republic.

The accounts of the capture of Texas cities by Mexican armies and the threat of invasion by European powers were the main topics of discussion among worried Texians wherever they happened to gather. Virtually ignored by Texians, and only briefly noted in the newspapers, was the passage into law by the Texas Congress of a proposal submitted by President Lamar to make abolitionist activity in Texas a crime punishable by death. Anyone convicted of assisting a slave to run away from his owner would be executed and his property would be confiscated by the court to be sold at public auction. The method of execution prescribed for those convicted of violating the laws against abolitionist activity was hanging.

IV

As soon as the rain stopped, I went outside to make certain my chickens were safe. Two of my hens were setting, and I had to keep an eye on them until the eggs hatched. Torrents of rain, such as we had been having in a summer of Gulf storms, caused snakes to seek higher ground. Sometimes the snakes got my chickens' eggs before my hogs got the snakes. Since I knew what could happen, I was anxious to get to my pens. Everything was in order and the hens clucked and ruffled their feathers as a warning not to come too close.

After raking out the goat sheds, I went to the front yard to watch Cata Valeria prune her rose bushes. My mother was beginning to spend more time outside. Now that she had stopped wearing only mourning dresses, she had begun to make cotton blouses and skirts in a variety of colors. When I had admired the designs of flowers and birds she sewed on her blouses in red and green and blue threads, she had offered to teach me how to do needlework. After a couple of lessons, I found ways to avoid any more and hoped she would forget I had ever mentioned it.

Presently, she looked at me and asked, "Where is your brother?"

"You gave him permission to go to the farm with Alma and Binu Seru. Do you not remember?"

"I remember. I just wanted to make certain you know where he is at all times."

Sometimes I wondered if my mother expected me to know when Esteban went to the privy house. He was now bigger than me. Someone who could race a horse as fast as my brother did not need his sister looking after him every moment of the day and night.

"Teresa," Cata Valeria asked, "did you know your grandmother is still asleep? It is almost noon."

I knew Carmen was asleep, and I knew why. She had been up all night helping a runaway who had just given birth to twin girls. If Cata Valeria would talk to her own mother, she might know why certain things happened in her parents' house. It seemed wrong to me that a mother and a daughter could not confide in one another.

Before the issue could be pursued, we both raised our heads at the sound of approaching horses. Two riders were coming up the west road.

The sun was in my eyes, and so I could not make out who they were. Both riders appeared to be wearing light-colored uniforms.

For a moment, I panicked because President Lamar's Ranging Companies, who had been given the task of crushing abolitionist activity in the Republic, wore tan uniforms. We had recently learned that Chandler Watts and his Carolinians had joined the Rangers. My grandfather and Lebe Seru were at the farm, and Esteban and Alma were on the way there with Binu Seru. The only people at the house were myself, Cata Valeria and Carmen. Our lives could be in danger if the riders were Rangers.

I thought of going for my grandfather's long-rifle until the men drew closer and I was able to see that their uniforms were not tan, but a brilliant white. And when the larger of the two men drew his sword to wave above his head, I recognized who it was.

Dismounting before his horse had come to a complete halt, Sam Houston resheathed his sword just in time to catch me as I raced to him and leapt into his waiting hands. Up I went, and I snatched the hat off his head and placed it on mine before he set me to the ground. The left brim of the hat was fastened to the crown, and a red plume was attached to the leather hatband.

"Teresita!" he shouted. "How you've grown! How old are you now?"

"You know I am ten years old, Kalanu. You sent me a letter on my birthday along with the gold medallion with your face on it!"

Kalanu's riding companion had dismounted and stood holding his hat in his hands. I had initially thought he was an older man with white hair. Now that he was closer, I could see that he was a young man. His neatly trimmed beard, mustache and hair were a very light color, gold like the sun. I saw, too, that his pale blue eyes were fixed on my mother.

Kalanu bowed to Cata Valeria. "*Buenas tardes, Señora.*"

My mother nodded, but her gaze was on the man wearing what I knew was the uniform of an officer in a European navy. I had seen such uniforms worn by officers on the great warships anchored in Galveston harbor. The uniform was exactly like the one Sam Houston was wearing. I knew the former President was not a naval officer and suspected he was wearing the apparel because it was very handsome with gold shoulder-cords, black wrist-bands and a crimson sash. The only difference was that Kalanu did not have a Maltese Cross suspended from a green ribbon around his neck.

"Teresita," Kalanu said. "You're going to have to help me introduce my friend here to your mama." He turned again to Cata Valeria. "Señora, permit me to introduce my friend, Baron Jacob von Gorlitz."

After I had translated, my mother said, "Buenas tardes, Señor von Gorlitz."

"Jacob, this is Señora Cata Valeria Sestos y Abrantes."

The young man bowed, took my mother's hand in his and kissed it. Stepping back, he said, "The señora is more beautiful than you described, General Houston. But even a man of your eloquence would be unable to invent the words to portray such loveliness."

His voice was deep, and he spoke English with a German accent. I did not know if I should translate his words to my mother. I did not have time, because Kalanu then introduced me and the Baron kissed my hand.

"I am delighted to meet you, Teresa. General Houston has told me many things about you and your brother."

"Teresa," Kalanu asked, "do you think your folks might put us up for the night?"

"The night, Kalanu? You can stay forever!"

"Maybe we'd better ask your mama."

Knowing how my mother viewed Sam Houston, I hesitated to comply with his request. However, I could not think of a way to avoid making the translation since I could see Cata Valeria understood I had been requested to put a question to her.

To my surprise, she told me to say, "You are welcome in our house, *señores.*"

My grandmother was very surprised to see our former president as was Coalter and Lebe Seru when they returned that evening. It was only when I saw my grandfather whispering to Carmen in a room away from the parlor that I remembered runaways might be coming to our house that very night. When I noticed Lebe Seru slip away in the direction of the pine forest beyond our house, I suspected some previously made plans were undergoing a change as a result of the unexpected arrival of our guests.

My mother again surprised me by appearing at the dinner table to take a seat across from Sam Houston. When Kalanu asked why Lebe Seru had not come to the table, Coalter told him he had gone to the farm to help his son with a mare in foal. He would return later that evening.

Carmen asked, "How are Esau and Tom Blue, Houston? Why did they not come with you?"

"They were too busy. Esau and Tom Blue are building houses in Nacogdoches these days. They're quite in demand. Esau is a master carpenter, and Tom Blue's a stonemason. They build houses all day, sunup to sundown, every day of the week. Everybody wants them to build them a house."

"They will be rich."

Kalanu's smile faded as he looked at Carmen. "Well, I get paid the money, of course. I hire them out." His eyes brightened. "But they do all right. There's nothing they want for. I take good care of 'em both. There's nothing neither wants that I don't get 'em. Esau and Tom Blue do all right."

Baron von Gorlitz could hardly keep his eyes off my mother except when she looked at him. Cata Valeria was wearing a yellow silk dress that I had never seen. I sat next to her and tried to translate what was being said.

"These are delightful," the Baron said, holding up a tortilla. "What is it called, Señora Owens?"

"It is called a tortilla."

"They are made from ground-up corn," Kalanu explained and proceeded to detail the use of the *metate* and how the corn is mixed with lime and flattened by hand.

"It is delicious, Señora Owens," Jacob said. "We have nothing like it in Austria. I wish I could take some home for the Emperor. He enjoys the foods from the Americas."

Esteban, who predictably had fallen in love with Jacob's naval uniform, asked, "Does the Emperor get to wear a uniform like yours, Jacob?"

"Esteban," my mother said. "Do not call Baron von Gorlitz by his first name. He is your elder."

After I translated my mother's words, Jacob said, "It is quite all right, Señora Sestos. I do not mind. And yes, Esteban; Emperor Ferdinand does wear a uniform similar to mine, as do his nephews, Franz Josef and Maximilian."

"Are the Emperor's nephews in the navy?"

"No, Esteban. They are too young. Maximilian is the same age as you. But when his brother, Franz Josef, becomes our Emperor, Maximilian will become the Archduke; and the Archduke is the Grand Admiral of the Austrian navy."

Carmen asked, "And you, Houston? You look very dashing in that uniform. Have you joined the Austrian navy?"

Grinning broadly, Kalanu said, "Jacob brought me the uniform, Carmen. Don't you think it looks handsome?"

"It is even prettier than the uniform the Sultan of Turkey sent you. You remember the uniform with those pointy-toe, silk shoes and long purple tassels? That was a handsome uniform."

Despite my grandmother's playful taunting, I thought Kalanu looked grand. I also thought Baron von Gorlitz was very shrewd to have given the uniform to a man who, though he was no longer the President of Texas, still had considerable influence with powerful men in the Republic, especially those engaged in commerce. Jacob was on a mission for his Emperor to explore trade with the Republic of Texas, and he was wise to get on the good side of Sam Houston.

After we ate, I accompanied my grandfather when he went outside so that Kalanu would not have to smoke his cigar by himself. We could see through the window that Carmen had taken my place as translator between Cata Valeria and Jacob. It appeared that my grandmother was being kept very busy in her task, and my mother was smiling.

"Don't let that uniform fool you," Kalanu said after lighting his cigar and taking out his whittling knife. "That young man is not just a naval officer. I made inquiries when I first received a letter from him that he wanted to meet me. His father is one of the most powerful bankers in Europe and a close advisor to their Emperor, Ferdinand von Hapsburg. The Austrians are wanting to invest in Texas."

My grandfather said, "I thought the Austrians were preparing to go to war with France again. How can they afford to make investments in Texas if they're going to war?"

"That's all a rumor, Coalter. France and Austria are on good terms. In fact Jacob's father helped to arrange the marriage between Napoleon Bonaparte and Ferdinand's daughter, Maria Louise. It was Jacob's father that brought their son to Vienna when Napoleon was exiled."

"What happened to Bonaparte's son?"

"He died a couple of years ago. He was only about eighteen or nineteen when he died. Jacob told me the story in Vienna is that the Emperor's youngest nephew, Maximilian, is Napoleon's grandson. He said the boy's mother, Archduchess Sophie, fell in love with Napoleon's son and bore his child." He picked up a stick and began to whittle. "If it's true, I hope that the little Archduke or whatever he is, this Maximilian, meets a better fate than his granddaddy."

The next morning it was hard to get Sam Houston up at the early hour he had requested because he had stayed up late talking to my grandfather and Lebe Seru about the disaster Lamar had made of his Republic; but he had to get up in order that they travel to Galveston where Jacob was scheduled to depart on his ship for the return voyage to Austria. Kalanu was bleary-eyed as I brought Proclamation and Esteban brought Jacob's horse, both saddled, to the front gate where we had all gathered to bid farewell. Jacob had stayed up most of the night talking to my mother, but he looked fresh and bright-eyed.

My mother tried to get Esteban to return the Maltese Cross that Jacob had given him, since it had been presented to him by his emperor for bravery. Jacob insisted my brother take it and that I take a gold jewelry box that played music.

"It is too expensive," Cata Valeria said. "Thank Baron von Gorlitz, Teresa, but return it to him."

He knelt before me when I tried to give it back. "I wish for you to have it, Teresa. You can use it when you put your pendant away for the night. It is a very beautiful pendant and very unusual. Is that a cross under the woman's head?"

"It is the Toltec Cross," Carmen explained. "The pendant has been handed down in my mother's family from mother to daughter for generations. The head is of Chimalma, the mother of Quetzacoatl. She has been likened to Our Lady. She will protect those who come to her in time of need."

Lebe Seru asked, "Will you be returning to Texas, Jacob?"

"I had not planned to return after making my report to the Emperor, but I think now I will return to Texas. Yes, I think I will be coming back to Texas very soon."

"How about you, General?" Coalter asked. "You need to come see us more often."

Kalanu placed a boot in the stirrup and slowly raised himself to the back of the big stallion. "I expect I'll be coming back real soon. I didn't tell you? I'm going to run for president again, and I sure as hell don't intend to have my capital in that swamp Lamar stuck it in up there on the

Colorado. I'm bringing it right back here to Houston Town where it belongs." He took the reins in his hands. "Besides, I want my bride to live here where you can breathe good salt air. You need to have good salt air if you expect to breed healthy chil'run."

Carmen was as stunned as I was. "You're getting married again, Houston?"

"I didn't tell you? I found me a right pretty little gal over in Alabama. I figure I better get myself hitched up again if I ever 'pect to have some younguns 'round to take care of me when it comes my time to be let out to pasture."

As we watched them ride away, I felt odd about what Kalanu had said about getting married again. I suppose I had come to believe that some-day I would be the one he would marry. I was not so sure I liked hearing the news about this woman in Alabama.

The long and disastrous administration of Mirabeau Buonaparte Lamar finally drew to an end. It came none too soon for most citizens of the Republic. President Lamar's failed expeditions and his military cata-strophes were bad enough, but the people of Texas were dismayed that he had bankrupted the government and almost ruined the economy of a nation blessed with so many resources. The Lone Star Redback was now worth less than three U.S. cents to the dollar. Texas money was so worth-less, people resorted to barter. European nations demanded restitution be made to their citizens who had invested in Texas revenue bonds. Ships of the Texas Navy that had not been captured by the Mexicans were sold to pay debts.

Lamar's vice president, David Burnet, angrily accused Sam Houston of working behind the scenes with Andrew Jackson to destroy President Lamar's plan to build a Texas empire. He said Houston and Jackson had used their influence to block foreign loans to Texas. Since Lamar could not succeed himself, Burnet stood for the office of president but was soundly defeated as the people of Texas voted once again to entrust their destiny to the Hero of San Jacinto.

Though Sam Houston secured from his Congress the authorization to return the capital to his namesake city, he remained in Austin for a few months after his inauguration to assemble his government and to negoti-ate loans from bankers in the United States and Europe. He traveled to the frontiers to reestablish peace with the Indian Nations and wrote letters to assure the Mexican generals he would not invade Mexico if they would cease making raids into Texas. Finally, to the surprise of most people in the Republic, he announced he had wed Miss Margaret Lea of Alabama but that she would not travel to Texas until he had built their new home at Cedar Point, just north of Houston Town.

Of course, Sam Houston himself could not build the new house; he had neither the time nor the resources. While he worked in Austin or traveled the frontier, he sent Esau and Tom Blue to Houston with the specifications for a house he wanted constructed at Cedar Point on the bayou. Esau and Tom Blue were accompanied by one of Mrs. Houston's slaves, Joshua, who had been sent ahead from Alabama to make certain the house would conform to the needs and requirements of his owner.

We were delighted to have Esau and Tom Blue back home and insisted they stay with us while building the president's new house. We welcomed Joshua, a young man of eighteen years, into our home and soon came to appreciate him even though he at first seldom said more then 'yes' or 'no.' He was a giant of a man, and his somewhat rough appearance made it difficult for us to realize he was very homesick for the people he had been forced to leave in Alabama. When Lebe Seru discovered Joshua was a skilled wheelwright, he was able to get him to talk to us a little more; and it was not long before the young man began to feel at home in what must have been for him a forbidding land.

At breakfast one morning, I asked, "What is Mrs. Houston like, Joshua? Is she a nice lady?"

Without hesitation, he answered, "Oh, yes. Miss Margaret is a very nice lady."

We waited for him to say more, but he did not.

Carmen asked, "How old is Mrs. Houston, Joshua?"

"She's seventeen, ma'am."

President Houston was near his fiftieth year.

"Miss Margaret is a fine Christian lady," Joshua volunteered. "I don't know how they gonna run that Baptist Church without her. That preacher gonna be lost without Miss Margaret tellin' him what to do. He wouldn't have ever been able to have that Temperance League in Alabama without her help."

If Esau, Tom Blue and Joshua had had to build the new house by themselves, it would never have been completed in time for the President's arrival with his new wife. The specifications for the two-story house required the felling of hundreds of yellow pines; and Mrs. Houston wanted the logs squared, which was no easy task. Lebe Seru and Coalter said they would help, and Binu Seru asked for volunteers from among his teamsters. It was not long before we were using teams of eight to twelve yoke of oxen to haul the timbers to the bayou, float them across, and then up to Cedar Point, where the carpenters squared them into planks and began construction.

Each night, the volunteers building President Houston's house would come home, tired and hungry. Waiting for them, we always had pots of beans and rice and a kettle of Alma's steaming gumbo. There was always pokesalad, collards and plenty of cornbread and hoecakes. For desert Alma would make apple or peach fritters over which could be poured fresh cream mixed with scorched cane sugar.

It was inevitable that Esau and Tom Blue, eating and sleeping at our house for weeks, would become aware of what took place almost every night under the cover of darkness. Very often, my grandparents and Lebe Seru had to make hurried trips to the barn with bandages and medicines.

One evening, after Lebe Seru returned to the house and sat down on the front porch, Esau, who was smoking his corncob pipe, said, "You know that seven abolitionists were hung up near the Sabine last month."

Without looking up, Lebe Seru nodded his head.

Esau glanced at Tom Blue. He knocked the ashes out of his pipe and set it down to dry.

Tom Blue said, "You people are taking a big chance in what you're doing here."

Lebe Seru said nothing.

"You can get yourselves hung," Esau said.

Lebe Seru looked at the two men. "Tonight, we tried to help an eight-year-old girl whose master poured scalding water on her head to correct the girl's insolence. A little girl's scalp was burned off her head because she was insolent."

"Will the girl be all right, Lebe Seru?" I asked.

"Your grandmother is helping the mother prepare the body for burial when it gets darker, Teresa."

For a long while, we sat on the porch and listened to the sounds of the gulls returning to Galveston Bay for the night.

Esau asked, "Where do the folks go that you help to escape?"

Lebe Seru explained about the land between the Nueces River and the Rio Grande.

"What do they do in this place?" Tom Blue inquired. "How do they live?"

"It is difficult for them," Lebe Seru said. "The land is hard, which is why few people live there. Our people are able to raise some vegetables, and they fish and they hunt. Their life is not easy, but they are free."

"Why do they not go to Mexico? There is no slavery in Mexico."

"Some do go to Mexico. Some find peace there. But although there are laws against slavery in Mexico, all of the land that is productive is owned by just a few men. The people who work the land are called *peones*, and they are not paid for their labor. They are expected to work for a place to live and food to eat. It is not called slavery, but it is not so different from what we have here."

"And so," Esau asked, "what will your runaways do in this land south of the Nueces River? They will forever live in a place so harsh no one else will go there?"

"Not forever, Esau. Someday, slavery will end in Texas, and peonage will end in Mexico. Then our people can choose where they wish to go. We are trying to prepare a place for those who wish to return here to Texas. In the meantime, our people will ready themselves to play whatever role we can to end slavery here and, if we can, in Mexico."

Esau narrowed his eyes. "What kind of role, Lebe Seru? I don't understand."

"We believe the time is not far off when there will be fighting to end slavery, Esau. Our people must be prepared to take up arms, if necessary, to assist in the struggle for freedom both here and in Mexico."

Esau and Tom Blue asked to be allowed to go with the burial party for the little girl that night. Alma and I took a yellow rose from my mother's garden and placed it in the little girl's hands before Coalter and Lebe Seru closed the grave which would remain unmarked.

President Houston's return was celebrated in grand style by the people of the town named after him. The people of Houston Town were happy to have the money associated with having the seat of government back in their city. Everyone settled back to watch the explosion of new saloons and gentlemen's parlors required to meet the needs of a new crop of representatives and senators elected to replace the Congress that had supported Mirabeau B. Lamar.

Since the president's new house was some distance from town and across the bayou, I did not see him everyday. Some days he did not even come to his office across from the Hall of Congress. He allowed his vice president to run the government on a day-to-day basis while he spent most of his time putting the finishing touches on what I thought was a truly magnificent house, one befitting the status of a growing nation's Chief Magistrate.

Binu Seru and his teamsters volunteered their time and wagons to unload furnishings off the ships in Galveston, put them on steamers to Houston Town and then haul them to Cedars Point. On one trip they brought a yellow carriage the president had ordered all the way from New York, and on another trip they carefully unloaded Mrs. Houston's rosewood piano. I was not at Cedars Point when Mrs. Houston finally arrived from Alabama, but my grandfather came home one day with an invitation for a party the president was giving in her honor to be attended by all those who had helped to build their house.

At the party, Mrs. Houston wore a blue silk dress under which she must have been wearing a dozen petticoats. She was very pretty and had violet-colored eyes.

When I was introduced to her, Mrs. Houston grasped my hand tightly and said, "You're the girl President Houston has told me so much about." She spoke in a slow drawl. "You and I are going to be good friends, Teresa. I just know it. Won't we? Won't we be good friends?"

"Yes," I said quickly as she squeezed my hand even tighter. "We will be good friends."

It seemed peculiar she would call her husband 'President Houston,' but I realized she was from a culture where the people were more formal than we were in Texas. Kalanu stood behind her and beamed proudly as she greeted my grandparents and my mother and Lebe Seru and his family. The president was wearing a maroon colored frockcoat and a leopard-skin vest.

As they chatted about how hot it was in Texas, I noticed Mrs. Houston did not introduce the negro woman whose sole function seemed to be to fan her from time to time and give her a glass of water to sip. Away from the others, Joshua told Alma and me the young woman's name was Eliza. She had been Margaret Lea's personal slave since they were babies.

"Is that all she does?" Alma asked. "She just fans Mrs. Houston and gives her water?"

"Mostly Eliza tries to keep Miss Margaret from gettin' the melon collies."

"The what?"

"The melon collies. Miss Margaret gets real sad sometimes. She cries a lot, and so Eliza sits with her and holds her hand and tells her not to be sad."

"Why does she get sad?" I asked.

"I don't know. Nobody knows. Even Miss Margaret say she don't know why she gets sad."

I was standing by the back door of the house when Kalanu waved at me to join them at a big table in the back yard where he and his wife were dining with my mother, my grandparents, Lebe Seru, Alma and Esteban. Eliza stood behind Mrs. Houston and waved the fan.

"Did you not get some food, Teresa?" Mrs. Houston asked after I took a seat between my mother and grandmother.

"I'm not hungry, Señora Houston."

"*Señora,*" she said sweetly and smiled. "What a beautiful word. I love the Spanish language. You must help me with my Spanish, Teresa."

"She can sing in Spanish," the President said proudly. "Why don't I get your guitar, Margaret. You can—"

"Later, Mr. Houston," she interrupted with a gentle pat of her hand on his arm. "First . . ."—her eyes narrowed—". . . Mr. Houston, what is that you are drinking? What is in your cup?"

Kalanu's expression was that of a little boy caught with candy he was not supposed to have. "Uh . . . it's nothing, dear. Just some bitters and orange."

Esteban, who was next to the president, leaned over and put his nose to the cup. "Smells like whiskey, Old Chief."

"It's just bitters and orange," Kalanu repeated and smiled awkwardly. "Maybe just a small touch of brandy to dissolve the bitters, nothing more."

Even from where I sat, across the table, the drink reeked with the aroma of alcohol.

"We shall discuss it later, Mr. Houston," Mrs. Houston said and turned to my grandmother. "Mrs. Owens, did I tell you about the dreadful incident that occurred before we left Alabama?"

Kalanu said, "No need to bring that up just now, Margaret. This is not the time nor the place."

Ignoring him, she continued, "We found poor Mrs. Littlefield hanging by the neck from a rope tied to the chandelier in the parlor. Isn't that dreadful?"

"Yes," Carmen said when Mrs. Houston seemed to be waiting for her to answer. "That is dreadful."

"She hung herself," Mrs. Houston explained and looked to see that each of us had understood what she had said. "She hung herself by the neck until dead, and her two little babies were in the next room."

"They were not exactly babies, Margaret," the President said. "Her sons are fifteen and sixteen years old."

"Her two babies were in the next room," Mrs. Houston repeated. "She hung herself by the neck until dead, and those babies had to discover her hanging there by that rope. I just don't . . ." Her lips began to quiver. "I can't—"

"There, there, Miss Margaret," Eliza whispered and gently applied a damp cloth to Mrs. Houston's face. "It will be all right. It will be all right, Miss Margaret."

Esteban was all eyes as he watched Mrs. Houston struggle to regain her composure. "Were her eyes open when they found her?"

"Esteban!" my grandmother said.

"Yes!" Mrs. Houston said, turning to the only person who seemed interested in her story. "She was staring right at them when they opened the door! Her eyes were open and staring right at them!"

"Margaret, please," Kalanu whispered and gulped down his bitters and orange. He looked across at my mother and, smiling, said, "That is a mighty pretty necklace, Cata Valeria. Are those diamonds?"

My mother looked at me as I translated, and then she blushed and placed her hand to the necklace.

"The necklace is a gift sent to her by Jacob von Gorlitz," Carmen explained. "If Jacob does not stop sending us gifts from Austria we are going to have to add a room to our house."

Pleased that he had been able to change the topic of conversation, Kalanu said, "I've had a couple of letters from Jacob. He wants to come back to Texas, but the Austrians are having some problems in their Empire. The Hungarians and the Czechs have been trying to win their independence. Jacob is commanding a fleet of gunboats on the Danube."

"Jacob's going to whip them Hungarians and Czechs!" Esteban shouted. "Then he's coming back to Texas."

"There's trouble all over Europe," the president said. "Jacob wrote that Napoleon's nephew, Louis Bonaparte, is in prison for trying to overthrow King Louis-Philippe in France. Jacob said his father likes this Louis Bonaparte and thinks he would be a good leader for the French."

"That poor woman," Mrs. Houston said. "She was hanging by the neck when her babies found her. Don't you think it was a dreadful thing, Mrs. Owens?"

Everyone, except Esteban, wished they were someplace else as Mrs. Houston continued to talk about the woman in Alabama until several of Binu Seru's teamsters began playing fiddles on the other side of the grounds. Following the president's lead, we saw this as an excuse to step away from the table. I followed Kalanu, Lebe Seru and my grandfather to an island of oleanders swaying in the night breeze. When I looked back, I saw that Carmen and Cata Valeria had not been able to get away and were still listening to Mrs. Houston talk as Eliza waved the fan and my brother looked on with great interest.

After wiping his sweaty face, Kalanu removed a whiskey flask from his coat pocket and said, "I dearly love that woman, but she does have some peculiar notions. You should see her mother. The woman's coming here to live with us. Her and her coffin will be here any day now."

"Her coffin?" Coalter asked.

"Margaret's mother has been dying for the past twenty-five years. She's already selected her coffin and her shroud just to make certain her funeral will be the way she wants it."

The president took a healthy swig from his flask and was about to continue talking, but he looked up when Esau and Tom Blue emerged from the darkness beyond the oleanders.

"Governor," Esau said, "we need to talk to you."

Both Esau and Tom Blue had on their jackets and hats and were carrying bundles tied with ropes.

A blind man could see what Esau and Tom Blue were about to do, but Kalanu asked, "Why are you all packed up like that?"

"Governor," Esau said, "me and Tom Blue, we've decided to . . ." —he glanced at Lebe Seru and Coalter— " . . .we've decided to move on."

"Move on?" Kalanu looked at Lebe Seru and my grandfather. "Move on where, Esau? You all going back to Nacogdoches? Well, that's all right, I guess. I know you promised some folks up there you'd build some houses. That's fine. You all go back to Nacogdoches and—"

"No, Governor," Esau interrupted. "We're not going to Nacogdoches. We're going south."

"Going south? What are you talking about, Esau? You and Tom Blue been drinking? I've told you both not to start drinking this devil's brew. You don't know what it can do to a man. Don't take up spirits, Esau and Tom Blue. It's been the ruination of many a good man. It's a filthy habit, and it's unchristian."

"We haven't been drinking spirits, General," Tom Blue said, lowering his eyes. The poor man looked so sad. "We're going to . . ." —he took a deep breath and closed his eyes— "we're going to run away, General Houston."

"Run away?"

"We have to, Governor," Esau said quickly. "I'm not a young man anymore. I was born a slave, and I want to live free a little while before I die. You know I have to do it, Governor. Don't make it hard."

"Esau, you and Tom Blue can't run away. You're both slaves. I own you. I paid money for you."

"We'll send you the money when we get where we're going and start to work," Tom Blue said.

"Lebe Seru," the president pleaded. "Coalter. Tell them not to run away. They'll get out there and get themselves killed. Every rotten piece of dogskin in Texas is out there trying to catch runaways for the bounties being offered. You can't go. Have I been bad to you? Are you running away because I don't treat you right?"

"You're a fair man, Governor," Esau said. "And you're a good man, most of the time. But it just isn't right for one man to own another man. I don't think you believe it's right."

President Houston tried mightily to persuade Esau and Tom Blue not to leave. Finally, he seemed to realize nothing would change their minds. He put the now empty flask back inside his coat and said, "All right then. If you must go, wait a minute till I come back."

He walked briskly to his house and entered.

Tom Blue said, "Maybe we should go ahead and leave. He might have went for his gun. You can't predict what the General might do. We better get on our way."

"He didn't go for a gun," Esau said.

It was not long before Kalanu came back out the door and walked to where we stood. In his hand was a leather pouch. He opened it and removed gold coins to hand to Esau and Tom Blue.

"No, Governor," Esau said, backing away. "We can't take your money. We'll do all right on our own."

"Don't argue with me," Kalanu said and grabbed Esau's wrist. He started putting coins in his hand. After dispensing a few, he paused, put them back in the pouch and handed it to Esau. "Take it, Esau. You and Tom Blue take it all."

"I can't, Governor. It—"

"Take it! It's not even a fraction of what I owe you and Tom Blue. This is the money I collected off hiring you and Tom Blue out to build houses in Nacogdoches. I already spent most of it on my house here. I'll never be able to repay you and Tom Blue what I owe you after all these years. You take this, and I'll send you some more."

Esau tried to say something, but he could not talk. He turned quickly, took Tom Blue's arm, and began to walk away from us. Just beyond the glow of the pitch-pine torches, he looked back and said, "Take care of yourself, Sam Houston. You hear me? You stop that drinking and stay out of trouble, or I'll come back and . . . I'll . . . I'll—"

He turned again and, Tom Blue at his side, disappeared into the night.

When I looked up at Kalanu, I saw he wanted to say something but could not. There were tears in his eyes. I took his hand and walked him back to the house.

V

All the work the volunteers put into building the president's new house went for naught. The new Congress voted to return the seat of government to the interior. More people than ever were coming to Texas now that it was once again governed by a man committed to making the Republic a part of the United States, and these people were settling in the unclaimed lands to the west. Members of Congress wanted to have the capital more centrally located than was Houston Town. Sam Houston refused to live in Austin, the town founded by Mirabeau Lamar; but he agreed to move the government to Washington-on-the-Brazos, the little village where Texas independence had been declared.

On the day of their departure, we all helped to load the Houston's belongings into Binu Seru's wagons. Mrs. Houston made us promise to come visit her. She said, "I want all of you to be there when the baby comes."

My grandmother asked, "Have you decided on a name yet?"

Mrs. Houston smiled. "I think Nancy or Mary would be good names."

"Those are girls' names," the president said. "We can use those names later. We'll call the first youngun Sam Jr., and the second'll be Andrew Jackson Houston."

Joshua helped Mrs. Houston to the deck of the lead wagon. Sitting beside her, Eliza fanned Mrs. Houston's face as the oxen trudged forward.

We always intended to go to Washington-on-the-Brazos, but never found the time to make the trip even after we received word the Houstons' first child, Sam Houston Jr., was born. We sent gifts and a promise to come, but our work kept us at home. Binu Seru's wagons and drivers were in demand to haul goods between Houston Town and San Antonio, and we were short-handed at the farm. As I grew older, my responsibilities for minding the chickens and goats grew until I was tending all the livestock. Alma expanded her vegetable garden so that she was able to sell produce in Houston Town and Galveston.

Gifts from Jacob continued to arrive almost every week along with his letters telling us about revolts occurring within the Austrian Empire and at other places in Europe. One of the gifts was a painting of the

Emperor Ferdinand and his family. I was drawn to the portrayal of the young Prince Maximilian and remembered Kalanu's telling us how the boy might be Napoleon's grandson. I had seen pictures of Napoleon Bonaparte, but I saw no family resemblance in the representation of Maximilian, who was tall and had blonde hair and blue eyes.

Cata Valeria made shirts and sashes to send to Jacob. On them she used green and red and gold threads to embroidery elaborate designs common to the Indians of ancient Mexico. I had never seen such designs and was amazed at my mother's skills. One of her favorite subjects was the Toltec god, Quetzalcoatl, symbolized as a plumed serpent. Quetzalcoatl was the son of Chimalma, the goddess of dawn depicted on the jade pendant I wore around my neck. Everyone who saw them admired the beauty of the designs Cata Valeria made on the articles she sent to Jacob.

As her translator, I knew what my mother wrote in her letters to Jacob. Usually, she would tell him about her garden or birds she had seen flying south for the winter or north for the summer. She wrote about how hard we were all working and the people that were coming to Texas, many of whom came from Europe. We often heard people speaking the German language as they stopped in Houston Town just long enough to purchase supplies. The letters sounded boring to me, and one day I suggested to my mother that she write something Jacob wanted to hear.

She looked at me with suspicion. "Such as what, Teresa? What would he want to hear?"

"You could tell him that you love him."

One would have thought I had uttered a blasphemy. "What do you know of love?" she asked. "You are just a child!"

"Jacob loves you. It is obvious."

"I love only your father. You know that."

"Father has been dead for seven years. Jacob loves you. He wants you to be his wife."

"I will not discuss such matters with you," she said and left the room.

It turned out that my mother had to discuss such matters with me. Alma was reaching the age where her body was changing and since her mother was dead, Binu Seru asked my mother if she would talk to his daughter. Cata Valeria at first tried to get her mother to take on the task, but Carmen told her she should do it and that it would be good if she would talk to both Alma and me at the same time. My mother was very nervous when she set us down to tell us the facts of life. She would look at neither of us as she spoke.

Anyone who had grown up around barnyard animals and the Congress of the Republic of Texas knew all about the facts of life. My poor mother made the unfortunate choice of mules as an illustration of how little mules came to be born. I had to say, "Mules don't do that, Mother."

"Don't do what?"

"What you're telling us."

She looked at me as if I were crazy. "Then how do we get mules, Teresa? Do they grow on trees?"

I had to explain to her that mules were the result of breeding horses and donkeys. My mother shook her head in exasperation, and our brief lesson on the facts of life was over.

Since the government was no longer in Houston Town, I had to rely on the newspapers to keep up with what Sam Houston was doing as time began to run out on his second administration as President of the Republic. He built roads and improved the rivers and harbors in Texas, making it possible for commerce to expand and open more land for settlement. He managed to put an end to almost all of the Indian wars. The President even published a beautiful tribute in the newspapers on the occasion of the death of Flacco, the great chief of the Lipan Apaches. Sam Houston proved all those people wrong who said the white men and the Indians could never live together in peace.

I knew President Houston must have been disappointed that his second term ended without Texas becoming a part of the United States. The representatives and senators from the northern states fought to keep Texas out of the Union because it would enter as a slave-holding state. The issue of slavery was becoming more divisive of the people in the United States. Sam Houston thought that by overturning Lamar's laws against allowing free negroes to live in Texas he had demonstrated his commitment to the eventual end of slavery, but he left office for the second time without Texas being a part of the United States.

President Houston's successor, Anson Jones, had been a member of the Houston cabinet and could be counted on to continue his predecessor's policies. I hoped the Houstons would come back to Cedar Point, but Mrs. Houston preferred to move to a house near the small town of Liberty in east Texas, where she hoped her husband would retire from politics and become a gentleman farmer. Knowing Kalanu's boundless energy, I could have predicted he would not be content to farm; and I was not surprised when I read in the newspaper that he had gone to Washington City to personally direct the campaign for Texas' annexation into the Union.

We received a letter from Mrs. Houston asking us to come to visit her in Liberty where she was expecting the arrival of their second child. She said that since her husband was gone so much, she was very lonely. My grandmother wrote her that we were sorry we had not been able to visit but that we would try to come later. We were all having to work harder than ever at the house and at the farm because my grandfather had come down with the fevers and was slow to recover. Carmen suggested Mrs. Houston come to stay with us for a while after the baby arrived. Mrs. Houston quickly sent a letter accepting the invitation.

It was a visit that would never happen.

Late one evening, I noticed our goats and cows were acting spooked. I scanned the edge of the forest, thinking I might spot a wolf or a cougar. Something was upsetting all the animals. The hogs raised their snouts to the air as if catching an unfamiliar scent. The dogs had gone with Binu Seru and Alma to the farm earlier in the day, or I would have turned them loose to chase off any predator. Even a wildcat will run from a pack of yelping dogs. I went to the house to tell my grandparents and Lebe Seru what was happening. We were the only ones at the house other than Esteban and my mother. Coalter reached for his rifle, but Lebe Seru said he would go with me, since my grandfather was still trying to regain his strength after another bout with the fevers.

Outside, we walked to the goat sheds and then to the barn. We were about to open the door when we both heard a sound behind us. Turning, we saw that a man was approaching us with his hands raised.

"Don't shoots me!" the man said. "Please don't shoots me!"

The man looked familiar, but I could not place him. His eyes were fixed on the long-rifle in Lebe Seru's hands.

"I know you," Lebe Seru said. "You're Chandler Watts' slave."

"I's Lightnin'. I's Mr. Watts' nigger."

Lebe Seru asked, "What do you want?"

"I wants to runs away from Mr. Watts. He mean to Lightnin'. He whups me and whups me, and I wants to gits away to Messico. Ol' Lightnin' gotta git—"

"You don't need to talk like a fool," Lebe Seru interrupted. "There are no slaveowners here."

Lightning's expression was one of puzzlement. "Suh?"

"And you don't need to call me 'sir.' My name is Lebe Seru. Why have you come here? Why do you think we can help you run away?"

"Everbody know you helps the niggers what wants to runs away. And I wants to runs away to Messico real bad. I gotta, 'cause that Mr. Watts, he gonna kill ol' Lightnin'!"

Lebe Seru took a step backward. "We can't help you. You'll have to go somewhere else."

I stepped back as well.

Lightning walked toward us. "Oh Lawdy, you gonna help me git to Messico! Thanks you, suh!" His voice grew louder. "Ol' Lightnin' goin' to Messico! Lawdy! Goin' to Messico and be a free nigger!"

Lebe Seru said, "Teresa, get in the house."

Before I could comply, I froze in place, because Chandler Watts had come from around the corner of the barn. He gripped a coiled whip in his hand.

Lebe Seru raised the rifle, and Watts stopped walking. He was wearing the tan uniform of Lamar's Ranging Company, which had been disbanded by Sam Houston.

"What are you doing here, Lightnin'?" Watts demanded.

"Oh, Mr. Watts, suh. I didn't wants to do it. This here nigger talked me into runnin' 'way to Messico!"

Judge Foley emerged from the corner of the barn along with six more men wearing the uniform of the Ranging Company. Each man carried a rifle, and they had knives and pistols at their belts. All stared angrily at Lebe Seru.

"Teresa," Lebe Seru said, "go in the house."

This time, when I turned to comply, I saw that both my grandparents had come outside. Coalter carried a rifle.

More men came from the opposite side of barn. I heard horses and saw that still more men were arriving on horseback. A wagon was being driven to where we stood. In the dark, I could not see who was in it, but I heard a woman crying. Behind the wagon, there were men in chains.

"Put down the rifles," Watts ordered.

Coalter aimed his rifle at Watts.

Looking in the direction of the wagon, Watts shouted, "Do you have them, Possum?"

I could not see him, but I recognized the voice when Possum Lanfer yelled, "We got 'em, Chandler! Had to cut a couple of 'em. They tried to put up a fight out at the farm."

"You got the girl?"

"Yep."

"Let her talk."

"Grandfather!" Alma shouted. "Grandfather, they killed my daddy. Daddy's dead!"

There were more than two dozen guns aimed at both Lebe Seru and Coalter. Several men ignited pine-pitch torches, and I could now see Alma in the bed of the wagon. She was tied, and Possum Lanfer held a knife to her throat.

"Are you going to put the rifles down," Watts asked, "or do I have to tell you what will happen to that girl if you don't?"

Lebe Seru and my grandfather dropped their rifles to the ground. Bob King ran to retrieve both rifles; and when he did, he thrust the butt of one into Lebe Seru's stomach, knocking him to his knees.

King started toward Coalter, but Watts said, "That's enough. Be patient. We'll take care of him in due time."

Several men bound both of my grandparents and Lebe Seru with ropes. There were so many bodies moving about in the faint light I could barely make out that three men had gone in the house to quickly return with my mother and Esteban. Cata Valaria was clutching my brother to her. I ran to them, and Esteban put his arms around me.

I did not see where she came from, but Mrs. Foley suddenly appeared and was talking with her husband and Watts. In the light of the torches, I recognized that Binu Seru's teamsters were in chains. They were being forced to kneel on the ground. I saw Binu Seru's body being removed from the wagon and tossed on the ground like a sack of potatoes.

After the activity settled, Watts shouted, "Boys, we've decided to have us a trial."

A table was brought from the house, and Judge Foley seated himself behind it as if he were holding court. He called for order.

"This court," Foley said, "is called to session to hear charges brought against Coalter Owens for violating the laws of the Republic of Texas against aiding and abetting slaves to escape their rightful owners. Who brings the charge?"

"I do," Watts said. "This man here is guilty of attempting to aid my slave flee to Mexico."

"Present your evidence."

"Lightning," Watts said, "tell the judge what happened here tonight."

"Judge," Lightning said. "I comes over here to buys some eggs like my massa tells me, and this ol' nigger tries to gets me to runs away to Messico."

"And did what you describe take place here on this man's property, the property of Coalter Owens?"

"Yassuh, Judge Foley, suh. This is wheres it happen."

Foley looked at Watts, who was now standing over my grandfather. Using an official tone, the Judge said, "The court finds Coalter Owens guilty of violating the laws of the Republic of Texas against aiding and abetting the flight of a slave from his lawful owner. He is sentenced to death by hanging and forfeiture of all his properties to the court."

Several men swung open the doors to our barn and threw a rope to a man in the loft who tied it to a rafter and let a noose drop back to the men below. Three men lifted my grandfather and carried him to the barn where Watts placed the noose over Coalter's head and tightened it around his neck. The men let my grandfather drop. His feet did not touch the ground.

Cata Valeria ran to the door of the barn and attempted to hold her father up. Esteban and I ran after her and tried to help. We were pulled away and knocked to the ground. I looked back at Carmen, bound hand and foot, frantically trying to make her way to where Coalter was hanging. One of the men stuck her forcefully in the head with a rifle butt and she fell to the ground, unconscious. I was thankful my grandmother had been spared from witnessing the death of her beloved husband. I would forever wish that I had.

I looked for Lebe Seru. He had been chained and was being drug to the wagons where Alma was crying and holding her father's body. When I looked up again at my grandfather, I saw that his face was swollen and discolored. His body was limp.

Glancing at the men who held my mother, Watts said, "Take her in the house. I'll take care of her myself."

Cata Valeria fell to her knees and had to be drug to the house. Apparently thinking that Esteban and I posed no threat, the men holding us loosened their grip. Immediately, Esteban ran to attack Watts, who was now talking casually with his sister as she displayed to him the jewelry she had discovered in the house. When my brother hit him, Watts swung the handle of the whip into Esteban's head, knocking him to the ground. He then stepped forward and kicked Esteban in the head. My brother tried to get up but fell backward.

Getting to my feet, I ran at Watts. He kicked me in my stomach. For a moment, I was unable to draw my breath. The blow to my stomach knocked the air from my lungs, and I could do nothing but sit on the ground and gasp. Gradually and in short gasps, I began to breathe again. I crawled to my brother's side and put my hand on his face.

"Esteban?" I whispered.

He had a terrible cut under his right eye, and blood was coming out of the wound. He moaned and his eyes flickered, but he did not answer.

We were too unimportant for further notice. Watts was listening to Judge Foley, who was explaining how the court would dispose of my grandfather's property.

"The house is ours," Mrs. Foley said. "You can have all the wagons, the animals, and all of that. I don't want any of it. I want the house. The house is mine."

"There is more than enough to go around," Judge Foley said. "Everybody will get their share."

"What are you all going to do with the niggers?" Mrs. Foley asked. "Did you decide on that?"

Watts said, "We're going to take them to Austin and sell them. The sooner we do it the better. We'll start moving them first thing tomorrow. I'll send Bob and Possum with some of the boys."

"I want to keep a couple for the house," Mrs. Foley said. "That house is bigger than it looks from the outside."

"I promised the girl on the wagon over there to Lightnin'," Watts said. "We'll keep her and her grandfather. That old buck's good with his hands. I might just use him to build me a house."

"Chandler?" one of the men in the house called. "We're having trouble with this woman in here."

"I better go take care of it," Watts said.

"You get that Mexican woman out of there, Chandler!" Mrs. Foley said. "I don't want no meskins in my house, you hear?"

When Watts went into the house, I looked down at Esteban. His eyes were partially open. "Esteban," I whispered. "Can you hear me?"

"Teresa?"

I touched my fingers to the ugly bruise forming under his eye. "Esteban, can you get up? We've got to get out of here and go for help. Can you—"

I stopped because I could hear our mother's screams in the house. And then I heard the sounds of another woman's voice. Watts was cursing and in a moment the back door flew open, and a woman came running out, followed by Watts. He was trying to hit the women.

"Oh look," Mrs. Foley said. "It's Constance. What's she doing here? Chandler told her stay home. He is going to be fit to be tied."

Watts ran to where his wife had stumbled to the ground and slapped her in the face. He then went back into the house, and the men who were inside came out. A few moments later, I again heard my mother's screams. I got to my feet and started to the house, but one of the men near my grandmother saw me and knocked me to the ground. I crawled back to Esteban.

Mrs. Watts got to her feet and reentered the house. The shouting stopped. Presently, Watts stumbled outside, holding his hand and yelling terrible blasphemies.

Bob King and Possum Lanfer ran to where Watts was bending over.

"What happened, Chandler?" King asked.

Watts stomped his boot to the ground several times and shouted, "That bitch bit my hand!"

"I'll take care of her," King said and started to the house.

"Leave her," Watts ordered. "Go and get the Mexican woman and put her in the barn with that one over there. I think that one is her mother. Put 'em both in the barn, and we'll take care of them later. Get me a rag or something before I bleed to death!"

Judge Foley and his wife went to help Watts while King and Lanfer rushed to the house and returned, dragging my mother, who was unconscious. Her face had been bloodied. Watts and the Foleys then went into the house, and Lanfer and King returned to the yard to drag my grandmother to the barn. Some men lowered my grandfather's body to the ground and shut the doors.

There was still much milling about, but it seemed that my brother and I were unnoticed.

"Esteban," I asked. "Can you walk?"

"Yes," he whispered. "I think I can."

I helped him get to his feet and put his arm over my shoulder. As quickly as I could, I walked him around the side of the barn and away from the light cast by the pine-pitch torches. I hurried to the goat sheds before stopping to look back to see if we had been noticed or followed. I watched two men carry my grandfather's body to the wagons and toss it close to where Alma and Lebe Seru knelt next to Binu Seru's body.

"Teresa," Esteban whispered. "We have to help Mother and Grandmother!"

His right eye was now swollen shut. "We cannot help them, Esteban. We must go for help."

"Go where? Who will help us?"

I could taste blood in my mouth and tried to spit it out.

"Teresa? Who will help us?"

"I do not know, Esteban. But I do know we cannot help Mother or Abuela if we go back. We must get away from here."

Again placing my brother's arm over my shoulder, I half-carried him as fast as I could away from our house and to the pines. Once in the forest, I stopped to again survey the scene at the house. I thought about going into town and asking for help but dismissed that option because there were many men in Houston Town who would approve of what Chandler Watts had done, and there was no assurance they would not turn Esteban and me over to him and his men.

I realized that hiding in the trees was not a good idea, especially at night. The forest was home to wolves, bears, wildcats and other predators. Moreover, once Watts realized we were gone, he might send a search party into the woods to look for us. The only way out of the forest was to go toward town or head for the bay. With one hand holding Esteban's arm over my shoulder and the other around his waist, I took us in the direction of Galveston Bay.

It seemed to take forever until we finally worked our way through the pines and beyond the islands of mesquites and salt cedars to the open field bordering the beach. Catching the aroma of the seaweed, I staggered the last few yards to the water's edge and lay Esteban down on the sand.

For a very long time, we lay on the damp sand and tried to catch our breath. We were both weak. I kept trying to spit the blood from my mouth. I felt a sharp pain in my chest and when I put my hand to the ache, I could not touch it without it hurting more. A rib was broken. There was no time to worry about my aches and pains. The entire left side of Esteban's face was swollen into a puffy mass of discoloration that I could see even in the darkness. The flow of blood from the cut beneath his eye had slowed, but it continued seeping. And when I touched his face, I could feel heat.

"Esteban, we have to keep going."

He did not respond.

"Esteban!"

For a horrible moment, my brother did not move. He did not even seem to be breathing. Finally, his eyes flickered and he whispered my name.

"We have to keep going," I said. We were now miles from Houston Town; but I knew that if Watts set out to locate us, he would have horses. "We have to keep going."

"Where, Teresa?"

"I don't know, but we have to keep moving."

With my help Esteban somehow got to his feet, and we proceeded along the beach in the direction south of Houston Town, which took us into a desolate stretch of salt flats and shifting sand dunes. It was for good reason it was an uninhabited area, because nothing could live there except rodents and sandrattlers.

Stopping from time to time, we continued for the better part of two hours until it was apparent Esteban could go no further. I found a small inlet along the beach and let him down onto the sand and collapsed beside him. I was exhausted. I did not even have the energy to look again into my brother's face to see the terrible bruises caused by the blows he had received. I grasped his hand in mine, put my head on my arm and began to doze. Several times I awoke, startled by the sound of the low and steady roar of the surf or the cry of a sea bird. I would watch Esteban long enough to satisfy myself he was still breathing and then fall asleep again.

Finally, I awoke and could not go back to sleep. I knew dawn was approaching because of the increased activity of the birds. Gulls and terns were circling schools of mullet near the shoreline. After checking to see that Esteban was still breathing, I jumped up with a start when I became aware that the tide was surging. The water was rising rapidly within the inlet. It was coming toward us.

"Esteban!"

He did not move.

"Esteban, the tide's coming in."

All I could do was grasp his hands and pull him along the sand further up the beach. The exertion of pulling Esteban to safety made me sink to my hands and knees and pant for breath. Only when I felt the cool dampness of a fog did I open my eyes again. A thick fog was rolling in from Galveston Bay. Sinking to my knees, I again tried to rouse Esteban until I thought I caught a whiff of the aroma of smoke. Suddenly, I saw the glow of a fire in the direction of the dunes we had earlier crossed. I knew I had to investigate. My brother was very ill, and I had to get help.

Cautiously, I edged toward the glow. I froze in place when the fog thinned at the spot of the glow, which I saw was caused by a small fire on the sand. A metal pot was on the fire and was emitting the aroma of food. I sensed someone was standing a few feet from the fire, but I was reluctant to look for fear of what I would see. My body relaxed when I saw that the person by the fire was a woman, a small woman not as tall as me. Her complexion was as dark as mine, and she had straight black hair. I assumed she was either Tejana or Indian. It was difficult to tell from her clothes, because she was wearing a dark cape that hung to her feet.

"*¿Señora?*" I ventured. "*Buenos dias, Señora.*"

There was no response. I was not even certain she was looking at me. The sky was beginning to lighten, though the sun had not broken the horizon. I moved closer but took a quick step back when I saw the woman's face. She had a very sharply defined scar across her forehead. I was not exactly frightened, but it was disconcerting how she made no movement.

"Good morning," I said in English.

Again, there was no reaction, but I could now see her dark eyes were fixed on mine.

I returned to Spanish. "Señora, I need help. My brother" —I pointed behind me— "has been hurt. Can you help him? Perhaps we could have some of your food."

It seemed unlikely Esteban would be able to take any food, but I did not know what else to do. It did not matter because this small woman continued to do absolutely nothing but stare at me. Maybe, I thought, she was Indian; and I tried to devise a sign language that would convey what I wanted her to understand. No effort I made to communicate evoked a response. Frustrated, I started to turn to go but stopped when, finally, she took a step toward me. No longer was she looking into my eyes. Her gaze had shifted to the pendant around my neck.

The cape she had been clutching to her throat parted and she extended her hand, palm up. She seemed to be asking for my pendant. When she pointed to the pot over the fire and then again extended her hand, I knew what she was saying.

"You want my pendant? You want to trade your food for my pendant?"

She nodded.

The pendant was mine. It had been given to me by Cata Valeria, just as she had received it from her mother. I knew, however, I was in no position to refuse. Something had to be done to help Esteban.

"Very well," I said and removed the pendant. I stepped forward to hand it to her. Without looking at it, she placed it into a pocket inside the cape.

I started for the pot, but the woman made a sign of caution with her hand. I thought she was going to renege on her end of the bargain, but she took a cloth to lift the pot. Realizing I would have burned my hand on the handle, I followed as she led the way back to where Esteban lay.

The fog lifted, and I was able to see the first orange sliver of the sun's orb over Galveston Bay. A line of brown pelicans glided across the surface of the leaden water.

Reaching Esteban, I knelt beside him and saw that his eyes were still closed. In the faint light, his swollen face was almost unrecognizable.

"Esteban," I whispered. "I'm back. Esteban, wake up! It's me. Teresa. Wake up!"

His breathing was faint. I looked across at the small woman, who had knelt on the other side of my brother. She was watching me.

"Please, Señora," I pleaded. "Help him! Do something."

She put her hands to his forehead. For a long time we sat like that, her hands to my brother's head. And then Esteban began to stir. His eyes opened.

"Esteban!" I whispered. "I'm here."

"Teresa?"

"Yes, I'm here. I've brought someone to help you."

The woman removed the lid from the pot. Seeing a ladle inside ended my puzzlement as to how we would get the food into my brother's mouth. She dipped up some of the steaming liquid and motioned for me to raise Esteban's head. When I did, she placed the ladle to his mouth. Esteban swallowed. After giving him several more servings, the woman motioned for me to let his head down.

It was not my intention to eat any of whatever was in the pot. How could I? My grandfather had been brutally murdered. My mother and grandmother were being held by vicious men who would not hesitate to do unspeakable things to them or kill them, and I did not know if my brother was dying. I was confused and sad beyond measure. How could I think of food at such a time?

But the woman insisted I eat. Kneeling in front of where I was sitting, she dipped the liquid from the pot and fed it to me the same way she had fed my brother.

"Thank you, Señora," I said when I had had enough, but I did not resist as she continued to feed me. The broth warmed me inside, and I no longer felt the pain in my chest.

I lay back on the sand and listened to the gulls. The sun looked so red and so huge as it rose on the horizon, and the wind whipped some of the foam across the shoreline to dance over the strands of seaweed beginning to dry after the tide had receded. Knowing there was someone to watch over Esteban, I thought I might be able to close my eyes for just a short while. My body was craving sleep.

When I awoke, I looked up into my brother's face. He was sitting by my side.

"Esteban," I said and raised myself to a sitting position. Looking to the sky, I could see the sun was now directly overhead.

"Teresa," Esteban said. "We must go. We must go and help Mother and Grandmother. Hurry!"

"Esteban," I said. "Your face." The swelling had greatly reduced, and there was little discoloration. I put my hand to his forehead. There was no fever. "Are you all right? How do you feel?"

"I am fine."

"Your face, it is—"

"Hurry, Teresa! We must go to help Mother and Grandmother."

Getting to my feet, I looked about for the small woman, who was nowhere to be seen. "Esteban, where is the woman?"

"What woman?"

On the sand was the small pot from which we had eaten. I knelt and touched it. It was cool and only a small amount of clear broth was in the bottom.

"The woman who brought this pot, Esteban; where is she? Where did she go?"

"I do not remember a woman. Hurry, Teresita. We must go back to the house."

I ran to the dune where I had first seen the woman in the dark of night. The only thing I found were the cold embers of the fire over which had sat the pot.

"Señora!" I shouted. "Where are you?"

Esteban followed, insisting that we must return to Houston Town to help our mother and grandmother. I knew he was right, and I must waste no more time looking for the woman who was now in possession of my pendant. We had to do something to help not only our mother and grandmother, but Lebe Seru and Alma and the people that had been put in chains and were to be sold in Austin. What I did not know was what that would be. I did not see that we were any more prepared to do anything than we had been the night before.

"Teresa," Esteban said. "Let's go. We've got to get back to the house. Hurry!"

"We cannot go back to the house, Esteban. We must go to the wharfs and try to find someone who will help us. Maybe one of the steamer captains will help us."

We followed the coastline north toward Houston Town. I was not at all certain that I had made the right decision. Many men who worked on the wharfs and on the steamers had been friends to my grandfather and Lebe Seru, but what could they do against a force of some thirty or forty armed men? It was one thing to be a person's friend but quite another to risk your life for that person or that person's family. All I knew was that Esteban was right. We had to do something.

It was late afternoon by the time we reached the wharfs. We tried to remain out of view of the many people working to load and unload cargos. For all we knew, some of Watts' men might be at the wharfs looking for us at that very moment. I had not recognized many of the men he had recruited to assist him in what he had done. There were two steamers that had just tied up when we arrived, but I did not know the captains. Discouraged, I was ready to suggest we leave when I heard a familiar laugh on one of the gangplanks. At once I knew the prayer I dared not to voice, for fear it would not come true, had been answered.

"Old Chief!" Esteban cried. "Teresita, look! It's Old Chief and Jacob!"

VI

Kalanu knelt before us and patiently waited for me to tell him and Jacob what had happened. While I spoke and his fingers gently touched the bruises on our faces, I saw the sadness in his eyes. Behind the compassion, however, I could see the rage. Encouraging me to relate what had happened at the house in as much detail as possible, he tried to smile; but his lips trembled and his chest heaved. He urged me to tell him the details of everything that had happened, no matter how insignificant. When I told him all I could remember, he stared toward Galveston Bay and said nothing.

"General," Jacob said, "we must recruit some men and go to the house. We must hurry!"

Slowly, Kalanu got to his feet.

"General Houston?"

"No, Jacob. It will not be necessary to recruit men. I will go by myself." He unbuckled his holster belt with his ivory-handled pistols and handed them to the Baron. "Keep an eye on these while I'm gone. You stay here with Teresa and Esteban."

"I'm going with you!"

Sam Houston studied the young man, who was dressed in a blue frock coat, grey trousers and riding boots. Jacob had come to surprise us, but now his joy had turned to apprehension for my mother. He was, of course, distressed about my grandmother, Lebe Seru, Alma and the others; but it was obvious who was the focus of his urgency.

"All right," Kalanu said. "You can come, Jacob, but leave your weapons here with Teresa and Esteban."

"Leave our weapons? We must prepare to fight these men, General Houston!"

"Jacob, these men used the law in what they did. I know Judge Foley. He does everything within the bounds of the law. The fact is, Coalter knew what he was doing violated the law and he knew the penalty. I guess it was a price he was willing to pay. Everything that has happened, including the confiscation of Coalter's property and putting Lebe Seru and his folks in bondage, has been done within the boundaries of the law. There is no court in the Republic that will go against Judge Foley's ruling. And if we go on that property and use force or the threat of force, we will be in violation of the law and will be subject to prosecution."

"Then what do we do? They have Cata Valeria! And they have Mrs. Owens and Lebe Seru and his granddaughter. We have to do something, General Houston! Immediately!"

"Oh, we're going to do something, Jacob. And we are going to do it right now." He looked at the darkening sky. "It's a safe wager most those men that came to the Owens' place stayed up most of last night drinking and celebrating. Right about now, they're feeling mighty groggy and sick to their stomachs. They haven't been able to drink too much just yet, so they're not drunk. We're going to go over there and give them something to think about before they have a chance to get back to some serious drinking. Teresa, you and Esteban watch our weapons 'til we get back."

"I'm going with you, Old Chief!" Esteban said.

"So am I," I said. "They have our mother and our grandmother. If you try to make us stay, we will follow when you are gone."

He stroked my hair. "I believe you would, Teresa. And maybe you and Esteban have a right to see what is going to happen to Mr. Chandler Watts. But you stay close to me at all times. You hear?"

We made no effort to conceal ourselves as we approached the house from which the glow of lamplight could be seen through the windows. No one was in the front yard as we walked through the gate and around to the back. There were eight men lounging near the stable and corral, and they looked up when they saw us pass.

"It's Sam Houston!" one of the men at the corral gasped, but no one offered to interfere as we continued to walk slowly toward the barn.

Near the chicken coops, I saw Alma. On her knees over a steaming tub of water, she was plucking feathers off a freshly killed chicken. Standing near her, yelling at her, was Lightning, dressed in a green and gold striped frock coat and wearing a beaver-skin hat.

"Hurry up with that!" Lightning shouted. "You got four more birds to do, gal. And stop that squallin'! That's all you been doin' all day. You shut it up, or I'm goin' whup you good!"

"Alma?" Sam Houston said quietly. "Put down the chicken and come over here to us."

Lightning looked up quickly and then appeared to shrink when he saw who had spoken.

Alma dropped the chicken into the tub and ran to me. I held her tightly and tried to soothe her as she buried her face against my shoulder and
sobbed.

"Where's Chandler Watts?" Kalanu asked.

Twisting his body into a crouch, Lightning said, "Massa in da house,
suh. He havin' his supper in da house with Judge Foley and his Missus."

"Go in the house and tell Mr. Watts and Judge Foley I will see them
both out here."

"Yassuh!" Lightning cried and ran into the house.

"Alma," I asked, "where is your grandfather and my mother and
grandmother?"

"They're in the barn. They've kept them there all day. They took
everyone else to Austin." She began crying again. "And they made us take
my daddy and your grandfather out in the woods and bury them. They
didn't even let us put them in coffins."

"Alma, is this all the men who are here, the ones outside? Where are
all the other men who were here last night?"

"They took our people to Austin."

"Where are King and Lanfer?"

"They were with those who went to Austin."

We walked past a startled guard posted at the barn's door and went
inside. Esteban and I ran to our mother and grandmother, both of whom
were bound with ropes. Dazed and disoriented, Cata Valeria seemed at
first not to recognize us. She was like someone awakening from a deep
sleep and uncertain of where she was or what had happened.

Carmen, her face swollen and caked with dry blood, knew what had
happened. I could see that she knew. There were no tears or even a sign
that she had been crying. My grandmother did not cry. Soldiers do not
cry. But I could see the emptiness. In her dark eyes I saw the void that
could never be filled, the hurt that could never be healed; not in this
world.

Jacob rushed to Cata Valeria and began helping Esteban loosen the
knots. Alma knelt beside her grandfather, who had been secured with
chains.

"Teresa," Carmen said when I began to untie her. "You should not
have come back." She looked up and tried to focus. "Houston? Is that you,
Houston?"

"Carmen," he said, kneeling to hold her hand. "I . . . I'm sorry about Coalter." He looked toward Lebe Seru, whose face was cut and bruised very badly. "And I am sorry about your son, Lebe Seru. We'll get these chains off in just a little bit here. There's something I have to do first."

I had to look away from my grandmother to avoid breaking into tears.

We heard Chandler Watts shout, "Houston? Come out here, Sam Houston!"

Kalanu walked to the door. I helped my grandmother to her feet, and we followed.

Outside, it was now as dark as it had been when Watts and his men had arrived the previous night. The eight men at the corral had ignited pine-pitch torches. In the amber glow we could see Watts, who was standing with his hands on his hips and his feet planted wide apart. Judge Foley and his wife were just a few paces from the back door of the house.

"Well, well," Watts said. "Look who's come to pay us a visit. The high and mighty Sam Houston himself! Aren't we the honored ones."

Kalanu picked up a rope that was lying in the dirt next to the barn door. It was the rope that had been used to take away my grandfather's life.

"The mighty Sam Houston!" Watts repeated. "Friend of the Cherokees! Did you hear what we did to your Cherokee friends, Mr. Mighty Sam Houston? We ran them out of Texas and killed the ones who wouldn't leave. I never enjoyed anything more in my life. I even got to kill old Chief Bowles. I had the honor of doing that. Did you know it was me that killed him? I even . . ." —Watts narrowed his eyes— "What are you doing, Houston?"

Kalanu had begun to tie a hangman's noose at the end of the rope. "I'm just tryin' to keep my hands busy, Mr. Watts. What is it they say? Idle hands are the devil's workshop? Go on with what you were saying."

"What do you want here, Houston?" Watts demanded, his tone suddenly one of anger. "This is private property. You don't have any business here. And you sure as hell don't have the right to come in here and set loose prisoners detained under a lawful order of the court. Are you planning on interfering with the lawful action of a court?"

"You seem to know something about the law, Mr. Watts. Are you an attorney?"

Watts folded his arms. "I'm no damned lawyer, Houston, but I know what we did here last night was all legal and above board. We were enforcing the law. We did what you should have done a long time ago when the people of Texas were stupid enough to twice elect you president."

"Enforcing the law," Kalanu said slowly and tugged the last knot secure on his noose. "Yes, sir. We must enforce the law impartially and swiftly. The traditions of our English common law heritage require that we enforce the law impartially and swiftly. Did you know that, Mr. Watts?"

Watts laughed. "We did that last night. We carried out the law very swiftly! Right, boys?"

None of the men around Watts said anything or joined in his laughter. Several had stepped back from where he stood.

"A swift trial and a speedy execution of sentence," Kalanu said and moved to the table that had been used by Foley to preside over what had been called my grandfather's trial. "Both are guaranteed in the English common law tradition, and they are in the constitution of the Republic of Texas. I happen to know, because I had a little something to do with writing that constitution. Did you know that, Mr. Watts?"

"I don't care."

"Well, I think you should, because I propose to enforce that provision of the constitution and do so by having your trial right here and now. Judge Foley? Come on over and sit down at your table. Call your court to order."

Foley inched toward the table.

"Stay where you are, Delford," Watts said.

"Get over here and sit down, Foley," Kalanu commanded in a stern voice.

Watts feigned a laugh. "You're drunk, aren't you, Houston?"

"This court is now in session," Kalanu said. "As twice Chief Magistrate of the Republic of Texas, I will assume the right to bring the charges against the defendant, Mr. Chandler Watts."

Watts took a torch from one of the men near him and lit a cigar. "What charges, Houston?"

"The charge is attempted rape. In the Republic of Texas, we have a law against rape, and we have a law against attempted rape. And the penalty for both crimes is death by hanging."

"What are you talking about?"

"I'm talking about your attempt to rape this woman," Kalanu said and pointed at my mother, who was now standing with Jacob's support at the entrance to the barn. "I charge you with that crime, Chandler Watts. How do you plead?"

I saw movement at the back door of the house, and it occurred to me that someone might be at the door with a rifle. For the present, the men in the yard were making no threatening motions with their weapons.

"How do I plead? I don't know what you're talking about, Houston."

Kalanu approached my grandmother and asked, "Señora Owens, please ask your daughter if this man here, Mr. Chandler Watts, attempted to rape her."

Carmen posed the question in Spanish. In English, my mother said, "Yes. He did."

Kalanu looked at Foley and said, "You have the evidence, Judge."

"That's the testimony of only one person," Foley said. "You know you can't convict a person of this crime on the testimony of only one witness, especially if it's the woman in question."

Taking a few steps toward the house, Kalanu asked, "Who here witnessed the attempted rape of this woman last night?"

The men in the yard were silent.

"You are a fool, Houston," Watts said. "You're a damn drunken fool."

Raising his voice, Kalanu repeated, "Who here witnessed the attempted rape of this woman last night?"

The back door to the house opened, and Mrs. Watts walked slowly down the steps. "I saw what happened."

"Constance!" Mrs. Foley gasped.

Mrs. Watts walked within the flickering glow of light cast by the pine-pitch torches. When she did, ugly bruises and cuts on her face became visible.

Kalanu stepped to her and in a gentle voice asked, "Ma'am, you saw Chandler Watts attempt to rape this woman last night?"

"He tried to rape her, and he beat her when she fought back. He beat me when I tried to help her."

Watts shouted profanities and started toward his wife. He stopped when Sam Houston stepped between them.

Turning to the men around him, Watts yelled, "Why are you standing there? You're not going to let a couple of unarmed men walk right in here take away what's ours, are you?"

The men stared at one another as if waiting for someone to make the first move.

"Kill him!" Watts ordered.

Kalanu took one of the torches from the man nearest him and raised it so that all could see his face in the light. "He wants you to kill Sam Houston, boys. Ask him how long the man who kills Sam Houston will live. Ask him if there is any place on the face of the earth the man who kills Sam Houston can go to avoid the Texans who will come looking for him. He wants you to kill Sam Houston and forfeit your lives. Why doesn't he kill Sam Houston?"

Several of the men stepped further back into the shadows.

"Damn your eyes!" Watts shouted and drew a long-blade knife from the scabbard on his belt. "I will do it! Prepare yourself for hell, Sam Houston!"

Watts was unable to take more than one step before Jacob seized his arm and both of them fell to the ground. After a brief struggle, Jacob took away the knife and plunged it into Watts' chest. When Jacob got up, it looked for a moment as though Watts was also going to get to his feet. He got to one knee and held both hands to his heart. Blood poured around his fingers. He uttered a vile curse and crumpled to the ground.

We took my mother, grandmother, Lebe Seru and Alma to Cedar Point, where Sam Houston opened his house for our use. I did not understand why we could not return to our own house, but Kalanu said Judge Foley's ruling against my grandfather would stand unless we could have it overturned in an appeal to a higher court, which he would file on our behalf. He said, however, it was likely we had lost all of our property. Worse, there did not seem to be anything we could do about the teamsters who had been taken to Austin and sold into bondage. Kalanu said he would try to obtain the bills of sale so that we would at least know where they had been taken.

Jacob went to Galveston to ask a friend of his, a French naval captain in command of a warship, to send a contingent of his men to stay at Cedar Point to guard against the possibility that Bob King and Possum Lanfer might return to do us harm or attempt to recapture Lebe Seru and Alma. The Foleys were claiming that Lebe Seru and Alma were their property. Kalanu insisted he could protect us, but he appreciated having the men at his house because it freed him to return to Liberty to be with Mrs. Houston for the birth of their second child.

Before leaving, Kalanu summoned a physician to Cedar Point to attend my mother and my grandmother. My mother had been the most seriously injured, and she grew worse as the days passed. The physician said Cata Valeria had internal injuries and should go for treatment in New Orleans. Carmen wanted to go with my mother, but she had herself suffered several broken bones and was not up to the trip. My mother and I agreed I should stay with my grandmother while Esteban went with her and Jacob to New Orleans.

In the weeks that followed, I stayed close to my grandmother. Her spirit had been crushed by my grandfather's death. We arranged for Coalter's body and Binu Seru's body to be moved to the cemetery where my father and Alma's mother were buried. Carmen planted roses at the graves and visited each day, but she did not cry. We began to receive letters from Jacob, and were encouraged to learn that the physicians in New Orleans said Cata Valeria would recover completely. Esteban wrote me a letter in which he said they had a wonderful surprise in store for us when they returned to Cedar Point.

Carmen wrote the Montemayors in San Antonio to tell them what had happened. Santiago and Pilar Montemayor sent a letter requesting that we come to San Antonio to live with them. They urged caution when we traveled, because Tejano teamsters were being attacked between San Antonio and Austin. They said that anger toward Tejanos had become so great among Texians in the interior that Juan Seguin had moved his family to Mexico. Many Texians wanted all Tejanos to leave the Republic and go to Mexico even if they had lived in Texas for generations.

Because Pilar Montemayor and my grandmother had been good friends for such a long time, I was surprised when Carmen wrote her that we would remain in Houston Town for the time being. Finally, I asked her what we would do. We no longer had our house and farm or our wagons. How, I inquired, were we going to make our living in Houston Town.

"What do you think we should do, Teresa?"

"We could go to Liberty, Abuela," I suggested. "We could live with Kalanu. He would like for us to live with him in Liberty."

"Houston is married, Teresa. He has his own family. It would not be right for us to live with him."

"Mrs. Houston wants us to live with them, Abuela. She has written you many letters to ask that we live with them."

"Mrs. Houston is a kind and generous woman, but it would not be right. We will stay in Houston Town for the present."

I sensed that my grandmother's refusal to live with the Montemayors or the Houstons was for a reason she was not willing to share with me. In the weeks that followed, I began to suspect that Carmen was making plans for what we would do. One night, after everyone had gone to sleep, I happened to see Lebe Seru slip away from the house. I watched him run to the bayou before disappearing into the darkness. He returned before dawn and was met at the door by my grandmother. I was reluctant to ask her what was happening after witnessing the same thing occur several nights in succession. I had learned there were times when it was best not to question my grandmother. I suspected it had something to do with what they had been doing before my grandfather was killed.

Whatever Carmen and Lebe Seru might have been planning was pushed even deeper into secrecy upon the return of Cata Valeria, Jacob and Esteban. None of us were surprised that my mother was returning as Señora von Gorlitz and that Esteban and I had a new father. They had decided to be married in New Orleans because there were no priests in Houston Town. After we had a celebration, Jacob took me aside.

"Teresa," he said, "I know you loved your father very much. You are old enough to remember him. Esteban does not remember him. He was too young."

"Yes," I said. "I loved my father very much."

Jacob continued, "I can never replace your father, Teresa. But I think you know I love your mother very much, and I love you and Esteban. I will try very hard to be a good father to you both."

Jacob von Gorlitz was a good and kind man. I could understand why Esteban felt so close to the man who had avenged our grandfather's death and was in a position to protect us from harm and give us anything we would ever need or want. Jacob was now Esteban's father in every sense, including name. I knew, however, it was different with me; but I did not want to hurt him, so I said, "I am honored to be your daughter, Jacob."

He hugged me. "You will love Vienna, Teresa. You will become good friends with the young Princes of the Royal Family. Franz Josef and Maximilian are your age. They will love you."

I was not certain I had heard correctly. I had no intention of leaving Texas, certainly not for Vienna. "Did you say Vienna?"

"Yes, Teresa. Vienna. And we must begin preparations for our departure immediately. The United States is on the verge of annexing Texas. The Mexican navy may attempt to blockade Galveston. We must be at sea before hostilities commence."

Esteban, of course, was happy he would be crossing the Atlantic Ocean on a French warship. Jacob was already teaching him his first words of the German language. My brother discovered he and Maximilian von Hapsburg were exactly the same age, both having been born on July 6, 1832. Jacob said the coincidence must mean the two boys were destined to be great friends and share a common destiny.

Carmen was pleased that Esteban and I would accompany our mother and new father to Vienna. A burden of responsibility had been lifted from her shoulders. However, when she learned it had been assumed she and Lebe Seru and Alma would also reside in the Austrian Empire, her response was quite different.

"Cata Valeria," she said. "I cannot go to Vienna. It is out of the question."

"You cannot stay in Texas," my mother said. "You have violated the same laws for which my father was murdered. They will do to you what they did to him. These Texians hate Mexicans. They kill the Indians and enslave the negroes. Why would you even think of staying in such a place?"

When my grandmother did not answer, I knew my suspicion of what she and Lebe Seru were planning had been confirmed. They intended to somehow carry on with what they had been doing before my grandfather's death. I now knew why Carmen had been so insistent that Sam Houston obtain the bills of sale of Binu Seru's teamsters. She and Lebe Seru were going to try to free them.

Over the next several days, my mother supervised the packing of trunks, including several that contained dresses and other clothes she had purchased for me in New Orleans. Jacob made several trips to Galveston to put our belongings on the French warship. He said we must hurry because everyone now said that war between Mexico and the United States was inevitable.

A few days before our scheduled departure, Sam Houston came to Cedar Point. We were saddened to learn he had just returned from Tennessee, where he had reached the Hermitage only moments after the former president's death. I knew this was a terrible blow to Kalanu.

Andrew Jackson had been like a father to him. His sad expression changed when he told us that he had just come from Liberty where his second son, Andrew Jackson Houston, was doing well. He said Mrs. Houston had sent him with wedding gifts for Cata Valeria and Jacob. He was pleased to learn of Jacob's plans to take us all to live in Austria.

"That's good," Kalanu said. "We're in for some unsettling times over the next year or so here in Texas."

Jacob asked, "You believe there will be a war between the United States and Mexico, General?"

"I expect so, Jacob. The boys up in Washington City finally approved annexation. I wish we didn't have to have a war, but the generals in Mexico think the Nueces River is the southern border of Texas. We're going to have to convince them it's the Rio Grande."

My grandmother said, "This war will not be about whether the Nueces or the Rio Grande is the southern border of the United States, Houston. This war will be about the United States taking all the land that belongs to Mexico between Texas and the Pacific Ocean."

Ignoring Carmen's words, Kalanu asked, "Did you folks hear that as soon as Texas becomes a state, I'll be going up to Washington City?"

Esteban shouted, "You're going to be the President of the United States, Old Chief!"

"Well, not right off, Esteban. James Knothead Polk has a claim on that office for the next four years, but I'm gonna be the first United States Senator from Texas! Then maybe I'll step in and be president for a spell."

Kalanu joined Jacob and my mother in trying to persuade Carmen and Lebe Seru to change their minds about going to Europe, but they remained steadfast in their refusal right up until the day we were to depart. I finally had to tell my mother that I, too, would remain in Texas. Her reaction was predictable.

"You are coming with us, and I will hear no more about it."

It was not easy telling my mother that I was fourteen years old and she could no longer make me do what I chose not to do. She threatened to have Jacob carry me on the ship, but I think both she and Jacob understood that I meant it when I said I would leave the ship the first opportunity I had and come back home. It was only when the wagons were loaded for the ride to the wharfs that my mother agreed to a compromise that I would come to Vienna in six months, when my grandmother's health was better.

We were late in our arrival at the wharf and had little time for good-byes. Esteban's excitement about his first ocean voyage faded when he had to bid farewell. After hugging our grandmother, he came to me and asked, "You will write to me, Teresita?"

"Yes, Esteban," I said and held him as tears came to my eyes. I loved my brother and did not want to be apart from him. I had no idea of when I would see him again. It was possible I would never see him again. "And you must write to me, Estebanito. Write as often as you can. Write to me everyday!"

My mother looked very stern when she said, "I will expect you in six months, Teresa. Do you understand? Six months."

Back at Cedar Point, Kalanu lit several candles, and he and I were ready to settle in for an evening of checkers when Carmen approached me with a blanket and some of my clothes.

"We are ready to leave, Teresa," she said. "Wrap your clothes in the blanket and secure it with these cords."

Something in my grandmother's tone warned me not to argue with her the way I had with my mother. In the next room Lebe Seru and Alma were also wrapping items in blankets.

"Carmen," Kalanu asked, "what are you doing?"

"We're leaving."

"Leaving? Tonight? I thought you were going to stay here a few months and then go to Austria."

"We're not going to Austria, Houston."

He followed us out the door and to the front porch where Lebe Seru extended his hand. Kalanu did not anymore understand what was happening than did I. He tried to persuade Carmen and Lebe Seru not to leave since it was getting dark and looking as though it might rain.

Stepping from the porch, Carmen said, "You may take a moment to say good-bye to Houston, Teresa." She glanced at the man she had known for so many years. For an instant her eyes softened just enough to confirm my suspicion that she had always liked Sam Houston. It made me very happy. "Tell the old rascal to take care of himself and stay out of trouble."

Kalanu watched Carmen, Lebe Seru and Alma walk to the gate where they waited for me. He glanced at me and then back to my grandmother. "I guess she knows what she's doing."

"I guess she does."

He looked at me again and then at the ground. "I have a feeling we won't be seeing each other for a spell, Teresa. That makes me feel a little poorly."

It made me feel very poorly, but my throat was too tight to tell him so without crying.

His eyes brightened. "Wait here, Teresa! I'll be right back."

I stood on the front porch as Kalanu ran inside the house. He returned carrying a canvas bag.

"What is it, Kalanu?" I asked weakly.

"It's for you. Look inside!"

The bag contained the books he had used to teach Alma, Esteban and me to read. His copy of *The Iliad* and *Robinson Crusoe* were in the bag, along with *The Pilgrim's Progress*.

"Kalanu," I said, shaking my head, "I cannot take these books. They are your books. You have had them since you were a boy. You should give them to your children."

He said, "That's what I'm doing."

Carmen called for me to hurry.

"Good bye, Teresa," Kalanu said and embraced me. "You be real careful now, you hear? Just because I dunked you down in the River Styx don't mean you still don't have to be real careful and watch out for things. And if you run into some trouble and need help, you come to me. You hear, Teresa? You come to me."

My voice failed. I could say none of the things I wanted to tell him. All I could do was nod before I ran to where Carmen, Lebe Seru and Alma were waiting. We began to run down the trail toward the bayou. When I paused to look back, my teacher waved.

Over the next several weeks, we learned firsthand the hardships faced by the fugitive slaves we had helped flee to the land south of the Nueces River. We went by foot to a place on the beach some fifty miles south of Houston Town where Lebe Seru had hidden a sixteen-foot boat in the dunes. Traveling at night to avoid detection, we made our way down the Laguna Madre, the long stretch of intercoastal waterway between the mainland and the line of barrier islands that run parallel to the Texas coast. The Laguna Madre is like a wide river of salt water. In most places it is shallow and filled with reefs and sandbars; but using detailed charts that had been drawn by runaways for those who would come later, Lebe

Seru was able to steer us through a maze of channels that carried the little boat ever southward.

Also noted on the charts were the rivers and creeks that emptied into the Laguna Madre and provided us with the fresh water needed to fill our canteens. The charts indicated places where we would find pecan trees, mustang grapes and other edible plants. Lebe Seru had brought a seine, which we used to scoop up the shrimp that were our main source of food along with fish we caught on troll lines. There were plentiful supplies of driftwood to use to cook our meals. Lebe Seru had brought a long-rifle, but we dared not fire at game for fear of the sound being heard.

The most bothersome thing were the insects that frequently descended on us in swarms until we began covering ourselves in the dried entrails of sharks we caught on the troll lines. The smell was enough to make you want to vomit, but it solved the problem of insects. It was a device Lebe Seru said he had learned from the Karankawa Indians, a tribe that had lived on the islands until exterminated by Lamar's Ranging Companies. When we reached a fresh water stream or river, we could not wait to wash the smelly concoction off our bodies. As soon as we encountered the next swarm of insects, we put it back on.

It was a difficult and uncomfortable undertaking, especially trying to sleep during the day with one eye always on the lookout for predators, animal or human. On land, we would use the boat as a shelter for protection against the sun or rain. Thanks to the charts and instructions of those who had gone before us, we did not suffer unduly. It was not long before I could even imagine that the life that had been led by the Indians in and around these coastal waters had its good points. They were able to live very close to the huge variety of birds that made their homes in the estuaries and coves of the Laguna Madre. There was nothing more thrilling that to see the long-winged whooping cranes glide gracefully over the waters.

At night when we were rowing or using a small sail to catch the wind, we did not talk because the sound of a human voice traveled over the waters. Most of the time there were probably no people within miles of us, but we did not want to take a chance. During the day, we were usually too exhausted to talk or do anything but sleep. Sometimes, when we were on one of the islands, we felt secure enough of our isolation to speculate on where we were and how much further we had to go.

One day, I tried to get my grandmother to talk about what we were going to do when we reached our destination, wherever that might be.

I asked, "Do you plan to try to help more slaves escape when we get to this place south of the Nueces River, Abuela?"

"It is not a matter of what we plan to do, Teresa. We will do what we have to do. We will do what we can."

"I hope we can find Binu Seru's teamsters and help them escape."

Carmen looked at me for a moment and then asked, "What happened to your pendant, Teresa?"

It was the question I had been dreading. I knew what the pendant meant to my grandmother. It was the only thing we had that had belonged to her mother. I saw no reason to go into the details of how I had traded the pendant to a woman for nothing more than a pot of broth.

"I no longer have it, Abuela."

The disappointment was evident in Carmen's expression, but she said nothing more.

When we passed the mouth of the Nueces River, we stayed far away and near the islands because the town of Corpus Christi was located on the south bank of the Nueces and was known to attract the worst sort of outlaws, the kind that would be only too eager to capture runaways for the bounty money being offered for their return. The night we passed Corpus Christi the sky was bright from the light of many fires, and we noticed lights from large ships anchored outside the entrance to the channel to the port. We were puzzled because Corpus Christi was not a port of call for ocean-going merchant ships. Later, Carmen said the fires on the shore might have been campfires of Comanches who sometimes traveled this far south to hunt or trade. There looked to be hundreds, perhaps thousands, of campfires.

The stretch of the Laguna Madre south of the Nueces was through a particularly harsh land. We no longer saw thick forests on the shoreline. As far as we could see the land was flat and barren, almost like a desert. There were isolated stands of mesquites or wind-swept oaks that did not grow very tall. As we went even further south, we began to see palm trees and red sage. Occasionally, we thought we saw gigantic purple mountains, but Lebe Seru said they were a mirage. The land between the Nueces and the Rio Grande was a vast and level coastal plain. Some mornings, we spotted families of javelinas trotting about amongst the chaparral and poking their tusks at prickly pear.

On our foraging trips ashore, we picked some of the prickly pear and were able to cook them with our fish. We also chewed on mesquite beans and the stringy but sweet fruit of yucca stalks. We soon learned to be extremely leery of rattlesnakes. They were not as numerous as around Houston Town, but the ones we saw were huge. Some were as long as six feet and as big around as a man's leg. It was truly a harsh land, but in its own way it was pretty. I had never seen flowers with such rich colors, and some of the white or yellow cactus blooms could be seen in the dark like the glow from a lantern.

We finally arrived one morning at our destination several miles north of the mouth of the Rio Grande. We hid the boat and went inland. It was a desolate place with no vegetation and a parched soil broken only by ponds of brackish water. We followed a dry river bed and made a camp at a place marked on the charts. Lebe Seru built a small fire with dry mesquite wood and then added green leaves to make a thin trail of white smoke for a few moments before extinguishing it. He repeated this once every hour until dusk.

After sundown, we heard a shrill whistle. It sounded like a whippoorwill. Lebe Seru answered with the same call. In a few minutes, three men appeared from the darkness and approached us, their hands raised to show they carried no weapons.

Lebe Seru got up, walked forward a few steps, and then began to run. Following, we caught up with Lebe Seru and saw he was embracing the men.

"Carmen!" he called. "Teresa and Alma! Look who's here!"

I was thrilled beyond words when I saw that two of the men were Esau and Tom Blue. The third man was younger. I did not immediately recognize him until I heard Alma whisper, "Teresa, it's Ralph!"

We ran to the men, and they grabbed and hugged each of us in turn. They looked to be in excellent health.

When we had finished our greetings, Esau asked, "Did you see them? You must have passed them on the way. They are right behind you. Did you see them?"

"Who, Esau?" Carmen asked.

Esau was very excited. "An army from the United States. They have crossed the Nueces River and are coming here to the Rio Grande. You must have passed them on the way."

VII

Esau, Tom Blue and Ralph escorted us south to a plankwood house on the north bank of the Rio Grande across from Matamoros. Behind the house was a grove of lemon trees and a field of about ten acres planted with corn, tomatoes, beans, squash, onions and an assortment of melons and peppers. From the rise of the embankment, we could see the spires of cathedrals in Matamoros and the red-tiled roofs of white adobe structures set among green citrus trees and swaying sycamores. Just outside the city were thatch-roof *jacales* and beyond them were fields white with cotton. On the opposite bank of the river, women were washing clothes in the shallows and keeping an eye on children playing in the reeds.

"This is an excellent soil for cultivation," Lebe Seru said. "Are there only three of you here?"

"Many of our people were in this valley until a short time ago," Esau said. "When we heard the American army was coming, we decided it would best for them to go to the farms inland. The soil is not so good there, but we cannot take a chance on being captured."

"If the American army is coming," Carmen asked, "why are the three of you still here?"

Tom Blue said, "Somebody has to be here to meet our people when they come from the Laguna Madre. They must direct them to our farms inland. We thought we would stay until the American army arrives. We don't know what will happen when they get here. They may leave us alone."

Ralph said they had received word of what had happened to my grandfather and Binu Seru at Houston Town. Esau and Tom Blue joined him in expressing their sorrow for our loss.

"We need to get word to the teamsters who were captured and sold in Austin," Esau said. "We need to let them know of how to come to us."

"We know where they are," Carmen said. "We have the bills of sale. We will get word to them."

"Did you and Tom Blue build this house?" Lebe Seru asked while admiring the workmanship on what was really two houses connected by a dog trot.

Esau put his hand on Ralph's shoulder in a fatherly gesture of affection. "With Ralph's help, we did."

Ralph glanced at Alma and then looked down at the ground when he saw she was smiling at him.

Esau was about to say more but stopped when a dozen men on horseback suddenly appeared on the south embankment. Even at a distance of some three hundred yards, we could see their bright red and blue uniforms. They wore the plumed helmets of Mexican dragoons. The soldiers reined their horses to the right, raced along the embankment for a hundred yards and then spurred their mounts toward Matamoros.

Tom Blue said, "The one in front is General Arista, the Commander of the Northern Army of Mexico. He's massed an army of about ten thousand over there. Arista sent a message to Zachary Taylor to return to the north bank of the Nueces. If he does not cross back over, there will be a fight."

"Zachary Taylor?" Carmen asked.

"General Zachary Taylor," Esau said. "He's the Commander of the Military Department of the Southwest United States. President Polk sent him across the Nueces with about four thousand men. The word is Polk wants a war. He's ordered Taylor to do whatever is necessary to provoke the Mexicans. There's a rumor that Winfield Scott, General of all American armies, will then land at Vera Cruz and march on Mexico City. Polk doesn't just want Texas. He wants California and all the land between here and the Pacific."

Carmen asked if any word had been received from the Montemayors. For years, the Montemayors had been helping fugitive slaves in San Antonio much as we had done in Houston Town.

"Yes," Tom Blue said. "The Montemayors sent a message with some of our most recent arrivals that they will soon be coming to live with us. They're having to leave San Antonio. The Texians have been burning down Tejano houses there. They think the Tejanos will be on the side of the Mexicans in this war that is coming. The Montemayors fear for their lives."

"The Montemayors are coming here," Carmen said and looked at me. "Did you hear, Teresa? The Montemayors are coming here to live with us."

It was the first time I had seen Carmen smile since my grandfather's death. I was happy to see my grandmother so pleased. It would be good for her to be with the friends she had known since before she had come to Texas. She and Pilar Montemayor were like Alma and me; they were like sisters. And I was happy the Montemayors were coming. It had been years since I had seen Jorge. I had never had a chance to thank him for the comb he had sent me.

Lebe Seru and Carmen decided that we would stay at the house on the Rio Grande with Esau, Tom Blue and Ralph. Using the information on the bills of sale, Tom Blue and Ralph would slip back into Texas to make contact with as many of Binu Seru's teamsters as possible and help them make their escape. Lebe Seru, Carmen and I would help Esau watch the contact point for the smoke signal and then assist escapees to make their way to the places the runaways were farming in the chaparral. We would raise vegetables and fruit so we could supply the fugitives with provisions on the trip inland.

Our immediate concern now became what effect the threat of war would have on our plans. The advance elements of the American army were just north of us, and each morning we heard the guns of warships being fired near the mouth of the river, some ten miles south of our farm. Lebe Seru said they were firing the guns to intimidate the Mexicans. The fact remained that Esau, Lebe Seru and Alma were fugitive slaves; and the United States army had in the past been used to capture runaways. We hoped the soldiers would be too preoccupied with the Mexican army to worry about a few people tending a small plot of land. We knew, however, that we must be prepared to flee inland if we detected any sign we were being viewed with suspicion.

Alma was delighted to be working again in a garden. Each day, we made many trips to the river to fill buckets and bring water to the plants. I was overjoyed on the days it rained because that meant I could spend more time building my pens and chicken coops. Esau said we would buy chickens and some milk goats. Lebe Seru found some scrap metal not far from the village of Point Isabel further down the river and began to construct a forge he could use to make the tools the runaways needed on the farms. He hoped we could eventually begin to trade and haul freight again in order to make money to buy rifles and other items we could not make.

Early one morning, two months after our arrival, the American army began a sudden and rapid advance to the river. Without fanfare, soldiers in blue uniforms quickly deployed artillery on the banks and aimed the tubes at Matamoros. Infantrymen dug trenches and erected earthworks.

Dragoons and cavalry mounted patrols on the roads that ran parallel to the Rio Grande. No drums were sounded or bugles blown. It was obvious they had been ordered to move into their positions with dispatch and without calling undue notice to their presence.

Their presence, of course, was quickly noted. The women who daily washed clothes in the shallows on the south bank ran back to Matamoros. Very quickly, Mexican dragoons and a detachment of cavalry appeared and commenced to monitor the activities on the north bank. When the Mexicans brought their artillery forward, I began to think the war was about to start right then and there in our front yard. We discussed the advisability of leaving the farm before the fighting began. Thus far, none of the soldiers had seemed to take much notice of our presence.

"I don't think they're going to fight right off," Esau said. "No one wants to fire the first shot in a war."

Esau's observation proved correct because no weapons were fired and by the end of the third day of the advance to the river it was possible to see soldiers on both sides relax and move about as though they were not within range of weapons that could end their lives in the blink of an eye. So secure were the Americans that fighting was not about to commence they began to float barges up the river with supplies from their warships anchored near the mouth of the river.

One afternoon, we stopped work to sip lemonade and watch the unloading of a flotilla of barges not far from our house. The cargoes were being transferred onto wagons pulled by mules. Since none of us were unfamiliar with the work of teamsters, we knew the steep banks presented a formidable challenge to whoever was in charge of moving the artillery and crates of ammunition and gunpowder up to the roads where they could be deployed to the men now encamped for miles up and down the river.

We were unable to tell which of the fifty or so men in the operation were officers because in the heat most of the men had stripped off their shirts and none wore jackets. About the only distinguishing feature of an officer's uniform, other than shoulder-insignia, seemed to be the darker color blue of the jacket. At first, the scene below was one of confusion. The mules, as is often the case with mules, were not cooperating. When mules are harnessed in single file, the mules in front will almost always try to run while the ones behind will sit on their haunches. Because of the weight of the cargo, the Americans were having to harness four teams to a wagon.

After awhile, we began to notice that one of the men in the platoon did seem to be in charge of the others. We were some distance away, but we could discern he was a rather small man. This officer did not appear to be issuing many orders; rather, he moved from place to place, demonstrating how to handle the mules and make them do what was required. He was teaching his men by example what to do as the situation demanded, and he was slowly bringing order to what had promised to be a catastrophe.

So intensely were we watching the operation at the river, we did not at first notice an elderly man on a mule riding sidesaddle up the trail to our house. When we saw him, Carmen and I walked to where the man had halted at the edge of Alma's garden. It was peculiar to see a man with both legs on the same side of his mount as though he were sitting in a chair and not on a saddle. He had one leg hitched over the pommel as if to insure he would not fall off the animal.

On the old man's head was a frayed straw hat that looked as if it had been chewed on by the mule who promptly went to sleep with the man still on its back. It was the kind of hat common among slaves who worked in the fields. The man wore a ragged linen jacket that might have once upon a time been white just as his faded denim pants had probably once been blue. The pants were rolled almost to his knees, revealing white and scrawny legs. When he removed his hat in a gesture of greeting, a flood of grey curls fell in all directions over his ears and his collar.

"Mornin', folks," the old fellow drawled. "How you folks be this fine mornin'?"

His red, weather-beaten face was as creased with seams as the beat-up saddle on his sleeping mule. It was not an unpleasant face, and the hard lines around his large mouth were those of a man used to smiling. His eyes were so deeply set beneath bushy eyebrows, it was impossible to determine their color.

"*Buenos dias, Señor,*" my grandmother said. "Welcome to our house."

"Thank you kindly, ma'am," the man said cheerfully. "Is that lemonade you folks are drinkin' thar? Did it come from those handsome trees?"

"Yes, Señor," Carmen said. "Please. May we offer you a glass? Won't you join us?"

The old gentleman seemed thrilled to have someone speak to him with kindness. I was now guessing he was some sort of itinerant merchant, hoping to find customers in the ranks of an army. All sorts of people were arriving daily from the United States to pitch tents and sell goods and services to the soldiers who had very little to do except spend their meager pay. Already, there were dozens of taverns and gentlemen's parlors around Point Isabel.

Struggling to dismount, the man said, "Ma'am, I must confess I truly love lemonade. It's my favorite libation since my wife, a wonderful and god-fearin' woman, put me on nonspeakin' terms with John Barleycorn. I will take you up on yoar kind offer."

Lebe Seru rushed to help me assist the man get off the mule without falling into the dirt. Grasping his arm, I realized he was not as decrepit as he looked. He was a sturdy fellow with a barrel-chest and thick arms. Standing, he had a somewhat odd appearance which I attributed to the shortness of his legs relative to the rest of his body. When he walked toward the porch, he rolled in a manner similar to a sailor.

When Carmen poured a glass of lemonade and handed it to him, the man downed it quickly and made no pretense he did not wish to have another.

Making himself comfortable in a wooden rocker, he nursed the second glass and said, "Fine lookin' garden. Mighty well tended. I admire that. You can generally tell the cut of folks by the kind of garden they keep."

We looked at each other, no one certain as to what to say to this bizarre fellow. I think we all thought he might be a little crazy in the head, although his sharp eyes were not those of a dull-witted man. He was observing us closely.

Suddenly, he leaned forward and peered down toward the soldiers loading the wagons with the munitions taken from the barges. "Look at that boy," he said, referring to the officer who now had the wagons moving up the incline. "I'd say he knows what he's doin', wouldn't you?"

"He is a fine teamster," Lebe Seru said.

The old man looked at Lebe Seru as if pondering his words very seriously. "You know, sir, I agree. That young man down thar is doing the most difficult job in the army. He's in the quartermaster corps. He's gettin' the weapons of war where they need to be when they need to be thar. The man who does that best wins the war. Do you not agree?"

"I am not a soldier, sir," Lebe Seru replied. "But it does stand to reason."

"It do indeed," the man said. "That young feller down thar does it better than anybody I've ever seen do it, and I'm not jist talkin' 'bout loadin' wagons."

It was hard not to think we were indulging old-man talk. On the other hand, he seemed to be speaking from some background of experience.

Suddenly, he sprang to his feet and shouted, "Lieutenant Grant! Come up here!"

I was embarrassed when all the soldiers below turned to look up at us. They had an important and difficult job to accomplish and here was an old codger yelling at them. To my surprise, the officer in charge quickly began to run up the embankment, stopping only to grab his coat and slip it on as he ran. He moved with the grace of an athlete and was at our front porch before my grandmother had a chance to refill the old man's glass.

The officer stopped in front of the old man, drew himself to attention and saluted. "Sir! Lieutenant Grant reporting as ordered, sir!"

"I didn't order you, Lieutenant. I jist wanted you come up here to meet my friends. You need to take a break ever now and agin. Don't do no good to work without stoppin' in this kind of heat. You'll get a lot more done if you let the men take frequent breaks."

"Yes, General Taylor."

Our eyes met as we realized we had been entertaining Zachary Taylor, the Commander of the Army Department of the Southwest. He was certainly not like any general I had ever seen. There was nothing in his casual manner of dress to indicate he was a soldier, much less a general.

General Taylor asked us each to introduce ourselves to the young lieutenant. I think it was his way of learning who we were. I began to appreciate there was a very cunning intelligence at work behind this old man's rough appearance.

After we had said who we were, General Taylor looked at the lieutenant and said, "This here is Sam Grant. Of course, that ain't your real name is it, Lieutenant? Stand at ease, son, and have a glass of the best tasting lemonade this side of Eden. What is your real name, Lieutenant Grant?"

Relaxing, the lieutenant took the glass of lemonade my grandmother offered and thanked her with a boyish grin. He did not look to be much more than a boy to me though, as an officer, I knew he would have to be in his early twenties. He was thin, of medium height, and had a round, smooth face with ruddy cheeks. His hair was reddish-brown, and his eyes were clear, almost devoid of color, except for a hint of blue.

"Sir," Lieutenant Grant said and shuffled his feet awkwardly. "My name is Hiram Ulysses Grant." He took a quick drink of the lemonade. "This is good, ma'am." His eyes lingered on my grandmother. "The soil must be good here. I mean, for the lemons to taste this sweet, the soil must be good."

"How'd you come to be called Sam, Lieutenant?" the general asked in a manner that suggested he had heard the story before and wanted it repeated for our benefit.

"Well, sir, when our congressman got me an appointment to West Point, he couldn't remember both my names. He knew my mother's name had been Simpson, so he put down Ulysses Simpson Grant. I tried to tell them the truth of it at the Academy, but they said that if I got appointed as Ulysses Simpson Grant then my name would have to be Ulysses Simpson Grant."

Taylor laughed and held out his glass for yet another refill. "Ain't that jist like the army? That's jist the way things are done in the army, 'specially at West Point. I'm shore glad I never went thar." He laughed again. "So how'd they get to callin' you Sam?"

Lieutenant Grant shrugged and smiled at me and Alma. He had a nice smile. "On all rosters, I was listed as U. S. Grant, and the boys called me Uncle Sam Grant. Pretty soon, they dropped the Uncle. It's as good a name as any. You've got to be called something, I guess."

"Just like the army," Taylor repeated. He looked at Lebe Seru and Carmen. "And it was the same thing with his assignment. Grant here was considered to be the best horseman to ever come out of the academy. So what do they do? They stick him in the infantry! You asked for the cavalry, didn't you, son?"

"The dragoons, sir."

"Well, thar you are. I've never seen a man with a way with horses like this boy here. 'Course, ifen he'd been put in the dragoons or the cavalry, I might not have come to know his abilities as a quartermaster, and it would have been the army's loss."

"General Taylor, sir," Lieutenant Grant said. "I've been meaning to ask you. I'd like to return to infantry now that it looks like we're going to fight."

"You wanna fight, do you, Lieutenant Grant?"

"I don't want to fight, sir. I don't really want to be in the army. I never have. But I'd like to do my part to get this over so we can all go home. And I have some ideas on how we might get this thing down here over real quick. I—"

Sam Grant cut his words short, because three officers were hurrying toward us. One of them, a corpulent young man, raced ahead of the others, drew himself to attention and executed a smart salute. "General Taylor, sir!" he said as the other young officers came to attention on either side of him. "We did not know where you were, sir!" His small eyes darted toward Lebe Seru and Carmen. "Is the General safe, sir?"

A scowl formed on the hard face of Zachary Taylor. "Safe?" he growled. "What do you mean 'safe,' Lieutenant Meade?"

"Well, sir" —he glanced at me in a most disapproving way— "I mean, these civilians, sir. They are *grisos*, sir. They may be acting in concert with the enemy."

Grisos meant one of mixed blood, Indian and Spanish. I was a *grisos*. It literally meant 'grey,' a mixture of colors. It was a common term among Mexicans and Tejanos alike, but it had been corrupted into the word "greaser" by some Texians and had become a word of derision.

"Lieutenant Meade," the general said, getting to his feet. "These folks here invited me into their home. You will demonstrate courtesy to them. Do you understand me?"

"Yes, sir!"

Meade's small eyes were now seeming to cast their disapproving gaze on Lieutenant Grant's uniform, which had been buttoned in the wrong holes; whereas Meade's uniform gave evidence of having been the object of considerable attention. He was wearing braids and epaulets. It was an impressive uniform, except for the heavy stains of wetness under his arms and at his stomach.

Turning to Lebe Seru and Carmen, General Taylor said, "Allow me to present these boys. Lieutenants Meade, McClellan, and Beauregard."

Lieutenants Meade and McClellan doffed their hats and executed quick, shallow bows. Lieutenant Beauregard bowed with a gallant fourish of his hand. He was a very handsome man and sported a blue silk sash around his waist.

"What is it you boys want?" General Taylor asked. "You jist out lookin' for me? You don't have anythin' better to do?"

"Well, sir," Meade said, "now that you ask. I would—"

"Meade," Taylor interrupted, "don't ask me again about bridges and pontoons."

"Uh . . . well. Yes, sir!"

"We're here to fight a defensive war," General Taylor said. "I'm not goin' across that river unless I can help it. I don't need no damn pontoons and bridges. That little . . ." —he cleared his throat— " . . . President Polk says this river is the southern boundary of the United States, so we're here to keep anybody from comin' 'cross that ain't invited. That's our mission, Meade, unless you know something I don't know. Do you know somethin' I don't know?"

"No, sir!"

"So you boys go find somethin' else to do. That's an order, gentlemen. You are dismissed."

The young men saluted and ran into each other in their dash to scamper out of the yard and head back in the direction of Point Isabel. Lieutenant Grant saluted and returned to his work on the embankment.

General Taylor put his hand on one of the porch beams for support. Nodding in the direction of the officers going to Point Isabel, he said, "Those are my Topogs. Topographical engineers. General Scott says they're the best in the army, except for his fair-haired boy, Captain Robert E. Lee, who he's sending to me as quick as he can get him down here. Scott says Lee's the best soldier in the army." His gaze drifted toward the river, where Lieutenant Grant had resumed moving the wagons to the road. "I might jist argue with him on that. Give me a man who wants to get the war over real quick, so's he can get home. I have a hunch that man will be the best soldier in the army."

Alma and I had finished supper and had gone to the garden to harvest corn in the cool of the evening. Lebe Seru and Carmen were at the contact point off the Laguna Madre, and Esau was escorting a family of escapees to one of the inland farms. I was taking a basket filled with ears to shuck to the house when I looked up and saw Lieutenant Grant standing in our lemon grove.

"Lieutenant?" I said to get his attention. He seemed lost in thought. "*Buenas tardes.*"

"*Buenas tardes, señorita,*" he said and rushed to take the heavy basket. "*¿Cómo está usted?*"

"*Muy bien, gracias.*" We walked toward the house. "Are you learning to speak Spanish, Lieutenant?"

He smiled. "Oh, I purchased a book. I've learned a few phrases, I guess."

There was a forlorn quality about this man. A smile came to his lips easily enough, but he would quickly retreat to an expression that made it seem as if he were somewhere else or perhaps lost in abstract thought.

"Señorita Sestos," he asked, "is your grandmother at home?"

"My grandmother?"

"Yes, señorita. I—"

"You may call me Teresa."

"Teresa," he smiled, pronouncing my name correctly. "I would like to see her if I may."

The request puzzled me. "Why, Lieutenant Grant?"

"Please call me Sam," he said with his boyish smile. "I'm not sure why I want to see your grandmother, Teresa. I guess that somehow" —he struggled for words— "your grandmother reminds me of my mother."

Now I understood. He was far from home, and he was homesick. He missed his mother. His words made me think of my mother, who was by now probably very angry I had not kept my promise to her.

"I guess," Sam continued, "I thought I could talk to your grandmother like I've always been able to talk to my mother. All my life I've always gone to my mother in times of trouble. She told me what I should do. I can't do that now. Texas is a long way from Ohio."

It was not difficult to know what was going through the young soldier's mind. Right across the Rio Grande, no more than a quarter mile from where we were standing, were thousands of young men, not so different from Sam Grant; and they were most likely each thinking the same thing. Would the battle begin tomorrow? Was there someone across the river whose life they would end? Was there someone across the river who would take their life?

"This war," Sam said, "is wrong. It troubles me. This is going to be a war of conquest to take land away from a people who do not have the resources to defend their land. And once the land is taken, I fear it will be used to spread the scourge of slavery."

The sun was setting, and it was beginning to grow dark. "If you think this way, why are you here, Lieutenant . . . Sam?"

"I've thought of resigning my commission, but I cannot bring myself to do it. I'm an officer in the United States army, Teresa. I swore an oath at West Point. I have an obligation to fulfil."

"Do other officers in your army view this war the way you do?"

"Some do. For most, however, I'm afraid the war is an opportunity for promotion and advancement. They plan to make a career in the army. Wars are the way you advance in the army. Some are eager to fight this war."

"I do not believe your General Taylor is eager to fight this war, Sam. He may be a little too old to be fighting wars."

"General Taylor will fight, and he will fight hard when the time comes. Don't let his appearance deceive you. We call him Old Rough and Ready. He's the best general in the American army. Zachary Taylor will never back down, and he'll never ask his men to go where he wouldn't lead them." He folded his arms behind him. "But you're right. The General doesn't approve of this war anymore than I do. What's ironic is that his own son-in-law helped get us down here."

"His son-in-law?"

"Zachary Taylor's son-in-law is a congressman named Jefferson Davis. Davis is one of the leading warhawks in Congress. They've beat back men opposed to this war, men like Congressman Abraham Lincoln from Illinois. Now I hear Davis has resigned to lead a militia of Mississippi Rifle down here."

"Why are you in the army, Sam? You don't seem to like it."

"The army was my father's notion. He liked the idea of having a son who was a graduate of West Point. Besides, my family is not wealthy. The military academy was the only way I could afford to go to college. My father always insisted I would go to college, despite what I wanted to do."

"What did you want to do?"

His expression softened. "I always dreamed about going West and raising horses. I love horses." He smiled. "Horses don't talk much, you know."

The remark made me laugh. "None I ever met did."

He retrieved a small pocket knife from his pocket, reached down for a mesquite branch and began to whittle. "I even thought of being a teamster. That's what I did as a boy in Ohio. I hauled folk's stuff for them from town to town. Some said I was pretty good at it. I made enough money to buy me some horses. Of course, I'd a done most anything not to be in my father's business. He was a tanner. I hated that line of work."

"Maybe you should have gone out west instead of going to West Point."

He stopped whittling. "I don't know, Teresa. Circumstances always did shape my course different from my plans. A practical man can never expect fate to fulfill his hopes. I wound up at West Point and spent most of my time wishing Congress would abolish the Academy so I would have an excuse to come home without disappointing my father. Now, here I am on the Rio Grande, hoping this war will not happen. All I want to do now is go home and find a little college where I can teach math. I was pretty good at math at West Point."

"I never learned much math," I said. "Maybe you could teach me math. I'll teach you Spanish, and you teach me math."

His eyes brightened. "It's a deal," he said, offering his hand to shake on it. "Back at camp I've got lots of books on mathematics. I'll bring them over if you think it's all right with your grandmother."

"It will be all right with my grandmother, Sam."

We talked for some time about one thing and then another. Just as Sam was about to leave for his camp, my grandmother and Lebe Seru returned home. Because of the early hour, I knew no runaways had come that day or they would have taken longer and possibly Lebe Seru would not have come back for days. Carmen was surprised to see Lieutenant Grant. Knowing he wanted to talk to her, I excused myself to help Alma with shucking the corn.

Sam began to come to our house almost every evening. Whenever he was not on duty, usually moving equipment from one place to another or traveling to and from San Antonio on supply or paymaster missions, he would come to the house for his Spanish lessons and my lessons on mathematics. He started taking his meals with us. As a quartermaster, Sam Grant was not anything if not resourceful. Our pantry expanded to include molasses, eggs, cheese, flour, tea and sugar. He had no way of knowing, but a fair amount of what Sam brought us found its way far inland to be used by people he never saw.

We had been on the river for a little more than four months when the Montemayors finally arrived from San Antonio. I saw the joy in my grandmother's eyes when Pilar and Santiago Montemayor embraced her. Pilar and Santiago had known Carmen since she had been forced to flee Mexico to escape the Spanish who were trying to hunt down and kill all of the followers of the executed Miguel Hidalgo. Santiago had, in fact, met my grandmother when he was a Spanish soldier fighting against the *revolucionarios*. Because he came to believe in Father Hidalgo's cause, he joined the insurgents and helped Carmen and Lebe Seru escape execution. Afterwards, he returned to Texas to fight the Spanish and, later, the Mexican generals who opposed a constitution for Mexico.

The Montemayors told us that their son, Miguel, and their daughter, Josefa, were in Oaxaca, where Benito Juarez had just been elected Governor. Since they regularly received letters from their children, they were quite well informed of events in Mexico.

Carmen asked, "What will Benito Juarez do if Mexico and the United States go to war? Will he support the generals in Mexico City or will he try to form a new government?"

"Governor Juarez would like to see a change in the central government," Pilar said, "but he will be the first to oppose an invasion of Mexico by the United States."

"If there is a war," Santiago asked, "will the Americans be able to defeat the Mexican army? The Mexicans have assembled a very large army across the river. It is much larger than what the Americans have in place so far."

"The Mexican army is much larger," my grandmother said, "but the Mexican officer corps is the same as when we were children and Spain ruled Mexico. They are the younger sons of the aristocracy. They have had no training in modern warfare. And their equipment is outdated. The Mexican soldiers have only old English muskets and their cannons are what the Spanish left behind."

"The American officers are very well-trained and highly disciplined," Lebe Seru added. "Most are graduates of West Point. Their men are equipped with breech-loading rifles which enables them to get off six or seven rounds during the time it would take a man with a muzzle-loading musket to fire one shot."

"There is a rumor," Pilar said, "that the Mexican generals in Mexico City are asking Santa Anna to return from exile in Cuba to lead their armies against the Americans."

Carmen shook her head. "Santa Anna is very good at collecting taxes and conscripting an army. However, when the fighting starts, he will remain far from the scene of battle. He has nothing to lose except the lives of Indian farm boys."

"Santa Anna has no respect for the Indians," Santiago said. "That's why he hates Benito Juarez. Josefa wrote us that when Governor Juarez was in college, he worked as a waiter and had to serve at a banquet in Oaxaca for Santa Anna. Santa Anna made fun of Benito because he was an Indian and wore no shoes."

During the many discussions that occurred after the arrival of the Montemayors, I watched Jorge. I was amazed at how much he had changed. He was no longer the pudgy little boy I used to call Gallito Rojo, little red rooster, because of his red hair and green eyes. Now he was lean and muscular. Jorge had matured into a handsome young man. I was not unaware that he would from time to time watch me as our elders discussed the impending war and what was happening in Texas. I knew he watched me because I caught my eyes drifting to him even when I thought I was listening to what was being said. He would quickly glance away when I looked at him. When we were little, it was difficult to get him to stop talking; but now he rarely said anything unless someone asked him a question.

One morning before breakfast, just as I was returning from feeding the chickens and goats, I saw Jorge walking at the edge of Alma's garden. I decided to visit with him since we had not had an opportunity to be alone since his grandparents had arrived.

"Jorge," I asked, "why are you up so early?"

He was clasping a brown serape tight around his shoulders against the brisk wind blowing in from the Gulf. "I did not go to sleep last night, Teresa."

"Is your bed uncomfortable?" He was sleeping on a mat on the dog trot until Esau and Tom Blue finished building another house for the Montemayors. "Did the mosquitos bother you?"

"No," he said in his soft voice. "Everything is fine."

It was obvious that everything was not fine. Even as a little girl, I had known Jorge was a sensitive boy. Just as I had lost my father to yellow jack as a child, Jorge had not been much older when his mother had succumbed to cholera. Grief-stricken, his father had soon left for Yucatan where he had been ever since, fighting the opponents of liberty in Mexico. Jorge had been raised by his grandparents, and he had no brothers and sisters. He had probably been a little spoiled by Pilar and Santiago, but he was good-natured and kind. He had a deep love of animals and disliked that they were killed for food.

"What is wrong, Jorge? You have hardly said anything since you came here. Are you sick?"

He looked at me with those green eyes that made me think of a forest at dawn. "Yes, Teresa. I am sick. I am sick about what happened to my grandparents. They have lost everything. Their house was taken from them by Anglos who think we are evil because we are Tejanos. They took our wagons and our mules. My grandmother and grandfather worked very hard for what we had. It is not fair."

I should have guessed what was wrong. "I know how you must feel, Jorge. It happened to us."

He lowered his head. "I know, Teresa. You have lost even more. They killed your grandfather. Your grandfather was a very good man. I liked him very much. I should not be so angry when others have suffered even more."

"You are angry, Jorge?"

"Are you not angry? Look at what these Anglos are doing to us. They have burned out entire villages of Tejanos between San Antonio and Corpus Christi. They are making people leave Texas whose families have lived here for generations. My family lived in Texas for a hundred years, and now we have lost everything and must leave San Antonio just to stay alive."

"What you say is true."

"And now the Anglos are going to make war on Mexico so they can take more land that does not belong to them. It will be an unjust war."

"I agree."

"You agree? Then are you not angry, Teresa? Do you not hate the Anglos?"

"Anglos are the same as everyone else, Jorge. Some are good and some are bad. My grandfather was an Anglo." I looked toward the embankment where the Americans had anchored their artillery. "There is a man in the American army here, an officer by the name of Sam Grant. He is an Anglo, and he is a good man. I would like for you to meet him. The two of you are much alike. Lieutenant Grant has gone to San Antonio to pick up the army's pay but when he returns, I want you to meet him. He, too, does not believe this war they are about to fight is just. I want you to talk to Sam Grant. He is a good man."

Jorge looked so forlorn I put my arm around him to walk him back to the house. I did not want him to be sad and angry. I wanted Jorge to be happy.

Three days after I talked with Jorge in the garden that morning, he and I went with Lebe Seru, Carmen and Esau to wait for runaways at the contact point near the Laguna Madre. Santiago and Pilar remained at the house with Alma. We did not wish to arouse suspicion by too many of us being absent at the same time. Tom Blue and Ralph had again gone north to contact more of Binu Seru's teamsters and instruct them on how to come south. On their trips north, they would hide boats and maps in the dunes and make contact with abolitionists who helped us.

We knew we would have work to do when we spotted the trail of white smoke rising during the day. At dusk, we advanced to the dry river bed and discovered a lone woman with four children, one of which was a baby. We were amazed at how they had managed to make the journey alone. Carmen's skills with medicine were required to tend to sunburns, but she soon had them ready to be on their way. When we got up to leave, I noticed the woman had brought along an old musket. Thinking she had forgotten it, I picked it up.

"Careful, Teresa," Lebe Seru warned. He and Carmen were both carrying long-rifles, loaded and ready to fire. "That's an old gun. It might go off and hit someone."

The woman smiled. "It's not loaded. I don't even think it will fire. It's not been used in years. I brought it, thinking I might be able to scare someone off if we got stopped by the bounty hunters. It's all I had."

Lebe Seru examined the musket and told me to bring it along. He said he thought he could repair it and make it work.

We traveled west for two hours until we reached the road leading north to San Antonio. It was a place where great care had to be exercised because it was the route the soldiers took to bring in supplies. We hid among mesquite bushes and sage while Lebe Seru and Esau scouted up and down the road to make certain we could cross it unseen. After a short wait, they returned to our hiding place. I could tell from their expressions something was terribly wrong.

In a low voice, Lebe Seru said, "There's a squad of five American soldiers up ahead. They've been captured and tied up by desperados." He looked at Carmen. "Two of the outlaws are those men who were with Chandler Watts in Houston Town."

"King and Lanfer?"

"Yes."

Esau whispered, "They have the soldiers tied up, and two have been killed. Their throats slashed. I think the soldiers were bringing the army payroll from San Antonio. The desperados are drinking."

Lebe Seru said, "One of the soldiers is Lieutenant Grant."

I was afraid to ask, but I knew I must. "Is he one of the ones who have been killed?"

"Not yet, Teresa. But it's a matter of time. Those men will kill all the soldiers before they finish drinking and move on. They're having fun with them now."

We looked at each other for a moment until Carmen asked, "What do we do?"

"We can go on around south and cross over. They'll never see us. They've got what they want right now, and they're too busy getting drunk to care about anything else."

"And the soldiers?"

"They will kill the soldiers."

"We've got to help them," Carmen said.

"What can we do?" Lebe Seru asked. "We only have two muzzle-loading rifles. If we fire our weapons, we will not have time to reload before they kill us."

"I've got the musket," I said.

"It doesn't work," Lebe Seru reminded.

"You said they were drinking. If we're able to surround them and point our weapons at them, they will give up. They won't know this musket is not loaded. We'll bluff them. We've got to do something, Lebe Seru!"

"Teresa," Esau said, "these men are killers! You know what they are like. You've seen this King and Lanfer. They helped to kill your grandfather."

Again, we fell silent. Finally, Carmen said, "Esau, you take the woman and the children down below and cross over. Teresa and Jorge will go with you. Lebe Seru and I will see if we can't get the drop on those men."

Esau protested her plan, but my grandmother's resolve was firm. Reluctantly, he agreed. When they began to leave, both Jorge and I stayed where we were.

"Go with them," Carmen said. "I will not argue with you, Teresa."

"Abuela, if you go without us, I will follow."

"And so will I," Jorge said.

"Oh, Teresa," my grandmother whispered, but she knew better than to argue with me. We were too much alike.

As soon as Esau and the woman and children were out of sight, we turned and ran as fast as we could in the direction Lebe Seru and Esau had come from earlier. After about fifteen minutes, I could hear the voices of men laughing and cursing. And then we saw the light of their campfire.

We crept forward until we could see the men. Four of the men were sprawled on the ground some distance from the fire. Two of them appeared to be already passed out and the other two were close to that condition. These men had no guns in their grasp, in the holsters on their belts or near them. Another man was slumped over near the fire. His head was down as though he, too, might be asleep; a rifle rested on his lap. The sixth and seventh men were Possum Lanfer and Bob King. Lanfer was standing with a bottle in one hand and a pistol in the other. King had a long-blade knife in his hand. He was standing very close to Sam Grant, who was on the ground with both his hands and feet bound.

There were four other soldiers, each bound hand and foot; but now three of them had their throats slashed, not two.

"I'm gonna cut me a Yankee Doodle!" King shouted in the slurred voice of a man drunk on spirits.

Lanfer laughed and yelled, "Yankee Dooooodle Dandy!"

The other men appeared to be too drunk to care what King and Lanfer were doing.

King bent down and seized Sam's hair and jerked back his head.

Carmen was the first to step forward. She aimed her rifle at King and ordered, "Drop that knife!"

King looked up, saw my grandmother and shouted a curse. He brought the knife to Sam's throat.

My grandmother squeezed off the shot, and King's head exploded.

Lanfer dropped the bottle and raised his pistol.

"Drop it!" Lebe Seru yelled.

Lanfer did not hesitate. He was raising the pistol to aim at Carmen, who had already begun to pour powder in the muzzle of her rifle. If Lebe Seru fired his weapon, there would not be time for my grandmother to finish loading the rifle because the man on the ground was getting to his feet and raising his rifle.

Lebe Seru had no choice. He shot Lanfer in the heart.

We now had no loaded weapons, but I raised the musket and aimed it at the man who was getting to his feet. Two of the unarmed men got to their feet but froze in place when I pointed the musket at them. I quickly alternated my aim between those two men and the man who held the rifle.

The man with the rifle did not drop it, but neither did he raise it to take aim. He watched me intensely. He was trying to determine if I was capable of shooting him before he raised his rifle. I had the musket aimed straight at his heart. Carmen almost had her rifle packed with powder and ready to fire.

If the man decided to raise his rifle and shoot me, there was nothing I could do with an empty musket. The other men would then have an opportunity to reach for their weapons, and we would all be dead. I knew everything depended on my being able to bluff this man until Carmen and Lebe Seru had their rifles ready to fire. It would only take a few more seconds, but it would take less time for this man to kill me and allow the other men to get their weapons. I tried not to reveal any expression except my determination to blow his heart out if he made the slightest move to raise his weapon.

My bluff worked. Suddenly, the man dropped the rifle and raised his hands. "Don't shoot me," he pleaded. "Please don't shoot me!"

The two men who had gotten to their feet also raised their hands and begged to be spared. The other two did not even wake up.

When Lebe Seru and Carmen reloaded their rifles and aimed them, Jorge ran to Sam Grant and cut the cords around his wrists and ankles. Quickly, Sam grabbed a pistol and aimed it at the men while Jorge freed the other soldier.

As Sam and his soldier bound the desperados, I lowered the broken musket and walked a few paces away from the clearing around the campfire. I needed a moment of solitude to settle my confused thoughts. My hands were trembling and my legs were shaky. For a moment, I thought I might fall. And then I felt arms around me, strong arms. Jorge was embracing me and keeping me from falling. I buried my face against his chest.

"Teresa," he whispered, "you saved our lives. You were so brave."

My voice was thin but I managed to admit, "I was frightened, Jorge." It felt wonderful to have his arms around me. It was as though he was somehow able to draw the fear from me and replace it with a warm and comforting strength. I put my arms around him and held him tightly. "I was not brave. I was frightened."

"You are brave," Jorge insisted. "Never have I known anyone like you, Teresa. There is no one like you. I . . ." —his lips touched my face— "Teresa, I . . . I love you."

When I looked toward the camp, I saw my grandmother watching us. She smiled.

VIII

Two days after our encounter with the outlaws, a company of Mexican cavalry crossed the Rio Grande and attacked a patrol of foot infantry. Twelve American soldiers were killed. General Taylor issued the order for his army to prepare for battle. The United States and Mexico were now at war.

The next day an American field command post was established on a hill overlooking an open meadow extending from the river to a stand of tall trees called the Palo Alto. It was the ground General Mariano Arista had selected for a battlefield after crossing the Rio Grande. Using ferries and boats, General Arista had transported some 20,000 infantry, dragoons and cavalry across the river and established a mile long front. Standing his ground, Arista waited for Taylor's 5,000 man army to challenge his right to occupy the north bank of the Rio Grande.

Almost from the moment the artillery was anchored and the officers had begun to calibrate on their enemy's positions, I regretted going with Carmen and Lebe Seru to a place on the hill not far from General Taylor's command post. Though at first opposed to our going, Carmen said it might be good for Jorge and me to know something about war other than what we had read in books. A great sorrow seized me when I saw that thousands of Mexican soldiers had been positioned to stand in lines well within range of the Americans' howitzers and cannons.

We were some distance from where the armies were positioning, but not so far that I could not discern that most of the Mexican soldiers were not that much older than Jorge or me, and some looked younger. Carmen said it was likely that most of the boys had been, until recently, farmers' sons in the hills and villages of Mexico. Many were Indian boys who understood few of the words of Spanish used by their officers to direct them to the places where they were to stand and do nothing but await orders to put into use the old English muskets they had probably never fired even in practice. In the field in which they stood were clusters of a plant that bloomed little white flowers called Velas del Señor, Candles of the Lord.

"Abuela," I asked, "don't the Mexican officers know their men will be killed when the Americans fire their cannons?"

"They know, Teresa."

"Then why do they not move them further back?"

"They want the Americans to attack," Lebe Seru said. "It is the traditional Spanish battle plan. They will draw the enemy to them, fall back and
close in on him from the flanks. See how their cavalry is positioned on
the sides of their main force? They will wait in place until the Americans
believe the Mexican infantry is too weak to repel a frontal assault. When
the Americans advance far enough, the Mexican cavalry will close in from
the sides and surround them. The only way to get the Americans to attack
is to allow them to believe they are pushing back the infantry."

Jorge asked, "Do those boys know they are to be sacrificed?"

"No, Jorge. They do not know that few of those standing in that field
will live to see the end of this day."

Behind the Mexican infantry was their artillery, huge siege-guns that
hurled eighteen- and twenty-four-pound balls; and well behind the artillery
were the officers in their resplendent uniforms. Many of the officers sat
astride expensive silver saddles on the backs of Spanish *destruirs*.
Hundreds of colorful battleflags and banners waved in the wind. Tents
had been erected including one as large as a two-story house which we
assumed was the command post of General Arista. A military band played
processionals.

Zachary Taylor had no tent or military band. He sat sidesaddle on the
back of his mule, his left leg wrapped around the pommel so he would not
fall off. Most of the times I looked at him, he was studying maps and other
documents brought for his inspection by Lieutenants Meade, McClellan
and Beauregard. Couriers waited nearby, ready to mount their horses and
race to the battlefield to convey an order to reposition a unit of infantry,
dragoons, cavalry or artillery.

Other than General Taylor and his Topogs, the American officers
were in the field with their men. Their uniforms were virtually indistin-
guishable from the regulars. Taylor, who continually chewed on pieces of
straw, wore only denim trousers, a cotton shirt and his frayed straw hat.

Carmen asked Lebe Seru if he believed General Taylor would order
an attack.

"I cannot fathom his strategy. What is most odd is where he has
placed his artillery, right up front with his infantry. Notice those smaller
pieces, the ones they call the Flying Artillery. They are in front of his
infantry. That is very unusual."

I was aware of where the Flying Artillery had been positioned, because Sam Grant had convinced General Taylor to allow him to turn his quartermaster duties over to another officer that morning in order that he could command units of Flying Artillery, the two-pounder cannons, each pulled by one horse. For weeks, Sam had practiced his men in advancing the cannons at a gallop, and then reversing course to come to a quick halt and fire. It was a tactic Sam said Napoleon Bonaparte had used successfully, one which he thought would be very effective against the Mexicans.

As we watched, Jorge said, "You are worried Lieutenant Grant will be killed."

"Are you not worried for him, Jorge?"

Jorge had entered into the same arrangement I had made with Sam to teach him Spanish in exchange for lessons in mathematics. Jorge had proven to be a very quick learner, and Sam appreciated having someone who shared his interests.

"Yes," he said. "I am worried. I do not want Sam Grant to die. I do not want anyone to die on either side."

At midafternoon, the front line of the Mexican infantry began to advance. Their band played a slow dirge to provide cadence to their march across the field which in some places stood shoulder high with sharp-pointed grasses. Suddenly, in a deafening roar, the American howitzers blazed forth grapeshot. For a few seconds the soldiers continued to march in line until the deadly shards came raining down on them. It was then I heard for the first time the most horrible sound in the world: the collective scream of human beings crying out in agony. We were hundreds of yards from where the soldiers fell to the ground, many writhing in pain; but those screams entered my ears and went straight to my heart.

The soldiers who had somehow remained untouched by the pieces of metal tried to retreat but were blocked by a second line that had been ordered to advance. Their fate was the same as the men in the first line. At the spot where their comrades lay dead or mortally wounded, the men fell before the blast of a second cannonade. It was too horrible to behold and yet impossible not to watch. Perfectly healthy boys were one moment walking through flowered fields; and in an instant they ceased to exist, their bodies ripped apart like animals in a slaughterhouse.

When I turned to Jorge, I saw the tears in his eyes. Both of us wanted the horror to stop, but a third advance was signaled by a bugle blast. The drums beat cadence until drowned out by the roar of cannons. It made no sense. Nothing was being accomplished. Young men were losing their lives while the rest of us just stood there and watched and did nothing. I became very agitated and angry, though I did not know who was the object of my anger. I was angry at the Americans firing the guns. I was angry at the Mexican officers, some of whom used their swords to slash the infantrymen reluctant to take the place of their comrades whose bodies were beginning to pile up in the field.

I was even angry at my grandmother for allowing us to come to the battlefield. Having witnessed battle many times, Carmen knew what we would see. She wanted Jorge and me to learn a lesson from what we were witnessing. She thought there was no way we could come to hate war unless we saw for ourselves what it was like. But when I saw the sadness in my grandmother's face, my anger toward her ceased. Carmen was right. No one who had never witnessed such horror could ever know the ugliness, the senselessness of it. If the pain and misery and unfairness of battle could be described in words, there could never occur another war on the face of the earth.

The Mexican generals ordered the firing of their big guns, thinking perhaps they would be able to do to the American lines what had been done to theirs. We heard the thunderous sound of the Mexican cannons being fired. We heard the whine of the balls cutting through the air. And then we saw the balls land harmlessly on the ground some hundred feet or so from the most forward of the American lines. Inertia propelled some of the balls on the ground to the soldiers' feet, but they were able to step aside as they rolled harmlessly into their ranks. The Mexican artillery fired round after round at the Americans until it became obvious they were succeeding only in wasting their ammunition.

The Mexican generals next ordered a contingent of fifty dragoons to mount a full charge at the American lines. This tactic proved more successful than the infantry advance because though many of the horses and their riders fell under the cascade of artillery, a number reached the American lines. Forming squares to absorb the impact of the charge, the American infantrymen fired their rifles pointblank at the horses and then killed the fallen riders; but about a dozen dragoons came close enough to fire their weapons, and the first American soldiers were killed. Three dragoons returned to their lines on hobbling mounts to the cheers of their comrades.

Encouraged by their success, the Mexican generals ordered a full-scale charge of the most elite unit of their dragoons, the Red Lancers. In formation, a thousand Red Lancers mounted their charge. Many fell under the shot belched forth by the American howitzers. Their ranks were unbroken, however, as they continued at an accelerating gallop toward the infantry squares the Americans had shaped under the direction of their officers, some of whom stood outside the squares in order to get a full view of what was bearing down upon them.

The Americans' Flying Artillery advanced in a gallop toward the Red Lancers. Within a hundred yards, the horses were reined to an about face, halted and the guns were fired as the horsemen were almost upon them. The Mexican dragoons charged into a wall of metal, and their horses buckled beneath them. The charge was broken. Seeing the deadly effect of the Horse Guns, the American infantry officers reformed the squares into lines and gave the order to fire immediately after the Flying Artillery had returned to the protection of their ranks. The dragoons who had not been killed by the artillery fell before a steady hail of bullets from the American sharpshooters.

Behind the Red Lancers, who were in disarray, came the Mexican foot soldiers. They took aim with their Brown Bess muskets. Upon firing, many of the soldiers dropped the weapons because the powder pans had flared into their faces. Those who managed to reload began to fire their weapons, bracing them not against their shoulders, but their hips in order to avoid the flameup that burned their eyes; thus, they fired over the heads of the American infantry who, using breech loading rifles, had no problem in taking aim, firing, and reloading at a rapid clip. Though some of the Americans fell, once again the Mexican soldiers were suffering too many casualties to continue an effective assault.

When another wave of Red Lancers met the retreating foot infantry, they did not have enough time to form a line before the Flying Artillery had once again raced forward to throw up another wall of grapeshot. At the very front of the Horse Guns was Sam Grant. He was in the thick of the battle; and soldiers, Mexican and American, were falling all around him. Somehow, in all the confusion, he continued to effectively direct the use of the Flying Artillery in such a way that neither the Mexican dragoons or foot infantry could mount a serious threat to the American front line. Sam seemed to be in several places at once.

When the Mexicans began a retreat, the American foot infantry pursued. Now it was impossible for either Mexican or American artillery to be used because the field of battle was mixed with soldiers of both armies, many in hand to hand combat with swords and knives. The dry grass caught on fire and the field was rapidly engulfed in flames and smoke. The American officers were leading their men up the hill to where the Mexican officers were watching the battle. Soon, the men in those magnificent uniforms and plumed helmets were digging their spurs into their mounts in a frenzied attempt to get off the hill and away from the Flying Artillery, which was now being moved to within range of their tents and banners.

After nightfall, the pursuit was broken off because the Americans were outdistancing their ammunition wagons. Returning to camp, the American commanders held a Council of War by the light of lanterns. Most of the officers urged they regroup and await another Mexican attack. Some feared that the entire Mexican retreat had been part of an elaborate strategy to draw them into a massive trap further down the river where more Mexican troops had been crossing even while the battle raged.

General Taylor listened to each of his officers and then announced: "I shall go ahead or stay in my shoes." It was another way of saying he would attack or die trying.

At dawn, the American army, four hundred supply wagons in tow, advanced in the direction of the Mexican retreat. By midmorning they caught up with General Arista, who had deployed his army behind a dry river bed, the Resaca de la Palma, surrounded by a dense tangle of dwarf oaks and thorny shrubs and cactus. It was a smart strategy since it would be very difficult to race the Flying Artillery toward his position as had been done on the unobstructed field the day before.

General Taylor delivered a short address to his army: "Men, today we are going to drive them back across the river. Use your bayonets."

When Sam Grant and the other officers in command of the Flying Artillery discovered the terrain and vegetation was an impediment to horses, they unharnessed the animals and pulled the two-pounder cannons by hand. Leading the way, they blasted a path into the heart of the Mexican positions and opened a corridor through which the foot infantry, bayonets fixed, could rush forward and engage the enemy, man to man.

The Mexican foot soldier, the Indian boys who had weeks before been farmers, fought bravely. For the most part they fought without the direction of their officers, many of whom had already crossed the river to the south bank. But they were no match for the American artillery and breech-loading rifles; and by late afternoon the Mexicans began a full-scale, disorganized retreat to the Rio Grande. At the river, men fought to get on the boats and ferries that would return them to the south bank and out of range of riflemen who stood on the banks and fired round after round at men trying to swim across the river, which was turning red with blood.

The sounds of gunfire continued throughout the night as the Americans came across pockets of Mexican soldiers who had not managed to get across the river and who refused to give up their weapons. General Taylor issued strict orders not to shoot prisoners and treat them according to the rules of war. The sounds of shots echoed throughout the night along with the noises of predators fighting over the bodies of dead and dying soldiers.

At dawn we were able to see the remains of hundreds of Mexican soldiers floating in the river. Schools of catfish attacked the bodies, making them twist and jerk as if they were still alive and writhing in pain. I shall never forget what I witnessed in those two days of fighting. I am certain that nothing in the deepest pit of hell could be more horrible.

The victories of the American army at what came to be known as the Battle of Palo Alto and the Battle of Resaca de la Palma were unqualified. Not only did the Mexican army retreat across the Rio Grande, it abandoned Matamoros and fell back toward Monterrey, two hundred miles to the south. Lieutenant Meade finally received permission to construct his bridges and pontoons, and General Taylor occupied Matamoros. All hope that the victories would bring a quick end to the war vanished when news was received that Santa Anna had returned to Mexico and announced he would march north to engage the Americans. Zachary Taylor was ordered to advance on Monterrey, while General Winfield Scott assembled another army on the Rio Grande in preparation for a sea invasion of Vera Cruz and a march on Mexico City.

Inevitably, the day arrived when General Taylor led his army south toward Monterrey. Before leaving, he came to our house for one last glass of lemonade. As expected, the glass turned into four or five as the general inspected Alma's garden one last time and sampled some of her radishes and carrots.

Kneeling in the dirt, he rubbed soil on his hands and said, "This is what I look forward to doing as soon as we get this war over. I'm goin' home and plant me some vegetables. Then I'm gonna sit back and do nothin' but watch 'em grow."

General Taylor said this even though we had already seen newspaper stories that hailed him as the "American Caesar" and called for his election as the next President of the United States. As he climbed up on his old mule and rode off side-saddle, he did not look anything like an American Caesar. He looked to be exactly what he was: an unassuming old man, who happened to be the best general in the United States army.

When Sam came to say good-bye, Jorge and I promised we would study the books on mathematics he was leaving for us. He joked that when he returned from Monterrey he would give us an exam. Sam embraced my grandmother and when he released her, he turned quickly, mounted his horse and spurred it to a gallop to join the army that was again marching off to war.

We tried as best we could to follow the reports of the fighting in Mexico. By the time we got the newspapers from San Antonio, they were many weeks old and reported events that had happened, in many cases, months earlier. When the stories of the war did begin to arrive, they told of hard fighting at Monterrey. The people of Monterrey would not capitulate and endured a long American bombardment. Finally, the city was surrendered; and General Taylor showed his respect for the Mexican soldiers by allowing them to leave with their weapons on condition they would no longer fight.

All during the Battle of Monterrey, rumors were rampant of Santa Anna's march northward through the desert to confront Zachary Taylor. He was said to have conscripted over fifty thousand men. Other reports contradicted these numbers and even told of state governors who refused to allow Santa Anna's officers entrance into their territory to force boys into his army and collect taxes. Santa Anna was a genius at organizing for war; but once the fighting began, his record of wasting lives through inept generalship was well known in Mexico.

After taking Monterrey, Zachary Taylor did not wait for Santa Anna to come to him. The general marched his army south of Saltillo and surprised Santa Anna at a place called Buena Vista. The reports we received, again months after the event, told of a vicious battle and great losses on both sides. Though there were conflicting accounts, it seemed the armies fought to a draw. What gave the Americans the victory was another loss of nerve by Santa Anna, who fled the battlefield. Realizing they had been abandoned by their leader, the Mexican soldiers melted away, leaving General Taylor's force in control of all of northern Mexico while Santa Anna, now in Mexico City, promised to raise an even larger army and fight to the last man any attempt by the Americans to occupy the capital. My grandmother said Santa Anna was always ready to fight to the last man as long as he was not that man.

With the cessation of fighting on the Rio Grande, commerce and trade were renewed. Boats and ferries began to go back and forth. The Montemayors visited friends in Matamoros to determine if they might be able to get back into the freight hauling business. There was much agriculture on both sides of the river that needed to be moved to market, and there were harbors on either side of the mouth of the Rio Grande that could accommodate ocean-going vessels owned by merchants eager to fill their holds with the cotton grown in the Rio Grande Valley.

Esau went with Santiago and Pilar on several of their trips to Matamoros and met people who recognized that he had a good head for business. Since he still had much of the gold Sam Houston had given him, money he and Tom Blue had earned, Esau decided to invest in a tavern in Matamoros. He said if there was one thing he had learned in his years with Sam Houston it was how to run a saloon. Even though he and Tom Blue would be spending more time in Matamoros, they wanted us to know they would continue to do everything they could to help the runaways.

On one of their return trips from Matamoros, Santiago and Pilar came to the house with letters that had just arrived from their sons and their daughter in southern Mexico, including one to Jorge from his father. While Jorge silently read his father's letter, his grandparents read their letters to us; and we were glad to hear everyone was healthy and doing well. Josefa was studying at the Oaxaca Institute of the Sciences and the Arts, where her older brother, Miguel, was now a teacher.

After the joy and excitement of reading the letters, Pilar wiped tears from her eyes. It had been many years since she had seen her children, and she missed them very much. Seeing that Jorge had finished his letter, I asked what news his father had sent.

"Yes," Pilar said. "We read our letters, but you did not tell us what your papa has to say."

Jorge glanced at me, and I saw that he was troubled. He looked down at his letter. "Papa says he has gone to stand with Benito Juarez if the Americans invade Oaxaca."

"Oaxaca is south of Mexico City," Lebe Seru said and looked at my grandmother. "Why would the Americans invade Oaxaca?"

Carmen replied, "They may decide to occupy the areas around Mexico City. Cut off from the rest of the country, Santa Anna would be forced to surrender. I do not know if the state governors will fight the Americans. Many, such as Benito Juarez, have long been enemies of Santa Anna."

"My father," Jorge said, "writes that Benito Juarez has condemned the American invasion. Governor Juarez is opposed to Santa Anna and will not allow him to conscript men in Oaxaca or collect taxes. But if the Americans come to Oaxaca, he will lead volunteers against them."

The Montemayors were not the only ones who received unexpected letters. On one of his trips north, Tom Blue decided to chance a visit to Joshua and Eliza. Senator Houston was in Washington, but Joshua assured Tom Blue that Mrs. Houston would not turn him in to the authorities. Mrs. Houston treated him with kindness and asked how we were. She gave Tom Blue a packet of letters that had come to us from Austria. They had been addressed in care of the Houstons at Cedar Point. Mrs. Houston said to tell us that if we wished to correspond with our mother, she would send and receive the letters through her husband's office in Washington City.

My grandmother and I could hardly wait to open the first letter from my mother, which turned out to be little more than a recitation of the events of their trip to Vienna. Cata Valeria's words revealed impatience and then anger in subsequent letters as it became apparent to her that we had not kept our word to travel to Europe. At the anniversary of their first year in Vienna, my mother wrote how disappointed she was in both me and my grandmother, and her letters abruptly ceased.

Esteban's letters were much more pleasant, and he continued to write after my mother had stopped. As might be expected, my brother provided Carmen and me with detailed descriptions of every uniform he saw. What most impressed him were the uniforms worn by the Emperor's nephews, Franz Josef and Maximilian.

In his bold and ornate penmanship, Esteban wrote:

> Maxl has ordered his tailors to make me uniforms just like his.
> Maxl loves horses and insists I take lessons with him at the Spanish
> Riding Academy. Everyone likes for me to tell them about Texas. They
> want to know all about Old Chief. Everyone in Vienna has heard about
> Sam Houston. Do you think you could get Old Chief to send me a bowie
> knife to give to Franz Josef? Maxl wants to meet Teresa, because I told
> him how pretty she is. Teresa, you must hurry and come to Vienna.

> Father takes me to the Palace everyday to attend lessons with Franz
> Josef and Maxl. Our tutor is Count Heinrich Bombelles, a Frenchman
> who was the tutor of Napoleon II. Count Heinrich is very interested in
> Texas and Mexico. He asked if I could obtain books and newspapers
> from Texas and Mexico. I told him I was sure my sister could send us
> many books and newspapers, because she likes to read. I do not care so
> much for the books, and neither does Maxl. Franz Josef must study,
> because he will become the Emperor when his uncle dies.

He closed his letter by sending his love and signed his name, "Stefan
von Gorlitz."

After reading the letter, Carmen said, "Your brother is no longer our
Estebanito. He is Stefan von Gorlitz."

I said, "He and Maximilian seem to have become very good friends.
He calls him Maxl."

"Perhaps," my grandmother said, "it is time you go to Vienna, Teresa.
After all, we did promise your mother."

"There is much work for me to do here."

"Yes. That is true. There is much work, and there is going to be even
more when this war is over. But in Vienna you would have an opportunity to receive an education. Your father would have liked that."

"Perhaps I will go later, Abuela. Lebe Seru says that slavery will end
someday. I will go when there is no more slavery." I looked again at my
brother's letters. "But I will write to Esteban. We must both write. In each
letter, he begs for us to write to him and to send books on Mexico and
Texas."

I had just let my chickens out for the morning and was returning to
the house for the milk buckets when I saw a lone man standing on the
north embankment of the river. When my eyes adjusted to the faint light,
I saw that he was wearing the uniform of an American army officer. His

hands clasped behind his back, he stood facing the river. Thinking I recognized who it was, I started across the field. From behind he looked like Sam Grant. But just as I got to him and he turned, I drew back. This man wore a beard, and his face was gaunt and leathery. And this man was smoking a cigar.

"Teresa," he said and quickly tossed the cigar to the ground.

"Sam?" He looked so different. "Is it you?"

"It's good to see you, Teresa."

I ran and put my arms around him. The aroma of tobacco was on his jacket, which now bore the insignia of a first lieutenant. But there was another aroma, one I had never detected on Sam Grant. The smell of alcohol was on his breath.

"Sam," I asked, "are you all right?"

I stepped back to look at him. His face was no longer that of a smooth-faced boy. The beard and the creases in his sun-darkened face made him look very much like a man.

"Yes, Teresa," he said softly. "I am fine. At least, I am all in one piece."

"Is the war over, Sam? Is that why you are back? The war is over?"

"No. The war goes on. It goes on and on and on. I have been ordered back to the Rio Grande to join General Scott's army for the invasion of Vera Cruz."

We had seen the troops arriving daily, though most quartered in Matamoros and drilled south of the city. There had been a grand parade when Winfield Scott came to assume command of the force.

"General Scott is here," I said.

"Old Fuss and Feathers. Have you seen him?"

"From a distance. He is the tallest man I ever saw in my life."

"He is six feet, four and one-quarter inch. Don't forget the one-quarter inch. He never does."

I laughed. "He walks like a turkey gobbler."

"He's a good soldier," Sam said. "He will have to be. He has his work cut out for him in Vera Cruz and Mexico City. We understand that Santa Anna has raised at least a hundred thousand men, and this time it is no bluff. The people will be fighting for their honor. Even those who hate Santa Anna will fight us in this unholy war. Who could blame them?"

"General Scott sent for you, Sam? He must be an excellent general if he sent for you."

He shrugged and looked toward the house, from which the faint glow of candles shown through the windows. "Is your grandmother awake, Teresa? I thought I might speak with her before I have to report."

Carmen was at one of the farms on the chaparral, helping several of the escapees who needed medical attention. "She is away, Sam. She will return later today."

"I understand."

"Can you come back this evening? There will be a celebration. Alma and Ralph are being married! Come be with us for the celebration."

A smile crept into his lips almost hidden by the beard and mustache. "I would like that. I have to report this morning. We have a staff meeting with General Scott. I expect we will be leaving very shortly for Vera Cruz. Yes. I would like to come this evening, Teresa. I will be here."

"We will expect you."

Before leaving, he asked, "Would it be all right if I brought one of my fellow officers? He was not here when we were on the Rio Grande before. He came back with me to join General Scott. I've told him about you folks. I think he would enjoy meeting you."

"Of course, Sam. Bring whomever you like. Our house is yours."

When Sam returned for our celebration, I did not have an opportunity to immediately greet his friend because I was busy helping with the food that had to be prepared for some fifty guests who had gathered at our house, many from Matamoros. Since it was her wedding, we would not allow Alma to do any of the cooking. Pilar spent most the day making tamales and the other foods common at a Mexican wedding. Carmen and I helped the best we could, which meant grinding corn, making tortillas and stuffing tamales.

A priest from Matamoros conducted the wedding ceremony which, strictly speaking, violated the laws of the state of Texas that negroes, slave or free, were forbidden to marry. Esau, Tom Blue, Lebe Seru, Santiago and Jorge worked hard to put the finishing touches on the cabin they had built next door for the newlyweds. They drove the last nail and moved in the last piece of furniture just before Alma and Ralph exchanged vows and everyone went to out to see the decorations strung in the lemon grove and to dance and listen to music.

When I finished my work and helped my grandmother carry the trays of food outside where our guests had gathered, my eyes were immediately drawn to Sam's friend, a Captain who had the most noble appearance of any man I had ever seen in my life.

Sam went to Carmen and took both of her hands in his. He said, "Mrs. Owens. Teresa. Please allow me to present my friend, Captain Robert E. Lee."

Captain Lee was several years older than Sam. A streak of grey ran along the temples of his dark hair which extended to his jaw in long sideburns. He carried himself with such a regal bearing that he looked as though he should be the general of the American army, though he gave no hint of arrogance. He was an exceedingly courteous man and bowed to my grandmother and then to me. He was very complimentary of the food and said he wished his wife in Virginia could sample the flavors.

Sam said, "Captain Lee's wife is the granddaughter of George Washington."

"His step-granddaughter," the captain said. "As a matter of fact, my wife came very close to becoming a Texan. She was once courted by Sam Houston. He asked her to marry him. Fortunately for me, she declined the offer. Of course, if she had accepted, she may well have had the opportunity to be the wife of a president as well as being one's step-granddaughter."

"The wife of a president?" Carmen asked.

"Yes, Mrs. Owens," Captain Lee said. "I believe Senator Houston will be the next President of the United States."

It was not long before Sam escorted my grandmother away from the festivities to sit with her in the lemon grove. I watched him talking to Carmen and could sense that he was sharing with her the contents of his troubled heart. The war had made Sam Grant a very unhappy man, and I hoped my grandmother could say something to give him some measure of comfort.

In the meantime, Captain Lee situated himself with the older men who had gone to the front yard to smoke their pipes and cigars away from the noise and music. Jorge and I decided to join them as neither one of us was much inclined to dancing.

Captain Lee turned to Jorge's grandfather and asked, "Am I correct in my understanding that you once served in the Spanish army, sir?"

"Yes," Santiago replied. "I was a soldier in the Spanish army for many years. But I left that army when I learned of Miguel Hidalgo's dream of liberty and equality for the people of Mexico. I then joined the army of those who fought the Spanish."

"Santa Anna," Captain Lee said, "has destroyed the Constitution that the followers of Miguel Hidalgo wrote. Why would the people of Mexico fight for this man?"

"There are men in Mexico, the same as men everywhere, who will fight for whoever puts gold in their pocket. There are men of high station in Mexico who support Santa Anna because they know he will preserve their privilege.

"There are still others, Captain Lee, men and women, who will fight not for Santa Anna, but against your army because they do not think you have a right to take away the lands that are the heritage of their children. Whether they can defeat you or not, I do not know. Mexico is a poor country. Her resources have been squandered by men like Santa Anna. But that will not stop many Mexicans from opposing an invader with their bare hands, even if that is all they have, to preserve their heritage and their honor."

"Perhaps," Captain Lee said, "we Americans can help the Mexicans to get rid of men like Santa Anna who have wasted the nation's resources and prevented the realization of Miguel Hidalgo's dream of liberty and equality."

Lebe Seru, who had been smoking his pipe, leaned forward in his chair. "Do you believe in liberty and equality, Captain Lee?"

"Of course. As you know, our country had to struggle against the tyranny of the English king. In our Declaration of Independence, Thomas Jefferson, who was from my state of Virginia, wrote, 'We hold these truths to be self-evident, that all men are created equal, that they are endowed by their Creator with certain unalienable rights, that among these are life, liberty and the pursuit of happiness.' Mr. Jefferson believed in the same things as Miguel Hidalgo. That is why we can stand shoulder to shoulder with the Mexicans and defeat tyrants such as Santa Anna and those opposed to the rule of law."

Lebe Seru said, "I lived in your country for many years, Captain Lee. I was taken to your country in chains. I did not find widespread the belief that all men are created equal. You gained your independence from England as did Mexico from Spain, but perhaps you have yet to experience the civil war over this question of equality that the Mexicans have been fighting these many years."

Captain Lee said, "I pray we do not have to experience the civil war that the people of Mexico have been fighting for so long. If it comes to our country, it will be a thing too awful to contemplate."

Sam was correct in his assumption that his stay on the Rio Grande would be a short one. General Scott was anxious to transport his force to Vera Cruz and achieve a victory before the hot weather brought with it the diseases and epidemics that could conquer an army without the firing of a single shot. Unlike Zachary Taylor, Winfield Scott *did* believe in pomp and ceremony. For days, military bands played grand processionals as the soldiers marched to the harbors on both sides of the Rio Grande and boarded the ships that would carry them to what was anticipated to be the largest sea invasion in the history of the world.

For the second time, we had the sad task of bidding our farewells to Sam Grant. As he prepared to mount his horse for the ride to the harbor, he said, "Maybe I'll come back here after this war and farm. This is good land. You can raise fine crops in this valley."

"We wish you would come here, Sam," Carmen said. My grandmother had grown very close to this young man. "You will always have a home with us."

Three days after the departure of the last American troops for Vera Cruz, I was awakened in the night by the sound of Pilar's crying. In the morning when I started outside to tend my animals, I found Jorge standing at the back door with blankets secured with cords around bundles.

"Jorge," I asked, "what are you doing?"

He avoiding looking at me. "I am leaving, Teresa. I am going to Oaxaca to be with my father."

"No, Jorge. It is too dangerous!"

"I must, Teresa. I must be with my father and those who will stand with Benito Juarez to defend Oaxaca if the Americans go there."

Jorge's decision came as no surprise to me. Ever since he had received the letter from his father, I knew he was troubled. I had come to know Jorge's thoughts as if they were my own. I had come to know his heart.

"No, Jorge," I said, putting my arms around him. "I cannot let you go. I will not let you go. You are just a boy. What if the Americans do go to Oaxaca? Will you fight them? You have seen their weapons."

"I know, Teresa," he said weakly. "I don't want to fight the Americans. I don't want to fight anyone. But I must stand with Benito Juarez."

"Why, Jorge? You were not born in Mexico. You were born in Texas and have lived here all your life. The problems of Mexico are not your problems. You know nothing about Benito Juarez or Mexico."

Finally, he looked into my eyes. "You are right, Teresa. I know very little about Benito Juarez, and I know nothing about Mexico. But I . . ." – he struggled to find the words to express what he wanted to say–" . . . Teresa, my father left Texas when I was just a little boy. I hardly remember him. I want to know why he left me. What is there about Benito Juarez that would make him leave me, to leave his family and his home, and go far away? Why did his brother and sister go with him? I must know, Teresa."

"Then I will go with you. Together, we will find your father and–"

"No," he interrupted, pulling from my embrace. "You cannot."

"Why not? I was born in Mexico. Mexico is more my land than yours. My grandmother and my grandfather fought for Miguel Hidalgo and Jose Morelos. I will go with you."

He gently took my hand when I turned to go to the house to pack my things. "Please, Teresa. You must stay. You must look after your grandmother. Is this not why you did not go to Europe with your mother and Esteban? You must stay with your grandmother. She has no one else." He embraced me. "Besides, Teresa, it will be dangerous. There will be fighting in Mexico. I do not want for you to be in danger. I could not stand it if something happened to you. You must remain in Texas."

I did not know what to do. Emotions were stirring in me that I had never known. I kissed Jorge and held him to me even tighter. If he had not gently pulled from my embrace, I think I would have held him forever.

"Teresa," he whispered, "I will come back. I promise you I will come back to you. I will come back because I love you, Teresa. I have always loved you, and I always will love you."

Such an ache gripped my heart as I watched Jorge gather his bundles and walk across the road to the embankment. Too quickly he was over the rise and out of my sight. For a moment, I considered racing after him. I was confused. Everything had happened too quickly, and I felt dizzy as though I might fall to the ground.

"Teresa?"

I turned and saw my grandmother at the corner of the house.

"Abuela, Jorge's going to Oaxaca."

"I know, Teresa."

She came to me and put her arms around me.

"Abuela," I said. "I do not want Jorge to go. I want him to stay here. I want him to stay with me."

"I know."

"I do not feel good, Abuela. I feel sick inside. Why do I feel this way?"

"Because you are in love."

I peered across the river to the land where Jorge was going. More than anything, I wished I had told him what was in my heart. I wished I had told him that I loved him.

IX

Many weeks passed before stories on the war in Mexico began to appear in the newspapers Tom Blue and Ralph brought to us from San Antonio, Austin and Houston Town. European observers said Santa Anna's fortress guns would make a sea assault on Vera Cruz impossible. Knowing this, General Winfield Scott landed his troops unopposed several miles south of Vera Cruz, marched them overland to surround the city on the land side, where there were no fortress guns, and began a bombardment. The city was surrendered, but not before Santa Anna escaped and fell back to Mexico City to prepare an even larger army with more big guns to hold off the Americans if they dared to approach his capital.

It was with enormous relief that I read that the Americans, after securing Vera Cruz, were marching straight to Mexico City. That meant for the time being there would be no fighting in Oaxaca where I prayed Jorge was safe with his father, his aunt and his uncle. My relief was soon tempered by the stories of vicious fighting on the outskirts of the capital. Young cadets at a military preparatory school were defending Chapultepec Castle against the Americans. Several hundred boys, most younger than twelve years of age, refused to surrender the cannons that guarded a major highway into the city. The Americans broke into the castle and killed all of the cadets, some of whom retreated to the towers and jumped to their deaths on the rocks below rather than surrender.

The fighting in Mexico City itself lasted for weeks and came down to hand-to-hand combat, street by street and house by house, until all resistance was crushed. Once again, Santa Anna managed to slip away into the night and retreat south, vowing to raise yet another army and continue to battle the Americans and their artillery, which had proven decisive in every campaign. When I read of his decision, my fears for Jorge were renewed because I knew that Oaxaca was south of Mexico City.

At last the news we had been awaiting arrived, news of Oaxaca. Governor Juarez refused to allow Santa Anna to enter the state. He would not permit the conscription of Oaxaca's young men or the collection of tax revenues from its citizens to continue the disastrous war. If the American army came to Oaxaca, Benito Juarez said, he would himself lead his people against them; but Santa Anna could not come into Oaxaca unless he was on his way out of the country. Calling Benito Juarez a traitor and vow-ing revenge, Santa Anna had no option but to comply. He fled the country and took refuge in Venezuela.

When General Scott declared he had no intention of invading Oaxaca or any other state, the war was over. For a brief period there was no central government in Mexico to negotiate the terms of surrender and a peace treaty. Finally, an ad hoc government was assembled to work out the terms with representatives sent by President Polk. Mexico had to rec-ognize the annexation of Texas to the United States and the Rio Grande as the southern border. Additionally, Mexico had to cede California and the vast territories between Texas and California to the United States. In effect, Mexico was forced to yield over one third of its territory to the United States. In return, the United States paid Mexico an indemnity of fifteen million dollars.

Though the war had from the beginning been unjust and its outcome a travesty, I was relieved it was over. My apprehension about Jorge, how-ever, did not lessen until his grandparents received a letter written after the end of hostilities that he was safe in Oaxaca.

I was so happy and relieved I did not at first hear Pilar when she said, "There is a letter to you, Teresa."

My hands trembled as I opened my letter.

"Dear Teresa," Jorge wrote:

> By the time you receive this letter, you will have learned that the war is over. It was a war shameful to all involved. The United States has taken lands that rightfully belong to Mexico. The only consolation may be that Mexico is at last rid of the madman who has brought her peo-ple such hardship.
>
> I have decided to stay in Oaxaca and enroll in a course of study at the Institute of Sciences and Arts, where my uncle and my aunt are teachers. I hope to complete my course of study in three or four years, because I want to return to you as quickly as possible. You are never far from my thoughts, Teresa, and you are always in my heart. I will always love you.
>
> Yesterday, I had the honor of meeting Governor Juarez. He is a kind man. He told me that it is only through learning and respect for the law that we will make this a world free of injustice. When I return to Texas, I want to be able to do what I can to bring justice to our land.
>
> Your eternal servant,
> Jorge

I read and reread Jorge's letter and the others that followed in rapid succession. At night, I kept them under my pillow. His letters were the only way I had of holding him in my arms and caressing him. I wrote him long letters telling him of my love for him and assuring him that he had made the right decision in enrolling in the course of study at the Institute.

Some friends of the Montemeyors in Matamoros were teamsters who hauled goods between the border and the interior of Mexico as far south as Oaxaca, and they carried our letters. They assured us that our letters to Jorge and his to us would arrive safely, though a lapse of two months or more between the sending of a letter and its arrival would be usual. Each day I awaited the arrival of a letter from Jorge, but now at least I knew he was safe and no longer under the threat of the horror of war.

My peace of mind was short-lived because, after a lapse of several months, we received a batch of letters from Esteban that Tom Blue had retrieved from Mrs. Houston, who now lived in Huntsville. After looking through the letters and sorting them into an order based on the dates Esteban affixed at the beginning of each letter, my grandmother began to read them aloud.

"Dear Abuela and Teresa," she read. "Victory is ours! We have crushed the Hungarians and the Czechs, and in Italy the Venetians and the Lombards have surrendered. My wounds have healed, and I have been given command of my own gunship in the fleet that Father commands."

My grandmother put the letter down, and we looked at each other. We knew nothing of Esteban's being wounded or in any way being involved in a war. Some of his letters must have been lost in route. It angered me that my mother had stopped writing. She should have let us know that Esteban had been wounded.

Carmen continued to read: "His Imperial Highness, Czar Nicholas I, personally led the Russian army to aid in the complete destruction of the Hungarian Republic. He decorated both Maxl and me for bravery. At present, the only resistance comes from the Serbs and the Croats, and they will soon capitulate. They are no match for our artillery.

"I am sorry to have to pen such a short letter, but we must prepare for battle. Mother is fine, and Father sends his love.

"Pray for our Victory! Stefan." Quickly, Carmen opened the second letter and began to read:

> Wonderful news! How can mere words convey the magnificence of what has occurred? Emperor Ferdinand has transferred the Crown to

Franzl! It is true. If only you could hear the bells ringing throughout all of Vienna and the guns being fired around the clock in salute, you would know it is true! Bands are playing. People are dancing and singing. Franzl is now Franz Josef I, Emperor of Austria!

After our glorious victories over the Serbs and the Croats, Emperor Ferdinand realized the time for leadership from a new generation had arrived. Maximilian is now the Archduke and will succeed Franz Josef should anything happen to him.

When I told Maxl I must now address him by his title, he said he would use his royal Hapsburg foot to kick me in the seat of my pants if I ever call him Archduke Ferdinand Maximilian. However, he does not object to my calling him Admiral of the Austrian Navy, which is his new position. Nor do I object to my new title of Commodore of the Fleet!

Esteban's letter and the ones following continued with a deluge of information about titles and ranks and descriptions of uniforms and medals. Esteban and Archduke Maximilian seemed to spend a considerable amount of time at the nightly balls at the royal palace, where people danced to waltzes played by the court orchestra under the direction of Kapellmeister Johann Strauss.

Carmen paused after she began yet another letter announcing more of Esteban's wonderful news. She was reading ahead.

"What is it, Abuela? Not another war?"

"He writes that he has just returned from Paris where Maximilian represented his brother at the inauguration of Louis Bonaparte as the President of France."

"Napoleon Bonaparte's nephew."

"Apparently, he is no longer in jail," Carmen said and returned to Esteban's words:

I was very nervous when presented to President Bonaparte. He put me at ease and insisted I tell him everything about Texas and Mexico.

Maxl told Monsieur Bonaparte he should not be a mere president and that he should abolish the Republic and make himself Emperor like his uncle. Monsieur Bonaparte said that everything happens in its own season. He will soon marry Princess Eugenie of Spain. She attended the inauguration. She was delighted to be able to use her native language with me. She said she was saddened by the unhappy lot of the Mexican people since their separation from Spain.

I was glad that Count Bombelles had made Maxl and me study our lessons in the French language. I had no problem in conversing with Monsieur Bonaparte. I am helping Maxl to become proficient in

Spanish. Like President Bonaparte and Princess Eugenie, he is fascinated by Mexico. Maxl devours the books you sent on Mexico, Teresa. Please send more!

I was relieved to learn that my brother was no longer in danger, but there was something about the tone of the letters I found unsettling.

"Abuela," I said, "I think Esteban's head has been turned by these kings and emperors that are his constant companions."

Carmen smiled. "Esteban is not so different than I was when I was young, Teresa. I dreamed of going to Europe to battle for the King of Spain. It was my highest ambition."

"You, Abuela? You have spent your entire life fighting for the cause of liberty."

"Not my entire life, Teresa. My father was Don Esteban, the Marquis de Abrantes. Your mother named your brother after him. Don Esteban believed in the divine right of kings. When I was a girl, I agreed with him."

"Then how did you come to be a follower of Miguel Hidalgo, Abuela?"

"Coalter came to my father's house in 1810 to enlist his help in establishing a colony of *norteamericanos* in Texas. Lebe Seru was a slave of one of the men who came with Coalter. Coalter and Lebe Seru admired Father Hidalgo. At first, I did not share their views. It was only later, after I had come to love your grandfather, that I understood that Miguel Hidalgo's cause was just."

Since Carmen seemed to be in a mood to recall past events, I decided to inquire about something that had long puzzled me.

"Abuela," I asked, "who took care of my mother when you came to Texas? Surely, your father could not do it alone. Was she raised by his servants?"

For a moment, she pondered my query. "I suppose it was Lupita who looked after Cata Valeria."

"Lupita?"

"You do not remember Lupita? Your mother called her Doña Lupe."

"I do not remember anyone by that name."

"She came with your mother from Mexico. She took care of you and Esteban. Soon after we moved to Houston Town, she left to return to Mexico with a friend of your father's. I suppose you were too young to remember."

"Who was she?"

"I first met Lupita in Dolores when she was just a girl. Her parents had been killed by soldiers because the people of her village had been unable to pay a Viceregal tax. Lupe had been struck in the head with a sword and left for dead. She was brought to Father Hidalgo who cared for children whose parents had been killed by the Viceroy's soldiers. He believed her life had been saved by the Virgin, which is why he called her Guadalupe. No one knew her name because she never spoke a word.

"Lupita appeared at my father's house after I had gone to Texas. She seemed to take it upon herself to be with Cata Valeria as she grew up in Guanajuato."

"So she was like a mother to Cata Valeria."

"I would not say she was like a mother. It is difficult to know what to say about Lupe. Your father believed the Virgin had given Lupita the power to heal. Arturo once told me that Doña Lupe promised him she would always protect you and Esteban. I do not know how she could tell him this since she did not talk. But your father said she made that promise to him, and he believed her."

Captain Lee proved to be a poor predictor of political events. On the day he came to Alma's wedding, he had said he believed the next president of the United States would be Sam Houston. If one had read only the newspapers in Texas, it would have been impossible not to draw the same conclusion. According to the Texas newspapers, the people of the country had fallen in love with the senator from Texas. They adored his exotic clothing. No one knew if he was going to appear on the floor of the Senate wearing a Cherokee turban, a Mexican serape or the yellow buckskin of a frontiersman. The fact that Senator Houston wore ornate rings on each finger of both hands and could often be seen on the floor of the Senate whittling hearts out of peach pits was widely reported in newspapers throughout the country.

People packed lecture halls in New York, Philadelphia and Boston to hear the Hero of Horseshoe Bend and the Hero of San Jacinto. Many said it was only natural that Sam Houston be President of the United States; he was the heir of Andrew Jackson, and Old Hickory's dying wish had been for Sam Houston to be president. The stories of his drinking, his ex-wives, his dueling, his caning of congressmen and his trial before the United States Senate only made him more attractive to a population tired of the colorless James K. Polk. The people of the United States loved a showman.

Unfortunately for Sam Houston, what the people of the United States loved even more than a showman was a war hero. The majority of Americans hated the Mexican-American war and had never wanted to become involved in the conflict. However, the war had turned out well for the United States, giving the country an empire that now stretched to the Pacific Ocean and included California which, it was soon discovered, contained rich deposits of gold. The war had turned out well, but the people were still angry at the man and the party that had gotten them in the war. The voters decided to look to a new political party, the Whigs, to govern the country; and for president, they turned to the man the war veterans loved. The people of the United States elected Zachary Taylor to be the first professional soldier to serve as president of the country.

Of course, I had wanted Kalanu to be the new president. I knew he would make a great president. More than that, I was confident he would somehow bring an end to slavery. But if Sam Houston had to wait four more years to occupy the Executive Mansion in Washington City, I was glad that Zachary Taylor would be president. After all, we had known him. He had spent many an hour at our house drinking lemonade and puttering in Alma's garden. I thought he would make a fine president.

Unfortunely, Zachary Taylor did not have an opportunity to demonstrate whether he would be a fine president because a little more than a year after assuming office, he died of complications brought on by a heat stroke suffered at a Fourth of July celebration. We were greatly saddened by his death.

The new president was Zachary Taylor's vice president, Millard Fillmore. Almost as soon as Mr. Fillmore was sworn in as president, the campaign began for who would be elected president in 1852. No one gave serious thought to Mr. Fillmore as anything but a caretaker until a real president could be chosen. This meant that Sam Houston was once again viewed as the logical choice to be the nation's chief executive. Almost every newspaper that we received contained the text of brilliant speeches the senator gave at important gatherings throughout the country. I was absolutely certain that Kalanu would be the next President of the United States.

My skills as a political prognosticator proved to be on the same level as Captain Lee's. Not only was Sam Houston not elected president, he did not even win his party's nomination. The leaders of the Democratic Party were paying less attention to what Sam Houston said about such things as the importance of national unity than the votes he was casting in the Senate that blocked the expansion of slavery into the territories acquired as a result of the war with Mexico. Sam Houston had played a key role in the Congress in implementing a series of laws that, among other things, allowed California to enter the Union as a state that prohibited slavery.

Southerners had begun to believe there was a national conspiracy to isolate them and allow the country to expand westward in a manner that would lessen their strength in the Congress and, therefore, lead to the abolition of slavery. Some of the southern congressmen, including John Calhoun, accused Sam Houston of being a traitor to the south; and they blocked his nomination to be the Democratic Party's candidate for president. After much squabbling and 50 ballots, the nomination went to Franklin Pierce, who had been a general of volunteer militia in the Mexican-American war.

Mr. Pierce was elected president over the Whig candidate, General Winfield Scott. The nation wanted no more war heroes. It was easy to forget an ugly and unpopular war, since what was now on everyone's minds was the issue of slavery, which was dividing the nation into enemy camps. Although he was from the north, Mr. Pierce did not take a stand against slavery and named Jefferson Davis as his secretary of war. President Pierce vowed to uphold the recently passed Fugitive Slave Law, which mandated the full power of the national government be employed to return runaway slaves to their rightful owners. Secretary of War Davis directed that the army be used to track down runaways and return them to their owners. The population of Texas was once again surging and more federal troops were being stationed in the state. Their central mission was to protect settlers on the frontiers from being harassed by the Comanches, but their presence freed the Texas Rangers to hunt down runaways and try to seal off the possibility of their escape into Mexico.

It was not long before Lebe Seru and Carmen saw the necessity of a change of strategy. Because of the ever westward movement of immigrants to Texas, it was only a matter of time before our inland farms, no matter how isolated in the harsh and forbidding chaparral of south Texas, would be discovered and reported to the state or federal authorities. It was decided to relocate the runaways south of the Rio Grande in the sparsely populated and remote areas of northern Mexico.

Once the move south of the river had been accomplished, the question arose as to who should stay on the farm across from Matamoros. We were not far upriver from the new town of Brownsville, named after the Major who had been the first American to lose his life in the war. The Rio Grande Valley continued to be overwhelmingly Tejano in population, but more Anglos were arriving to farm and ranch the fertile land. So far they had posed no threat, but it would take only one person to report the suspicion of abolitionist activity. Nevertheless, our location remained essential to helping runaways use the escape route down the Laguna Madre. Some of us had to stay at the farm.

There was no small amount of debate on the wisdom of Lebe Seru, Alma and Ralph remaining where they might be arrested by the Texas Rangers or captured by men who called themselves 'nigger-thieves.' These men would capture fugitives for the bounty paid by the state of Texas. Carmen urged they go to Mexico and said that she, the Montemayors and I could do what was required to assist the runaways. Esau and Tom Blue had taken up residence in Matamoros, but they were always available to help when needed. It was Lebe Seru, Alma and Ralph who were especially vulnerable to capture on the farm.

When Alma gave birth to a little boy, which she named Binu Seru after her father, the necessity of their going across the river seemed even more apparent. Alma and Ralph argued that the money they were making in operating the farm was critical to buy the medicines, the weapons and the other items needed by the runaways to the south. We now had almost six hundred acres of land under cultivation. Furthermore, Lebe Seru was making plows and other farm equipment on the forge, something that would be difficult for him to do in Mexico away from the scrap metal we were able to obtain at the harbors on both sides of the river. The farm equipment he made was vital to the survival of the fugitives in Mexico.

Finally, it was decided that Alma, Ralph and their baby go across the river to one of the settlements the runaways were establishing. Lebe Seru would stay with us on the farm; but to lessen the chance of his being arrested, he would be registered as a slave belonging to Santiago Montemayor. The Texas legislature had passed a law against allowing free negroes to live in the state. Although Santiago hated slavery, he understood that the only way Lebe Seru could remain with us without fear of arrest was for him to register as a slave.

It was sad saying good-bye to Alma, Ralph and their baby. We could go across the border to see them from time to time, but it was not the same as being together everyday. Before they left, I held Binu Seru in my arms as one of the wagons was being loaded.

"Teresa," Alma asked, "will you be my son's godmother?"

"Of course I will, Alma. I will be honored to be Binu Seru's godmother."

"If anything happens to Ralph and me, you will have to take care of him. You will have to raise him."

"If anything happens, I will take care of him. But nothing is going to happen. That is why you are going to Mexico. You will be safe there."

She took Binu Seru into her arms. "It is not right that you have to be separated from Jorge. If you did not have to stay here to help the runaways, you could go to Oaxaca."

"Jorge's course of study at the Institute will soon be over. He will come back then." Alma looked so sad. I wanted to say something to bring her cheer. "We will be married, and you and Ralph will be the godparents of our children!"

"I would like that, Teresa."

When Alma climbed onto the deck of the wagon next to Ralph, I saw her looking at her garden.

"I will look after your vegetables, Alma. Don't worry. I won't let my chickens and goats eat them!"

We watched them drive slowly down the road in the direction of the ferry that would take them across the Rio Grande and into Mexico.

Taking care of Alma's garden along with my chickens and goats was a challenge. Over the years, I had acquired many customers for my eggs and milk among the people who operated freight boats on the Rio Grande between Brownsville, Laredo and Eagle Pass. Up before dawn, I was kept busy all day tending my animals and making deliveries. I took turns with Carmen, Lebe Seru and the Montemayors on going to the contact point to watch for the smoke signals of the runaways. Most days there were no signals. However, when fugitives did appear, we were often up all night taking them to a place on the river where they could cross and be met by Esau and Tom Blue, who would then escort them to one of the settlements in Mexico.

Lebe Seru and Carmen helped me with the garden as much as they could, but they both worked at the forge to produce the tools, guns and other items needed by our people in Mexico. Sometimes we all had to pitch in to help Santiago and Pilar with freight hauls they made up and down the north bank of the river. Together with the money Esau and Tom Blue earned with their tavern and hotel in Matamoros, we were beginning to accumulate the resources Lebe Seru said would be needed when slavery drew to an end.

Despite all of the hard work, I was more than compensated when I saw the relief in the faces of the people who had escaped slavery. The horror many of them had suffered was beyond description. Most of the newspapers in Texas defended the institution of slavery, and they often published stories maintaining that negroes benefited from slavery and were treated well. Some of the newspapers attacked books, such as Harriet Beecher Stowe's *Uncle Tom's Cabin*, that told of the brutal nature of slavery. Tom Blue returned from one of his trips north with a copy of *Uncle Tom's Cabin*. That book did by no means overstate the cruelty and horror of slavery.

Not all of the newspapers in Texas defended slavery. Many of the people who had come to Texas from Europe abhorred slavery. German language newspapers in Fredericksburg and New Braunfels called for the end of slavery. Most Tejanos opposed slavery, and there were Spanish language newspapers that lobbied for universal manumission. As a result, actions were taken in some Texas cities against European immigrants and the Tejano communities. Attempts were made to ban immigration from Europe and attacks were made on German settlements. In 1853 the city council of Austin, the state's capital, banned Tejanos from residing within the city's boundaries, and other municipalities enacted similar ordinances.

After a long period of no letters from Jorge, Esau made a special trip across the river one day to bring one addressed to me. He knew how much Jorge's letters meant to me, and he was too kind to make me wait until Santiago and Pilar made one of their regular freight runs to Matamoros. Even before opening the sealed envelope, I suspected the news was not good. My intuition proved correct.

Dear Teresa,
I am sorry I have been unable to answer your last three letters. Please forgive me. I have been out of Oaxaca on a tour of the state with Don Benito, whose term as governor has come to an end. As governor,

he was often too busy to go to the countryside to witness the effects of all the things he has led us in doing over the past several years.

Everywhere you look, there are roads that make possible the free movement of commerce and the rise of prosperity of all the people. Wells have been dug and aqueducts have been constructed that are enabling people to make productive land that was once little more than a desert. There are no more hungry children in Oaxaca.

With the increased prosperity, the people are able to build schools. For the first time anywhere in Mexico, we have a system of free public education. Everywhere, even in the smallest villages, children are learning how to read. When the children learn to read, they go home and teach their parents and their grandparents. Don Benito's goal is that everyone learn to read, and it is happening. You should see how hungry everyone is for knowledge. The future is unlimited. Compared with other states in Mexico, Oaxaca is poor. What we have done here can be done everywhere, and we have only just begun.

Don Benito has so much more he wants to do for Oaxaca and for all of Mexico, and he has asked me to help him. As I wrote to you in my last letter, I have successfully completed my course of study at the Institute of Sciences and Arts. Several of my teachers were kind enough to tell Don Benito that I show talent in my studies. He seems to believe that I have abilities that would help him in the work that he wishes to undertake throughout all of Mexico.

If I help Don Benito in his work, I shall have to remain in Oaxaca for a while more. What am I to do? I want to be with you. Is it possible that you could come to Oaxaca? I know the work you are doing is very important. I know, too, that you are watching after your grandmother and my grandparents. A heavy responsibility has been placed on your shoulders. Is it possible there are other people who can do the work you do and that you and your grandmother and my grandparents could come to Oaxaca?

Please tell me what to do. If you want me to return to Texas, I will come as fast as I can. Without the thought that we will someday have an opportunity for happiness together, I do not think I could find the motivation to do any work, even this work which Don Benito wants me to share. I pray each night that the people of the United States will end slavery. If it would only come to an end, we could be together.

I love you, Teresa, and will abide with whatever you decide I must do.
Jorge

Never had I felt such an emptiness as I did when I folded that letter and clasped it to my heart. The happiness I had anticipated for what seemed an eternity was not going to happen. Benito Juarez had asked

Jorge to help him in his work. How long was that going to be? A year? Two years? Ten years?

As for my going to Oaxaca, I knew it could not be. What we were doing in helping the runaways was much more than simply important work. In many cases it was a matter of life and death. And I knew my grandmother would never leave. She would not go to Oaxaca. I wished she would, if only for a little while. She was not old, but the rigors of her life were beginning to exact a toll.

For a long time, I debated in my mind whether to ask Jorge to return to Texas. I understood what his teachers meant when they said Jorge showed special ability. What Benito Juarez was doing in Mexico was important. The future of an entire nation depended on what this man was doing. If Jorge could help him, he must do it. There was really no decision to be made. I found my pen.

> Dear Jorge,
> I am proud that Benito Juarez has asked you to help him with his work. What he is doing will benefit not only the people of Oaxaca and Mexico, but wherever people are striving to make this a better world. When you return to Texas, I will be waiting. Our work here will detain us for yet a little while longer. The day is coming when slavery will end. When it does, I will come to you as fast as I can. Continue to write as often as you can, and I will write you.
> I love you,
> Teresa

One day, after Tom Blue had returned from a trip to Huntsville with a letter from my brother, I asked if he ever saw Senator Houston. I was beginning to think about going to see Kalanu. I wanted to know his assessment of the chance of slavery coming to an end and when it might happen. Also, I just wanted to see him and hear his voice. I wanted to hear him laugh and spin his tales.

"General Houston doesn't spend much time in Huntsville, Teresa," Tom Blue said. "Joshua says Mrs. Houston is real upset because the Senator spends all his time in Washington City. He doesn't want Mrs. Houston and the children to come to Washington City because he says the climate is unhealthy. But the General, he don't hardly every come to Texas anymore at all."

"Is there anyway of knowing when he might be in Huntsville?"

"I don't think so. Joshua says Senator Houston believes he's finally going to become president in the next election. The General's giving speeches up north everywhere he can. He's not liable to come back to Texas until that election is over."

I thanked Tom Blue and gave him several sacks of lemons to take to Esau in Matamoros. I took Esteban's letter to my grandmother, and she read it aloud.

"Dear Abuela and Teresa," Esteban wrote:

Maximilian and I have just returned from Paris, this time for the Coronation of Napoleon III. The people of France have demanded that Louis Bonaparte accept the Crown that his uncle wore. His Empress, Eugenie, wears the very Crown worn by Maria Louise, who was Maxl's cousin.

Napoleon and Eugenie promised to come to Vienna if we have a royal wedding. Negotiations are even now being conducted for the union of Maxl and Princess Charlotte of Belgium. I believe she is exactly the woman he needs. Charlotte is ambitious and will help the Archduke realize his destiny.

Maxl may not be the only one to be led to the altar. I have been keeping company with a very charming young lady in Paris.

Carmen looked up at me and smiled.

Her name is Jeanne Lavoisier. She is the most beautiful woman in all of Europe. She is a favorite of Napoleon and Eugenie. In fact it was the Empress who introduced us. Jeanne's father is one of the most successful bankers in all of France. Maxl joked that if we join the House of Lavoisier and the House of Gorlitz, his brother shall be forced to come to us to finance our next war, which may be with Russia if they attempt to take advantage of the weakness of the Turks.

Mother is in good health. She went with us to the Coronation in Paris, but Father had to stay home. Jacob has developed a persistent swelling in his legs that makes it uncomfortable for him to walk and impossible to travel.

Write to me often and send newspapers from Mexico.

My grandmother and I were, of course, most interested in Esteban's revelation. It did not seem possible my little brother was old enough to marry, but he was. He was a man, and apparently he was destined to be a wealthy man. It pleased us both he had found happiness.

Lebe Seru made regular trips south of the river to bring equipment and supplies to the settlements being established by the runaways. Because it had been too long since I had seen Alma and her family, I decided to go with him on one of the trips. Driving a team of mules hitched to a buckboard, we crossed the river by ferry and traveled north, parallel to the Rio Grande. It was a country not unlike where we lived, the soil fertile and productive. When we turned south, the terrain changed and we entered a more arid, desert-like land, marked by islands of mesquite and cactus. One could see why it was a region of sparse population.

Alma and Ralph ran to greet us as we drove into their settlement. I realized how much time had passed when Binu Seru ran to his great-grandfather and leapt into his arms. Alma and I were so glad to see each other we almost could not let go our embrace. We went to their little house, a jacal made of thin mesquite branches driven vertically into the ground and lashed together with horse-hair rope. The roof of the house was corn-thatch. Considering the materials available to use, they had made a comfortable dwelling place.

Alma prepared a special meal of cornbread, okra, squash, beans and melon. Somehow, she had managed to nurture a garden in the dry soil. She watered it from a well they had dug and shared with the eleven other families who comprised their settlement. Ralph introduced us to their neighbors, many of whom I had met at the contact point near the Laguna Madre. I renewed my acquaintance with the woman who had come down the Laguna Madre with the four children and had been with us the night we happened upon the desperados threatening Sam Grant. Ralph took Lebe Seru to see the horses they had captured and were training for farm work.

When Alma and I were alone, I asked, "How is my godson?"

"He is fine, Teresa. He bears more than my father's name. He has his strength and his strong will to survive."

I could see that Alma was happy, but she was also tired. It was a hard life. As I had so many times before, I reflected on what Alma could accomplish if she were not forced to live her life in fear of being captured and made to become someone's property. Why should she have to raise her child in a desert just because other people did not believe she had the right to live free, the same as them? I had deep admiration for the former slaves who had the resolve and the ability to carry on and stay alive in such a difficult situation. They were literally making the desert bloom.

Alma, Ralph and Binu Seru traveled with Lebe Seru and me to other settlements to deliver farm equipment, guns, gunpowder, and other items the runaways needed. Alma told us that there were over six thousand fugitive slaves living in small settements in the area between the Rio Grande and the Sierra Madre mountains. We came to what Ralph explained was the headquarters settlement at Santa Rosa, some fifty miles south of Piedras Negras, which was across the border from Eagle Pass. A Council House had been built at Santa Rosa, and Ralph and Alma introduced us to a number of people who had come from the smaller settlements for a meeting.

Not all those who fled south were negroes. A group of fugitive slaves had come to Mexico all the way from Florida by way of the Indian Territory. They had formed an alliance with Seminole Indians who had lost their ancestral homes as a result of war with the United States. The negroes were led by a man by the name of John Horse, who was part Seminole; and the Seminole leader was Chief Wild Cat. Some two hundred of these people had come through Texas; and on the way, they were joined by a band of Kickapoo Indians led by Chief Papicua. The Kickapoo Indians, who were famed for their accuracy with both bow and arrow and the rifle, helped the fugitives fend off attacks by Comanches, some of whom would prey on runaways.

As the elected representative of his settlement, Ralph attended the Council House meetings. Alma and I attended some of the meetings but spent most of our time helping Lebe Seru make what repairs he could of farm equipment and guns. What he could not repair would have to be taken back to his forge at the farm on our return trip.

One afternoon, we noticed about two dozen uniformed men enter Santa Rosa and ride to the Council House. They were led by a well-dressed man who sat astride an Arabian stallion on an expensive saddle not unlike those used by the Mexican generals in the war. From the deference exhibited by the men in uniform, the man appeared to be someone of importance. Lace cuffs protruded from the sleeves of his frock coat, and a gold-hilted sword gleamed in the jeweled scabbard at his side. Brushing the dust from his riding cape, the man waited for one of his men to open the door to the Council House before going inside.

"Who is that man?" I asked.

"That is Governor Vidaurri," Alma replied. "He is the Governor of Coahuila and Nuevo Leon."

"Both states?"

"Yes. He combined them. And the Governor of Tamaulipas serves at his pleasure. He is the *caudillo* of all the states in northwest Mexico. Those men with him are part of his private army. He owns many great estates and mines. He is a very powerful man."

"Why is he here?"

"At first he was opposed to our coming to this region. Even though no one lives here and the land is worthless, he did not wish to risk the hostility of the Americans for harboring fugitive slaves. When he discovered we are armed and know how to fight, he began to change his mind. Several months ago, Wild Cat, John Horse and Chief Papicua led a group of our people who defeated and drove back into Texas a large force of Texas Rangers who had crossed the river looking for runaways.

"The people of Mexico remember the war. They don't like for Americans to come across the river for any purpose. Therefore, our people have the respect of many of the Mexicans. Many have gone to Governor Vidaurri and asked him to grant us refuge in exchange for us protecting the people against the Comanche tribes that conduct raids into northern Mexico. The Governor has agreed to this arrangement. He comes to the council meetings to make certain everyone understands he is in charge of this part of Mexico."

When the meeting was over and Governor Vidaurri came out of the meeting house, I watched as he berated a boy who did not bring his horse to him quickly enough. Riding past where we were working, he glared down at us as though we were unworthy of the trouble of an acknowledgement. There was something about this man that troubled me.

Upon our return to the farm, we saw an unfamiliar horse hitched outside and heard a woman's sobs from inside the house. Lebe Seru and I rushed into the front room where we found my grandmother with her arm around Pilar, who was crying. Santiago was also trying to comfort her. Immediately, I thought of Jorge. Standing apart from the others was a woman who looked familiar. Though not a tall woman, she stood with a bearing that made her seem taller. Around her waist was a leather belt to which was attached a hostered pistol.

"Abuela," I said. "What has happened? Is it Jorge? Has something—"

"No," my grandmother said quickly. "It is not Jorge, Teresa. He is safe."
She looked at Pilar and stroked her hair. "It is Jorge's father. He has been
killed."

The woman who had been standing in the corner, holding a broad-
brimmed sombrero in her hand, put the hat on a table and walked to
where I was standing. She grasped my hands firmly in hers. Though her
eyes were sad, there was a smile on her lips.

"Teresa," she said. "I am Josefa. I guess you do not remember me. You
were just a baby when I left Texas."

"Josefa," I said and embraced her. I did not remember Jorge's aunt, but
he had written about her often in his letters from Oaxaca. "I am sorry
about your brother."

Josefa went to her mother and held her hand for a moment. Then she
returned and asked me to join her on the front porch.

Outside, I inquired as to the circumstances of the death of Jorge's
father.

"Santa Anna has returned to Mexico, Teresa, and reclaimed the presidency by force. There has been fighting. Jorge's father answered the call
of those in the capital who were trying to resist Santa Anna's return to
power. He was killed there in the fighting. Hundreds have been killed or
executed. After consolidating his victory, Santa Anna issued arrest orders
for those who have oppposed him in the past. Benito Juarez was at the top
of the list."

At the mentioned of the name of Benito Juarez, I was seized by a terrible fear. "Jorge is with Benito Juarez! Tell me of Jorge, Josefa! Is he all
right? Has he been hurt?"

"Jorge is in New Orleans, Teresa. He has not been hurt."

"New Orleans?"

"Yes. Both he and Benito Juarez are in New Orleans."

I was not certain I had heard correctly. "New Orleans? I do not understand. Why would they go to New Orleans?"

"Santa Anna decided to send Benito Juarez into exile rather than
stand him before the firing squad. Perhaps he did not wish to make of him
a martyr. For whatever the reason, I am thankful. And it saved Jorge's life.
He and several of Don Benito's aides were allowed to accompany him. Just
before I left Oaxaca, we learned they were in New Orleans.

"And that is where I am going. My brother, Miguel, remains in Mexico
to help organize the fight against Santa Anna. I have messages that must

be delivered to Don Benito. He must be kept informed of what we are doing."

Carmen came to the front yard to tell Josefa that her mother wanted to see her.

When we were alone, I said, "Josefa is going to New Orleans, Abuela. Benito Juarez is in New Orleans." I took her hand. "Jorge is with him."

My grandmother looked across the field to the embankment above the river. "In that case, Teresa, we must pack your things."

"Abuela, I cannot leave you."

"We will manage for a while without you. But you must return soon. The time is fast approaching when we will face a great test, and you will be needed." She embraced me. "But for now, Teresa, you must go to Jorge. He will need you. He will need your strength."

X

Esau wanted to pay our fare to go by passenger ship, but Josefa said we could reach New Orleans just as fast on a freighter, and pay for our passage by loading wood and stoking the fires necessary to drive the steam engines. We made such an arrangement with a captain who was unable to secure a crew to man his boat loaded with uncured hides. No seamen wanted to be around the stench of the hides for the meager wages the captain was paying. We became his only crew.

Slowly, the little boat advanced up the Texas intercoastal waterway until we reached the Sabine River, after which we hugged the Louisiana coast to the mouth of the Mississippi. The work was not especially hard, though we had to make frequent stops to search for driftwood to fire the engines. The captain, who had once been the master of merchant sailing vessels before wrecking three ships on reefs, spent most of his time drinking spirits or sleeping. Josefa was the kind of person who could adapt to any circumstance. She had never been on a boat in her life, but she took the wheel and steered as I manned the bow to let her know when we were coming too close to sand bars.

Though it seemed much longer, it was just a little over a month before we reached the Mississippi Delta and plied our way upstream past the swampy lagoons and canebrakes to solid land supporting stands of willows and poplars. Approaching the city, we saw large live oaks on which strands of Spanish moss hung like mourning crepe. My first glimpse of the city was the huge burnished cupola of the St. Charles Hotel. Soon, Josefa was threading our vessel among the sea-going clippers and riverboats anchored near the waterfront of the city.

After securing the boat and waking the captain to bid him farewell, Josefa and I walked along the bustling wharfs and listened to the babel of languages of those buying and selling every kind of goods one could imagine. There was much more French and Spanish being spoken than English. I recognized German and Italian, but there were a good many languages that I had never heard, even at Galveston which was much smaller than this city of New Orleans with its cobblestone streets and boardwalks. Josefa had the address of where the Mexican exiles were living and, after asking for directions, we set out to find Jorge. We entered the French

Quarter and walked past the marketplace, which was filled with vendors offering a variety of produce, spices, breads, candies and pastries.

Just beyond the market were stately, multi-story, stone and brick houses with long balconies and ornate wrought-iron balustrades. We walked pass mahogany-wood doors, some open to reveal indoor patios with stone fountains and lavish gardens. We saw well-dressed men and women exit the houses to walk to elegant coaches drawn by magnificent barouche horses. Slaves opened doors for their masters and carried packages or babies. In the narrow streets, vendors pushed carts and called out the names of the products they were selling.

The house we were seeking was on a dirt street several blocks from the French Quarter in an area of older wooden structures. Peering through a broken glass pane, I saw a young man on his hands and knees, scrubbing the floor. My heart raced when I recognized who it was.

"Jorge!"

Turning quickly, Jorge squinted his eyes against the sunlight and then dropped his brush and scampered to his feet. Though he was trying to dry his hands on an apron, I did not allow him the opportunity before I embraced him. Over and over, I whispered his name and kissed him.

When I drew back to get a better look, I saw the joy in his face; but I also detected sadness deep within those beautiful green eyes. He was older, of course. He was no longer the boy who had run across that field to the ferry crossing on the Rio Grande so long ago. His face was now lean and there were lines around his eyes, all of which only made him more handsome. I knew the lines were not those caused by age. There was disappointment and discouragement in Jorge's face, much discouragement.

"Teresa," he whispered. "It is really you. It is not a dream. It is you?"

"Yes, Jorge. It is me."

He looked over my shoulder. "Tia?"

"How are you, nephew?"

Never letting go of my hand, Jorge stepped to his aunt and embraced her.

"Your grandparents send their love," Josefa said. "They are well. And Miguel is well. He remains in Oaxaca."

I told Jorge of my sorrow over his father's death. He closed his eyes and nodded.

"Jorge," Josefa asked, "where is Don Benito?"

For a moment, it seemed Jorge could not bring himself to answer. Finally, he said, "He is at a place called Jackson Square, Tia. He is selling cigars to people on the street."

We did not need to prolong Jorge's distress by asking pointless questions as to why he was scrubbing floors and Benito Juarez was selling cigars. It was obvious they were having a difficult time in this strange and foreign land.

"Teresa," Jorge said. "Tia. I cannot tell you how happy I am to see you, but you should not have come. Our situation is not good. No one will give us a decent job. The people in this city hold Mexicans in the same low regard as the slaves."

Josefa asked, "Is Don Benito well?"

"No, Tia. Don Benito suffered from an attack of yellow fever when we first arrived. He has recovered, but he works constantly doing what he can to earn money. Most of it he places in a fund to purchase the arms and powder that will be needed to defeat Santa Anna. He eats too little and does not get enough sleep. He tries to make the rest of us eat more and work less, but we attempt to follow his example. And though he never complains and says little, we know he is heartsick with worry about his wife and children."

"They are fine," Josefa said. "Margarita and the children are well and in a safe place."

"He will be relieved. You must go and tell him at once. I would go with you, but I must finish the floors and do those in the house next door. All these houses on this street are owned by the same man. He allows Don Benito and me a room in the attic if I keep the houses clean."

"Only one room?" I asked. "There must be at least thirty houses on this street, Jorge. You clean them all for only one room in the attic?"

"We are lucky to have it, Teresa. New Orleans is very crowded, and the landlords charge very high rents for even squalid houses like the ones on this street."

"Is there another room here, Jorge?" Josefa asked. "Teresa and I will need a place to sleep until Don Benito decides what is to be done."

"There is one, Tia, but it is even smaller than ours."

"Tell the landlord we will take it."

"But the rent, Tia. He will charge too much."

"We have a little money," Josefa said. "Enough for a few days. In the meantime, we will find some way to earn money." She looked at me. "I might even be able to roll a few cigars. What do you say, Teresa? If we can bring a steamboat five hundred miles across the Gulf of Mexico, we should have no trouble with rolling a cigar. No?"

Jorge gave us directions for how to get to Jackson Square and promised to join us after work at a park where the Mexican exiles gathered to share a meal and discuss the latest news from home. Everyone, he said, would be anxious to hear Josefa's report. Before we left, I embraced Jorge again and kissed him. It did not matter to me the condition of the old broken-down house in which we would be living. No palace in the world could look so beautiful. Finally, we were together again.

Retracing our steps, Josefa and I returned to the marketplace and located Jackson Square, which was on the east side of a great cathedral and adjacent to the river front. The square was crowded with hundreds of people. We were almost bowled over by several young men carrying roosters in a cage to a cockfight arena near one of the riverboat wharfs. Josefa's small stature made it difficult for her to look over the crowd.

Finally, she said, "There he is! Over there!"

As we approached the location Josefa had indicated, I saw several men carrying large boxes on which had been hand-printed the word: CIGARS. Since I had never seen Benito Juarez, I had no idea which he was. One man stood out among the rest. He was a tall and distinguished-looking gentleman with wavy silver hair and a neatly trimmed beard and mustache. Shoulders erect, this man had the bearing of a statesman; and I concluded he must be the former governor of Oaxaca, particularly since Josefa was approaching him.

"Señorita Montemayor!" the man exclaimed in a deep voice. "Is it you? Benito, look who's here! It's Señorita Montemayor! How wonderful to see you!"

Behind the silver-haired man, a much smaller gentleman turned to respond to his friend's summons. I remembered Benito Juarez was an Indian. There could be no mistake. This bronze-skinned man with the high cheekbones, broad nose, strong jaw and black hair and eyes was Benito Juarez.

Josefa hardly allowed them to put down their boxes before she embraced them.

"Ignacio," she said to the first man, "how are you, you old scoundrel? You look well, hombre. And Don Benito! Ah, Benito! How good to see you!"

In traditional Mexican fashion, the man called Ignacio expressed his pleasure at seeing Josefa with great fanfare.

Though a man of middle years, Benito Juarez seemed boyishly shy. "It is good to see you, Señorita Montemayor," he said in a soft baritone voice. He removed his hat and extended his hand. "How are you?"

Josefa would have nothing to do with formality. She hugged Benito Juarez again with great vigor. If he had not been a rock-solid and broad-shouldered man, I think she might have swept him off his feet. His eyes focused on me, and I had to force myself not to look away from his gaze. Only a kind smile prevented Benito Juarez from appearing to be an aloof, even cold, man. He had the eyes of a man who, come what may, would not, could not, be moved. A will of iron was evident in this man's face.

"Teresa," Josefa said, taking me by the hand. "May I present Ignacio Comonfort."

"*Buenas tardes, Señor,*" I said to the tall gentlemen.

As I somehow expected, Señor Comonfort bowed and paid me many compliments for my appearance. He was a good and sincere man but much in need to be noticed for his striking good looks and manly voice.

"Teresa," Josefa said, "this is Benito Juarez."

"Governor Juarez," I said and shook his hand. "It is my pleasure."

The kind smile deepened when he said, "I have heard much about you, Señorita Sestos. Jorge speaks of you often. And he has told me of your grandparents who followed El Señor Hidalgo." He said the words 'El Señor Hidalgo' with reverence and devotion. "Someday, I hope to have the honor of meeting your grandmother. We are indebted to those of her generation who made such enormous sacrifices. I pray that we can be worthy of their example."

Initially, it had been necessary for me to fight to keep from averting my eyes from this man's intense gaze; now I hoped I did not seem impolite by my inability to cease staring at him. There was some intangible and rare quality about this man that drew one to him. I could understand why Jorge had chosen to follow Benito Juarez and wanted to serve his cause.

When Josefa relayed the news that his wife and children were safe and well-hidden in Mexico, Don Benito closed his eyes and a benediction of thanksgiving swept over his face. And though his expression changed but slightly, one could see the pain when she told him of her brother's death and the deaths of so many other of the people who had been their friends and compatriots. He sought detailed information about all of their compañeros who remained in Mexico.

"Benito," Ignacio Comonfort said and gestured to a large group of men who were waiting nearby. "Your customers."

After excusing himself, Don Benito picked up his box and began to sell packages of cigars to men who seemed eager to purchase his product.

Señor Comonfort explained, "Benito rolls the best cigar in New Orleans. Each morning we go to the tobacco warehouses and he purchases a little of this tobacco, and some of that, and a little bit more of a different one. Brown tobacco. Yellow tobacco. White tobacco. He has developed this unique blend and rolls them just so: not too tight, not too loose. Those who know cigars swear that his are cooler and sweeter than the finest cigars from Havana. Leave it to Benito Juarez to discover the science of the perfect cigar!"

After the men had sold all of their cigars, we accompanied them to the market where Don Benito carefully selected a variety of inexpensive breads and cheeses, vegetables and fruits. He had held back several of his cigars to exchange for a large bag of apples. We took the food to a place up the river where gradually, one by one, and in small groups of three or four, the Mexican exiles, each tired after a long day's work at menial jobs, gathered to share their meager fare and discuss the latest news from Mexico.

When Jorge arrived, I could sense the tiredness in his body as I hugged him and followed him to a spot where he spread a serape for us to sit on the ground. He was almost too exhausted to eat the cheese and bread Don Benito gave us.

"Eat, Jorge," Don Benito said with fatherly concern. "You must keep up your strength. We have many apples. They are good for you."

Everyone listened as Josefa told of the events in Mexico just prior to her departure. Most of the exiles were men, forced to leave their families behind; and they were grateful for news that their wives and children were being helped by those in opposition to Santa Anna and the aristocracy which had returned him to power. Several had been officials in state governments that had begun to challenge the power of the landowners.

Josefa told the group how Santa Anna was now calling himself "His Most Serene Highness" and had revived the titled aristocracy in Mexico. The country once again had its marquises and condes and holders of the Order of This or the Order of That. Elaborate ceremonies and formal banquets were being staged almost every night at the National Palace to honor the nobility under the watchful eye of Santa Anna's Elite Guard, which he called "The Supreme Protectors of the Universe."

Benito Juarez shook his head sadly and said, "The money spent on just one of those banquets could operate a school for an entire year."

Ignacio Comonfort sighed. "It will play itself out, Benito. It always does with Santa Anna. After he has squeezed every last centavo of taxes out of the people and transferred it to his accounts outside of Mexico, he will leave the country to live at one of his plantations in Cuba or Venezuela."

"Yes, Ignacio," Don Benito said. "What you say is true. But then he will return to Mexico in a few years to plunder the country once again after the people have labored to restore some small measure of prosperity. Or perhaps the aristocracy and their generals will select a younger man to rule on their behalf and plunge our nation once more into ruin. When will this cycle end? It will end only when we have firmly established a constitution and the rule of law."

After we had eaten and the exiles were engaged in discussions about what course of action they should take in light of the latest news of Santa Anna's activities in Mexico, Don Benito suggested Jorge and I take a walk along the riverbank. He knew we wanted some time alone but were reluctant to leave the others. He cautioned against going too far from the group in order to avoid the danger of robbers who might take advantage of the darkness.

Hand in hand, we went to the bank and found a quiet place near a stand of magnolia trees whose aromatic blooms glowed a soft white in the night.

"Don Benito is like a mother hen," I said. "He watches over everyone."

"He is what holds us together. We would be lost without him." Jorge's eyes saddened, and he shook his head. "Mexico would be lost without Benito Juarez."

"What is he going to do, Jorge?"

"He will return to Mexico. It is only a question of when. Already, there are pockets of resistance against Santa Anna in the countryside. People like my uncle, Miguel, are fighting a guerilla war. Eventually, we shall have to organize larger forces and retake the states, one by one, until not only Santa Anna, but the power of the aristocracy who support him is broken. Señor Comonfort spoke the truth. Santa Anna will only stay until he loots the treasury. The real problem are the younger officers ready to take his place, men like Miguel Miramon and Tomas Mejia, ruthless men hungry for power."

"Miramon? That is a French name. He is an officer in the Santa Anna's army?"

"Miramon's family is French, though he was born in Mexico. He is a great admirer of Louis Bonaparte. In the end, it is men like Miramon that we shall ultimately have to defeat."

"And you, Jorge? What will you do?"

He lowered his head. "I, too, must return to Mexico. Don Benito needs me."

"I need you, Jorge."

"Then come with me to Mexico, Teresa," he said, grasping my hands. "Marry me!"

It was what I wanted more than anything. But I knew I could not leave Texas. I was needed there just as Jorge was needed in Mexico. The struggle was the same. A boundary on a map meant nothing. Men and women on both sides of the Rio Grande were struggling for the same cause, the cause of liberty and justice. Victory could not be achieved in one place and not the other. No one could be free until everyone was free.

I kissed Jorge and held him tightly. There was no use in torturing ourselves in pointless debate about what we must do. We both knew what we must do. For now, we were together and that was all that mattered. We were together.

Josefa and I became cigar makers. Each morning we would leave our tiny little room at dawn and meet Benito Juarez outside where he was always patiently waiting in his freshly washed and ironed white shirt, black pants, necktie, and stovepipe hat. We would go with him to the warehouse district and watch as he carefully selected the various kinds of tobaccos he would use to make his special blend.

Most of the morning was spent in shredding the leaves just the right way and mixing them according to Don Benito's exacting standards. Rolling them—not too firm, not too loose—was the final stage of production before we packed them in the boxes, ready to be sold on the street to the former governor's ever expanding clientele, most of whom probably did not realize that the money they were spending for cigars would eventually buy weapons and gunpowder to bring down a dictator in Mexico.

On Sundays, we enjoyed a respite from our labors. We would accompany Don Benito to the Ursuline Academy where he knew the rector. We would attend mass in the academy's small chapel. Benito Juarez was not an atheist, as was claimed by the bishops in Mexico who were angered by his call for the church to give up its land holdings used in peonage farming. Don Benito wanted the church and state to be separate in Mexico and for there to be freedom of religion.

One Sunday after mass, the exiles assembled in a field next to the Ursuline Academy to have lunch and enjoy the afternoon. Josefa and I had set a trot line the night before, and we were able to treat everyone to a meal of fried catfish, cornbread and poke salad. I had managed to recall a thing or two of what Alma had taught me about cooking. We even made fresh tortillas, which made everyone happy, though more than a little homesick.

Adjoining the field was a small plaza in which a puppeteer was performing for children. While some in our group took naps or conversed, others of us, including Don Benito, were charmed by the puppeteer's clever antics. More than the performance, we enjoyed watching the delight of two negro children at the edge of the crowd. They loved the puppets.

Suddenly, a white woman appeared with a stick and began to strike the negro children. "I told you not to come out here!" the woman screamed while hitting the children again and again. "You lazy niggers! You're supposed to be in the house working. I'm going to sell you both as field hands! You hear me? I'm going to sell you both to the meanest man I can find, who will work you in the fields until you drop dead! You hear me?"

As the woman continued to hit the children, Don Benito walked toward the woman and, in English, said, "Do not hit the children."

Though not very tall, Benito Juarez was a broad-bodied man, and he sometimes reminded me of a bear. I think the woman must have thought of something similar, because she stopped beating the children. After telling them to go home, she hurried away. The children obeyed, but not before returning the smile of the man who had come to their defense.

Back in the field, Don Benito sat next to Jorge and me and shook his head. "Man is born free," he said, "and yet we see him everywhere in chains."

"Rousseau," Jorge said, ever his teacher's student.

"Yes," Don Benito said. "Jean-Jacques Rousseau. It is the first sentence of his *Social Contract*. And how true are his words. We are born free. It is God's intent that we be free, but soon man is in the chains of injustice and man's inhumanity to man." He looked at Jorge and me. "Do either of you recall the second sentence in Señor Rousseau's book?"

Neither of us did.

"Those who believe themselves the masters of others cease not to be even greater slaves than the people they govern." He nodded his head. "Greater slaves. What do you think, Teresa? Is that woman who was beating those children a greater slave than the children?"

"That woman is not bruised, Don Benito. She is not bleeding. She can beat the children without fear of the law. She can buy and sell them. It is the law of the land. I do not think she is a greater slave than the children."

"Yes," he said. "The lot of a slave is a terrible one. But I cannot help but wonder what Rousseau meant when he said those who believe themselves masters are even greater slaves than the people they govern."

"What do you think, Don Benito?" I asked.

"Do you recall the account in the scriptures when Christ told his disciples to 'call no one on earth your father; for one is your father, who is in heaven'? To call anyone but God your father, he seemed to be saying, is to fail to understand that we are each of us created in God's image and, therefore, we are equal.

"Christ also told his disciples, 'neither be called masters'; and I wonder if it was not for the same reason. If I think I am the master of other men, I am living a lie. I am failing to recognize the truth that all men are equal, that truly we all have the same father.

"Could this be what Rousseau meant when he said, 'Those who believe themselves to be the masters of others cease not to be even greater slaves than the people they govern?' That woman who beat those children does not know they are the children of God, does she? How could she? Could you beat a child of God? Neither can she know she is a child of God, for a child of God could never buy and sell his brothers and sisters. That woman is a slave to a lie. She may for the present be able to buy and sell those children and to beat them with no fear of the law, but she is a far greater slave than they are."

The day Jorge and I had been dreading came too soon. The news arrived that the forces opposing Santa Anna had captured Acapulco on the Pacific coast. They were holding the city but were in desperate need of reinforcements. Benito Juarez assembled the exiles and told them he was returning to Mexico. He and those who chose to go with him arranged to take a freighter to the Isthmus of Panama where they would go by land to the Pacific and take another ship to Acapulco.

It was perhaps merciful that everything happened quickly, because it did not give Jorge and me time to dwell on the fact that once more we would be parted without any idea of when we would see each other again. I tried not to think of the fact Jorge would be going to where battles were raging. At the dock, I held him as long as I could until just before the gang-plank was to be hoisted. Even when the ship was only a fading spot on the horizon, I continued to wave, thinking that he could still see me. My only consolation was in knowing that Jorge was with Benito Juarez. I had faith Don Benito would let nothing happen to the man whose life was more precious to me than my own.

Since Josefa had gone with Benito Juarez and Jorge to Acapulco, I had no traveling companion on my return trip. It did not seem prudent to try to work my way home on a freighter, so I took a passenger ship to Brownsville. When I arrived at the farm, Carmen embraced me for a long time before she held me at arm's length to look into my face. I was glad to see her, though I was a little shocked to see that her hair was now almost entirely white. In my absence, my grandmother had reached her sixtieth year, but she was still very strong.

Carmen's first news was that I now had a sister-in-law and would soon become an aunt. Esteban had married Jeanne, and they were expecting a child. When Carmen gave me my brother's letters to read, I noticed the information about his marriage came after he had detailed the elaborate ceremony held for the marriage of Archduke Maximilian and Princess Charlotte of Belgium. Even the letter informing us of his impending fatherhood was prefaced with descriptions of visits with Napoleon III and Empress Eugenie. Esteban seemed to be spending more time in Paris than Vienna. His father-in-law was deeply involved in financing Napoleon's effort to make the French army the most powerful in all of Europe.

The Montemayors were happy to learn that Jorge was in good health and, though concerned for his safety, understood why he had returned to Mexico with their daughter. They had received word from Miguel that he was involved in the fighting that was slowly forcing Santa Anna out of the western states of Mexico.

Esau and Tom Blue were continuing to do well in Matamoros, and Lebe Seru said Alma and Ralph wanted me to come to see them as soon as I returned. He said I would understand why they no longer referred to Binu Seru as "the baby." Lebe Seru said his great-grandson was not only walking and talking, but was riding horses like a vaquero.

Within days of my arrival, I was at the contact point, watching for the signal from runaways that had made their way down the Laguna Madre. The number of slaves attempting to find their way to Mexico was increasing. Two and three nights a week, we were involved in helping escapees cross the Rio Grande and make their way to one of our settlements in northern Mexico. Our work was even more dangerous because more bounty hunters were seeking the money the state of Texas was promising in ever increasing amounts for the return of fugitive slaves. Texas Ranger units patrolled the riverbanks and sometimes crossed into Mexico in search of the runaways. They did not go too far because they knew our people were armed and prepared to fight with their allies, the Seminoles and the Kickapoos.

Tom Blue continued to make trips north to hide boats in the dunes for the fugitives. In Huntsville, Joshua told Tom Blue that Mrs. Houston was very upset her husband continued to seek the presidency, election after election. I read in the newspapers that Senator Houston was considered to have a good chance of being elected president in 1856. Franklin Pierce had proven to be a weak president, and many people said the Union needed a strong leader like Sam Houston to avoid breaking into pieces over the question of slavery. Though disliked in the southern states, the Texas senator was held in high regard in the north.

Sam Houston was not elected president in 1856. Once again, he did not receive the nomination of any of the political parties. Before the conventions, he delivered a speech in which he said the Indians should not be forced off their lands in violation of treaties they had made with the government of the United States. Since many people in the northern states were anxious to immigrate to the lands the Indians were being made to vacate, they became hostile to the senator who was virtually the only friend the Indians had in Washington. Combined with his attempts to block the spread of slavery, Sam Houston's support of the Indians' rights to their land destroyed any chance of his being elected President of the United States.

The man elected president in 1856 was James Buchanan, who had been Secretary of State at the time of the Mexican-American War. Buchanan defeated John Fremont, the nominee of the newly formed Republican Party. The Republicans were angry that slavery was being extended into the western territories. Fighting had erupted and blood had been spilled in Kansas over the issue of slavery.

Buchanan proved to be yet another weak president, not up to the task of dealing with the nation's problems. Soon, the newspapers were filled with speculation that the presidential election of 1860 would be a turning-point. The Union's future would depend on who was elected president in 1860.

Not only did Sam Houston fail to be nominated for president in 1856, he was not selected by the Texas legislature to continue to be one of the state's United States Senators. Texans were angry with The General for his votes that were at odds with other southern senators and for his efforts on behalf of the Indians. The degree of anger was evidenced by the fact that when the now ex-senator Houston returned home and stood for election as governor of Texas, he was defeated. He waited two years and stood again for the office, this time reminding the people of Texas of all the things he had done for them. He won the election by a very narrow margin. I resolved to pay a visit to my old teacher in Austin the first chance I got.

The new governor of Texas had no way of knowing, but I found a way to put to good use the books he had given me upon our departure from Houston Town that night so many years ago. On one of my trips with Lebe Seru to the settlements in northern Mexico to deliver supplies, I remarked to Alma on how fast my godson was growing.

"I know," she said. "He seems to get bigger everyday."

I watched Binu Seru caring for the settlement's horses. The people had acquired a small herd of range cattle, and the horses were vital to moving them from place to place where there were water holes and grasses. It was no small task to keep the horses and cattle fed and watered and in good health, but Binu Seru had a way with animals.

"He reminds me of your father, Alma. I remember how your father loved animals."

"His grandson is just like him. And he asks so many questions. I think if he had an opportunity to learn to read and write, he could prepare himself to go to college and learn how to treat sick animals. That was my father's dream. He wanted to go to college and learn how to treat sick animals."

I did not know why I did not think of it sooner. "Alma, we must start a school!"

"A school? Here?"

"Yes. Here and in all the settlements. We have to teach the children to read! We will teach them writing and arithmetic and science and geography. We have to have a school!"

Alma liked the idea, but she had always been very practical. "Teresa, in order to have a school, you must have books. You have to have slates and chalk and pens and paper. You need many things for a school."

"I have books," I said. "Do you remember the books Kalanu gave me? You and I learned to read out of those books. And I have the books Sam Grant gave Jorge and me. We can teach arithmetic from those books."

I could hardly wait to get started. When I told Esau what we were doing, he found more books for us in Matamoros. Some of my egg and milk customers on the riverboats gave me books. Tom Blue brought slates and chalk from Austin, where he now had to go to make connections with Joshua since Kalanu had assumed his new office. He said Joshua shared with Governor Houston why he was looking for slates and chalk and, before long, supplies of these and other school items began to make their appearance.

At Carmen's suggestion, I wrote to my brother in Vienna to ask if he could send us materials for our school. After all, I had sent him many books and maps on Texas and Mexico over the years. If his father-in-law were able to finance Napoleon's army, it seemed little to ask for a small contribution to a school for fugitive slaves in northern Mexico.

Since the distances were so great, I did not think much about it when I did not receive from Esteban an immediate response to my request for materials for our school. However, after six months passed without any word from him, I began to worry. From a time shortly after my return from New Orleans, Esteban's letters had become increasingly few and far between. What's more, whereas he had once written pages detailing everything that was happening in his life, he had begun to confine his letters to a few brief sentences on a single page.

Even the letter in which he told us of the birth of his son seemed to be little more than a hurried note from someone preoccupied by other things. He informed us that he and Jeanne had named their son Ferdinand Maximilian. After the letter telling us of the birth of his son, we heard nothing more from Esteban. When a year had elapsed without hearing from him, Carmen wrote to my mother, pleading with her to let us know if something was wrong. We feared Esteban was sick.

We heard nothing from Cata Valeria. It had been many years since we had heard from my mother. When two years passed without hearing anything from Esteban, I gave serious consideration to writing to Maximilian von Hapsburg. He and Esteban were like brothers. Surely, he would let us know if something had happened to Esteban. With the passage of more time, however, I abandoned the idea of writing to the Archduke. I had to agree with Carmen that if something were seriously wrong, my mother would put aside her pride and write to us. Reluctantly, I concluded that Esteban had become so involved in the affairs of his life in Europe, he no longer had time for his sister and his grandmother.

Though I continued to be concerned by the absence of letters from my brother, I was distressed beyond measure by the lack of any word from Jorge in Mexico. The fighting had cut off all communication from the western regions of Mexico. What news we had came from sketchy reports in the newspapers of Matamoros, which Esau would rush to us anytime something new was available.

Ignacio Comonfort had been correct in his assessment of Santa Anna. When his forces began to be driven back toward the capital, the dictator looted the national treasury and sailed for one of his plantations in Venezuela. Santa Anna, a master of collecting taxes and conscripting young men, could plan for a war; but he had no stomach for fighting one. In truth, the Mexican aristocracy was probably as happy to see Santa Anna leave as those who had been fighting him.

Unfortunately, Benito Juarez was correct in his prediction that younger men were only too eager to take Santa Anna's place. Jorge was on the mark when he had identified Miguel Miramon and Tomas Mejia as the new champions of Mexico's powerful aristocracy. After Santa Anna's departure, Miramon and Mejia, acting with the support of the notables, challenged the processes that led to the selection of Benito Juarez as the first civilian president of the Republic of Mexico. Only for a brief period was Don Benito able to commence a program of reform that would bring the rule of law to Mexico before Miguel Miramon pronounced against Benito Juarez and proclaimed himself the president of Mexico.

What then ensued was a full-scale civil war, one much more severe than anything that had occurred previously because, unlike Santa Anna, Miguel Miramon and Tomas Mejia were generals who not only knew how to prepare for a war, but how to fight one. Neither Miramon nor Mejia would abandon their soldiers on the battlefield to flee for a plantation in another country. The final confrontation had finally arrived between the defenders of privilege and those who wanted to bring to fruition Miguel Hidalgo's dream of a Mexican Republic governed by the rule of law and dedicated to the principles of liberty, equality and justice.

With my head, I understood the gravity of what was happening, and I knew why it must happen. In my heart, I understood one thing, one overwhelming fact: Jorge and I would continue to be separated until the issue was settled after a protracted struggle of many years on many battlefields. I prayed that we could somehow survive and at last be able to begin our lives together and never again be separated.

Just as Mexico was beginning to demonstrate to the world the horrible destructiveness and human suffering of civil war, the United States seemed to be intent on charting the exact same course. In 1860 the Democratic Party split into two factions. The northern Democrats nominated Stephen A. Douglas of Illinois for president. The southern Democrats nominated John C. Breckinridge of Kentucky. Neither man opposed slavery, but Douglas wanted to prevent its spread to the territories. Breckinridge endorsed the Supreme Court's *Dred Scott* decision, which effectively stripped all negroes, free or slave, of citizenship and allowed slavery in the territories.

The Republican Party nominated Abraham Lincoln of Illinois. As a congressman, Lincoln had strongly opposed the Mexican-American war. He said slavery was wrong and its spread to the territories should be stopped. He believed that if slavery were restricted to the south, it would die a natural death. His position was not different from that long held by Sam Houston, whose name was placed in nomination to be the candidate of a new party called the Constitutional Union Party. Even this small party would not accept a man who opposed moving the Indians to the west, and they nominated John Bell of Tennessee.

Abraham Lincoln won the election by a narrow margin. Because the vote was split among four candidates, he was elected president by less than a majority of the popular vote. Receiving no more than a scattering of votes throughout the south, Mr. Lincoln did not receive one recorded vote in Texas. Although the election was held in November, Mr. Lincoln would not be inaugurated as president until March of the following year. Within days of his election, several of the southern states began the process of selecting delegates to conventions called to authorize the withdrawal of the states from the Union.

Shortly after the election, Lebe Seru and I were returning from a supply trip to the settlements when we were passed by a company of federal soldiers. We did not think much of it because the U. S. army had been sent by President Buchanan to the Rio Grande Valley in pursuit of a group led by a man named Juan Cortinas. Cortinas had killed a city marshall in Brownsville. When the Texas Rangers came after him, Cortinas and his friends fought back. At one point they seized control of Brownsville and threatened harm to Anglos who had for years swindled Tejanos of their land and property. To most Anglos, Juan Cortinas was nothing more than a bandit. To most Tejanos, he was a folk hero who was leading his people to take a stand against the injustices they had suffered at the hands of the Anglos.

As Lebe Seru and I drew near the farm, we were alarmed to see that the soldiers which had passed us were outside the house. They were dismounted and moving about. It occurred to us that the army had somehow come to believe that Juan Cortinas had supporters at our farm, and they were going to burn the house down. It was not unusual for people suspected of supporting Cortinas to have their houses burned or even to be killed.

At the gate to the front yard, we saw my grandmother and the Montemayors in the yard. They were talking to an officer. I was greatly relieved when I saw that Carmen was smiling. When she saw us, she waved and gestured for us to join them. The soldiers were exceedingly polite. They tipped their hats as we passed, and several of them insisted they be allowed to unharness our team and take the mules to the corral.

As we walked to the house, the officer came toward us. His hair and mustache were almost entirely grey. A red silk sash was around his waist and there was an ostrich plume attached to the black hat he held in his gloved right hand. Tall and broad-shouldered, he cut a striking figure. In terms of appearance, one could not have imagined a more perfect soldier.

Suddenly, I recognized who he was. "Captain Lee?"

Robert E. Lee smiled and pointed to the shoulder brass on the dark blue officer's jacket.

"Colonel Lee."

He embraced me and then grasped Lebe Seru's hand with both of his and shook it with much vigor.

"Colonel Lee," I said, still unable to believe it was him. It had been fifteen years since he had attended Alma's wedding at our house. "What are you doing here?"

"As I was telling your grandmother and Señor and Señora Montemayor, I am the Commander of the Army's Department of Texas. I'm on an inspection tour of our facilities in the Valley."

"It is good to see you, Colonel Lee."

"I am delighted to see all of you, Teresa. I'm sorry Alma and Ralph are not here. I understand they have a son." He looked at Lebe Seru and smiled. "You are a great-grandfather, sir."

"I am indeed, Colonel Lee."

"And you, Teresa?" he said, looking at me again. "Where is your young man? I thought by now you would have made Mrs. Owens a great-grandmother, although I understand your brother has already accomplished that feat. Where is Jorge?"

I explained where Jorge was and what he was doing.

"He is serving a good man. I have heard many good things of Benito Juarez. Our president-elect, Abraham Lincoln, has expressed great admiration for President Juarez. I hope the war ends very soon and Jorge will be able to return home. I will pray for his safe return."

Carmen said, "We have invited Colonel Lee to have dinner with us this evening. And he has accepted."

"I must admit," Colonel Lee said, "it is an invitation I was hoping would be made. I have never forgotten the wonderful food that lovely evening. And I have never forgotten your hospitality. I have looked forward to seeing you all for a long time."

It was necessary for Colonel Lee to go into Brownsville and meet with some of his officers, but he returned later that day for dinner. We expended no small effort to prepare the traditional Mexican fare that he had enjoyed. From the way he ate and the compliments he lavished on the food, our labors were not in vain.

After eating, we retired to chairs in the front yard and watched the stars emerge. Lebe Seru lit his pipe, and the Montemayors served fresh coffee, *pan dulce* and fruit.

Finally, I raised the question that had been on my mind since the Colonel's unexpected arrival. "Colonel Lee, what happened to Lieutenant Grant?" We had not heard from him since the war, and I feared he had been killed.

"Sam Grant is no longer in the army, Teresa. After the war, he was sent to the Pacific coast. He spent some time in the Washington Territories." He drew a deep breath. "Perhaps it is not my place to say this, but I know how you folks were friends with Sam. I certainly know he had a deep affection for all of you. He fell on hard times. The horror of the war weighed heavily on him, and he took to drink. It got the better of him, and he had to resign his commission."

"Where is he now?"

"The last I heard he was back in Ohio. He's married and has two children."

I was glad to receive this last piece of information. I hoped that Sam was raising the horses that he so loved and perhaps teaching mathematics at a small college. "What is he doing, Colonel Lee? Do you know?"

"I understand he tried his hand at farming and then shopkeeping, neither of which worked out. I believe he has gone into his father's business."

I remembered what Sam had said about how he hated the tannery business.

Colonel Lee said, "It is a shame that Sam Grant had to leave the army. He was a fine soldier. If I were ever to lead men in battle, I would want Sam Grant by my side. I would not want him on the other side."

One of our cats strolled up and, without any hesitation, jumped up onto Colonel Lee's lap. I started to chase her away.

"No," the Colonel said. "Let her stay. I love cats."

Lebe Seru asked, "Do you expect that you will be leading men in battle again, Colonel Lee?"

We all understood what Lebe Seru was asking. Just that afternoon, the news had arrived that Conventions in South Carolina and Mississippi had voted to leave the Union.

"I pray that I will not."

Carmen asked, "Would you lead men against the United States?"

"I will never bear arms against the United States, Mrs. Owens. By the same token, I hope it will never become necessary for me to carry a musket in defense of my state, Virginia."

Not long after Robert E. Lee's visit to our farm, we read in the San Antonio newspaper that he had been summoned to Washington City by Winfield Scott, who was still the General of the Army. More states were leaving the Union in the final weeks before Abraham Lincoln's inauguration. Many officers from these states were resigning their commissions and returning home to take positions in their states' militias. Robert E. Lee's successor as Commander of the Department of the Army in Texas was General David Twiggs. A Georgian, Twiggs began to immediately transfer all facilities and property of the United States army in Texas to state and local authorities. He made the transfers without the authorization of the United State's government or of Governor Houston, who was refusing to call a convention to consider the succession of Texas from the Union.

We were uncertain as to what these events meant to our efforts to help fugitive slaves. We heard reports from throughout Texas of lynching of slaves suspected of planning insurrection. Though the slave owners had always tried to pretend the slaves were content with their lot, they lived in fear that a slave revolt could sweep across the south. They were afraid that Abraham Lincoln's presidency might be interpreted by the slaves as a signal for a general uprising against the people that had kept them in bondage. Consequently, the slave owners were determined to block any insurrection by killing anyone, white or negro, who might lead such a revolt. The result was an increased number of slaves willing to risk the uncertainties of escape to Mexico.

In our settlements in Mexico, there was discussion of the wisdom of conducting raids on military supply depots before General Twiggs could turn them over to the Texas authorities. If a civil war between the northern states and the southern states was inevitable, it might be advisable to seize as many armaments and as much gunpowder as possible before hostilities commenced. What to do with such materials could be decided later, but for the time being they would not be in the hands of those who were determined to take Texas out of the Union and maintain slavery.

Colonel Lee was correct in his assertion that much depended on Governor Houston. Could he keep Texas in the Union? If Texas left the Union, could he keep the state from joining the newly formed Confederate

States of America, which had named Jefferson Davis to be its president even before Lincoln was sworn into office in Washington? My grandmother and I decided that the time for our visit to our old friend was overdue. We would go to Austin and seek his assessment of the situation. What he had to say would help us decide what course of action we would take and what role our people in the settlements might play in the coming conflict.

On the morning we had planned to leave for Austin, Carmen and I were in the house when we heard the sound of riders approaching. We went outside, thinking that it might be Texas Rangers looking for Juan Cortinas. The riders were not Rangers. In a double-column formation led by a man on a beautiful Spanish *destruir*, some fifty men reined their horses to a halt just short of our front yard. They wore brown dusters that matched in color their narrow-brimmed, low-crown hats. Though there was a distinct military quality to their apparel, it was unlike any uniform I had ever seen. At first I thought they might be from the other side of the border. These men, however, were conversing not in Spanish, but in French.

The man on the *destruir* bounded off the big horse. He was a tall, strapping fellow and very obviously in charge. Speaking French, he issued orders to the men to dismount and then turned to face us while the men began to loosen the cinches on their saddles. There was a broad smile on his handsome face. He withdrew a rifle from his saddle-holster and gripped it in his leather-gloved hand. His hair and thick beard were a rich golden-red hue like the color of the morning sun.

"Oh," Carmen said softly and drew her right hand to her mouth.

"Abuela? What's wrong?"

She whispered, "He looks just like my father."

Following her gaze to the man whose smile had broadened into a grin, I asked, "Who, Abuela? This young man? He looks similar to your father?"

"Not similar, Teresa. He looks exactly like my father when he was a young man. Exactly."

I wondered if the heat was affecting my grandmother's head. I had never seen her quite so taken aback. Normally, she was quite the stoic, ever in control of her emotions. Now her hands were trembling. Surely, I thought, she was not intimidated by this man's rifle. He was not holding it in a threatening way. There was a bit of a swagger in this broad-shoul-dered giant, but he looked friendly.

"Don't you recognize him, Teresa?"

"Recognize him, Abuela? I don't—"

My grandmother laughed and so did the man. He had a deep-chested laugh.

Suddenly, I saw it. There was something about the tilt of his head and the cadence of his laughter.

"Esteban?" I whispered. "Esteban!"

XI

My brother hugged me and then lifted me into the air. He did the same with Carmen. She landed with a bounce and sprang forward to embrace her grandson again and again.

"Estebanito!" I cried. "What happened? Did you forget to stop growing, little brother? You're so tall!"

"You're not exactly Teresita anymore."

"Abuela says you look like her father."

"Oh?"

"Yes, Esteban. You look like my father when he was a young man. Even the beard. It's cut precisely the same."

"I see," he said, touching his long fingers to the thick beard. "Now I know why Mother insisted I have it cut this way. I was going to style it like Maxl's, but Mother directed the barbers to cut it this way. She was remembering her grandfather. I did not know."

Carmen asked, "How is Cata Valeria?"

"Very well, Abuela. She sends her love."

"Really?" I asked. "Is that what she said, Esteban?"

He shrugged. "Well, Teresa. Not in so many words."

"But she is well," Carmen insisted. "That's good."

"Yes, Abuela. Mother is quite well. She spends most of her time in Paris with the Empress Eugenie. They spend much time together and with Charlotte. Mother and the Empress call her Carlotta. The three of them are great friends."

"And your wife and your son?" Carmen inquired.

"Both are fine, Abuela."

"Your son," she asked, "he must be what? Four years old?"

"Five, Abuela. Little Max is five years old."

Reminded of his wife and son, I looked about. Escorted by more armed riders, a train of several dozen ox-drawn wagons was now arriving. I thought Esteban's family might be with them. The cargoes of the wagons were concealed with canvas wraps.

"Where is your wife and son, Esteban?" I asked.

"They are in Vienna."

"Why did they not come with you?"

"They will come later."

We both asked Esteban many questions about his family and about Jacob who, sadly, was now unable to walk. Even as he responded to our queries, Esteban's focus seemed not entirely on what we were saying. His eyes were exploring the house, the barns, the stables, the corral, and the fields beyond. Several times, he turned to look toward the riverbank and the city of Matamoros. He looked up the road toward Brownsville.

Finally, I asked, "Esteban, who are these men?" Even more wagons, larger ones, some drawn by teams of as many as six yoke of oxen, were arriving. "Why are they here?"

My brother had not lost his ability to charm with a boyishly innocent smile. "They are friends of mine, Teresa. Who do you think they are?"

"These are all your friends?" I asked, looking out over the crowd of men, some of whom had removed from saddle-holsters rifles exactly like the one Esteban continued to grip in his right hand. "Are they hunters?"

"Yes, Teresita," he said and laughed. "They are hunters. You guessed it! We have come to the great frontier to hunt the buffalo and the antelope."

I could see by Carmen's expression she was also troubled by this large assemblage of men who in no way, other than their weapons, appeared to be hunters. Despite the fact that these men did not wear uniforms, they reminded me very much of professional soldiers. There was a high order of discipline in even the manner in which they walked their winded horses.

"Abuela?" Esteban said and pointed toward the area beyond the garden. "Who owns that land?"

Turning to look, Carmen replied, "Santiago Montemayor."

"Señor Montemayor? Ah, wonderful! Where is he? Is he inside?"

"No. He and Pilar are in Laredo."

"Do you think he would mind if we set up a camp on his land? We will stay clear of the garden and the plowed fields. We will use only that pasture beyond the garden."

Carmen assured him the Montemayors would not mind. The land, in fact, belonged to us all, though it had to be registered in Santiago's name.

Excusing himself, Esteban walked to a group of men who seemed to have been awaiting his orders. He spoke to them in French, after which they returned to the main body of men with the horses, oxen, and wagons. The entire group of men moved the animals and vehicles to the field and quickly began to unload equipment and set up rows of tents.

Returning to the front yard, Esteban said, "It will be only until I have had the opportunity to purchase some land up river from here."

"You're going to buy land on the Rio Grande?" I asked.

"Yes. We're going to be neighbors! How does that strike you, my sister?"

"Wonderful!" I shouted. "It's wonderful, Esteban! But why? Are you going to farm? I do not understand. Surely you do not need so many people to farm."

"No," he said and put his arm around me. "I am not going to farm, Teresa. We are going to build warehouses here and in Laredo. You see, I intend to go into the business of exporting cotton. We'll move it down the river and then to that little Mexican village below Matamoros on the Gulf. Bagdad?"

I nodded.

He laughed. "What a strange name for a Mexican town. In any case, it has a deep natural harbor. We are going to build wharfs and docks and use it for our exports. That's what these men are about. They are going to build warehouses here and develop the harbor at Bagdad in order that I can go into the business of exporting cotton to France."

I watched the men who were methodically setting up the camp. They kept their rifles near them, regardless of what they were doing. Esteban, too, had never stopped holding his rifle.

"Esteban," Carmen said. "There is very little cotton grown in the Rio Grande Valley. There is some, but hardly enough to require warehouses. And I know of no cotton grown near Laredo. How many warehouses are you going to build?"

"Many, Abuelita!" he said in a tone almost as if our grandmother were a child. "A hundred to begin with. And then we will add more. We may build a great many more!"

Carmen was perplexed. She turned to me to help her find what she wanted to say.

"Esteban," I asked, "why did you not write to us for the past two years? We were worried. We did not know if you were sick. Why did you not answer our letters?"

"I received none of your letters. I have been traveling. I always intended to write, but I was moving from place to place. I did not mean for you to worry." He smiled. "Most of the time, I was not that far from you. I should have written. It is just that I have been so busy."

"You were not far from us? You have not been in Europe?"

"Not for almost three years."

"Where have you been?"

"Oh," he said, looking toward where the camp was rapidly taking shape, "most of the time I have been in the United States."

"The United States?" I glanced at Carmen. "Where, Esteban? Where in the United States have you been?"

"Oh, for a while I was in Virginia. Then I went to Charleston. And then to Atlanta. A little while in Montgomery. Then on to New Orleans before coming here."

"Why were you in those places?"

For a moment, I thought Esteban was going to shout at the men at the camp. Something they were doing appeared to displease him.

"Teresa," he said, "I will explain everything to you later. I must go and help these fellows over there. When we get things organized and I've had a chance to bathe and freshen up, I'll come back. I see you still have your chickens and goats. And Abuela, you still grow pretty little flowers. I'll come back this evening, and you can tell me all about your animals and your garden."

He kissed us both, rushed to the *destruir*, mounted and spurred the big stallion to a gallop to the camp. After stopping to help a squad of men raise the poles of a large tent, he joined another group of men bent over a table covered with papers. They pointed toward the riverbank, where several of their companions were now stationed with surveyor's instruments and binoculars.

My grandmother and I did not know what to think. On one matter we were in accord; our journey to Austin would have to be deferred to another day.

We returned to the house and began to prepare food. We wanted to make those things, such as okra gumbo and hoecake, that Esteban had loved as a boy. It was still difficult for me to think of my little brother as a man. All during the day, I would go to the door or a window and look across at him as he directed the men in their activities. They were building a tent city, complete with an elaborate field kitchen and a corral for the animals. Though the cargoes in the wagons remained under wraps, I happened to be watching when several men lifted a canvas to expose what appeared to be a cannon tube. Esteban rushed to where they were and quickly had them secure the wrap.

That evening, Lebe Seru returned from the lookout point with word that he had seen no smoke signals during the day. We would be guiding no fugitives across the Rio Grande that night. Lebe Seru was, of course, surprised by the sight of a small army of men camping in the pasture beyond our gardens. When we told him about Esteban, he was elated and started to go to the field to greet him. He stopped when we happened to notice Texas Rangers arriving at the camp. At first we thought they had come to investigate the sudden appearance of an armed force of men on the Rio Grande. We feared there could be trouble. But the way in which the Rangers greeted Esteban seemed to indicate they were not unfamiliar with him. It was as though they were paying a courtesy call.

Not long after the Rangers had departed, Esteban came to the house and warmly embraced Lebe Seru, who could not believe my brother had grown into such a big man.

"What kind of a rifle is this, Esteban?" he asked.

My brother handed the rifle to Lebe Seru. "A Winchester Repeating Rifle. The bullets are stored in the rifle. You simply pull down the lever to bring a bullet to the breech and close it when you wish to fire. You can fire as quickly as you are able to operate the lever and squeeze the trigger A man would be able to fire five bullets in the time it would take another man to hand load one bullet in a breech-loading rifle. He could fire twenty bullets in the time required to pack a charge in a muzzle loader."

"I've never seen such a rifle."

"It has just been developed," Esteban said. "Ten men with Winchester Repeating Rifles will equal a hundred men with breech loaders! Is it not amazing, Lebe Seru?"

"Yes," Lebe Seru said and glanced at Carmen. "Soldiers will now be able to kill more of each other faster than ever before. It is truly amazing."

"Where is Alma?" Esteban inquired.

"You do not know?" I asked.

"No."

I explained to Esteban about Alma and Ralph and the settlements across the river, even though I thought I had written to him about every-thing we were doing. Either he did not get my letters, or he had not read them carefully.

"And Jorge?" he asked. "You wrote me something about the two of you getting married. Where is that Gallito Rojo who used to pin my shoulders in our wrestling matches?"

I related what I thought I had written in many letters. I told him of the death of Jorge's father and that he and his aunt and uncle were with Benito Juarez.

For the first time since he arrived, Esteban's happy smile vanished entirely. "That is not good, Teresa."

I looked at my grandmother's puzzled expression. "What do you mean, Esteban? What is not good?"

"They should not be in Mexico with Benito Juarez. It is very dangerous. Juarez is going to be defeated. His armies will be destroyed. Jorge and Miguel and Josefa should come back to Texas at once. They must leave Mexico immediately."

None of us knew what to say. Finally, Lebe Seru said, "I do not think Benito Juarez is going to be defeated, Esteban. The armies of Benito Juarez have been victorious. President Juarez is in the capital. There are pockets of resistance here and there in the mountains, but they are contained and will soon surrender. General Mejia is in hiding, and General Miramon has fled the country. He is—"

"General Miramon," Esteban interrupted, "is in France."

"I do not know where he is," Lebe Seru said. "But the civil war is almost over. Many of our people in the settlements fought with the armies of Benito Juarez. They are returning home. They are no longer needed."

Everything Lebe Seru said was true. We had finally received a message from Jorge. He was in Mexico City with President Juarez, helping to reestablish the government and prepare for new elections.

"Jorge wrote to me, Esteban," I said. "He will be returning home very soon. The civil war is almost over. He said we can begin to plan our marriage."

My brother's smile returned. "That is good news." Relaxing, he got up from his chair and put his arm around our grandmother. "We will give Teresa the grandest wedding in the history of Texas. Yes, Abuelita? I will write to Jeanne immediately. She will send us the most beautiful gown in all of Paris! We will spare no expense."

Over the next several days, we saw little of Esteban as he traveled to the Mexican village of Bagdad to put his engineers to work on enlarging the harbor. After buying several hundred acres of land on both sides of the Rio Grande, he then proceeded to direct the construction of warehouses and wharfs. Barges, laden with lumber taken from ships anchored offshore, were towed by steamers up the river and unloaded at the construction sites. Hundreds of laborers were employed to do the manual labor while Esteban's men stood guard over the wagons whose contents remained under wraps. As soon as the first buildings were completed, the cargoes in the wagons were transferred to them. During the transfer, I saw more cannon tubes and kegs of gunpowder.

At first I was reluctant to approach my brother about what I had seen since he had not volunteered to explain. My curiosity, however, finally got the best of me and I asked, "Esteban, why do you have need of artillery and so much gunpowder?"

As usual, he tried to charm me. "Why do you think we need artillery and gunpowder, Teresa?"

"I do not know. That is why I am asking."

"It is simple, my sister. We shall be transporting cotton up and down the river. We will be an inviting target for bandits and Comanches. We shall need to defend ourselves. We will protect our property. For that, we need weapons. Do you not agree?"

There was a measure of logic in what he said, although I was not at all sure I understood why so many men and weapons were necessary to defend against bandits and Comanches.

It was difficult to obtain a straight answer from Esteban. Each time Carmen or I would raise a question, he was evasive and quick to turn us to some other topic. Usually, he would begin talking about something he had done or seen in Europe with his friend, the Archduke. Esteban never tired of talking about Maximilian von Hapsburg.

One morning, Esteban insisted that I take a ride with him. He had one of his men saddle for me a beautiful, flaxen-maned palomino from their corral. We raced for several miles before he signaled for us to rein our mounts to a stop. I had forgotten how Esteban loved to ride horses and complimented him on his skill. But I was still his older sister, and I warned him about riding his horse so fast.

Stroking the *destruir's* black mane, Esteban said, "Maxl says to walk one's horse is death. To trot is life. To gallop is bliss! It is not given to me to ride slowly."

Two weeks after his arrival, Esteban announced that he was going to Laredo to buy land and start the construction of warehouses and wharfs near that city. Again, Carmen and I questioned the wisdom of such an endeavor since his facilities were likely to sit unused. I had begun to suspect that my brother's seemingly limitless abundance of resources were not matched by common sense, a hazard not uncommon among wealthy young men. When I tried to find a tactful way to suggest this suspicion, he put his arm around me and said I was probably correct but that I should indulge him.

With Esteban away in Laredo, a trip he did not invite us to share, there was no longer a reason to postpone our journey to Austin. Accompanied by Tom Blue, my grandmother and I struck out on what proved to be a long and arduous trek across the arid south Texas chaparral. It was not until we came to the Nueces River that we found the terrain to be less hostile to travelers. Further on, the Colorado River valley was lush with streams and islands of great oaks standing above tall prairie grass that billowed in the wind. Tom Blue guided us along back trails to reduce the possibility of encountering bounty hunters.

The city of Austin was enchantingly beautiful. I could not understand why Kalanu had said it was the most miserable place on the face of the earth, unless it was because Mirabeau Lamar had chosen the site for the capital of Texas. On the north bank of the Colorado, the city was surrounded by wooded hills from which flowed clear-water creeks. Most of the houses were simple wood-plank cabins, and there were brick buildings housing commercial establishments. The main street was a wide boulevard called Congress Avenue, which led to the three-story Capitol building made from an attractive soft cream limestone. Just southwest of the Capitol was the two-story Executive Mansion.

We waited until dark to approach the Mansion. This was, after all, the city that a few years earlier had prohibited Tejanos from residing within its precincts and regularly hosted the lynching of abolitionists and suspected slave insurrectionists. Two Tejano women and a negro man would be viewed with suspicion.

Our entrance onto the Mansion grounds was unnoticed not so much because of the hour, but because it appeared that virtually the entire population of the city was gathered outside the Capitol, from whose windows glowed bright lights. A meeting was occurring in the building, and the people outside were making their presence known by much shouting and yelling.

At the door of the mansion we were met by Joshua, who embraced my grandmother and me. No longer the awkward young man that had accompanied Margaret Houston and her other slaves from Alabama to the Republic of Texas, Joshua was a distinguished-looking gentleman with greying hair and a mustache.

"I am so happy to see you!" he said. "It has been such a long time. Please, come inside!"

The mansion was an elegant house with a winding staircase and high-ceiling rooms. Soft candlelight illumined lovely blue-velvet drapes and mahogany-wood furniture. Mrs. Houston rushed into the room and threw her arms around us. She hugged first my grandmother and then me. She hugged Tom Blue. Tears ran down her face. Sobbing, she was unable to talk. Behind her with a glass of water and a fan was Eliza.

Finally, Mrs. Houston cried, "They want to kill Mr. Houston! They are going to kill Mr. Houston!"

We looked at Joshua. "The Governor is at the Capitol," he said. "The succession ordinance has been approved by the legislature. Texas is no longer a part of the United States. They have also approved Texas' being a state in the Confederacy. Governor Houston has agreed to succession, but he wants Texas to be an independent republic. He refuses to sign the legislation making Texas a part of the Confederacy."

"They're going to kill Mr. Houston!" Mrs. Houston repeated. "They are. They said they are!"

Joshua explained, "There have been threats against the Governor's life."

"Tell them about that horrible man in Georgia!" Mrs. Houston gasped as Eliza dabbed her face with a damp cloth. "Tell them about that man, Joshua!"

Joshua said, "Governor Iverson of Georgia has called for the assassination of Governor Houston."

Mrs. Houston began to scream, and it required all of Eliza's efforts to calm her. Several of the Houston's eight children peeked from behind doorways. Finally, Eliza said she should take Mrs. Houston to her bedroom to rest.

When they had left, Carmen asked, "Houston is at the Capitol building?"

"Yes," Joshua answered. "The legislature is in special session. They are requiring all state officials take an oath of loyalty to the Confederacy. Those who do not will be removed from office. Governor Houston is preparing to give them his answer."

"Is he alone?" I asked. "That mob outside the Capitol is very angry. His life could be in danger, Joshua."

"It could indeed, Teresa. I was preparing to go over there when you arrived."

"We'll go with you," Carmen said.

Joshua took us around a back pathway to the Capitol where he ushered us into the building through a small side door which he used a key to open. He lit a candle and led us down a narrow passage to a long stairway to the basement. We advanced to a closed door. A small man answered Joshua's knock and gestured for us to come in quickly. Inside the room, dimly lit by the light of a single lantern, were about a dozen men who relaxed when they saw Joshua.

And then I saw Kalanu. He was sitting at a table with his back to us, whittling on a stick.

"That you, Josh?" he said without looking up.

"Yes, Governor."

"Be careful, Houston," Carmen said. "Don't cut yourself."

Sam Houston's eyes widened when he focused on my grandmother. Turning quickly, he jumped to his feet and rushed to embrace her.

I was amazed at how little he had changed. He was, of course, older. His hair was grey, and he was heavier; but his rugged face still had the look of a sly and mischievous little boy mulling his next prank. Over my grandmother's shoulder, he stared at me.

And then, releasing Carmen from his bearhug, he whispered, "It can't be. Teresita? Is that you, Teresita?"

"Hello, Kalanu."

He grabbed me and effortlessly lifted me into the air. He could no longer set me on his shoulder; but for a moment, I thought he might try, as he performed a war dance around the room while holding me above him. Finally, he let me down and embraced me for a long time.

"Teresa," he said. "Oh, Teresa! You've grown into a beautiful woman. I knew you would, but I did not know how lovely you would be. How wonderful to see you!"

"Houston," Carmen said. "Are you safe? That is a very angry mob out-side."

From what I could see, none of the men in the room were armed, and the Governor was not wearing his pistols.

"That crowd," Kalanu said and waved his hand as if swatting away flies. "I'm not afraid of them. Bunch of dimwits, that's what they are. Dimwits!"

Joshua said, "Perhaps we should leave the Capitol building, Governor. It might be the best thing to do at this point."

"Dimwits!" Kalanu repeated, ignoring Joshua. "Everyone's gone mad, Carmen! Mad!"

"I gather you do not intend to take the oath of allegiance to the Confederacy."

"I'm not going to have anything to do with that illegality led by Jeffy Davis!" He spoke the name "Jeffy" as if it were something dirty. "That piece of dogskin is going to get a lot of my boys killed. I hate that man! He's a cold man. He's so cold he would freeze a lizard's blood!"

There was a knock at the door, which Joshua answered. When he returned, he said, "They're ready for you upstairs, Governor Houston."

"Well, let's go! Carmen, you and Teresa come with me. It isn't often you get to see such a passel of dimwits all herded up in the same place."

Along with his small cadre of loyal supporters, we followed Kalanu up to the Hall of Representatives, where the state legislature was waiting to learn if the Governor was going to take the oath to the Confederacy. We found a place to stand at the edge of the platform, on which was the podi-um of the Speaker of the House.

After climbing the platform and gripping the podium with both hands, Kalanu stared down at the hundreds of angry people packed into the room. People outside were shoving each other to get a place at the win-dows that would enable them to see what was about to transpire. Men shouted insults at the Governor, and there was much booing and jeering.

"I am here tonight," Governor Houston said in a loud voice, "to deliv-er my answer to your demand that I swear an oath of loyalty to the Confederate States of America. Well, my answer is no! I will never do it!"

There was a thunderous outburst of angry shouts and jeers.

One man in the front demanded, "Hang him! Hang the miserable trai-tor!"

Under our serapes, my grandmother and I both had pistols. I knew we would stand no chance of protecting the Governor against such a large crowd, many of whom seemed more than prepared to carry out the man's demand on the spot.

"You want to hang Sam Houston, mister?" Kalanu said. "Then you come up here and get him! He's waiting for you!"

The man in the front row melted back into the crowd.

"Any of you!" the Governor shouted. "Any of you who think you can hang Sam Houston, come on up here! One at a time. Two at a time. I don't care. Come on up here and try to hang Sam Houston. He's standing right up front. Right up front! The same as he was at Horseshoe Bend and at San Jacinto. Right up front! Come on up and hang Sam Houston. Just try it!"

It was not long before all the noise and jeers died away. The room fell silent.

"What is the matter with you people? Whenever you listen to me and follow my advice, you prosper and do well. But whenever you turn your backs on me and ignore what I tell you to do, you lose everything."

Many of the men began to shuffle about nervously and stare at the floor.

"Well, I'm telling you now; don't go and do this stupid and illegal thing. Don't join up Texas to the Confederacy. If you must leave the Union, then do it. I am opposed to it. You know I'm opposed to it. But you voted on it, and you left the Union. There is a legal basis for doing that. But stay independent! We've been independent before. Let's go back to being the Republic of Texas!

"But if you enter this Confederacy, you will take Texas down with it. And it will go down. It will be a disaster!" He paused to allow time for his words to be absorbed. "There's gonna be a war, Texans. And I am here to tell you, the Confederacy will lose that war."

"We'll win it!" a man in back yelled.

"No you won't!" Kalanu shouted before the cheers had a chance to build. "The states in the north will be able to field an army of two million men."

"Hell," another man shouted. "One Texan can whup ten Yankees!"

"No we can't," Kalanu again said over the yells of approval. "We can't do it. And do you know why? We don't have any factories. We can't make guns or repair the ones we have. We can't make gunpowder. We can't make railroad engines to haul supplies to our men on the battlefield. All we've got is cotton."

A man at the window yelled, "We'll sell our cotton and buy all them things, General!"

"Can't you people think? The Confederacy doesn't have a navy, and it has no shipyards to build one. The United States Navy will blockade all our ports. We won't be able to sell one bale of cotton. We'll go broke in a year's time. Flat broke! Our money will be worthless. Even if we find someone stupid enough to sell to us on credit, we can't get anything because the United States Navy is not going to allow ships from England or France or from anywhere to come into our ports. Think about it, Texans! Don't let Jeffy Davis and his crowd ruin you."

No one other than the Governor was doing much thinking that night. When Kalanu had hugged me in the basement, I had been surprised that I could not detect the aroma of spirits on his breath. But I could smell it in this hall. Men were passing bottles and jugs one to another.

"This war that's coming," the Governor continued, "is going to be a horrible thing. With all these new guns that you fire as fast as you pull the trigger, there is going to be a river of blood flowing in our land. And for what? Slavery? Slavery is over, Texans!"

There was a cascade of jeers and curses.

"Listen to me, Texans!" Sam Houston commanded, and there was silence. "Slavery is over. It was never a good thing. Never! Millions of people suffered because of it. And now the time for its end has come. Are you going to send your boys out to die just so you can try to hold on to something that should have ended a long time ago, something that should never have started?

"You want to be able to own other people? Is that more important to you than your boys' lives? Because that's what's going to happen. Boys that are alive today and ready to start their lives are going to be in the cold earth a few months from now if you do this thing. Think about this now. Once your boys are gone, they're not coming back. You better think long and hard about this. What's more important to you?"

What was more important became evident very quickly. As soon as the Governor stepped back from the podium, the Speaker of the House called for a vote on whether to declare the office of governor in the state of Texas vacant. The vote was unanimous. Sam Houston was no longer the governor of Texas.

We gathered around Kalanu to escort him back to the Mansion, where Mrs. Houston threw her arms around him and would not let go until he gently pulled free and asked Eliza to take her upstairs to her bedroom. In the drawing room, he sat down, took out his knife and began to whittle.

Sitting on the floor at his side, I asked, "Kalanu, what will you do now?"

He smiled and stroked my hair. "I reckon I'll move Mrs. Houston and the chil'run back to Huntsville." He made a silly face. "Can't stand to live in the toadfrog's town. It's an unhealthy place. There's no pine trees here to clean the air."

My grandmother sat down in the chair across from him. "How long do you think this war that's coming will last, Houston?"

He put down his knife. "It can't last long, Carmen. Believe it or not, I was telling those people the truth. The south will be blockaded and won't be able to sell its cotton or buy guns and gunpowder from Europe. Oh, the Confederacy will win a few battles in the beginning because all the good generals went over to their side. Robert E. Lee joined them, you know."

I was surprised to learn this. I knew Robert E. Lee did not want to fight against the nation he had sworn to defend.

Kalanu continued, "As far as I know, the north doesn't have any good generals. That'll be a big problem for Mr. Lincoln." He looked at me. "Did I tell you Mr. Lincoln sent me a letter?"

"What did he say, Kalanu?"

"He offered to supply me with troops if I would keep Texas in the Union." He sighed. "If I was ten years younger, I would have took Mr. Lincoln up on that offer. I like that man. He might just make a pretty fair President; leastways, 'til folks come to their senses and send me up there to straighten things out."

Carmen, Tom Blue and I helped the Houstons pack their belongings and joined their friends who provided an escort to Huntsville. When we were satisfied they were safe in what Mrs. Houston insisted would be their place of retirement, we traveled to the coast where we returned home by way of the Laguna Madre. Upon our arrival at the farm, Lebe Seru told us that we had just missed Esteban. He was now on his way to Virginia.

"Virginia?" my grandmother asked. "Did he say why he was going to Virginia?"

"No, he did not say. And there's more. Two weeks ago, Esteban was spotted in Monterrey by some of our people. They did not know who he was, but they described him. There could be no mistake. It was Esteban."

"What was Esteban doing in Monterrey."

"He was meeting with Governor Vidaurri."

"Vidaurri?"

"Yes. And Vidaurri has been seen at Bagdad. He was there to inspect the harbor. Esteban's men are building wharfs and docks big enough to accommodate ocean-going vessels. They are building hundreds of warehouses there."

We were all troubled by these reports, but I did not want to assume that something bad was happening.

"It is understandable," I said, "that Esteban would meet with Governor Vidaurri. After all, what he is doing could be good for the economy of northern Mexico. What governor would not want a new harbor in his state?"

Lebe Seru said, "I do not trust Vidaurri, Teresa. He claims to be a supporter of Benito Juarez, but I think he is the kind of man who will support whoever will make him a wealthy man."

Shortly after our return from Austin, I received a letter from Jorge. With the cessation of hostilities, we would be able to hear from Jorge on a regular basis; and I hoped we would soon be reunited. Once again, however, my hopes were in vain.

"Dear Teresa," he wrote:

> The elections were held, and Don Benito has been elected for a full term as President of the Republic. The army had been reduced in numbers. Our very limited resources must be applied to building schools and roads and other facilities that will cause the economy to prosper. The generals President Juarez has retained are defenders of the constitution. One of our ablest is General Ignacio Zaragoza. He was born in Goliad, not far from my place of birth. We have become good friends.
>
> The treasury is empty. President Juarez has been forced to postpone all payment of foreign debts for two years. By that time, we should begin to receive new revenues. Some of the debts that were incurred by Miramon are staggering. In his short tenure as President, he issued revenue bonds to French investors that will be impossible to repay.

Because of the need to restore stability to the national treasury, Don Benito has asked me to stay a little while longer in the capital. He apologizes to you and begs your forgiveness for keeping us apart.

Once again, Benito Juarez was the reason Jorge and I would have to defer our plans. However, I was almost thankful Jorge would not be returning to Texas, at least not immediately. There was too much uncertainty as to what was going to happen in the United States, and the threat of violence was in the air like the stillness before a storm. For a change, peace seemed to have come to Mexico. Jorge was safe, and for that I was very grateful.

One day, without fanfare, soldiers in the United States Army marched out of Fort Brown, boarded their ships and sailed for home. A few days later, soldiers of the army of the Confederate States of American, dressed in their brand-new grey uniforms, took possession of the fort and began regular patrols of the border. They established a military guard at critical places such as government buildings and the harbor facilities near the mouth of the Rio Grande. Confederate soldiers were also posted as guards at all roads leading to Esteban's warehouses.

Three weeks after the Confederate soldiers took control of Fort Brown, we read the newspaper accounts of the bombardment of Fort Sumter by the Confederate Army at Charleston, South Carolina. The commander of the Confederate force that received the surrender of the Union fort was General Pierre Beauregard, who had been one of Zachary Taylor's Topogs on the Rio Grande fifteen years before. Many of the young lieutenants and captains of that war were to be the generals of the war that had now begun with the lowering of the United States flag at a small fort on an island in Charleston harbor on that April day of 1861.

In was not until several months after the fall of Ft. Sumter that the United States began to advance an army south with the intent of capturing Richmond, the capital of the Confederacy. The first reports indicated the Union army was successful in early skirmishes and speculation began to build that the war would quickly be over. However, the Union army was met at a place called Bull Run by a southern force under the command of General Thomas Jackson, another veteran of the Mexican-American War. The newspapers reported that General Jackson held the Union army like a stone wall. The Union army panicked and fled the battlefield. It was evident that the war would not soon be over.

After Bull Run, the command of the principal Union army, the Army of the Potomac, was given to General George B. McClellan, still another of Zachary Taylor's Topogs. McClellan proved to be a little like his old enemy, Santa Anna; he was good at preparing for war, but he did not like to fight. Month after month, the newspapers reported on McClellan's preparations, but the General made no move toward the south even when Abraham Lincoln accused him of having "the slows" and asked if he could "borrow" the army. Finally, McClellan led an army of 100,000 men to the south, but was met and forced to retreat by the Army of Virginia under the command of General Robert E. Lee.

Sam Houston's prediction had proven correct. The Confederacy was winning the opening battles of the war. Southern generals were able to repel Union armies, regardless of their superior equipment and numbers. However, by the end of the year, another of Sam Houston's forecasts was coming true. The United States Navy had imposed a blockade of the southern ports. Unable to export their cotton or import war materials, the Confederacy was in a stranglehold and, without a navy, was unable to do anything about it. Even the Texas newspapers, which had trumpeted the Confederate victories on the battlefield, began to express the fear that economic ruin could accomplish what Union armies had thus far been unable to achieve.

Early one morning before dawn, I was startled awake by what I thought was thunder. It was not an unwelcome sound, because I had just returned from delivering more books and supplies to our teachers in the settlements and knew the people in northern Mexico were greatly in need of rain to break a long drought. Alma and Ralph and their neighbors were having to spend much of their time hauling water to sustain even a small portion of their garden, and many of their animals were dying. It was with relief that I rolled back over in my bed and looked forward to waking up to the welcome sound of falling rain.

Moments later, I jumped out of bed when I realized the noise I was hearing was not thunder. It was the rumble of wagons, many wagons, being pulled by oxen, a sound I had heard many times as a child. Dressing quickly, I rushed outside, where I found Carmen and Lebe Seru looking toward the north sky. The horizon was glowing with a steady brightness as if the sun were about to rise in the north. I went to my grandmother, and she put her arm around my shoulder.

"It must be an army," Lebe Seru said. "It sounds like caissons, hundreds of them."

"Perhaps it is the American army," I suggested. "They are coming to retake Fort Brown."

"Yes," Lebe Seru agreed. "It must be. What else could it be?"

There was much activity in the area around Esteban's warehouses. Men were rushing about with lanterns. Their movement, however, was not that of soldiers preparing for battle. They were building bonfires to light the way to the wharfs on the river. As the fires began to illuminate the entire area, we could see more soldiers arriving from the direction of Fort Brown, and there were barges being towed up the Rio Grande. We saw men on the other side of the river. They signaled the men on this side with lanterns and also began to build bonfires.

"Vidaurri's men," Lebe Seru said.

"Are you sure?" Carmen asked.

"Yes. They are wearing the uniforms of his state militia."

Lebe Seru and I had been incorrect in our guess as to what was approaching. An army was coming, but it was not the American army. As we watched, a company of Confederate cavalry rode slowly into range of the bonfires. They were escorting not caissons, but wagons, hundreds of wagons, loaded with bales of cotton.

Neither my grandmother, Lebe Seru nor I had ever seen so many wagons; and they were large wagons, many pulled by as many as twelve yoke of oxen. Each wagon was filled with fifty or sixty bales of cotton. The teamsters led the animals to the wharfs where laborers, who had been walking on either side of the wagons, began to unload the cargoes onto the waiting barges. In the light of the fires, we could see that the teamsters and laborers were negroes.

"Slaves," Lebe Seru said. "And from the looks of them, they have come a very long way."

Standing in the yard, we watched as wagon after wagon after wagon arrived to await its turn to be unloaded.

At daybreak the process continued. We climbed to the top of a nearby hill and the line of wagons stretched as far north as we could see. I had never seen so many wagons and men, not even at Houston Town when the cotton was brought to be loaded on steamers for Galveston. There had not been this many wagons and men when General Taylor's army came to the Rio Grande. After a while, we stopped counting.

As we were returning to the house, an elegant barouche, pulled by four silver-maned horses raced up the road to our yard. The driver cracked a whip to make the high-stepping jobbers go even faster.

"Abuela," I said, "it's Esteban."

Running ahead, I reached the house just as my brother set the brake and leaped from the driver's deck. Six wagons were coming up the road behind him, none of which were loaded with cotton but appeared to carry lumber and other items.

"Teresa!" Esteban yelled. He grabbed me and swung me around in a circle. He let me down when our grandmother and Lebe Seru caught up with me.

"Esteban," Carmen said. "What is this?"

Gesturing to the beautiful coach and team, Esteban said, "This, Abuela? This is yours. How do you like it?"

"It very fine, Esteban, but—"

"Teresa," he said, "did you know that Abuela used to drive a team like this when she was a girl? Mother told me. She said her grandfather used to tell her about how his daughter loved to drive his team of Parisian Barouche horses. Well, Abuela, you now have your own team of Barouche horses!"

"They are very nice, Esteban," Carmen said. "But I did not mean the horses. Why are all these wagonloads of cotton being brought here?"

The wagons that had followed behind Esteban were now halted in the yard. Stepping to where they were, Esteban said, "Start unloading, men. Put the lumber over here. Take the things in those two wagons to the house. And be very, very careful!"

"Esteban," I asked, "what is this?"

"This, my sister," he said, "is your wedding present! I'm going to build you a new house. A very big new house! It will be big enough for you and Jorge and many, many children. And there will be plenty of room for Abuela." He pointed toward the bundles the men were starting to take into the house. "And this is new furniture and drapes and china. And in one of those packages is the finest, most beautiful wedding gown in the world, a gift to you from my wife, Jeanne. It is the most—"

"Esteban!" Carmen said abruptly. "Answer me! Why is this cotton being brought to the Rio Grande?"

"It is not being brought to the Rio Grande, Abuela. It is going to our harbor at Bagdad." He shook his head in amazement at the sight of all the activity at the river wharfs. "We have over a thousand wagons arriving just this morning. And an equal number should be arriving in Laredo within a few days."

Lebe Seru asked, "Is this cotton from Texas, Esteban?"

"Most of it is. But some is from Arkansas and Louisiana. Next month, we should start to see cotton from Mississippi and Alabama. And then there should be some coming from Georgia, the Carolinas and Virginia."

Carmen was very agitated. "There is a blockade, Esteban. Have you not heard of the blockade?"

"Yes, Abuela. I have heard of the blockade."

"The United States is not allowing southern cotton to be shipped to Europe."

"That is not exactly accurate, Abuelita. The United States is not allowing southern cotton to be shipped from ports in the Confederate States."

"Esteban," I said. "The United States Navy will stop any ships that have southern cotton."

"No, Teresa. The United States Navy is blockading southern ports because the United States is at war with the Confederate States. The United States is not at war with Mexico. It would be illegal to blockade Mexican ports. What is more, it would be very dangerous for the United States Navy to try to stop any ships leaving or seeking to enter Mexican ports. Why? Because at this very moment there are twenty French warships off the Gulf coast of Mexico. If the United States Navy attempts to interfere with any French merchant vessel, the entire United States Navy will soon be located at the bottom of the Gulf of Mexico and it will not be in a position to blockade anything."

It had been many years since I had seen our grandmother so distraught. "Esteban," she said, "you don't know what you are doing."

Esteban was either not aware of Carmen's displeasure or he chose to ignore it. "Abuela," he said cheerfully, "let's go for a ride. Show us how you used to drive a team like this when you were a girl in Guanajuato. Here, let me help you to the deck."

Pulling her arm from Esteban's grasp, Carmen shouted, "Get away from me! I don't want your horses or your coach. We don't want anything from you. Take your wagons and all your things and get off our property. You are not welcome here, Esteban!"

Before Esteban could react, Carmen ran to the house and went inside. Lebe Seru followed. Very quickly, the men who had been taking packages and furniture inside came out with those same items.

"Teresa," Esteban said, extending his hands. "What is wrong? I don't understand."

"I think you understand, Esteban," I said, pointing toward the wagons at the wharfs. "Abuela is upset with all this cotton you are bringing to Mexico."

"But I told her I was going to export cotton."

"Esteban, you did not tell us that you were planning to ship southern cotton out of Mexico. You must have been planning this for a long time. You knew what was going to happen. You knew a war between the states was coming."

Smiling, he said, "I am a shrewd businessman, Teresa. I have to know about such things."

"Are you in such need of money, Esteban, to do something like this? You know very well what this means. The Union has blocked the export of cotton from the south. The planters are losing money. Without money they cannot continue the war. With the money they receive for their cotton, they will be able to buy guns and powder. And I suppose you are not only in the business of export. I suspect the ships that come for the cotton at Bagdad will be filled with things that will find their way back to the southern states. Things such as guns and powder? Yes, Esteban? You are an importer as well as an exporter?"

"Yes, Teresa," he said cooly, and his face hardened. "Our ships are at this moment unloading guns and powder."

"Esteban, why? You have great wealth. Jacob's family is wealthy. Your wife's father is wealthy. Why do you need more money?"

"Do you think I am doing this for money?"

"Why else?"

He looked toward the north where the end of the train of wagons was still not in view. "I cannot tell you now, Teresa. Later, I will tell you, and you will understand."

"Esteban, I—"

"Teresa," he interrupted. "Please accept these gifts. I want to build you and Jorge the house. Will the wedding be soon? Jorge has returned?"

"He is still in Mexico City."

"Jorge must return immediately! Write to him!"

"Why must he return?"

He walked toward the coach. "Will you not accept my gifts? Can I not at least leave them here? The wedding gown?"

"It would be best if you take them."

Slowly, he climbed to the deck and took the reins. He motioned for the men to reload the wagons.

"Esteban," I said, "you are my brother. I love you. But what you are doing is wrong. It will cost many lives. It will extend slavery. Please. Stop what you are doing."

His face was sad as he looked down from the deck. "I may not see you for a while, Teresa. I have to go to Vera Cruz. It may be some time before we see each other again. Write to Jorge. Tell him to come home immediately."

Over the next several months, few days passed that more wagon trains did not arrive to unload their cargoes at the wharfs. We saw barges heavily loaded with bales of cotton that had been wagoned to Laredo and were now being towed south to Bagdad. And we saw the steamers headed north with barges laden with weapons, powder and other supplies intended for the Confederate armies. Some were unloaded at the wharfs not far from our house and others went on to Laredo.

Most of the materials unloaded near us were placed on wagons and shipped north, but a large number of big guns and thousands of kegs of powder were stored in the warehouses that remained under heavy guard. These warehouses contained no cotton; they had become a military arsenal, one far larger than what Zachary Taylor or Winfield Scott had assembled on these very banks before their invasions of Mexico.

Esau went to Bagdad to see the harbor. He said thousands of merchant ships were lined up to unload weaponry and powder destined for the Confederate armies and to take on the cotton bound for Europe. Not only were French warships standing guard off the harbor, but British, Austrian and Belgium warships patrolled the coast as a warning to the United States not to interfere with their merchant vessels.

I wrote to Jorge of Esteban's activities, and he wrote back that President Juarez was disturbed by the reports coming from the north. At present the national government simply did not have the resources to police the northern states or dictate policy to the governors. In effect Governor Vidaurri was the law in northern Mexico until the national government could begin to generate revenues. Jorge wrote that England, Spain and France were expressing anger at the president's moratorium on Mexico's payment of its foreign debts. In particular, Napoleon III was demanding the immediate redemption of revenue bonds. Jorge promised he would come home as soon as President Juarez solved the problem of finances.

Unknown to Benito Juarez, the problem of finances was soon to become among the least of his worries. His plans for rebuilding Mexico would have to be postponed. Without any warning, on January 7, 1862, a full division of the Imperial Army of France landed at several locations on the eastern coast of Mexico and seized the port of Vera Cruz. They began immediate preparations for a march on Mexico City.

XII

After the French invasion of Mexico, I wondered how I could have been so blind. Esteban had all but told me it was about to happen. The last time we spoke he must have known warships were at that very moment transporting to Vera Cruz thousands of the Zouaves, who had crushed the Russians in the Crimea at Sevastopol, and thousands more of the mercenaries in the newly created Foreign Legion, which had cruelly broken all resistance to Napoleon III's empire in north Africa. Now I understood why my brother had been so adamant in wanting me to write Jorge and urge him and his aunt and uncle to return to Texas.

If I had listened to Esteban and insisted that Jorge come home, I would not once again be waiting for some word as to whether the man I loved was in danger or, worse, whether he was alive or dead. Each time some new fragment of information on the invasion arrived in Matamoros, Esau would rush to the farm to notify us. The Montemayors had no idea where Josefa and Miguel were, but we had no doubt they would fight the French. Both had dedicated their lives to Benito Juarez's vision of liberty and equality in Mexico, and they would not allow that dream to be shattered at the very moment of its realization.

My impulse was to go to Jorge in Mexico City. I well knew that now, more than ever, he would not leave Benito Juarez. However, I had no intention of trying to make Jorge return with me to Texas. I, too, would stand with Don Benito. Jorge and I would fight together and drive the foreign invader from the soil of Mexico. In those first days of uncertainty after the French had taken Vera Cruz and were advancing inland, I made plans to go to Mexico City.

My plans had to be deferred because Carmen fell ill. Since the day she had told Esteban to leave our house, my grandmother had not been herself. Almost overnight, she seemed to grow old. She ate very little, and her once unlimited energy was no longer apparent. She appeared distracted, and I began to have to repeat myself before she could grasp what I was saying.

One evening, when Carmen did not return from the contact point, Lebe Seru and I went to see what had detained her. We thought she might have gone to be with fugitives who had made the smoke signal. Many of the slaves now fleeing had suffered severe beatings at the hands of own-ers who blamed them for the war, and Carmen always wanted to go with the medicines to escapees as soon as they arrived rather than wait until the cover of darkness.

We found my grandmother on the beach, unconscious, her body cov-ered with insects. After we revived her, she was unable to stand and walk. Lebe Seru gathered her into his arms and carried her back to the house. She would not allow us to send for a physician and said all she needed was a little sleep.

For days, Carmen was unable to walk without help. She fretted at not being able to go to the contact point or accompany us when we escorted fugitives across the border at night. It hurt to see my grandmother in such a helpless condition, and I knew it was painful to Lebe Seru. He was always cheerful in her presence and even made jokes about getting old, but there were times I saw him cry when he thought he was alone.

Eventually, Carmen was able to do some work around the house and in her garden, but I realized I could not leave her alone for any length of time. If I went to Mexico City, I had no idea of when I might return. I knew Lebe Seru and Pilar and Santiago would help my grandmother; they had stayed with her day and night when she was bedridden. But Lebe Seru and the Montemayors were also getting old. Jorge would want me to look after his grandparents; and Alma and Ralph would expect me to take care of Lebe Seru, who was now in his eighties. For the present, all I could do was pray that somehow the French would be persuaded that what they were doing was a mistake and withdraw their soldiers. Only if that hap-pened could Jorge and I be together.

Napoleon III had no intention of withdrawing his invasion force. After securing their hold on Vera Cruz, the Imperial Army advanced toward Mexico City. They were met at Puebla on the fifth day of May, 1862, by a volunteer militia led by General Ignacio Zaragoza. Incredibly, General Zaragoza's citizen army held the French force and made them retreat to Vera Cruz. It was a wonderful victory; and we hoped that Bonaparte's generals would send word to their Emperor that the people of Mexico could not be conquered, not even by the most powerful army in the world.

Unfortunately, Napoleon sent more thousands of battle-hardened vet-erans and placed the entire invasion force under the command of Marshal

Achille Bazaine, France's most able general and a man known for his strategy of killing civilians who gave support to his enemy's soldiers. Entire villages in Algeria had been wiped off the face of the earth by Bazaine's Legionnaires. Bazaine was the kind of man who relished combat. Entering the army as a private, he had risen to his country's highest military leadership by a proven ability to obtain victory at all cost.

Louis Bonaparte's willingness to send to Mexico his best general at the head of his most elite troops was an indication of his single-minded determination to subjugate Mexico. For some reason, Napoleon wanted to rule Mexico. The nonpayment of debt was only a pretense for the enormous costs to which he was willing to commit his empire. England and Spain, which had demanded payment of debts owed to them by Mexico, landed token forces to occupy customhouses in Vera Cruz; but both countries quickly withdrew their soldiers after realizing that Bonaparte's goals were much broader than the mere collection of debts and redemption of revenue bonds.

After long months of waiting, we began to receive the reports that Marshal Bazaine had launched a second advance to the capital. Mexico had lost Ignacio Zaragoza to malaria, but it is doubtful that even that gallant young general could have turned back the army of 60,000 French soldiers and Prussian mercenaries equipped with repeating rifles and the most advanced artillery in the world. Sweeping aside all resistance, Bazaine seized Mexico City early in 1863. When we heard the news of the fall of the capital, I thought my heart would cease beating. Was Jorge among the thousands of courageous men and women of all ages who were sacrificing their lives in what was proving to be a vain attempt to prevent their nation's conquest by the Empire of France?

For weeks, I went about my routines as though stumbling through a dream. I kept praying that what was happening was nothing more than a horrible nightmare. Finally, the news came that Benito Juarez had fled Mexico City in advance of the French takeover of the capital. He had reestablished the national government of Mexico in San Luis Potosi, some three hundred miles northwest of Mexico City. A week after hearing of this development, one of the Montemayors' teamster friends came to our house with a hurriedly scrawled note from Jorge that he and Josefa and Miguel were with President Juarez in San Luis Potosi. He said he would write more as soon as he had an opportunity.

Most of the news on what happened in Mexico came through reports in Matamoros newspapers. There were some stories in the Texas newspapers of the French invasion of Mexico, but Texans were preoccupied with accounts of the war to the north. Endless casualty lists in the Austin newspapers told of the ferocity of the battles that were being waged on several fronts. Though the southern armies continued to be victorious in the east, they were unable to deal a decisive defeat to the Union. One of the south's greatest victories, the Battle of Chancellorsville, proved very costly with the loss of Stonewall Jackson, the general Robert E. Lee said was his right arm.

While President Lincoln's generals could not give him a victory in the east, the story was very different in the west. In a campaign to divide the Confederate States, Union armies began to inflict defeats on southern armies and drive them from the Mississippi River valley. In the Spring of 1863, a Union army forced the surrender of Vicksburg, the strongest Confederate fortified point on the Mississippi River. It was a devastating loss to the Confederacy and led directly to the Union's recapture of New Orleans.

When I read the newspaper account of Vicksburg, I was astonished to learn that the campaign had been directed by a general by the name of Ulysses Simpson Grant. I stared at the name for some time before I realized it was Sam Grant. Finally, someone had recognized his ability. After his victory at Vicksburg, General Grant was named by Abraham Lincoln to be Commander of the Western Army of the United States. I was elated. With Sam Grant in the war and in a position of command, I knew it could not continue to drag on and on. Zachary Taylor had said it: It takes a man who truly hates war to bring one to a swift conclusion. Sam Grant was that man.

Shortly after the victories in the west, President Lincoln issued his Emancipation Proclamation in which those slaves in the Confederate states were declared to be "forever free." There were no reports of the Emancipation Proclamation in the Texas newspapers, and we understood that the Proclamation meant nothing until the northern armies could somehow achieve a final victory on the field of battle.

Tom Blue continued to make trips north to help escaping runaways. On each trip, he would stop at Huntsville to confer with Joshua, who had become an important link between our settlements in Mexico and the slaves, who were awaiting word of how the war was progressing and what they could do to aid a Union victory. Some of the slaves engaged in clandestine acts of sabotage of the southern war effort. They destroyed bridges and burned fields of grains that could be harvested and shipped to Confederate cavalry, which had proven to be the south's most effective weapon. Depriving the cavalry's horses of grain was a way of helping to speed a Union victory.

After returning from one of his trips north, Tom Blue came to me and said, "General Houston wants to see your grandmother."

I told him I did not think my grandmother could make the trip to Huntsville.

"The General knows Carmen's doing poorly, but he said it was very important that he see her. It has to do with your brother, Teresa. When he was returning from Virginia, Esteban stopped by to visit General Houston."

Esteban had said nothing to us about visiting with Sam Houston. I asked Tom Blue why he wished to see my grandmother.

"He wouldn't say. I asked Joshua, and he said he didn't know why the General wants to see Mrs. Owens. He said that when Esteban came to visit General Houston, he was with some Confederate soliders."

"Confederate soldiers?"

"Yes. Officers in the Confederate army. And Joshua said one of them was the son of John Tyler, who used to be President of the United States."

I realized that Kalanu would not ask my grandmother to make the trip to Huntsville if what he needed to tell her was not important. When I told Carmen of his request, I was surprised that she did not appear anxious to go.

"Why don't you go to Huntsville, Teresa," she said. "I'm sure whatever Houston wants to tell me, he can tell you."

What she was recommending was exactly what I was going to suggest. She was far too weak for such an arduous journey.

On the morning Tom Blue and I were preparing to depart, Carmen held my arm to prevent my mounting the mule I had selected for the trip north. I turned to face her, thinking she wanted to give me some last minute instructions. She looked at me for a moment and then embraced me.

"Abuela?" I asked. "Are you all right?"

She smiled. "I saw your grandfather last night."

"You had a dream, Abuela?"

"Coalter is very happy, Teresa."

Carmen seemed her old self, strong and vigorous. It may have been the dawn light, but she looked almost youthful. My grandmother was really a very beautiful woman.

"You and Tom Blue had better get started," she said, looking toward the eastern sky. "The sun will be up soon. You will not want to travel during the heat of the day. Give my regards to Houston and tell him I'll see him soon. Tell him I'm looking forward to it."

She embraced me again and helped me mount. There was strength in her arms, and I wondered if perhaps she should be making this journey instead of me.

Lebe Seru, too, embraced me. When I looked at him, there were tears in his eyes; but he was smiling. He hugged Tom Blue and said for us to be careful.

When Tom Blue and I reached the top of the hill north of our farm and looked back one last time, both Lebe Seru and my grandmother waved. They looked very happy.

The journey was not as dangerous as the one we had made to Austin two years before. Virtually all white men in Texas between the ages of fourteen and sixty were in the Confederate armies, the largest of which, according to newspaper accounts, was being led by Robert E. Lee into the state of Pennsylvania. He was hoping for a victory on northern soil that would cause the people in the Union to demand that President Lincoln negotiate a peace. Therefore, we saw very few men on the roads.

As we drew near Huntsville, we heard an unusual sound. It was a pounding noise and the low wail of human voices.

Reining my mount to a halt, I asked, "What is it?"

Tom Blue did not answer. There was sadness in his eyes.

"Tom Blue? What's wrong?"

And then I recognized the sound and understood Tom Blue's silence. It was an Indian chant, accompanied by the beating of drums. It had been many years, but I had heard this sound when I was a girl and the Cherokees came to visit Kalanu in Houston Town. It was the ceremony they conducted when someone was dying.

We dismounted and walked our horses to Sam Houston's two-story frame house, which was built to resemble a steamboat. The porches on both ends of the house looked like boatdecks. Some thirty feet from the house were two dozen Cherokees, sitting in a circle, beating rawhide drums and chanting. To the left of the house was an oak tree, its massive limbs providing shade for the man who had been the first President of the Republic of Texas.

Dressed in a simple white linen suit, Kalanu sat in a wooden rocker, his large hands resting on a cane he held between his legs. He raised his head slowly as we approached. I saw the smile on his ashen face deepen when he recognized us through eyes that were watery and swollen. Joshua, who was seated in a rocker next to him, got to his feet and greeted us.

I rushed to Kalanu to prevent his attempt to get up. He was too weak to stand. I knelt and took his frail hands in mine.

"Teresa," he said. "Thank you for coming."

"*Buenos días, Kalanu,*" I said as cheerfully as I could, determined I would not let my voice or any tears betray the sadness I felt at seeing him so near death.

Mrs. Houston came out of the house, followed by Eliza who carried neither fan nor water. Both were smiling.

"Teresa!" Mrs. Houston said and rushed to embrace me. "Oh, Teresa. How good to see you!"

I could see she did not want Kalanu's last hours to be sad and morose. She was being strong for her husband. He smiled as she asked about my grandmother and Lebe Seru and Esau. I told her everyone was fine and that my grandmother said she was looking forward to seeing her old friend very soon.

"Well," Mrs. Houston said, patting me on the shoulder, "we'll let you and Mr. Houston talk, Teresa. Tom Blue, come inside. Eliza has just baked one of her wonderful apple crisps."

"You don't have to leave, Joshua," I said when he started toward the house.

Smiling, he nodded and said, "I'll just go sit on the porch, Teresa. You all need to visit by yourselves for a spell. I'll be over here if you need me."

We watched Joshua walk slowly to the porch and lower himself to the steps.

Kalanu shook his head. "Look at that man there, Teresa. That man has been my slave for over twenty years. He belonged to me like this cane here. I was supposed to own him. And yet, he's the one that has taken care of me. I tell you the truth, if it weren't for that man, my family would have starved to death."

I stroked his hand. His skin was like paper. He looked much older than his seventy years, except for his eyes. His grey eyes still had the same sparkle they had when he used to prop me up on his shoulder and dance a jig.

"I don't have a penny to my name," Kalanu continued. "The state of Texas has not paid me any salary for my term as governor. When I die, my family has nothing. It's Joshua there who'll take care of them. He's fed my chil'run, and he'll feed them after I'm gone. And he doesn't have to. Joshua's a free man, Teresa. He can go anytime he wants, the same as Esau and Tom Blue. He's known that for years."

"He's your friend, Kalanu."

"Even while he was my slave and working for me, he earned money on the side, wheelrighting and such. He saved his money. He's already told Mrs. Houston not to worry. He'll take care of her and the chil'run." He shook his head. "He is my friend, isn't he, Teresa? What did I ever do to deserve such a friend?"

"You have many friends. Many people respect you. You've done many great things."

"I've done a lot of damn stupid things."

"Most of us have."

"I could have done a lot more good things. Your grandmother was right. I should have spoken out a long time ago against slavery. Maybe there wouldn't be so many boys getting killed if I had. I should have done that, but I didn't. And you know why? I wanted to be president. I wanted to be president so bad I wouldn't speak my mind on things for fear the people wouldn't vote for me."

"You spoke up for the Indians. You probably would be president today if you hadn't stood up for the Indians."

His gaze drifted toward the Cherokees who continued to chant. "And they are the only ones who are here to be with me as I draw near that narrow isthmus which separates this sorrowful world from the sea of eternity."

At that moment I was startled because a platoon of some fifty soldiers were marching on the road near the house. They were wearing the blue uniforms of the Union army. I soon saw the men were unarmed and being guarded by grey-uniformed Confederate soldiers.

"Prisoners of war," Kalanu explained when he saw where I was looking. "They keep them over at the penitentiary. They're taking them out to
clear off some farm land. Mornin', boys!"

"Mornin', General Houston!" the prisoners shouted in unison.

"You boys be careful out thar in them woods!" Kalanu yelled. "Watch
out for them snipes I been tellin' you 'bout!"

"Yes, sir, General Houston!" the young men responded cheerfully.

"They're good boys," Kalanu said. "My boy, Sam Jr., was a prisoner of
war up north. Did you know that?"

"No."

"He just got back home. He got wounded, and they treated him real
good up there in Ohio or Illinois or someplace. Isn't that something? We'll
treat each other's chil'run real nice, patch up their wounds, and then we'll
send 'em out to blow each other's brains out. Don't make sense, do it?"

"No, it doesn't."

His expression became serious. "Carmen couldn't come?"

"No, Kalanu."

"Tom Blue said she's doing poorly."

"She's not as young as she used to be."

"I understand." He reached into his coat and retrieved a set of folded
papers. "Maybe it's best you came. I'm not sure what Carmen could do. To
tell you the truth, I'm not sure what you can do. I don't know what anybody can do."

"What's wrong, Kalanu? Why did you want to see my grandmother?"

He shook his head. "Teresa, something very bad is happening. It
involves your brother."

"Tom Blue said he came to visit you."

"Esteban's grown up into such a fine-looking young man. Big and
strong. A born leader of men. Reminds me of myself when I was that age."

"Tom Blue said he was with some Confederate officers."

The smile faded from his lips. "One of them was Major John Tyler, the
son of former President Tyler, who just passed on a couple of months ago.
Did you know that?"

"No."

For a moment, he searched for words. "Teresa, I don't know how to
tell you this. Esteban is deeply involved in something that is very disturbing. Very disturbing. Louis Bonaparte is planning to help the Confederacy
in this war."

"What?"

"I didn't know what to make of it at first. They came to me because they thought I might give my support to the plan. I'm not sure how much good my support would be, but Esteban seemed to think it would help."

"Bonaparte is planning to help the Confederacy? Why?"

"For some years now, the northern states have had enough votes to get the Congress to impose tariffs on manufactured goods from France and England. It helps the industries in the north, but it is very bad for the French and the English.

"If the Confederacy could remain an independent nation, they would likely buy most of their manufactured items from the French because they could get them cheaper than from the United States. Bonaparte's not alone in Europe in wanting to see the United States taken down a notch or two. They would love to see the United States broken up into pieces. The last thing they want is one big country stretching from the Atlantic to the Pacific and from the Rio Grande up to Canada. The way they see things, that's just too much country in one place.

"Anyway, Bonaparte views this war as an opportunity to cut the United States down to a manageable size. If he comes in to help the Confederacy, it could just happen."

"France has the most powerful army in the world, Kalanu. If they help the Confederacy, the north will lose the war."

"Yes. The Union will be defeated. That's why Esteban and Major Tyler and the others came to see me. They want me to speak out in favor of French intervention when the time comes."

For a moment, I did not realize he had stopped talking. My thoughts were on the arsenal near our house on the Rio Grande. Now I understood its purpose. It would be there for the French when they came across the river. And there were other arsenals further up the river at Laredo and Eagle Pass.

"Teresa?"

"Kalanu, when are they planning to come across and help the Confederacy?"

He gripped the cane. "Louis Bonaparte is a very cunning man. He does not want to do this alone. He wants the support of other European nations. The English and the Spanish got cold feet. They are nervous about coming into a civil war, especially after something like Gettysburg."

"Gettysburg?"

"You didn't hear? I guess you didn't. It happened while you and Tom Blue were on your way here. Lee's army was defeated in Pennsylvania near a town called Gettysburg."

"Does that mean the war is over?"

"No. The Union won the battle, but they were hurt too bad to follow up on it and move south. Just the same, I would say it doesn't look very good for the Confederacy right now."

"So Napoleon will be less likely to come into Texas. The war is almost over."

"I would say he is more likely to come into Texas now. He knows the Union armies have been weakened, and the south is in desperate need of his help. Bonaparte has an army of over seventy-five thousand men in Mexico, and more may be on the way. His army is led by his best general, Marshal Bazaine. But Bonaparte still wants the backing of other European powers, which is why he is preparing to make the Archduke of Austria the Emperor of Mexico."

"Maximilian von Hapsburg," I said immediately. It was all beginning to make sense.

"Yes. Maximilian von Hapsburg."

"And when Maximilian becomes the Emperor of Mexico, that is when Bonaparte will send his armies into Texas."

"That is how I understand the plan, Teresa, but he is going to have to defeat Benito Juarez first. It won't do to intervene in a civil war if you are having to fight one in your own back yard. And you can't put an army up into Texas if someone is behind you cutting off your supply lines from Vera Cruz."

"And so Esteban and his friends wanted you to support the movement of French soldiers into Texas. That is why they wanted to talk to you?"

Kalanu unfolded the papers he had been holding in his hand. "Louis Bonaparte will not send his armies into Texas without at least some pretense of legality. This was brought to me." He handed the papers to me and I began to read them. "There was a provision written into the agreement by which Bonaparte's uncle sold the Louisiana Territory to the United States in 1803. That provision said that France would retain the right to reclaim the Louisiana Territory if the United States government ever acted to seize the property of the people of the territory.

"Major Tyler wrote this memorandum you have. The case is being made that when President Lincoln issued the Emancipation Proclamation, he was acting to seize the property of citizens of Louisiana, Arkansas and Texas, thereby activating the provision in the treaty Napoleon Bonaparte made with President Jefferson. He is saying there is now a legal basis for France to enter the states of Texas, Arkansas and Louisiana."

The document was written in a form of the English language I found difficult to follow, but I could discern that it said what Kalanu was relating.

"Teresa, if the French come into Texas and if they supply weapons to the Confederate armies, this civil war will continue for several more years. Tens of thousands more people will be killed. And it is likely the United States will lose the war."

My thoughts were disorganized. "Have you told anyone about this, Kalanu?"

He shrugged. "Who am I to tell, Teresa? I was the legally elected governor of Texas, and they ran me off. Most Texans think I'm a traitor. I may be the most hated man in the south. Who can I go to? I think you can see I'm not in any position to jump on my horse and slope up to Washington City to see Mr. Lincoln."

"What did you think my grandmother could do?"

"I don't know. Since it involves Esteban, I thought your grandmother might be able to think of something to do. Maybe she could talk him out of this thing."

When I tried to return the memorandum, Kalanu shook his head and raised his hands to indicate he did not want it.

"Kalanu," I said, getting to my feet, "I need to go back to Brownsville. My grandmother and Lebe Seru will know what to do about this."

He struggled to raise himself from the chair.

"Please. Don't get up."

"I will get up," he said firmly. "I don't want your last image of me to be of some an old man in a rocking chair."

"I'll see you again."

"It's my time to go, Teresa. I'm ready."

He stood tall, and I embraced him. Despite everything, my tears began to flow.

"Teresita, do you remember when I dunked you and Esteban in that bayou?"

"Yes."

"Maybe I should have jumped in there with you and got me a little bit of that immortality."

I looked up into his grey eyes. "You are immortal. No one will ever forget Sam Houston."

"Sam Houston," he said. "My name is Kalanu! It was given to me by people who loved me, and I loved them. If you ever have occasion to tell anyone about Sam Houston, tell them he was proud of the name Kalanu! Will you do that for me, Teresita?"

"Yes, Kalanu. I will do that for you. I will do it, because I love you."

Something compelled me to leave very quickly. It was not only because of the need to get back to Brownsville and tell Carmen and Lebe Seru about what I had learned. Mrs. Houston tried to get us to stay a little longer. I thanked her and told her it was very urgent that we get back home. Tom Blue and I rode away at a gallop. Something was pulling me away, and I knew what it was. We had ridden only a mile down the road when the drums and the chanting stopped. I had been spared having to witness my teacher leave this world. He would not have wanted me to see that. But I was happy. Sam Houston had crossed that isthmus into the sea of eternity. Kalanu had joined the immortals.

We were five miles from the Rio Grande when we began to detect a familiar aroma in the air. As we drew closer, it became unmistakable. It was the sickening smell I had learned to hate. It was the same sharp odor that had hung in the air for days after the battles that had been waged almost twenty years before between the Americans and the Mexicans. It was the aroma of gunpowder. Closer to the border, we encountered smoke, the kind of thin smoke that issues from embers after a fire has consumed wood. It was a suffocating smoke and, together with the acrid smell of gunpowder, we found it difficult to breathe.

A cold dread gripped me as we spurred our mounts toward a hill that would provide us with a view of the valley. Tom Blue had begun to speculate that a Union army had invaded Brownsville by sea and a great battle had been fought. The smoke, however, was not coming from the direction of Brownsville or the harbor at the mouth of the Rio Grande. It was coming from further up the river. It was coming from the direction of our farm.

At the crest of the hill, we looked down at where the warehouses had stood. They were gone. In their place was the source of the smoke and the fumes: a huge mass of charred ruins. It was apparent that we were witnessing the effects of what must have been an enormous explosion. The thousands of kegs of gunpowder that had been stored in those warehouses had ignited and nothing was left. Here and there among the blackened quagmire were the twisted remains of what had once been howitzers and cannons. The arsenal had been destroyed.

But our house was also gone. The barns, the stables, the sheds were gone. The debris was not quite so obliterated as at the warehouses. The blast from the warehouses had been so powerful, it had blown down everything on our property. Even trees and bushes were gone. There was no trace of any plants in the gardens, which were covered with a thick layer of black soot. There were no animals. There were no people.

"Tom Blue," I whispered. "Where is everyone? Lebe Seru. Santiago and Pilar. My grandmother. Where are they?"

"Let's cross the river, Teresa. Esau will tell us where they are."

I knew where they were. I did not know the particulars, but I knew. My grandmother was no longer alive. Lebe Seru and the Montemayors. They were gone. We would never see them again. They were dead. Somehow, I knew this. Something in me knew they were dead, and I thought I understood why. I knew what they had done. I prayed I was wrong, but I knew I was not.

Holding the reins loosely in my hands, I allowed my mule to follow as Tom Blue led the way to the ferry and we crossed to Matamoros. We rode down dirt streets where mothers were shouting at their children to come inside out of the hot sun. At the market, vendors bargained with customers and hawked their wares. When we reached Esau's tavern, he came running outside to meet us. If he and Tom Blue had not been there to help me, I would have fallen after I dismounted. My legs were weak, and I felt a trembling all over my body. Holding my arm, Esau escorted us inside, through a hallway and to a room in the hotel behind the tavern. It was only after I heard my name that I looked up. It was Alma. She embraced me.

After walking me to a chair in the corner of the room, Alma knelt before me and held my hands. I saw Binu Seru sitting on a chair on the other side of the room. He looked so sad.

I said, "My grandmother is dead."

Alma nodded, and the tears flowed from her eyes. She buried her face on my lap. I stroked her hair.

Esau, too, could not restrain his tears. Tom Blue sat down, closed his eyes and bowed his head.

"Lebe Seru?" I asked.

"He's dead," Esau said. "And Pilar and Santiago. They are all dead. They were killed in the explosion."

Tom Blue asked, "What happened?"

It took a few moments for Esau to regain his composure. Finally, he cleared his throat and said, "It was just a few days after you left for Huntsville. I should have known what they were planning. The way they said good-bye that last time; I should have realized what they were going to do. They had been planning this for a long time. I know that now."

"They blew up the warehouses," I said.

"Yes," Esau said. "Carmen. Lebe Seru. Pilar. Santiago. They went out there in the middle of the night and blew them up. I don't know how they did it. We'll never know. There's nothing left out there."

"You did not find their bodies?"

"No, Teresa. No bodies were found. Not theirs. Not the French soldiers or the Confederate soldiers who were guarding the warehouses. They sacrificed their lives. It was the only way to get close enough to do what it was they had to do. It was a powerful series of explosions. The whole valley shook. I've talked to people who were more than twenty miles from here that night, and they felt the explosions. It collapsed the wharfs on the river across from your house."

Never in my life had I experienced such a contradiction of emotions. There was a terrible emptiness at the same time I felt a deep pride. My grandmother was gone. The woman who had been more like a mother to me than my own mother was gone. I would never see her again, not in this world. But I was proud of what she had done. I was proud of Lebe Seru and Pilar and Santiago. They had destroyed those weapons and the gunpowder before they could be used to kill more people and prolong the wars on both sides of the border.

I looked at Binu Seru and could see that he had been crying. "Don't be sad, Binu Seru," I said. "Be proud of your great-grandfather. He wouldn't want you to be sad."

"Teresa's right," Alma said, getting to her feet. "Be proud. Be proud of your great-grandfather and Carmen. Be proud of Pilar and Santiago."

Binu Seru wiped away his tears. In a soft voice he said, "I am proud, but I miss them."

I went to him and put my arms around him. Looking at Alma, I asked, "Where is Ralph?"

"He and the men in the settlements have gone to join the Juaristas."

"That is where we will go. We will go to San Luis Potosi and join the Juaristas."

Esau shook his head. "Benito Juarez is no longer in San Luis Potosi, Teresa. The French have taken the city. President Juarez has once again gone north. No one knows where he is. Some say he is in the Sierra Madre. Others say he is in El Paso del Norte."

"Can he not come to Matamoros? He can establish the seat of government here in Matamoros."

"He cannot come here. Governor Vidaurri has declared his allegiance to the new government."

"The new government?"

"Miguel Miramon has returned to Mexico. He and Tomas Mejia convened a Council of Notables to organize a new national government for Mexico. The Council issued an invitation to Archduke Maximilian of Austria to rule Mexico as an empire under the protection of France."

"Do they not realize that is illegal? Mexico is governed by a constitution. Benito Juarez is the duly elected President of the Republic of Mexico."

"The Council of Notables has declared Benito Juarez an outlaw. The Pope has excommunicated him. Maximilian von Hapsburg is expected to arrive in Vera Cruz any day."

"Then we must find Benito Juarez," I said. "Wherever he is, we must go to him. We will join his forces. We will do what Carmen and Lebe Seru and the Montemayors did. It is not only the future of Mexico that is at stake. What Louis Bonaparte is doing is going to affect the war in the United States. He may prevent the end of slavery."

Esau asked, "Is that why Governor Houston wanted to see your grandmother, Teresa?"

I explained what Sam Houston had told me of Bonaparte's plan to help the Confederacy.

"I had begun to suspect something like that," Esau said. "I think Lebe Seru and Carmen did as well. That is why they blew up those warehouses. Those materials were being stored there for the French army when they enter Texas."

"Teresa," Alma said. "I know you want to go to Jorge. I can understand that. But we cannot join Benito Juarez. Before Ralph and the other men left, we moved the women and children in the settlements to Matamoros. All throughout the city, we have hidden them with families that are sympathetic to our cause. It is the safest place. We must stay and care for the children."

"I cannot, Alma. I must go to Jorge."

Esau said, "Alma's right, Teresa. We must take care of the children. And who will meet the fugitives when they arrive from the Laguna Madre? Dozens are arriving everyday. We need you to guide them across the river. There are so many Confederate soldiers on the other side, it has become very difficult for myself or Alma or Tom Blue or any of our people to elude them. A Tejana will go unnoticed. We need you, Teresa."

It was too much. It had happened too many times. "I can no longer stand to be separated from Jorge. I have to be with him! I will fight at his side."

"Teresa," Alma said. "Do you not think I want to be with Ralph? I want to fight at his side, but we each have to do what will be best for our cause. We need you here. Perhaps the time is not far off when the Union armies will retake Brownsville. Then our people can come here without fear of being captured and, in some cases, killed. I know it's hard, Teresa, but we have to be patient and do what we must."

Alma and Esau were right. For the present, my place was on the Rio Grande. It was where I could do the most good. Each dawn, I would ferry to the north bank and walk to the contact point up the coast. Very few days passed that I did not lead at least a dozen people up the river under the cover of darkness to a safe place to cross over. Tom Blue and Binu Seru would then take them to the farmhouses of Mexicans who were sympathetic to the runaways. These people were taking a great risk. Since Governor Vidaurri's defection to the Imperialists, he had declared it a crime for any Mexican to help the runaways. Any fugitive slave caught in northern Mexico was to be transported back across the river to the Confederate authorities at Fort Brown.

On the rare occasion I was not at the contact point or when there were no escapees to escort across the river, I stayed in my room in Esau's hotel, hoping to receive a message from Jorge. Some of the teamsters, who had been the friends of the Montemayors, traveled across the remote desert regions where Benito Juarez was rumored to be traveling. His government was always on the move, usually one step ahead of pursuing

French armies. The teamsters promised that if they came across Jorge, they would deliver my letters to him and bring back his to Esau's hotel in Matamoros.

Sometimes, on the way to the contact point in the mornings, I would purchase a newspaper in Brownsville so I would have something to read during the long hours of watching for signals. I hoped there would be news on the war in Mexico, but there was little. There were many stories about Maximilian and Carlotta. Their coronation at Chapultepec Castle was described in detail. Members of royal families in Europe traveled to Mexico to attend the event. Queen Victoria ordered British warships all over the world to fire their guns in salute to her cousin, Emperor Maximilian, and to her niece, Empress Carlotta.

As could be expected, most stories in the newspapers focused on the civil war that continued to rage to the north. After General Lee's retreat from Gettysburg, the south no longer had the ability to mount an offensive against the Union. The Confederate strategy was to fight a protracted defensive war, one that would cost so many lives the people in the north would be willing to call a halt to the war and recognize southern independence. Realizing this, President Lincoln knew he must mount a vigorous assault that would destroy the south's ability to resist. He did exactly the right thing; he named Ulysses S. Grant to be the supreme commander of all the northern armies.

In May of 1864, General Grant launched two offensives against the Confederacy. He sent over 120,000 men, under the command of General George Meade, into Virginia to seek and destroy the army led by Robert E. Lee. General Grant personally accompanied this army. He also dispatched an army of nearly 100,000 men, led by General William Sherman, to sweep through Georgia and defeat the other great Confederate army under the command of General Joseph Johnston. As reports began to reach the newspapers of the fighting in both campaigns, it was evident that the cost of ending the war was going to be very high for both sides. In engagement after engagement, thousands of men lost their lives. The United States was slowly winning the war, but in the process it was literally being bled to death.

Late one evening, after returning from the contact point where there had been no smoke sightings during the day, I was in my room with Alma, Esau and Binu Seru. We were making plans to deliver food to our people around the city. Esau had opened two more taverns and was using his profits to buy food to distribute to the women and children who were staying with families throughout Matamoros. Before the war, Matamoros was a town of about six thousand people; now it had swollen to a population easily ten times that number, and we were able to hide many fugitives amidst the hustle and bustle of a city where few people paid much attention to anything except the opportunity to make money from the wars on both sides of the border.

Just as Esau was about to leave, we heard a commotion outside the hotel. There were the sounds of horses and men outside. Esau went to investigate.

Moments later, he returned. "French soldiers! They've surrounded the hotel!"

Suddenly, the door to our room flew open. Two soldiers, rifles in hand, barged inside. They looked very menacing in their blue jackets, flowing red trousers and black boots.

Alma drew Binu Seru to her and held him tightly. I rushed to them and tried to help shield the boy. I did not know what else to do. Esau prepared to fight with his bare hands. The soldiers, however, did not aim their weapons. Holding the rifles at the ready, they moved aside to allow a tall man behind them to lower his head and come inside. It was my brother.

"Teresa," Esteban said, reaching for me.

I pulled my arm away from his grasp.

"Teresa, I must talk to you."

"I have nothing to say to you."

Looking at the others, Esteban said, "Esau. Alma. Could you please excuse us? I would like to talk to my sister alone."

Alma looked at me, and I nodded my assent. Taking Binu Seru by the hand, she and Esau left the room ahead of the soliders, who closed the door behind them.

"Teresa," Esteban began, "I need for you to come with me to Mexico City."

I stared at his sun-scorched face streaked with yellow dust caked by sweat. His beard looked like it had been washed in mud. He had been riding hard.

"Do you not even wish to ask about our grandmother, Esteban? You have not seen her in a long time. Do you not want to inquire of her health before you tell me what you need?"

His expression was one of puzzlement. "Abuelita? Yes. Tell me. How is she?"

"Carmen is dead, Esteban."

"What?"

"She is dead. Lebe Seru is dead. Santiago and Pilar Montemayor are dead."

"Dead?"

"You should write to Cata Valeria. Inform her that her mother is dead. Or perhaps you need not bother. I expect it would be of little interest to her."

There was genuine sorrow in his eyes. "Had she been sick?"

"She and Lebe Seru and the Montemayors blew up the arsenal you had prepared for the French army when they cross into Texas. They were killed in the explosion."

He straightened. "When the French army crosses into Texas? What do you mean?"

"You need not pretend with me, Esteban. I visited Sam Houston in Huntsville. He told me about your visit with your friends from Virginia. He told me about Major Tyler."

As much to himself as to me, Esteban said, "Abuela blew up the warehouses. We thought it was an accident."

"It was no accident. Carmen wanted to stop what you and Maximilian von Hapsburg are planning to do."

He shook his head. "If that is why Abuela blew up the warehouses, then her life was wasted. I am very sorry. I loved our grandmother. But we will rebuild the warehouses and stock them with more gunpowder and weapons. We will surround them with as many soldiers as it takes to guard them. We have many such warehouse along the Rio Grande."

"Then I will blow them up, Esteban. And when I am dead, others will follow. There are millions of us. Are you prepared to kill us all?"

"Teresa, you must come with me to Mexico City. I want you to talk to the Emperor. You will understand what we are attempting to do. The people of Mexico will support Maximilian when they understand what he will do for them. He is going to make Mexico strong!"

"I am not going to Mexico City."

"But you must! You must leave this place. Old Chief told you the truth. The French army will cross into Texas. Confederate armies will join us, and we will supply them with weapons and gunpowder. Together, we will defeat the Union. There will be much hard fighting. That is why I have come for you. I want you safely in Mexico City when the battle begins."

"I will not go with you, Esteban. I will be here when your armies cross into Texas. I will fight the French soldiers. I will fight the Confederate soldiers. I will fight them the same as our grandmother did. And if you are with them, I will fight you!"

Esteban paced to the door. He turned. "Teresa, I have just returned from Monterey where we almost captured Benito Juarez. Once again, he somehow managed to escape. But not everyone did." His face hardened. "Miguel Montemayor is dead. He was killed in the fighting. He would not surrender."

When he continued to look at me, I knew there was more. I could see it in his face. I could not stand it. He was going to tell me about Jorge. He had news about Jorge, and I did not know if I could bear it.

"Jorge was wounded, Teresa. His arm. His wound is severe, but he will recover. I made certain the best physicians in Mexico attend him."

Even my own body was fighting me. My chest was so tight I could not speak. My hands trembled, and my head was throbbing.

"Jorge is in Mexico City. I had him sent to Chapultepec Castle. Come with me, Teresa. I will take you to him. Will you come with me?"

I was having to struggle for each breath, but I was able to nod my head.

"I have a coach outside. We will leave immediately."

XIII

On the first leg of our journey to Mexico City, Esteban drove a barouche pulled by a team of six horses. I was the only passenger inside the elegant cabin upholstered in black leather. From the way my brother wielded the whip and drove the team, it was evident he was in a great hurry to get to the capital. We were escorted by two hundred Zouaves mounted on Spanish *destruirs*, which had been confiscated from the Mexican army. Zouaves were the elite troops of the French Imperial Army, and they were famous for their colorful uniforms. They wore green turbans, sky-blue tunics and billowing red trousers, which is why they were often referred to as the *pantalons rouges*.

Esteban would dispatch his fastest riders ahead to a town or military station to have readied a fresh team of horses for the barouche when we arrived. We would have time only to quickly attend to nature's require-ments before I was back in the coach and he was on the deck, cracking the whip to urge the new team to an angry gallop. Our escort, too, would be changed, and a new contingent of Zouaves on fresh mounts would try to keep up while scanning the countryside for any challenge to our progress. Esteban and I would consume whatever food or liquids we had managed to grab at the stop. Though I was seldom hungry, I knew I must keep up my strength. As soon as Jorge and I could get away, we would find a way to stop what was being planned. I had no idea what it would be, but we had to do something.

Finally, Esteban realized that even he could not drive a team of hors-es twenty-four hours a day. We began to take on a fresh teamster with each change of the horses, and he would drive while my brother rode in the coach with me and slept. When rested, Esteban would climb to the deck and take the reins because the driver was not pushing the team fast enough to suit him. He drove like a madman even as we began to ascend the foothills of the Sierra Madre.

When in the coach, stretched out on the seat opposite mine, asleep, Esteban would turn and toss and sometimes shout out words in German or French. Other times, he would lapse into a deep sleep and, as I watched him, I could not help but be reminded of when he was a little boy and I was his protector. Despite the beard and the manly lines to his face and the powerful body, Esteban was still my little brother. He was the Estebanito who used to urge me to hurry so we could get to the President's Mansion and play with Kalanu. He was the boy who had wanted to come to my defense when that horrible man threatened to whip me. I hated everything Esteban was doing. I could not understand why he was doing it, but I still loved him. I could not help it.

One morning, just after Esteban had climbed into the coach to get some sleep, we heard a cracking sound. At first, I thought it was the driver using the whip, but he began to rein the horses to a stop.

Opening the door, Esteban shouted, "Why we are stopping, *hombre?* Give them the whip!"

When the coach came to a complete halt, Esteban jumped out and began to berate the driver. He stopped when the officers of the escort rode up, dismounted and spoke with him in French. I climbed out to stretch my legs. The men were pointing ahead. One of the Zouaves, riding in the lead, had been shot by a sniper. The man was dead. Forming a protective shield around us, the Zouaves were scanning the surrounding hills in an attempt to determine from what direction the shot had been fired. They aimed their repeating rifles in all directions, but the hills were silent.

Finally, the men remounted. We climbed back inside the barouche. Just as we began to move, the crack sounded again; and the driver screamed. He had been hit.

Esteban jumped out of the coach. Again, the Zouaves surrounded us and aimed their rifles.

When I got out, Esteban said, "Juaristas. They've killed the driver."

I scanned the barren hills. The snipers were probably hiding in one of the islands of mesquites or the clumps of tall, blue *grama* grass. Taking my arm, my brother positioned me under the coach and knelt beside me.

"It's probably no more than two or three men," he said. "Two or three peasant farmers, armed with old breech-loading rifles, are able to pin down two hundred of Napoleon's finest soldiers. It's what is happening all over this country."

As I looked at the French soldiers, each unable to do anything but crouch and wonder if they were the next one to be killed, I saw their frustration and their anger. Esteban was correct. It was what was happening all over Mexico. The French armies had defeated Mexican armies time and again on the battlefield. They had burned down villages whose inhabitants they suspected were in support of the Juaristas, and they had demonstrated no reluctance to kill women and children. And yet they were being pinned down all over the country and themselves killed, one by one, by bands of guerillas.

Suddenly, we saw a rider galloping toward the crest of a distant hill. He was out of range of the French rifles. Thinking this had been the sniper, the Zouave officers dispatched a dozen of their men in pursuit. We watched as they gained on the rider, whose horse was apparently not as fast as the *destruirs*. And then more shots rang out. The Zouaves in pursuit fell. As we continued to watch, more riders appeared on the hill to capture the now riderless *destruirs*. Before the French could send more men, the riders had disappeared over the hill. However, just before following his *compañeros*, one of the riders paused, raised his rifle and shouted, *"¡Viva Juárez!"*

The hills around us echoed his cry.

After the return of a squad sent in vain pursuit of the snipers, we resumed our journey.

Mexico was the land of my birth, but I had no idea of its beauty and the great variety of its terrain and vegetation. As we climbed ever higher, we began to encounter large forests of oaks and fir trees. There were magnificent junipers whose bark was the texture of an alligator's hide. Higher still, we crossed alpine meadows covered with clovers and columbines; and we encountered stands of tall white pines. We negotiated among massive red boulders splotched with glistening blue and orange lichens. In regions so high we sometimes had to drive slowly and carefully through the mists of low clouds, I was enchanted by the rich pinks and yellows and purples of delicate orchids and bromeliads growing in moist glades.

Descending to a lower region, we passed through thorn forests composed of acacias armed with gigantic broad-based thorns. Most of the trees were scraggly and gnarled and bore all shapes and sizes of beans pods. Here and there among the thorn trees were clusters of fan palms and palmettos. There were hundreds of varieties of cactus, ranging from the ubiquitous prickly-pears to the stately yuccas that sometimes grew as tall as twenty feet and were crowned with ornate white blossoms that would glow in the dark like candle-lit lanterns.

There was an abundance of the wolves and bears and great cats that I knew in Texas; but as we went further south, I began to see animals that were unfamiliar to me. I was especially attracted to a odd-looking mountain cat that had rings around its tail like a raccoon. At several points, I caught a glimpse of rusty-colored jaguars and spotted leopards. Among the lacy ferns and tropical foliage of the wet glades, red parrots squawked and preened their long tail-feathers. In some regions the noise made by millions of migrating birds was so loud it drowned out the thunder of the hooves of our escort's horses. And everywhere circled *zopilotes,* long-winged vultures who did not care whether the bodies on a battlefield or those next to a bullet-pocked execution wall were French or Mexican.

Approaching Mexico City, we passed through a region that had been formed by once raging volcanoes. It looked as though a storm tossed sea had frozen into black rock. The capital itself was sprawled across a great basin surrounded by dark and rugged mountains. South of the city could be seen the snow-capped peak of Popocatepetl and its twin titan, Ixtacihuatl, a still active volcano that issued smoke from its cone. The city's white churches, spires and haciendas were attractively laid out and nestled among trees on a green plain broken by lakes that glimmered with a silver sheen in the sunlight.

The hooves of our team clip-clopped on the cobblestone roadway leading up the steep incline to the red stonewall Chapultepec Castle, which had been built on the high ground that had, four centuries ago, been the site of Montezuma's palace. Originally constructed as the summer residence for the viceroys, Chapultepec Castle was surrounded by a forest of gigantic cypresses, many of them three hundred feet high and fifty to sixty feet in circumference. Long drapes of blue Spanish moss hung from their limbs; and the air was thick with hummingbirds and butterflies attracted by the fragrant blooms of eucalyptus trees that bordered spring-fed pools and well-tended, terraced flower gardens.

Thousands of French soldiers, Zouaves and Legionnaires, were everywhere around the castle. Many of the Legionnaires were Egyptians, and they wore fezzes, from which dangled long, purple tassels. I saw hundreds of cannons and howitzers, aimed in every direction from which interlopers might approach. There was more artillery concentrated on the castle grounds than I had seen employed by both the Mexican and American armies in their war on the Rio Grande. It would be difficult to determine if Chapultepec Castle was now the world's greatest fortress or its most guarded prison. It had something of the look of both.

Inside the castle, Esteban shouted questions and instructions in French and German, depending on which bowing sycophant ran forward to do his bidding.

As we walked down a dark and cavernous hallway, Esteban said, "We will go immediately to see the Emperor."

"No," I said firmly and ceased my effort to keep up with my brother's long strides.

"You promised you would talk to Maxl."

"After I have seen Jorge."

Esteban inquired of one of the servants as to Jorge's whereabouts. The man said he would lead us to his room.

We followed the servant up a marble staircase and to a room guarded by two armed Zouaves. When I heard my beloved's voice respond to Esteban's knock at the door, I rushed inside. Jorge struggled to get up from a chair next to a tall arched window. I rushed to him and embraced him. He grimaced in pain.

"Jorge," I said, looking at his right arm which hung at his side. "Your arm."

"Teresa," he whispered. "It does not matter. Please. Just hold me. Please."

Esteban, who stood next to a rosewood table in the luxurious and spacious room, said, "His elbow was shattered. We were fortunate the physicians were able to save the arm."

My anger flared at the sight of Jorge's arm dangling at his side. Jorge had never hurt anyone in his life. He was the gentlest of men. Why should his body be mutilated by soldiers who had no right to enter a country that had done nothing to them or to their country?

"This is what the man you want me to see has done!" I shouted. "He is the reason for this!"

"Teresa," Esteban said, "Maxl and I regret the suffering that is necessary to—"

"The suffering that is necessary? If the French had not invaded Mexico, there would have been no suffering. Look at what you have done, Esteban. Look at Jorge's arm! Look at it!"

Stepping to the door, Esteban said, "There is a ball tonight. There you will meet Maximilian and Carlotta. I will send a servant to assist you with your bath and provide you with appropriate attire."

After my brother left, I embraced Jorge and we held each other for a long time. Finally, I told him of the deaths of his grandparents, my grandmother and Lebe Seru.

"Teresa," he said. "Miguel was killed. One by one, they are killing my entire family."

"Josefa? What of Josefa?"

"Tia Josefa helped the president escape." His left hand trembled as I helped him sit down. "Everything is going so badly for us, Teresa. Each day more French soldiers arrive. From this window I can see their movements to the north. They are sending hundreds of cannons and thousands of wagons of gunpowder. I do not know how we can defeat them. Our people have only muskets, and we have almost no gunpowder left."

The last thing I wanted was to compound Jorge's despair, but I knew I had to tell him about the plan for the French to cross into Texas and ally with the Confederacy.

After listening to my story and reviewing the document Sam Houston had given me, Jorge said, "The French will not go into Texas as long as the Juaristas are in a position to cut off their supplies from the Mexican ports."

"That is true. But as you said, the Juaristas have few weapons and little gunpowder. How long will it be before—"

I stopped because Jorge had put his left hand on his right arm and closed his eyes.

"It hurts?"

"Sometimes it hurts so much I can not stand it."

There was a knock at the door. I admitted a woman who was carrying a basin of water.

"Teresa," Jorge said, "this is Señora Olga Barrera. She is one of us."

My expression must have revealed my confusion because the woman explained, "I am a Juarista, Señorita Sestos. My husband is with Porfirio Diaz in the south."

Jorge said, "Olga cleans the rooms of Maximilian and Carlotta. She and many of the servants who work in the castle provide valuable information we are able to send to President Juarez and to General Diaz."

"We discover where the soldiers are being sent," Olga said, "and warn our people so they can flee the villages."

"Olga's father knew your father," Jorge said. "He knew your grandmother, too."

"It is true," Olga said. "My father's name was Hector Sandoval. He was a servant at the hacienda of the Conde de Sestos in Guanajuato. He knew your father very well and was one of his sergeants when your father was an officer in the army of Santa Anna. And he knew your grandmother when she was a girl at the Hacienda de Abrantes."

"Is your father with the Juaristas?"

"If he were alive, he would be with them. He died many years ago."

I remembered what Carmen had said about a friend of my father's returning to Mexico when I was a baby.

"Olga," I asked, "did your father ever say anything about a woman called Doña Lupe?" Why I happened to think of what my grandmother had said of the woman she called Lupita, I did not know. "Did he know her?"

"Yes. My father spoke often of Doña Lupe. He said she had the gift of healing. She had been touched by Our Lady."

"Did he return to Guanajuato with Doña Lupe?"

"He told us that he left Texas in the company of Doña Lupe, but they became separated in a storm one night at the Rio Bravo. He looked for her for many days but never found her. He came to believe that she perished in the river that night. It has been years since I have heard anyone speak the name of Doña Lupe. You must have known her in Texas."

"I was a baby when she left with your father."

Jorge struggled to get to his feet. We both rushed to help him stand at the window. "Teresa," he said. "Tell Olga what you learned about the plan for the French to go into Texas."

After I told what I had learned, Olga said, "This explains why Marshal Bazaine is sending so many of his soldiers to the north. We have wondered why so many are going there and with so many cannons. Our strength is in the south."

"I must go to Don Benito," Jorge said. "I must go tonight."

"Jorge," I said. "You are in no condition to travel."

"I must. If the French and the Confederacy have formed an alliance, both the Juaristas and the Americans will lose. I must go to Don Benito. He must be told."

"We can send a message to him," Olga suggested.

"I must go to him. I am of no use to him here."

"But how will you get out of here, Jorge?" I asked. "There are guards outside the door, and the castle is surrounded by French soldiers."

Olga said, "Some of our people can climb through the window tonight and lower Jorge to the ground. He can be smuggled out of the castle in one of the supply wagons. It can be done. But Teresa is right, Jorge. You are in no condition to travel hundreds of miles to the Sierra Madre. Your arm is far from healed. The physicians said you may yet lose it."

"It does not matter. I must go to Don Benito."

"What if you need help on the way?"

"Then I will help him," I said. "I am going with him. Can you smuggle us both out of the castle?"

Olga took a deep breath at the thought of what we were proposing, but she nodded. "It will have to be tonight after the Grand Ball has begun."

"What is this Grand Ball?"

"It is to celebrate the New Year, Teresa. Tomorrow is the first day of 1865. Did you not know?"

I had lost all track of time on our journey from Texas. I had not even known when it was Christmas.

"I will make the arrangements," she said. "Tonight will be a good time. After midnight, the soldiers will be drunk. The wagons that have brought the food from the city will be returning. We will disguise you as workers, and you will leave with the wagons. I must go now for the dress you are to wear to the ball."

I balked at having to wear a dress and having to go to the ball, but I knew it was necessary. If I did not comply with Esteban's wish that I meet Maximilian, he might not leave me alone long enough for us to make our escape. Moreover, I might be able to obtain more information to take to President Juarez. After returning, Olga helped me put on a white tulle gown trimmed in Belgium lace.

"You are beautiful," she said as she combed my hair. "Do you not think she is beautiful, Jorge?"

"Teresa is very beautiful. But it is not because of the gown."

"Olga," I asked after she had secured a jeweled tiara in my hair, "how do Maximilian and Carlotta spend their time? What do they do each day?"

"Since arriving in Mexico, Maximilian has spent much of his time writing a book called *The Regulations of the Court*. It's a guide of instruction to the Mexican aristocracy. Their duties and privileges are outlined, and a description is given of the dress they are to wear to the various court functions. He has even drawn diagrams of where everyone is to stand at ceremonies or receptions. Carlotta gives lessons on etiquette to the daughters of the wealthy Mexican merchants."

"Why would they waste time on such things?"

"Maximilian and Carlotta believe that if they can make the Mexican aristocracy act like the European aristocracy, the people of Mexico will be more governable."

When Esteban called for me, I did not feel comfortable going into the corridors now crowded with women in elegant gowns and men in tails and top-hats. My brother said I would be the center of attention. As I held his arm and we entered the Grand Ballroom, I did feel I was being scrutinized by every pair of eyes of the several hundred people assembling in the expansive high-ceilinged room awash in the glow of thousands of candles mounted on crystal chandeliers. In one corner of the room was an orchestra playing Viennese waltzes. It seemed to take forever to walk across the parquet floor polished so brightly the light from the candles reflected on its surface.

As we walked, I saw Maximilian and Carlotta standing before two thrones on a platform elevated a foot above the level of the floor. The ornate, high-backed thrones were canopied in crimson velvet and surmounted with an Imperial Crown. On either side of the couple stood guards wearing chest-armor amd plumed helmets, and armed with halberds. Both the Emperor and Empress wore purple robes. Maximilian's robe was parted to reveal a white uniform similar to the naval uniform Esteban was wearing. Carlotta's robe was worn over a yellow silk gown. A heavy brooch, fashioned from emeralds and diamonds to resemble the leaves of a water plant, hung across her bosom.

Though by no means a small man, Maximilian probably seemed taller than he was because his legs were disproportionately long to his upper body. The most striking feature about the man was his golden beard, which was parted in the middle and combed in a backward swirl that made it appear as if he had a beard on each side of his face, rather than one beard at his chin. His hair, like his beard, was parted in the middle and combed to the back. He had a high forehead, and his deeply tanned face framed powder-blue eyes that sparkled with friendliness as we approached.

Carlotta's dark eyes were not friendly. She was a small woman; even on the platform, she had to tilt her head back to look at me. She narrowed her eyes in what I at first interpreted to be a haughty pout. I soon realized she was near-sighted and had to squint in order to see. Her snow-white complexion made her look even younger than her twenty-four years. Her long, dark hair had been shaped into a twist that hung over the front of her left shoulder.

Stopping before the couple, Esteban said, "Excellencies, I wish to present my sister, Maria de Jesus Teresa Sestos y Abrantes."

There was an awkward silence. I was not unmindful that I would be expected to curtsy. Instead, I nodded my head and said, "*Buenas noches, Señor y Señora von Hapsburg.*"

"My sister has just arrived," Esteban explained in a low voice. "She is unfamiliar with the protocols of the court."

"Quite all right," Maximilian said in a perfectly accented Spanish. His voice was almost as deep as Esteban's. "We cannot remember the last time anyone addressed us as Señor von Hapsburg. Indeed, we believe you may be the first to do so, dear Teresa." His smile was a curious mixture of sincerity and arrogance. "May we call you Teresa, or" —he arched his right eyebrow slyly— "should we call you Señorita Sestos y Abrantes?"

From the manner in which Maximilian laughed and looked at the dozens of faces quickly posturing smiles around him, I assumed the question had been made to demonstrate his ability to use humor to defuse an awkward situation. I found it discomforting that our private conversation was the focus of attention of several hundred people I did not know.

"You may call me what you wish, Señor von Hapsburg," I said with a touch more harshness than I may have intended.

Stepping from the platform to my level, Maximilian took my hands in both of his and said, "I shall be pleased if you would allow me to call you Teresa. Stefan is as close to me as any of my brothers. I would like to think that his sister is my sister. May I think of you as my sister? May I call you Teresa?"

As I looked into Maximilian's eyes, I saw a man with a profound need to be loved. At the corner of his mouth was a nervous twitch, and his hands were cold and damp.

"Yes, Señor von Hapsburg," I said when I became aware everyone in the room was waiting for my reply. "You may call me Teresa."

"And you will call me Maxl."

Though I had taken his words as a directive, he was waiting for my assent. "I will call you Maxl if it pleases you, Señor."

"In that case," he said, raising his hand toward the orchestra, "I shall exercise my prerogative to dance with my sister."

Before I could object, Maximilian had swept me into a fast turning skip-step around the ballroom while the onlookers scurried to get out of our way. Esteban escorted Carlotta to the floor, and they began to dance. Everyone else crowded against the walls and watched.

Smiling, Maximilian said, "You are an excellent dancer, Teresa. Kappelmeister Strauss should be here. He would say that no one has danced his 'Blue Danube' more gracefully than you."

"I do not know how to dance," I said while trying to catch a glimpse of Carlotta as a model for what I should be doing, though it was easy to follow Maximilian's lead. He had the grace of an athlete.

"You are far too beautiful to have never danced, Teresa. The young men of Texas must be fighting duels to win the right to dance with you."

"I did not say I have never danced. I danced once."

"Once?" he asked, raising an eyebrow. "It must have been a special someone. Yes?"

"It was someone special to me."

We glided past my brother who towered over the diminutive Carlotta. It did not appear that dancing was one of her favorite activities. I could see that she was talking to Esteban, and neither were smiling.

"I can keep a secret."

"It is no secret. The man I danced with was Sam Houston. He showed me how the Cherokees dance to celebrate a successful hunt. I was eight years old."

"Oh, yes," he said. "Stefan told me many stories about . . . what did he call him?"

"Old Chief."

"Yes. Old Chief. Stefan told me many stories of the daring adventures and exploits of Old Chief. I can't wait to visit Texas. Do you think the Texicans will like me when I pay them a visit, Teresa?"

I sensed the question was not casual. This man expected me to understand that it was not his manner to speak directly. Behind the facade of tutored charm was a serious man.

"I understand there are many German-speaking people in Texas," he continued before I could respond. "What would be their attitude toward a German prince?"

"I do not know . . ." —I almost addressed him again as Señor von Hapsburg— " . . .Maxl. A great many of the German-speaking people in Texas immigrated to the Americas to get away from German princes. The

German-speaking people of Texas are ardent supporters of liberty. Many now serve in the Union armies against the armies of the Confederacy."

Maximilian's smile became labored. "I did not know. I suppose I should not be surprised. One of the inevitable outcomes of republican government has always been dissension among contending interests. It is the root cause of the present conflict in the United States. A generation ago, the same circumstance produced the loss of many lives in France before the present emperor's uncle was able to restore order."

"Is that what Napoleon Bonaparte did? He restored order in France?"

"Indeed. Much as we are doing in Mexico. We shall protect the interests of all our people and make of them one family. The monarch is like a father to his people, Teresa. He stands above contending interests. A monarch will work tirelessly to assure the happiness and prosperity of all his children. Otherwise, there will always be the kind of conflict and competition for advantage that results, at the very least, in poverty and hopelessness; and, at worst, in the senseless bloodletting we witness today in the United States."

"And under a monarch there are no contending interests? There is no senseless bloodletting?"

"Not to the degree we have seen in republics."

"What occurred in Europe after Napoleon ended the French republic and restored order?"

Maximilian's expression turned to puzzlement.

"There was," I said, "continual war in Europe for years after Napoleon made himself the Emperor of France. Hundreds of thousands of people lost their lives as a result of his wars. European history is written in the blood of countless millions of people killed in wars to satisfy their monarchs' lust for wealth and power."

"Stefan did not tell me you were an historian, Teresa."

"I learned history from Sam Houston, Maxl. I wish you could have known him. He might have helped you to avoid some very serious mistakes."

"Ah!" Maximilian exclaimed as the orchestra finished the waltz. Following his example, everyone applauded. "Bravo! Are they not marvelous, Teresa? I intend to dispatch them on a tour throughout all of Mexico. To the villages. They will bring such joy to our people! Do you not agree?"

Maximilian escorted me to the platform where Carlotta and Esteban were waiting. The orchestra began another waltz, and the ballroom was soon crowded with hundreds of finely attired men and women bobbing up and down in a twirling glide around the hall.

Watching the dancers, Maximilian smiled and said, "Teresa, please allow me to show you something in my library. I think it will help you to understand what we are trying to do in Mexico. Stefan, would you be so good as to escort the Empress?"

Everyone applauded as we left the ballroom and walked down a long corridor behind and ahead of a cadre of guards. The guards in front carried halberds at arms length in the manner of medieval knights, while other guards carried rifles and appeared to be anything but ceremonial in their function. We paused where passageways intersected to allow men to make certain no one hid in ambush.

Just before reaching our destination, a Zouave officer approached Maximilian, bowed to Carlotta, and said, "Marshal Bazaine wishes to see you, Excellency."

"Now?"

"Yes, Excellency," the Frenchman said. "Now."

Maximilian asked my brother to accompany him and excused himself after ordering the guard to escort Carlotta and me to the library.

In the library, I was so overwhelmed by the long rows of leather-bound books that covered the walls from the floor to the high ceiling, I almost forgot that I was alone with a woman who thought she was the Empress of Mexico. When I looked at her, I could see she was agitated and disturbed. She twisted a lavender silk scarf in and around the tiny fingers of her white-gloved hands.

For a moment, I thought Carlotta was oblivious of my presence as she paced back and forth across the beautiful persian carpets of the long room. And then, turning quickly, she stared in my general direction and shouted, "He summoned my husband! Did you hear it? He summoned the Emperor to him. He does not go to the Emperor!"

There was little doubt as to who was the object of her ire, but I did not know what else to do except ask, "Who, Señora?"

"That liverish man!"

I was uncertain as to what 'liverish' meant. "Marshal Bazaine, Señora?"

"Yes! That braying jackass summons my husband to him as though he were the Emperor and Maxl were his lackey. He does it to humiliate us! Just wait until we raise our own army. He thinks because we need him he can treat us as lackeys in our Empire!"

It occurred to me that Carlotta probably did not understand that, except for Bazaine and his army, she and her husband would very likely be in jail in what she called "our Empire."

"I do not trust the man," Carlotta said.

"Why, Señora? Why do you not trust Marshal Bazaine?"

She focused her squint several inches above my head. "He is too cautious. Maxl and I are engaged in a great endeavor, one that requires bold action. Risks must be taken! Bazaine will risk nothing unless he has a guarantee of success. He is a coward!"

From everything I had heard, Achille Bazaine was no coward. One did not advance from the rank of private to that of a marshal in the most powerful army in the world by being a coward. Nevertheless, I found it interesting what Carlotta was saying about Bazaine's reluctance to take risks.

I was hoping Carlotta would say more about Bazaine, but she had walked away from me toward a small window at the far end of the room. Suddenly, she turned and ran back to where I stood.

"Señora von Hapsburg, what is wrong?"

"He is out there!"

The window was dark. It was impossible to see anything outside. "Who, Señora? Who is out there?"

"That little man. That dark, little man. He is out there."

"A man is outside the window?"

"The Indian! Benito Juarez! He is out there. He is coming for us. He wants to kill us. He will kill us!"

"Señora von Hapsburg, Benito Juarez is not outside. He is the President of Mexico. He does not wish to kill you. He only wishes for you to respect the laws of this country."

Her eyes took on a bizarre wildness. "He will kill Maxl. He will kill my husband! And I will be left alone in the world. I do not want to be alone in this world!"

I started to go to her to give her comfort, but at that moment Maximilian and Esteban came into the room.

"We have returned!" Maximilian said cheerfully without looking at his wife, who withdrew quickly toward the window. "A small matter. Bazaine had a communication from Miramon and Mejia he wished for me to read. Now, where were we? Ah yes, the map!"

Saying nothing to her husband of her belief that Benito Juarez was outside the window, Carlotta cocked her head in a manner that suggested she might be listening to someone not visible to the rest of us. I realized this woman was living on the edge of madness. When Esteban looked at her and then at me, I sensed he had long before come to the same conclusion.

Maximilian crossed the room, retrieved a large roll of thick paper from a bin and began to position it on top of a table. "Please, Teresa," he said. "This is what I wish to show you."

I walked to the table and helped Maximilian place weights on the paper to prevent it from curling into a roll. On the paper was a beautifully drawn map of the North American continent. Political territories were designated in various pastels of green, red, yellow and blue. Lettering had been done by the hand of a skilled calligrapher. The map was a work of art.

"Do you know what this is, Teresa?"

"It is a map of North American of around 1800."

"Very good! It is a map made for Napoleon in 1802. It shows the political boundaries at that particular time. What we propose to do is to restore those boundaries."

"The Viceroyalty of New Spain will be returned to Spain?"

"Oh, no!" he said and laughed. "Not to Spain. We shall rule this territory. But that" —he pointed to the Louisiana Territory— "shall revert to its original owner."

"Napoleon."

"Napoleon III."

Though I knew the answer to my question, I asked, "And what of the United States? The Louisiana Territory was sold to the United States in 1803."

Maximilian began to explain the provisions of the treaty that called for the return of the Louisiana Territory to France should the United States ever violate the property rights of the inhabitants of the territory. Abraham Lincoln's Emancipation Proclamation had, he said, violated those rights.

As Maximilian explained the legal basis for the introduction of French soldiers into Texas and an alliance with the Confederate States, it occurred to me that there was only one man who could stop this project. The French army was considered to be the most powerful military force in the world, and it was led by the military genius, Achille Bazaine. There was, however, one man who was a greater general than Marshal Bazaine; and that man commanded an army of battle-hardened veterans. At least, in my view, there was such a man. His name was Ulysses S. Grant.

I did not think General Grant could defeat the French army and the Confederate army together, but I had a hunch he could defeat Marshal Bazaine alone if he met him before the French had an opportunity to cross the Rio Grande. If Sam Grant could block Bazaine before he crossed into Texas, there may not even be a need for a battle. A cautious general, a general who weighed risks and did not like to gamble, might avoid a war he was likely to lose, especially if he knew his army would do battle with an army led by Ulysses Grant.

"Do you understand," Maximilian concluded, "what we are attempting to accomplish, Teresa?"

"I understand."

"Stefan and I have been planning this for years. I know it is important to him that you understand what we are doing."

I looked at my brother who at that moment did not seem to share his friend's enthusiasm.

"If you ally with the Confederacy," I said, "you will enable it to continue to exist. That means slavery will continue. Is that your wish, Esteban?"

"No," my brother said. "That is not our wish. Slavery will eventually end, even in the Confederacy. But for now, it is necessary to allow its continuance. The Confederate States will be a counterbalance to the United States. It is not good to allow one nation to dominate the entire continent. If the United States defeats the Confederacy, it will be in a position to control the resources of Mexico and her people. You would not wish for that to occur, would you, Teresa? We both know how the Anglo-Saxons treat Mexicans. We learned that as children."

My brother was sincere in what he believed, but I knew I would have to do everything I could to oppose him. Slavery must not continue for even one more day in the United States or the Confederate States. Nor could I stand by while the duly elected President of Mexico was hunted down like an outlaw and imprisoned or executed. I placed my hand to my head.

"Teresa?" Esteban said. "What's wrong?"

"I don't feel well."

"Oh," Maximilian said and touched my arm in a gesture of sympathy. "We must allow you to retire. It is getting late, and you have had a long day. Take her to her room, Stefan. We will have many opportunities to visit and talk."

At the door, I looked back at Carlotta, who was staring out the dark window. Before I left, Maximilian took my hands in his and said, "I am so happy you have come to live with us, Teresa. Stefan spoke of you with such tenderness over the years. I believe that today I have acquired a new sister."

Upstairs, outside Jorge's room, I asked Esteban if he could instruct the guards that I not be disturbed.

"I understand," he said and smiled. "You and Jorge have had to sacrifice your happiness for so many years. I know what that is like. I have been away from Jeanne for almost five years. I have not seen my son since he was a baby. But it will soon be over, Teresa. You and Jorge will be married. I will bring Jeanne and little Max to Mexico. We will all be very happy."

"Yes, Esteban. It will be over very soon."

"And Mother will be coming here," he said as if remembering something he had forgotten to tell me. "She wrote that she is planning to come to Mexico. Jacob is better, and she will not be afraid to leave him for a while."

"That is nice, Esteban. It will be good for you to see your mother."

Before leaving, Esteban instructed the guards that no one was to disturb me for any reason. I went into the room and locked the door.

Jorge was already dressed in the clothing of a laborer. I quickly changed into similar attire that Olga had smuggled into the room. She had also managed to get a long rope past the guards. We anchored it to the bed and tossed an end out the window. Two men, who were servants at the castle, climbed into the room, tied the end of the rope around Jorge's chest and gently lowered him to the ground. They did the same with me and then scaled down the side of the building to join us where Olga was waiting.

So as not to arouse suspicion, we walked unhurriedly to the area near the kitchen where wagons were being loaded with items to be taken back to the city. The Zouaves and Legionnaires had begun their celebration of the new year, and they were in no mood to pay attention to what we were doing as we drove a team off the castle grounds and down the steep incline. In a darkened area beneath a stand of trees, we transferred to another wagon which was to take us north of the city to a back trail where we would be met by people who would provide us with mules to ride to the mountains.

After helping Jorge to the deck, I turned to Olga who had accompanied us to the road. "When they discover we are gone, you will be suspected. Your life and the lives of the other servants will be in danger."

"That is why we are leaving. We need no more information. We know what is going to happen. The time has come to fight."

"Where will you go?"

"I am going south to join my husband in the army of Porfirio Diaz. Our prayers will be with you, Teresa. I hope we meet again someday."

We embraced.

"*Viva Juarez*," Olga whispered.

"*Viva Juarez*," I said.

We traveled at night and slept during the day to reduce the risks of being seen by French soldiers. In the countryside, the nights belonged to the Juaristas. Word was sent ahead of our progress, and we were met at various places by one or more people with mules or horses. Occasionally, we rode burros. We were given food and drink and blankets for the cool nights. Most of the people who helped us were elderly or young children. Men and women our age were with the guerilla bands that harassed the French.

About three weeks out of the capital, one of our guides was a woman named Rosa, who said she had followed Miguel Hidalgo in 1810. When I told her of my grandmother, she said she had known Carmen and my grandfather.

"I remember them very well," she said. "Carmen and Coalter Owens were very brave. And they were very much in love."

Rosa told us that few people knew where Benito Juarez was. It was the way they wanted it in case they were captured by the French or the Mexican royalists led by Miramon and Mejia. Even if they were tortured, they would be unable to tell where the president was.

"Sometimes," Rosa said, "President Juarez goes to the mountains. Sometimes, the sea. Benito Juarez is everywhere."

If few people knew where the president was, we wondered how we were supposed to find him; but late one night, a twelve year-old girl became our guide and within an hour we found ourselves suddenly surrounded by fifty men with muskets. I knew by their manner of dress they were neither French soldiers nor Mexican royalists. We were being stopped as a precaution against the possibility of our being spies or assassins.

A man began to question us but stopped when a woman cried, "Teresa! Jorge!"

It was Josefa. Gripping a machete, she came running from the darkness and threw her arms around us both before we could warn her about Jorge's arm.

"Oh, poor one," Josefa said when she saw the limp arm. "Let us get you to camp. We have been expecting you. Hurry!"

Josefa looked the same as when we had lived in New Orleans; and at the camp of several hundred people, I greeted a number of the people who had been with us in New Orleans. Everyone embraced me and touched Jorge gently so as not to injure his arm. Soon, Jorge was being attended by a physician, and I was finally able to relax. Not once during the journey had he complained, but I knew that every step of the way had been painful for him.

Backing away from the crowd around Jorge, I bumped into someone behind me. Turning, I found myself looking into the dark, steady eyes of Benito Juarez. He was wearing a black suit, white shirt, black ribbon-tie, and a tall stovepipe hat.

"Don Benito!" I shouted and wrapped my arms around the President of the Republic of Mexico before he could remove his hat.

"Teresa," he said in his soft baritone. "How are you?"

"I am fine, Don Benito."

"And Jorge?" he asked, looking past me to where the physician was having to send away people who wanted to help. "His arm? It is bad?"

"Yes, Don Benito. It is bad."

He stepped to where Jorge had been placed on a cot and was being examined by a physician. When Jorge saw the president, he reached for his hand and would not release it. For several moments, Don Benito did not move. Before leaving, he bent down and kissed Jorge's forehead.

Returning to where I stood, he said, "You have come from the capital?"

"Yes, Don Benito. There is something I must tell you. It is very important."

He escorted me to a folding table that had been set up next to the small black carriage he used to travel around Mexico. The capital of the republic was wherever that carriage happened to be. President Juarez sat down on a wooden chair behind the table, and I sat on a chair across from him.

I hardly knew where to begin, so I took out the document Sam Houston had given me and explained its significance.

"May I see it?" he asked.

"It is in English, Don Benito."

"I can read a little English. My time in New Orleans was not entirely wasted." He smiled. "We did not spend all of our time rolling cigars, did we, Teresa?"

"No, Don Benito, but the cigars we did roll were good ones."

The president's smile faded as he read through the pages of the paper. When he had finished, he reassembled the pages, tapped the edges to make a neat stack and placed them on the table before him. He folded his hands and stared in the direction of the small campfires while I told him of what Maximilian had said in the library.

Finally, the president said, "All this should come as no surprise to us. We know that Marshal Bazaine is massing his troops on the border with Texas. We have had reports of increasing numbers of Confederate soldiers entering Mexico. They have established two camps: one at the city of Cordova outside of Vera Cruz and the other just south of Matamoros at a town they are calling Carlotta."

"They have stockpiled weapons and gunpowder on the Rio Grande."

"Yes," he said and his face saddened. "I know about those stockpiles, and I was told of what your grandmother and her friends did to destroy one of them, Teresa. I am very sorry. They sacrificed their lives for people on both sides of the border."

Josefa joined us. "The physician says there is nothing he can do for Jorge's arm. He says it may have to be removed."

"No," I said and started to get up.

"Stay," Josefa said, touching my shoulders. "The physician gave him something to make him sleep."

President Juarez related to Josefa the things I had told him and explained the meaning of the document.

"We must go to the border," Josefa said. "We cannot allow the French to go into Texas and join with the Confederate armies. If it happens, we will never drive them from Mexico."

"We do not have the resources to stop the French from entering Texas," the president said.

"Then the Americans must do it, Don Benito."

"I do not think they will. I have exchanged letters with President Lincoln; and our ambassador, Mateo Romero, has spoken with him many times. Mr. Lincoln is in sympathy with our cause, but he will not involve his nation in a war with France. On this point, his Secretary of State, Mr. Seward, is even more adamant. The Union is defeating the Confederacy on the battlefield. The war will soon be over, but Mr. Lincoln will not send his soldiers to the border."

"If he does not," Josefa said, "the war could begin again. The Confederacy is losing because they ran low on weapons and gunpowder. The French can provide them with both."

"I do not know what more I can do, Josefa. Ambassador Romero has conferred with President Lincoln on this matter many times."

"Don Benito," I said. "There is a man who can convince President Lincoln of the importance of sending his armies to prevent the French from entering Texas."

"Oh, Teresa? Who is that?"

"The General of his Armies, Ulysses S. Grant."

He looked at me. "Well, yes. Of course. If General Grant made the case, I think Mr. Lincoln would be inclined to follow his advice. But who will convince General Grant of the need to commit his army to a course that could involve the United States in a war with France?"

"I can convince him, Don Benito."

The president looked at Josefa and back to me. "I do not understand."

I related how I had come to know Sam Grant when he was a lieutenant in Zachary Taylor's army on the Rio Grande during the war between the United States and Mexico. I told of how Sam Grant had objected to that war and expressed his admiration for the people of Mexico.

"Sam Grant is a good man, Don Benito," I said. "He hates war. He will do what is necessary to prevent the war he is ending from beginning again and destroying more lives. I know I can convince him of the necessity of putting a Union army on the Rio Grande. I believe that if he were to do that, Marshal Bazaine will back down. He will not run the risk of losing to the American army. But it is vital that he be blocked before he comes into Texas and the Confederate soldiers can be supplied with more weapons and gunpowder. General Grant cannot defeat both armies."

President Juarez removed his hat and rubbed his temples with his fingertips. He looked at me. "Then you must go and see General Grant."

It was what I wanted him to say, but I did not have the first idea of how to do it.

Sensing my dilemma, the president said, "We can arrange for you to get to Washington, Teresa. We have friends who know how to elude the French. The quickest way will be by boat across the Gulf and up the Atlantic. We will send a message to Tampico to have a boat readied for you. However, I do not want you to go alone."

"She will not go alone," Josefa said. "Teresa and I have had experience with boats. I will go with her to Washington."

"Very good," the president said. "I will have a message sent at once to Tampico, and I will have a telegram sent to Ambassador Romero of your mission. You and Josefa can depart as soon as you get some sleep."

I looked across at where Jorge was now asleep.

"I think I had rather go now, Don Benito, before Jorge awakens. I do not think I can say good-bye to him again. I cannot—"

When I lost the battle to hold back my tears, Benito Juarez got to his feet, walked around the table and embraced me. He held me until I stopped crying.

XIV

Unlike on our previous voyage across the Gulf, Josefa and I were not required to stoke the fires in the engine room or steer the vessel around sand bars and reefs. Though by no means a luxury ship, our sturdy two-hundred-foot craft was designed to transport passengers between Mexico, Cuba and the Atlantic coast of the United States. The captain, a white-haired man we knew only as Saturnino, was a long-time supporter of Benito Juarez; he spared no effort to make certain our journey was comfortable and would accept no payment for our passage. Saturnino had no idea of the nature of our mission, but a handwritten note from President Juarez was all that was necessary for him to drop everything and speed us on our way as rapidly as the boat's engines and the weather would allow.

After a surprisingly smooth Gulf crossing, the weather became an impediment to our progress as we entered the Atlantic and advanced northward along the eastern seaboard. We wasted many precious days sheltered in coves along the Florida coast until winds died and waves subsided enough for us to resume our voyage. Storms made it difficult to secure the dry wood necessary to fuel the engines. Knowing only that we were on our way to Washington City in service of President Juarez, the five-man crew worked diligently to push the ship as fast as possible. Each told us that he, too, was a Juarista and had lost relatives or friends as a result of the French incursion.

Entering the harbor at Savannah to take on supplies and fuel, we were encouraged to see the flag of the United States flying at the customhouse. Was it possible, we wondered, that the war between the states was over? We prayed that it was because it would mean no more lost lives. It would also mean that slavery was finally at an end. What the cessation of the war signified as far as Mexico was concerned we did not know. It could mean that American armies were available to confront the French on the border. Or the defeat of the Confederate armies might make the southern states even more eager to embrace a powerful ally able to supply them with the guns and gunpowder they had lost in what could turn out to be only the first stage of the war between the north and the south.

We soon discovered the war was not over. The harbormaster told us that Savannah had been captured in December by the army of General

Sherman. Destroying everything along a sixty-mile front, Sherman's army of a hundred thousand men had crossed the entire state of Georgia. Sherman was now advancing north through the Carolinas while the Union Army of the Potomac was pushing General Lee's Army of Virginia to the south. Though under the command of General Meade, the Army of the Potomac's pursuit of Robert E. Lee was being personally directed by Ulysses Grant.

Josefa asked, "Does it mean the war will be over if General Lee is defeated?"

"Not necessarily," I replied. "Some of the soldiers at the customhouse said there are two large Confederate armies in the west. One is led by General Joe Johnston and the other is under the command of General Kirby Smith."

What we learned in Savannah was cause for concern, especially the news of the Confederate armies in the west. If the full power of the Union was being concentrated in Virginia to destroy Robert E. Lee's army, what was there to prevent the armies of Johnston and Kirby Smith from going to Texas to join forces with the French? If Grant defeated Lee, would his armies be able to march over a thousand miles to Texas and engage rested Confederate armies newly supplied and backed by a powerful French army under the command of Marshal Achille Bazaine?

We entered the mouth of the Potomac River on Thursday, April 13. It was late evening by the time we secured the boat at a pier on the outskirts of Washington City. Strangely, there were no people on the riverfront. Hearing the sounds of guns being fired from the direction of the city, Saturnino urged us to delay going into town for fear the war had come to the capital itself. As we continued to listen, we realized the shots were not those of a battle. Church bells were being rung, and we heard the sound of voices in song.

"The war is over," Josefa said. "People are celebrating."

Saturnino insisted he accompany Josefa and me into town. Though we realized the government offices would likely be closed, I wanted to locate the War Department so we would not waste time the following morning in trying to find where I hoped Sam Grant would be.

We encountered an assemblage of people gathered around a large bonfire in a vacant lot. They were singing a hymn. I approached an elderly negro woman and asked what was happening.

The woman had probably never seen anyone in a serape, and she looked at me and then at Josefa and Saturnino with a puzzled expression. "You don't know?"

"No, Señora. We have only just arrived in this country. We are from Mexico."

"Mexico?"

"We have been at sea. Is the war over? Is that why you are celebrating?"

She smiled. "Yes, young lady. The war is over. We were about to offer a prayer. Would you join us?"

We bowed our heads while a man delivered a prayer of thanksgiving. I then inquired if anyone could give us directions to our destination.

"See that wide street up there?" a man asked. "That's Pennsylvania Avenue. You go up there and turn right. The streets are numbered. You keep going until you come to 17th Street. You will see a red brick building surrounded by soldiers."

As we walked along the streets, we passed hundreds of people gathered in small groups and no small number simply standing alone, lost in thought. Many were singing or kneeling in prayer. In thousands of windows were lit candles, and lighted transparencies adorned the government buildings. The entire city was aglow with amber light made soft by a fine mist in the air. Lights were reflected on the water standing in the ruts of the dirt streets that intersected the broad, cobblestoned Pennsylvania Avenue. Up and down the streets, we heard the sound of laughter. And we heard people crying.

There was no difficulty in identifying which building was the War Department. Its red-brick facade shone brightly from the dancing flames of dozens of bonfires around which soldiers in blue uniforms had gathered to talk and laugh and celebrate. Many carried rifles, but most weapons had been stacked in tripods that circled the building like a long picket fence. The air was heavy with the aroma of the smoke from the bonfires and the tobacco many of the men were smoking.

We stopped at the entrance to the War Department. The heavy wooden doors were closed and guarded by armed soldiers standing at parade-rest. Seeing lights in the windows, I decided to inquire as to whether General Grant might not at that moment be in the building. A barrel-chested sergeant-major looked at me suspiciously when I posed my query.

"General Grant is in his office," the sergeant said and narrowed his eyes. "Why do you ask?"

"I would like to see him."

"The War Department is closed for the day, Miss," the sergeant said. "It will open tomorrow at seven in the morning."

"Sergeant, if General Grant is told I am here, he will see me. I am a friend of his, and I have just come from Mexico with information he will wish to have. It is extremely important."

"You are a friend of General Grant?"

"I am."

The way the sergeant's eyes smoldered, I knew he was not the kind of man to tolerate nonsense; but he was also a sergeant-major, that special breed of men who make armies function by knowing when to stand firm and when to bend. "How do you come to know General Grant, Miss?"

As briefly as I could, I related my acquaintance with General Grant during the Mexican-American War.

The sergeant studied my face. "Come with me," he said. "But just you. You other two wait outside. And you had best not be lying to me, Miss."

Josefa and Saturnino assured me they would be all right, and I followed the sergeant inside and down a corridor to a desk, behind which sat a young lieutenant.

Drawing himself to attention before the officer, the burly sergeant said, "Sir, this woman wishes to see General Grant."

The lieutenant, who had been reading a newspaper, raised his head slowly and looked at me. He then focused a disapproving scowl at the sergeant. "I thought I made it clear that the General is seeing no one tonight, certainly not a woman dressed like this. Who is this woman?"

"She says she knows General Grant from when he was in the Mexican war. She says she has important information for him." He looked down at the officer. "I believe her."

Fortunately, the young lieutenant understood the wisdom of trusting the intuition of a sergeant-major. After again looking at my serape, he said, "I'll tell the General."

The sergeant came to attention, saluted, and marched down the corridor and out to his post.

Rising from the desk, the lieutenant clearly did not relish the task of going into the office of the Commanding General of the American Army.

When he hesitated, I asked, "Is General Grant alone?"

"He is."

"I have not seen General Grant in a good many years. I would like to surprise him."

The young officer shook his head. "I don't know, ma'am. General Grant is not fond of surprises."

"Please. Don't announce me. Just open the door."

"Well," he said and pulled at his collar, "I'm probably going to be cleaning stables tomorrow, but follow me."

He knocked and opened the door. I followed him inside.

The large office was lit by only a single candle. Standing behind his desk, his back to us, and staring out a dark window as if lost in abstract thought was Sam Grant. I immediately recognized the reddish-brown hair and the slight but compact build. Calculating the passage of years since I had seen him as a lieutenant fresh out of West Point, I realized he was only forty-two years old. Sam was still a young man. He seemed especially young to be the first lieutenant-general in the American army since George Washington.

"Sir?"

"Yes, Lieutenant. What do you want?"

The young officer's eyes pleaded for me to speak up, so I said, "Sam? ¿Como esta usted?"

Sam had been smoking a cigar. Without turning, he removed the cigar from his mouth and cocked his head slightly to the right, revealing the beard he had first begun to grow on the Rio Grande.

"I have come for my math lesson, Sam."

When he turned, I saw the startled expression in those clear eyes almost void of color.

"Lieutenant," he said. "That will be all. Thank you."

"Yes, sir!" the officer snapped, drew a breath for the first time, and quickly exited the room.

Dousing the cigar in a half-empty whiskey glass on a desk piled with mounds of papers, Sam hurried across the room and embraced me.

Except for the stars on his shoulder insignia, his uniform did not look so very different from when he had been a second lieutenant. The jacket was buttoned wrong exactly as it had been the first time I had seen him in uniform outside our farm. Looking into his face, I was surprised at how little he had changed. The lines were a little deeper around now sunken cheeks, but his face conveyed the same youthful energy and quiet intelligence that I had witnessed as a fifteen year-old girl.

"How are you, Sam?"

Continuing to hold my hands, he stepped back to look at me and smiled. "Teresa, I . . ."–he shook his head–"I am so happy to see you."

"I am happy to see you, Sam."

"Please," he said, escorting me to his desk where he offered a chair, "sit down." He sat in another visitor's chair opposite mine. "Tell me why you are here. And . . . Your grandmother! Is Señora Owens here? Is she with you?"

I could see my own sadness reflected in his expression as I told him what had happened to Carmen.

"I am sorry, Teresa."

There was so much to tell him, I did not know where to begin. Of course, one thing came before everything else. "Sam, is the war over? The Confederacy has surrendered?"

"No, Teresa. General Lee has surrendered his army, but that's about it. Davis and his so-called government"–his eyes revealed anger–"have fled south and vow to continue fighting. Joe Johnston is still in the field with an army. Many of the Confederate soldiers are going west, vowing to fight on in guerilla bands." He leaned forward. "Why are you here, Teresa? I am glad to see you, but I know you would not come to Washington City just for a visit."

As much as I would have wished to visit with Sam and learn of what had happened in those years since the war on the Rio Grande, I knew we must waste no time. Handing him the document given me by Sam Houston, I told him of the secret alliance between the French and the Confederacy. As I talked, he read the pages of the document. I told him of how President Juarez had agreed I should come to him and explain the danger to both the United States and Mexico of a French incursion into Texas.

When I had finished, Sam got up an paced to the window behind his desk. For several minutes, he stared outside. Finally, he turned and asked, "How did you come to be involved in this, Teresa? Why were you given this document by Sam Houston?"

"I do not know if you recall, but my brother and my mother moved to Austria to live with my stepfather just before my grandmother and I went to the Rio Grande."

"Yes. I remember your telling me."

"My brother, Esteban, is very close to Maximilian von Hapsburg. They grew up together. They are like brothers. I'm afraid Esteban is deeply involved in what is being planned. Sam Houston gave me that document because he knew my brother, and because he was worried the plan could destroy the Union. My brother took me to Mexico City to meet Maximilian von Hapsburg. It is where they took Jorge when he was wounded."

His eyes narrowed. "Jorge was wounded? You did not tell me about Jorge."

"Yes. He is . . ." Suddenly, I felt very tired. "Jorge may lose his arm, Sam. He—I—"

Quickly, he knelt beside me at the chair and patted my hand as my tears flowed.

"Teresa," he said softly. "How long has it been since you have had any sleep?"

"I don't remember."

Sam helped me get to my feet. "How did you come here? I mean, how did you get to Washington City? You did not come overland?"

I explained about the boat and told him of Josefa and Saturnino.

"Teresa, I am going to arrange for you to stay in a hotel near here; you and your friends." He must have read the puzzlement in my expression, because he continued, "The information you have brought confirms something I have long suspected. But I need you to do something for me. Tomorrow morning, I have to be at a cabinet meeting with the president. I don't want to bring up any of what you've told me at that meeting, but I want you to come with me to see President Lincoln before we meet. I want you to tell him exactly what you've told me tonight."

"Sam," I said, shaking my head, "I can't meet President Lincoln. I do not have the proper clothes. I—"

"You look fine," he interrupted. "I'm going to have you and your friends taken to the Willard's Hotel. I want you to get a good night's sleep. I'll come for you at 6 a.m. sharp."

Before I left, I asked, "How is General Lee?"

"He is glad it is over. He is ready to go home."

That night, I was unable to sleep despite an aching tiredness in my body. All through the night, I lay in bed listening to the sounds of gun-shots, bells, horns, drums, people talking and laughing. They were convinced that because of Robert E. Lee's surrender of the Army of Virginia the war was over. They did not know Confederate armies were still on the move, some going west, ever closer to the powerful ally that could supply them with the means to launch the war anew in a fury as yet unknown on the North American continent.

Before dawn, I dressed and sat at the window. Just as the day was about to begin, the people in the city had finally gone to sleep. Every now and then, a wagon rolled by, its way lit by street lamps hung on poles at the intersections. Vendors were delivering fresh produce to the hotel's kitchen. I could see the Capitol building which was being renovated. Further down, I could see the partially completed white stone obelisk which was being constructed as a monument to the nation's first president. Everything seemed to be only partially completed in Washington City.

In the stillness of that hour, my thoughts were, as always, two thousand miles to the south. I wondered what Jorge was doing at that very moment. I tried very hard not to think he had lost his arm, or worse. Sensing what was going through my heart, Josefa came and sat beside me. She put her arms around me and held me.

"Do not worry," she said. "Jorge will be all right. Don Benito won't let anything happen to him."

I was thankful Jorge's aunt was with me. I do not know what I would have done without her.

Sam's carriage arrived ten minutes before six o'clock. An escort of dragoons surrounded the coach, and the soldiers, rifles in hand, watched in all directions as I rushed from the hotel and accepted a sergeant's hand to climb inside. I sat on the seat next to Sam. Once settled, he patted my arm but said nothing as we rode down the bumpy cobblestone street called Pennsylvania Avenue. From the puffiness around Sam's eyes, I suspected he had gotten no more sleep than I had. With an unlit cigar in his mouth, he spent most of the ride gazing out the window.

The team struggled to pull the carriage in the deep, muddy ruts of the driveway that took us to the main portico of the Executive Mansion. A doorman opened the carriage gate and extended his hand to help me to the ground. Exiting behind me, Sam took my arm and hurried me inside where I was immediately struck by the musty odor of the entrance hall. The rugs were caked with mud. Sam asked me to wait in a room wallpapered in red. The tall windows of the room were draped with shabby red damask curtains, and the chairs were upholstered in horsehide.

After a few moments wait, Sam returned and said the president was ready to see me. We climbed up a great staircase and walked down a long, dark corridor, the only light coming from a single large window. Servants rushed past us in all directions. Soldiers came to attention as Sam hurried ahead, pulling me gently by the hand. We came to a wooden railing with a gate, which was opened for our passage by an old negro gentleman. Sam paused to glance inside a large green room filled with servants placing glasses on a long table. He told me it was the room where the cabinet would meet later that morning.

Next to the cabinet room, we entered a small office lit only by a single kerosene lamp whose flickering wick made the shadows on the white plaster wall wave like grass in a field. In a dark corner of the room, sitting in front of a high-back pigeonhole desk, was President Lincoln. He had been reading, but he removed his spectacles and slowly got to his feet when Sam closed the door behind us. Though a tall man, he was stooped and appeared to be having difficulty in straightening.

Extending his hands in an offer to help, Sam asked, "Is it your back again, sir?"

Smiling, the president said, "No, General Grant. I have decided to become a closer student of the earth, and this posture accommodates that ambition."

I was surprised that a man of Mr. Lincoln's size would have such a high-pitched voice. He was a most impressive man to behold. His lean face was marked by many wrinkles and deep creases that told of a man who had borne a heavy burden for a very long time. The lid of his left eye drooped lazily, but the right eye had the sparkle of a man of good humor who enjoyed the company of people. His eyes were the same shade of grey as Sam Houston's, and I thought I could detect the same mischievous twinkle I had so loved in my old friend and teacher. I was reminded of Sam Houston because of a portrait of his mentor, Andrew Jackson, hung in Mr. Lincoln's office.

Twisting his back until it creaked and popped, which allowed him to stand a little taller, the president drawled, "Reckon I slept crooked last night. Got a ketch in my back. But I slept good, nonetheless. Had the most remarkable dream."

Sam asked, "What did you dream, Mr. President?"

Although we had yet to be introduced, President Lincoln looked at me when he said, "It was a strange dream. I was on the shore somewhere by a great body of dark water. A ship was coming toward me. I call it a ship, but it was like nothing I had ever seen. You'd have to say it was inde-scribable. It was coming to the shore, but the shore, too, was most peculiar. It was an indescribable ship moving over dark waters to an indefinite shore. Most odd, but quite enchanting."

"You've had that dream before, sir."

"I have. I've had that dream before some of our great victories. Antietam. Gettysburg. Stone's River. Your victory at Vicksburg, General Grant. It always seems to occur before some great and momentous event."

Mr. Lincoln had the most genuinely kind face I had ever seen. Though he wore chin whiskers, his upper lip was shaven, revealing a wide mouth always framed in a smile. The spectacles, still dangling in his long fingers, looked as though they had been broken and patched with pieces of wire and string.

"Well, enough of that," President Lincoln said. "Please introduce me to our guest, General Grant."

Sam made the introduction, and we both declined the president's offer of coffee or food. I explained to him about serapes after he showed great interest in mine. He inquired about President Juarez and spoke of his admiration for him and his desire to meet him someday.

After we sat down and the president had settled back into a battered old maplewood armchair, he said, "So you knew General Grant when he was just a shave-tail fresh out of the academy and down on the Rio Grande in that sad episode of our nation's history. Tell me, Señorita Sestos, what sort of man was General Grant back then?"

Looking at Sam, I was unsure of what to say. "Well," I began and hes-itated. "He was a quiet man."

"A quiet man," he said. "Yes. General Grant is a quiet man. Who was it that said, 'Blessed are they who have nothing to say and can't be per-suaded to say it'? Who said that, General Grant? Was it St. John or St. Peter who said that?"

"I believe it was St. Abraham who said it, sir; and I believe he has said it on more than one occasion."

President Lincoln brought his hand down on a bony knee and laughed with vigor.

"Sir?" Sam asked and glanced at me and back to the president. "Did you take a look at the document I brought you?"

The smile did not completely vanish from his face as Mr. Lincoln reached to his desk and retrieved what I recognized to be the document I had given Sam the night before. It was what he had been reading when we came in.

"Yes, I have. And just before you returned, I sent Robert over to the State Department to find me the original treaty that President Jefferson made with Napoleon to acquire the Louisiana Territory. I want to take a look at that."

"Yes, sir. You should. But suspect it's exactly as it was represented to Governor Houston."

"I expect you're right, especially if President Tyler had a hand in it. He was a right smart lawyer and one of our finest diplomats."

Sam asked me to relate to Mr. Lincoln everything I had told him, which I did as best as I could.

The president was clearly disturbed by what he was hearing. He drummed his fingers on his desk. "Señorita Sestos," he asked, "this Maximilian von Hapsburg is a fairly young man, is he not?"

"Yes, sir. He's in his early thirties."

"I think that accounts for part of this peculiar undertaking down there. Maximilian is young and ambitious. Young men dream big and often don't think ahead to the consequences."

I thought of my brother. President Lincoln could have been describing Esteban.

"With all due respect, sir," Sam said. "Maximilian von Hapsburg is not the problem. He would not last a month against Benito Juarez if he had to rely on his Austrian and Belgium troops. We're facing this threat because of Louis Bonaparte, no one else.

"Remember, Mr. President, Louis Bonaparte has already acquired territories in Africa and Asia. He is securing a vast source of inexpensive raw materials for his industries. Mexico gives him enormous mineral resources. But that is only half of the equation. He needs markets. Our industries in the north are his competitors. Our tariffs have cut him out of our markets. If the Confederacy stands, it would provide him an enormous market for his manufactured goods. If he reacquires Louisiana for France, it would be both a market and a source of raw materials.

"He would also succeed in preventing the United States from growing into a power that could challenge French industry. California, the entire Pacific coast, would be his. Bonaparte is playing for very high stakes, sir. This is something that has been planned for a long time. He has the full backing of his bankers. They would not be footing the bill for the army he has in Mexico if they did not expect a good return on their investment. This venture of his has not come cheap, although much of it has been paid for by southern cotton."

President Lincoln nodded solemnly. "He hurt us mighty bad with letting that cotton come out of Texas and into Mexico."

"Yes, he did," Sam agreed. "This war should have been over two, maybe three, years ago. Our blockade was only an inconvenience to the rebels. They were selling their cotton in 1863 and 1864 at a rate higher than before the war. That gave them the money to buy the weapons and powder they brought in through Texas from Mexico. Bonaparte is responsible for the deaths of tens of thousands of my boys, and I'll hate that man till the day I die."

The president rubbed his face. The smile was now gone from his lips. "What do we do, General Grant? What can we do? You know how I've been opposed to war with France. Seward's against it too. How can we go to the American people after all they've been through and ask them to sacrifice more of their boys. I don't believe I can do that."

Sam got to his feet and walked to the window from which could be seen the Potomac and the hills of Virginia beyond. He turned to face Mr. Lincoln. "Sir, we have no choice. When you made me the General of the Army, I guaranteed you a victory over the Confederate armies. That mission is almost accomplished. Marshal Bazaine has his troops massed in northern Mexico. If he comes across the border with munitions and supplies enough for the Confederates, they will join him. Together, they would have an army I cannot defeat. Bonaparte has warships in the Gulf of Mexico that could destroy our navy in days. He could bring those ships to our eastern ports, and we would be defenseless."

President Lincoln said, "What I don't understand is why Bonaparte has not sent Marshal Bazaine across the Rio Grande before now. He has his legal pretense in this treaty by which we purchased the Louisiana Territory. Why did they not come on across last year or the year before when we were fighting for our lives with the rebels?"

"The French have not been able to come across because of Benito Juarez, sir. The people of Mexico, armed with little more than machetes and muskets, have never stopped harassing the French armies since they came ashore at Vera Cruz. Bazaine could not come across into Texas as long as there was a threat that Benito Juarez would cut off his lines of supply from the ports."

Looking at me, the president asked, "Cannot President Juarez continue to keep them pinned down?"

"Not for long, sir," I replied. "The Juaristas are almost out of powder, and their weapons are falling apart in their hands. They will never stop fighting, but they will not for long be a threat to Bazaine's lines of supply should he enter Texas."

The president drew a deep breath. "I ask again, General Grant. What can we do?"

"We stop them before they can get into Texas, sir. We meet them at the Rio Grande. If necessary, we fight them and we defeat them before they can be joined by the rebels."

"Can you defeat them?"

"I can defeat Marshal Bazaine. If I can get a large enough force on the Rio Grande before he crosses, I do not think I will even have to fight him. He knows I can defeat him alone. And I'm certain he has conveyed this to Bonaparte. Louis Bonaparte cannot afford to have Bazaine's army defeated or even weakened in a costly victory. The Prussians are rebuilding their army. If Bazaine is defeated or weakened, the Prussians will attack France. If Bonaparte's gamble succeeds and he wins Louisiana and secures the independence of the Confederate States, the Prussians will then be very reluctant to take on the French."

President Lincoln looked weary. "Do we have to make a decision today?"

"Each day we delay works in Bazaines favor. I suspect he is waiting for remnants of the Confederate army to move toward him to Texas. Already, we have reports of large numbers of rebels crossing the Rio Grande and setting up camps in Mexico. That is why it is necessary for us to act as soon as possible. Last night, I looked at our deployments. I have troops in Mobile and in Arkansas that I could move to the Rio Grande in a matter of weeks. I have a surplus of fifty-thousand rifles that I could take to the Rio Grande and make available to Benito Juarez. We can provide him with gunpowder. But we must do it quickly."

"Why don't we bring this up at the cabinet meeting this morning?"

"I'd rather you didn't, sir. I would rather you not say anything about this or even our meeting this morning. We have intelligence that the capital is filling with rebel agents, hoping to do by other means what they could not accomplish on the battlefield. We cannot take a chance that word gets out that we are going to deploy a large force on the Rio Grande. Marshal Bazaine may move up his timetable before I am in place to block him. Let me organize my force before you say anything to the cabinet."

"Who will be your commander?"

Without hesitation, Sam said, "Philip Sheridan. He's my most aggressive general. With Sheridan in command of the operation, Bazaine will know we are ready to fight. And if Bonaparte does not order a withdrawal within a short period of time, I will personally take command of the army on the Rio Grande."

Again, the president shook his head at the prospect of sending his army into war so soon after seeming to win a victory in his country's most bloody conflict. He pulled a gold watch from his pocket and looked at it. "I guess I best go wake up Mrs. Lincoln. She wants to go buy herself a new dress for the theatre tonight. You and Mrs. Grant are coming with us, aren't you?"

"I don't know, Mr. President. Julia wants to go to Burlington to see the children. We've not seen them in a while."

Turning to me, President Lincoln asked, "How about you, Señorita Sestos? Would you like to come with us to the theatre tonight? It's a comedy. We could all do with a little lighthearted humor."

"I am very tired, sir."

"I understand," he said, taking my hands in both of his. "You've had a very long and arduous journey to come here. I know General Grant is most appreciative. I certainly am. You have rendered a great service to our nation. I'll look forward to meeting you again soon under more pleasant circumstances. Maybe I'll come visit you down there in Texas after I retire. I've always wanted to see Texas."

"You will be very welcome, Mr. President. I will look forward to it."

Sam escorted me downstairs and to the portico where he summoned his driver and escort. He ordered them to take me back to the hotel and place a guard at the door. I told him I was very anxious to return to Mexico, but he insisted that I remain under guard until he could organize his army for the Rio Grande. When he said I was not to leave my room, I thought he was being overly cautious and told him so.

"I can assure you," he said, "that rebel spies are aware that you came to my office last night. I cannot take a chance that they would capture you and try to discover why I took you to see the president. I am going to begin the immediate movement of troops to the Rio Grande. I will tell no one the reason, not even Sheridan, until I have everything in place. We cannot take a chance on the French coming across and linking up with the rebels before I'm in a position to block them. I'm sorry, Teresa, but I'm going to have to continue to confine you and your friends to your rooms until I have everything in place."

Back at the hotel, I explained to Josefa why we were confined to the room under a guard of soldiers outside our door and why more soldiers were at the entrance to the corridor leading to our room. Saturnino and his crew were in a room across the hall. Josefa urged me to try to get some sleep after insisting I eat a little of the fruit and bread that had been brought to the room along with coffee and pastries.

Though exhausted, I could not sleep and spent most of the day looking out the window at the coming and going of people on the streets of the capital. At Josefa's insistence I stretched out on the bed at dusk and made an effort to clear my head. When the night descended, the noise outside grew louder as more people took to the streets and commenced their celebrations anew. I began to doze, waking from time to time whenever I heard Josefa at the door talking to our guards. She had given them much of the food that had been sent to our room. It happened that most of the soldiers of our guard were from Ireland, and they took pride in guarding people of their faith. It was Good Friday, and some of them were planning to go to a midnight mass.

I awoke with a start when I heard a noise. The room was dark, and I thought perhaps the sound had been part of a strange dream I had been having. My father and I were gathering shells on the shore of Galveston Bay. As we walked on the beach in the company of a woman I did not know, he recited a beautiful poem to me. Awake, I was not certain where I was. When I heard Josefa talking to the soldiers, I relaxed and tried to go back to sleep so that I might again see my father and hear his voice. The words of the poem were important. My father wanted me to remember those words. And then I heard crying. A man was crying. Quickly, I got up and put on my clothes.

In the sitting room, I found Josefa trying to comfort several of the soldiers who were no longer in the hall but in our room. Standing with their heads bowed, Saturnino and the crewmen of his boat were also in the room. When Josefa looked up, I saw there were tears in her eyes.

"Josefa," I asked, "what's wrong? What has happened?"

For a moment, she could not find her voice. "Teresa," she said, "Mr. Lincoln has been shot."

"What?"

One of the young soldiers was crying uncontrollably.

"The president was shot in the head, Teresa. He is not expected to live."

My hands became numb. I walked to the window and looked outside. I placed my fingers to the dampness of a glass pane but could feel nothing.

Suddenly, the door to the room opened, and the sergeant-of-the-guard rushed to where I stood and pushed me from the window.

"Snuff those candles!" he ordered. "Now!"

The room became lit only by a light in the hall as the soldiers readied their rifles.

"I'm sorry, ma'am," the sergeant said. "I didn't mean to hurt you, but you can't be standing in front of the window. And we need to keep it dark in here."

"Why?" I asked. "What's wrong?"

"We've just received word that Secretary Seward and his son have been wounded, and an attempt on the life of Vice President Johnson was foiled. There are reports of gunfire all over the capital. We don't know what's happening."

"Where is General Grant?"

"He's on the way to Burlington, ma'am. Secretary Stanton has sent a telegram for him to return to Washington City."

We spent the rest of the night huddled on the floor in darkness. All through the night, we heard the sounds of gunshots from all regions of the city and the rumble of caissons racing up and down Pennsylvania Avenue. At the light of day, I risked a peek outside because it had become so quiet I wondered if the city had been evacuated. Soldiers, gripping rifles with bayonets affixed, were standing in small groups. One man was gesturing toward the hills of Virginia that were now coming into view. As more light became available, I saw the flags at the capital at half-mast.

Just before noon, there was a knock at the door. Josefa had gone across to Saturnino's room, and the soldiers were outside. When I opened the door, my heart ached. Sam was standing in the hallway, and he looked so alone and forlorn.

"Sam. Please come in."

He walked slowly into the room and to the window where he stood to gaze outside.

After closing the door, I said, "Sam, I am so sorry."

He turned to look at me. "This is the darkest day of my life, Teresa."

"It is a dark day for the world."

"He was the greatest man I ever knew. More than that, he was a good man."

I went to Sam and embraced him. He hands were trembling. Finally, I convinced him to sit down and poured him coffee that had just been sent from the kitchen.

Presently, he regained his composure. "Teresa," he said, "I've been in contact with President Juarez's ambassador, Mateo Romero. He has explained to me the best way to get the weapons to the Juaristas. I have forty-five thousand repeating rifles on the way to the border at this moment. I'll have sixty-thousand troops on the Rio Grande by the end of May. I've yet to tell President Johnson about any of this and when I do, he may not approve. But I will do it whether he approves it or not. I may face a court-martial, but it will be done."

"It has to be done, Sam."

"It's all I know to do, Teresa. I have to move straight ahead as hard and fast as I can." He looked at me and smiled. "I guess I learned that from General Taylor."

"He hated war as much as you, Sam. That's why he said you were the best soldier he had ever seen, That's why you will go down in history as a great general."

"A great general? No, Teresa. I will go down in history as a butcher. They already say that about me."

"You saved lives, Sam, by the way you fought the war. You are going to save many more lives by what you are doing today."

He got to his feet and held my hands. "I'm going to send you and your friends to City Point, Virginia, where you'll be safe until Sheridan gets ready to go to Texas. We'll send you home on one of our warships."

"I want to go to Mexico, Sam. I need to be with Jorge."

"I know you do, but I still can't take a chance on your being captured. It will be safer for you to go to Mexico across the Rio Grande than by sea. Be patient, Teresa. I think this will be over quickly."

I walked him to the door. "Will I ever see you again?"

"We will see each other again, Teresa. Who knows? When this is all over, I might buy a little farm down there on the Rio Grande. Some of the best soil I've ever seen is in that valley. I could grow orange trees and raise a few horses."

"And you can teach me mathematics."

"If you will teach me Spanish."

We embraced, and then Sam Grant hurried away with his escort running to keep up with him.

It was another two months before Josefa and I climbed to the top of the rise west of Brownsville that overlooked where our farm had once been. To my surprise, a new house had taken its place. The rubble of the burnt-out warehouses nearby had been removed. Not knowing what to expect, we approached cautiously until I saw a familiar figure working a well-tended garden.

"Alma!" I shouted and ran to her.

"Teresa!"

Running from the barn, Ralph and Binu Seru joined in our round of hugs and kisses. My godson had grown into a handsome young man, almost as tall as his father.

"You rebuilt the house!" I exclaimed when we had all settled down. "The barn. The stable. Everything has been rebuilt!"

Ralph said, "We rebuilt it exactly as it was. We wanted it to be the same as when your grandmother and Lebe Seru and the Montemayors lived here."

"It belongs to Jorge now," Alma said. "The land is in his grandparent's name. This is his farm."

"Have you heard from Jorge?"

"We've heard nothing since you left."

I looked at the house and barn and stable. Even my chicken coops had been reconstructed.

"This farm," I said, "belongs to us all, Alma. We will go and put it in all our names. Slavery is over. We will put this property in all of our names."

That night, Esau and Tom Blue, after learning that Josefa and I had returned, came across from Matamoros; and we celebrated. Alma made her okra gumbo and cornbread. It had been so long since I had had vegetables from Alma's garden, I was unable to stop eating. She made a pecan pie, and I nearly ate it all by myself. And I drank a pitcher of cold goat's milk.

Esau told us that a great battle had been fought just a few weeks earlier not far from our farm. The Confederates had driven back a Union force trying to take Fort Brown and Brownsville. When they got word of Appomattox, many of the rebel soldiers simply drifted away to return home; and the Union army was able to secure the fort and the city.

"Some of the Confederates," Esau said, "have gone across the river to join the French."

Tom Blue added, "Hundreds of Confederate soldiers are crossing the Rio Grande everyday to join Marshal Bazaine's army. All up and down the Rio Grande, they are crossing. We know of four Confederate generals that have gone across: Magruder, Shelby, Slaughter, and Walker. Shelby took almost four hundred wagons of supplies across at Laredo not more than a week ago."

I told them of what had happened in Washington City and that Sheridan's soldiers would soon be arriving.

"Well," Esau said, "they better get here real soon. Marshal Bazaine is bringing his army closer to the Rio Grande each day, and the French have warships right off the mouth of the river. General Miramon and General Mejia have assembled a small Mexican army loyal to Maximilian."

It was not long before General Sheridan's army began to arrive in force and take up positions all along the river. General Sheridan maintained a reserve army in Houston under General George Armstrong Custer and another in San Antonio led by General Wesley Merritt. Though his force in Brownsville was commanded by General Fred Steele, General Sheridan himself spent most of his time on the Rio Grande and personally directed the operations. He stopped by our farm from time to time to pay a courtesy call, but he did not spend too much time in any one place. It was not his way.

Philip Sheridan was a restless man. He reminded me a little of Sam Grant. Not much over five feet in height, he was like a stick of dynamite with the fuse lit. One could see the desire in his dark eyes to fight the French. He was eager to take on Achille Bazaine and the army of the most powerful nation on earth. Partly out of respect for his victories in the just concluded civil war and partly out of fear, his men obeyed his every order without question and without delay.

Through constant movement and maneuvers, General Sheridan made his army of 60,000 on the north bank appear to be twice that number to the French on the south bank of the river. Columns of his soldiers would march west for several miles parallel to the river, fall back into the south Texas chaparral and then parade into Brownsville as if newly arriving from the north. He kept his engineers busy with the construction of pontoons that could be thrown across the river to allow the swift movement of his troops to the south if warranted. In the meantime, he maintained a steady flow of weapons and gunpowder flowing south to the Juaristas in the Sierra Madre. General Sheridan also halted the migration of Confederate veterans into Mexico.

Sam Grant's plan worked. The combination of arms to the Juaristas, which allowed them to put more pressure on the French in all areas of Mexico, and the threat of having to battle a battle-hardened Union army under the command of Philip Sheridan resulted in Louis Bonaparte's abandonment of his dream of a North American empire. With the Prussian army threatening his eastern borders, he could not risk the defeat of his elite troops over half a world away. Gradually and in stages, Marshal Bazaine began a withdrawal. At first, we feared a trick. He might be shifting his army from one place to another to try to lure Benito Juarez into the open and then attack him. Such tactics had been employed before. But when reports began to arrive that the French armies had begun to board transports at Vera Cruz and sail east, we knew the end was in sight.

Early one morning, just after opening my chicken coops and the goat sheds, I saw movement in the darkness near the embankment. Someone was coming up the road toward the house. My eyes adjusted to the faint light, and I put my hand to my mouth. It could not be, but it was.

"Jorge!" I whispered and ran to him.

His right arm still hung loosely at his side. With his left arm he held me tightly, and I kissed him again and again.

"Jorge, you've come home."

He looked into my eyes and smiled. "I've come for you, Teresa. The war is over in this country. Slavery has ended. I need you with me in Mexico."

We walked back to the embankment and sat down on the bluff overlooking the river. When I inadvertently touched his right arm, he winced.

"It still hurts?"

"It does not matter."

"We will take you to physicians in New Orleans."

"There is nothing that can be done," he said and stroked my hair. "I am resigned to it."

I placed my head against his shoulder. "Jorge, why can we not stay here? We can have a good life here."

"We must return to Mexico."

"But the French, Jorge, they are leaving."

"Yes," he said, nodding his head. "The French are leaving. But Maximilian has decided to stay. He will continue to fight us. He has the support of his Austrian troops and the support of Miramon and Mejia."

I could not stand it. Would the fighting never end?

"President Juarez needs me," he said. "He is moving the government to San Luis Potosi. There is much work to be done, Teresa. Eventually, we will defeat Maximilian. It is only a matter of time. But we must begin now to plan for the future. We must organize our resources and begin to build schools. We have to build roads and harbors. There is so much work to be done. Don Benito asked for you to come. He needs you. He needs us both."

"He asked for me to come to Mexico?"

"Yes. Mexico can be our home. Marry me, Teresa. Return with me to Mexico. I—"

I touched my fingers to his lips and nodded.

"You will marry me? You will go with me to Mexico?"

"Yes, Jorge," I said. "I will marry you, and we will go wherever you wish."

XV

Ours was not the largest wedding ever held in Texas, but no couple was ever blessed with such loyal friends to stand witness to their marriage. An elderly priest from Matamoros, who had served with my grandparents in Miguel Hidalgo's army, performed the ceremony. Esau and Tom Blue provided food and drink for all of our guests, which included many of the teamsters who had carried our letters back and forth over the years. People we had helped flee slavery came from Mexico to convey their wishes for our happiness. Some had made their homes in norther Mexico, and others were planning to return to friends and family they had left behind in Texas or other southern states. Many told us how happy our grandparents and Lebe Seru would be.

It was, of course, extremely sad for me when the day came for us to climb into the new wagon Ralph had made for us and go south. Alma was my sister. I do not think we could have parted except for the agreement we made to visit each year regardless of the great distance. Binu Seru assured me he would take care of my chickens and goats, and I promised I would look for the books he wanted on how to treat sick animals. Esau and Tom Blue were not young men, and I held them both for a long time before I got into the wagon. We laughed when we remembered the time Sam Houston had dunked Esteban and me into the Buffalo Bayou and they had stood watch for alligators and cottonmouth water moccasins.

It was a comfort to me that Josefa was going with us to Benito Juarez's administrative headquarters at San Luis Potosi. I knew there was no problem that could arise that Josefa could not solve. She was the only one left in Jorge's family; all the rest had given their lives to the cause of liberty and equality in Mexico. Jorge and I walked most of the time while Josefa drove the team pulling the wagon filled with our food and clothes and the many gifts our friends had given us to start our new life.

We arrived in San Luis Potosi, a town surrounded by barren hills, to the excitement created by the news that Maximilian had been forced to flee Mexico City. Republican armies under General Porfirio Diaz and General Mariano Escobedo were closing in on Maximilian's army of six thousand Austrian Hussars, two thousand Belgium Dragoons, and a force of some ten thousand Mexican royalists led by Miguel Miramon and Tomas Mejia. Inexplicably, rather than attempting to escape to the port of Vera Cruz, Maximilian was heading north. The small army with Benito Juarez was preparing to defend San Luis Potosi should Maximilian somehow succeed in eluding the pursuing armies of Diaz and Escobedo.

Immediately upon reaching the President's headquarters in a municipal building, we were taken to his office next to an indoor patio filled with flowering plants. Don Benito was working at his desk, but he quickly got to his feet when we entered and embraced us, taking care not to touch Jorge's arm.

"I am so happy you are here," he said. "I was worried. We have received word that bands of royalist cavalry have circled north of San Luis Potosi and are attempting to drive toward the Rio Grande. Apparently, they hope to join with what is left of Vidaurri's army and seize the northern provinces."

Jorge asked, "Is that why Maximilian chose to go north rather than to Vera Cruz?"

"We believe it is. He continues to believe veterans of the Confederate army will come to support him if he can establish a stronghold south of the Rio Grande."

"Philip Sheridan," I said, "will cross the river and destroy Maximilian's army if he goes there. General Grant will not allow Maximilian to rule even a portion of Mexico."

Don Benito took my hand. "What you did in going to General Grant saved many lives, Teresa, both in Mexico and in the United States."

I related to him what President Lincoln had said about wanting to meet him.

His dark eyes saddened. "I would like to have met Abraham Lincoln. His death is a great tragedy for his country. It is a loss for the entire world."

Jorge told Don Benito about our marriage.

Again, he embraced us. "I am so happy for you. And I am happy to have you both here with me. There is much work to be done. Many children, whose parents were killed in the fighting, have been brought to San Luis Potosi. We must organize our resources for their care. They will be our first priority."

"Don Benito," I asked, "what of Carlotta? Is she with Maximilian's army?"

"Señora von Hapsburg has returned to Europe to solicit support for their misguided adventure."

I thought immediately of Esteban. He may have returned to argue Maximilian's case with Louis Bonaparte. "Is it known who accompanied her to Europe?"

"We do not know. I only wish her husband had gone with her. He has had ample opportunity to leave Mexico. We have been told that Marshal Bazaine delayed his departure at Vera Cruz for weeks in hopes of persuading the young man to sail with him."

We rented a small house near the municipal building and began our work with the children made orphans by the years of warfare. Our immediate task was to obtain food from farmers in the region to feed the children. We then set up a network of correspondence throughout the nation to determine where other children in similar circumstances were being assembled and how best to move food to them or transport the children to a place where there was food.

We made plans to move the children should the Imperial Army approach San Luis Potosi, but that threat ended with the news of Maximilian's capture, along with Miramon and Mejia, at the town of Queretaro, some two hundred miles to the south. Telegraph lines were strung to San Luis Potosi; and General Escobedo, now in control of Queretaro, requested instructions as to what to do with Maximilian and his officers.

President Juarez directed that Maximilian von Hapsburg and his principal officers be put on trial for crimes against the Republic but that the soldiers in his Mexican armies be sent home to plant crops. The Austrian and Belgium soldiers were to be marched to Vera Cruz and put on ships for Europe.

When the lists of those against whom bills of indictment had been drawn began to arrive in San Luis Potosi, I searched for my brother's name. Most certainly, Esteban would be among those considered important enough to be placed on trial; but his name was on none of the lists. I feared that Esteban was not among those indicted because he had been killed.

"Jorge," I said. "I must go to Queretaro. Esteban may have been wounded. I have to help him if I can. He is my brother."

"I will go with you."

"Our work here is too important. I will go alone and return as soon as I can."

Josefa insisted on going with me. There continued to be reports of royalist bands refusing to accept Maximilian's defeat. Though most of the units were reported to be in the north, near the border, Josefa did not want me to travel alone and unprotected. She carried a repeating rifle and even made me strap on a revolver.

Queretaro was on a high plain surrounded by hills. Its many towers and domes and red-tiled roofs made it look like a city in Moorish Spain. Immediately upon our arrival, we went to the headquarters of General Escobedo to deliver communiques from President Juarez. The general was very helpful and personally guided me on a tour of the hospitals in what proved to be a futile effort to locate Esteban. I talked to the men on the burial details, but no one could remember a man who conformed to the description I gave of my brother.

"Señora Montemayor," General Escobedo said, "there is, of course, one who may be able to tell you what happened to your brother."

"Yes, General?"

"Maximilian von Hapsburg."

Though I realized Maximilian was the logical source of information about what had happened to Esteban, I was reluctant to see him. By no means did I feel guilty about my role in his downfall, but I was very uncomfortable with the prospect of seeing him since he had been found guilty of violating the laws against taking up arms against Mexican independence and assisting in a foreign invasion. The penalty for violation of these laws was death. Despite appeals for clemency sent by Queen Victoria, Emperor Franz Josef and other members of royal families in Europe, President Juarez had refused to grant a pardon. Even a personal letter from Victor Hugo did not persuade the president the court's sentence should be nullified.

When I hesitated, General Escobedo said, "You had better see him tonight, Señora Montemayor. The execution is at dawn."

I was escorted to the Capuchin convent, where Maximilian was being confined to the burial vault under the building. It was a morbid and damp place, lit only by the amber glow of beeswax candles. Approaching the open door of the room housing Maximilian, I halted when I saw him on his knees with a priest. The ragged, Prussian-blue uniform he was wearing only served to accentuate the grey pallor of his skin. His once golden beard was dry and matted.

Maximilian must have sensed my presence, because he looked up and, a smile forming on his lips, exclaimed, "Teresa!"

"Please," I said, glancing at the priest. "Do not get up. I will come back later."

But Maximilian was already on his feet and extending his hands to plead for my return. The priest, too, was anxious to escape from what was essentially a crypt.

Under the watchful eye of armed guards, Maximilian directed me to a wooden bench and took a seat on an inverted wooden bucket opposite me.

"Dear Teresa," he said, "I am so glad to see you. How are you?"

I had never felt more awkward in my life, but I knew I must try to be cheerful for a man who had only hours to live.

"I am fine. You look well."

His puffy, red-rimmed eyes did have a glimmer of the sparkle I had witnessed that night at the Grand Ball in Chapultepec Castle. He looked at peace with himself and resigned to his fate.

"And your young man? How is his arm? Our physicians worked very hard to save his arm."

"Jorge and I are now married."

He appeared genuinely pleased at this news. "That is wonderful, Teresa. I wish you and Jorge much happiness."

I wanted to extend the courtesy of asking of Carlotta, but I knew it would only remind him of their separation. It was absurd to inquire of his health since he was to be executed.

Sensing my discomfort, he said, "Do not be sad about me, Teresa. We are all pilgrims on this earth. We must each return home sooner or later."

"That is true," I said too quickly and with more force than I intended.

"I only hope," he said wistfully, "that my death will bring peace to this beautiful land. Mexico is beautiful, Teresa. The people in the countryside and in the villages are the most gentle and kind people I have ever known. I wish I had had an opportunity to spend more time with them. Will you and your husband live in Mexico?"

"That is our intention—" I had almost called him Señor von Hapsburg but realized he needed someone to treat him as a friend. ". . . Maxl. Mexico will be our home."

"I am glad."

Leaning forward, I asked, "Maxl, what happened to my brother?"

"You do not know?"

"No," I said and braced myself for bad news.

"Stefan led a company of cavalry to the Rio Grande. It was his hope to organize a force in the north that could return south and make it possible for us to surround San Luis Potosi and capture Señor Juarez. We have many loyal supporters among the people in the north under Governor Vidaurri."

I did not see that it served any purpose to tell him that the people of northern Mexico did not support him and that Vidaurri had maintained his position of power only through force. Nor did I discern what purpose would be served in telling him that I had helped to bring an American army to the Rio Grande, one that would have crushed any attempt he might have made to continue his empire.

"Alas," Maximilian sighed, "I have been told that Governor Vidaurri, too, has been captured and sentenced to death. I pray that Stefan has been able to take his family across the Rio Grande where they will be safe in Texas."

"His family?"

"I guess you do not know. Jeanne and little Max came from Vienna." He smiled. "And your mother, Baroness von Gorlitz. They arrived just after you left us. I insisted Stefan take them with him to the Rio Grande. In case we were unsuccessful, as now seems to be the case, I wanted them to be able to enter Texas."

I was not surprised that Cata Valeria had come to Mexico. Even in Europe, she must have seen what was inevitable, especially after Louis Bonaparte had abandoned Maximilian and Carlotta. She had come to protect her son. They were, I suspected, at that very moment in Texas. At least, they were safe.

Maximilian moved his right hand toward mine, hesitated, and then touched my hand. "Teresa, I must ask a favor."

"Yes?"

"Soon, they will come for me. Somehow, I must walk through that door and face the firing squad. Part of me is relieved that it will soon be over, but I must confess I have fear."

"That is understandable, Maxl," I said and held his hand with both of mine. "Who would not have fear?"

"What I would deeply appreciate, Teresa, is for you to be near when the time comes. You see, I have no one in my family here to stand with me. Charlotte, thank God, is in Belgium. My mother, my brothers, all my family, are in Europe. Stefan is like a brother, but he is not here. You are his sister. It will help knowing that you are near. I hope to die with some measure of dignity. I am a Hapsburg. I cannot bring shame to my family. If someone I know is there, I will not be so alone. I am afraid of dying alone."

"I will be there, Maxl."

"God bless you, Teresa," he said and stood, gathering himself to his full height. He bowed crisply. "And now, if you will excuse me, I shall see the priest."

At dawn, Josefa and I joined the thousands of Republican soldiers who had come to the Hill of Bells outside the city to stand in ranks and witness the execution. I had never known such silence among so many people. All that could be heard was the crowing of the roosters at the nearby farms. Maximilian was brought to the hill in an open carriage along with General Miguel Miramon and General Tomas Mejia. The three were to be executed together.

They were led to stand before a crumbling adobe wall. Maximilian was situated in the middle, but he insisted that General Miramon, as a past president of Mexico, should have that place of honor. Just after the members of the firing squad were marched into place, Maximilian was permitted to approach them and distribute gold coins to each. He requested they aim at his heart. The officer in charge of the squad asked if he had any last words to speak.

In a strong voice, Maximilian said, "I die in a just cause. I forgive all, and pray that all may forgive me. May my blood flow for the good of this land. *¡Viva Mexico!*"

When the officer brought down his sword, the rifles sounded in unison. The two generals were dead before their bodies touched the ground.

Maximilian sank to one knee. Grasping his right hand to the bloody spot on his white shirt, he cried, "*¡Hombre!*"

The officer in charge of the stunned firing squad drew his pistol, rushed forward and discharged a shot into the back of Maximilian's head. The bodies of the generals were carried to the cemetery for burial. Maximilian's body was taken to a chemist to be embalmed in preparation for its return to Austria.

Later that morning, many of us went to the Cathedral to celebrate a mass for those killed in the war. In the streets there was little evidence of a spirit of vindictiveness, due in part to the way Maximilian von Hapsburg faced his death.

By afternoon, Republican soldiers were beginning to leave the city in small groups, departing for their homes in all corners of the nation. The fighting was over. What Father Miguel Hidalgo had begun over a half century before in the village of Dolores on September 16, 1810, had finally been achieved. Mexico was an independent nation, governed by a freely elected president and Congress under a constitution that upheld the principals of liberty and equality.

When Josefa and I entered the headquarters of General Escobedo to bid him farewell, he rushed to me with a paper in hand and said, "I was afraid we had missed you. You have just received a telegram from your husband."

I read the words on the paper: "Esteban in our custody."

It was evening when we arrived in San Luis Potosi. I went directly to our house where Jorge told me my brother had already been tried and found guilty of violating the laws against taking up arms against Mexican independence and assisting in a foreign invasion. Esteban was being held in the municipal jail pending his execution before a firing squad. Jorge tried to comfort me and offered to go with me to the jail.

"I do not know if I can see him, Jorge. Esteban is going to die. It is because of what I did that he will die. How can I face him?"

"He has asked to see you, Teresa. His wife and son are with him." He stepped back. "Your mother is with him."

When we arrived at the jail, I paused to clear my head and watch the sun set over the dark mountain peaks to the west. Inside, Jorge waited in the office while a guard escorted me to the cellblock where my brother was the only prisoner. Entering the corridor outside the cells, I saw Esteban reaching through the bars to hold the hands of an attractive woman with a boy at her side. There was no mistaking that the boy was his son. His golden hair was the same color as Esteban's. All three looked at me with wide eyes, and I could sense their fear.

Cata Valeria was seated on a straight-back wooden chair, facing the cell. She did not turn when I entered the corridor. After the guard had left, I walked to the cell and stood directly behind my mother.

"Teresa," Esteban said, gently letting go of his wife's hands and moving toward me. "Thank you for coming."

I nodded and looked down at the boy.

Smiling, Esteban said, "Teresa, this is Jeanne and our son, little Max."

Jeanne crept forward to extend her hand. Clinging to his mother's elegant silk dress, Max averted his eyes to the floor.

"*Buenas noches, Jeanne,*" I said, taking her hand. "*Buenas noches, Max.*"

Jeanne embraced me.

Cata Valeria abruptly got up from the chair and walked away a few feet to stand with her back to me.

"Mother," Esteban said. "Please. You have not seen Teresa for so many years. Please, Mother."

When Jeanne stepped back, Max worked up the courage to look at me. "Are you my aunt?"

"Yes, Max. My name is Teresa."

"Are you a Juarista?"

"Yes. I am."

Jeanne said, "You need not be afraid, Max."

He looked at her and said something in French I did not understand.

For a moment, Jeanne looked at the floor and then at me. "It is your pistol, Teresa. He is afraid of your pistol."

Cata Valeria turned, and her eyes fixed on the weapon I had forgotten I was still wearing. Looking at her, I was reminded how young she was when I was born. She was still an astonishingly beautiful woman, little changed from that day she had boarded the steamer at Houston Town to go to Europe. She looked at Esteban, and I became aware that I was standing close enough to my brother that he could easily reach through the bars and take my pistol. I did not move.

Cata Valeria spoke to Esteban in French.

"No, Mother," he said. "I cannot."

Her eyes blazed when she looked at me and said, "Your brother is to be executed at dawn. Use your gun to free him. Help him escape this terrible place."

"What would you have me to do?"

"Use your gun on the guards!"

"My husband is outside. He is an official in the government of Mexico. Would you have me shoot my husband?"

"You do not have to shoot him. There are only two guards. You can threaten them and lock them in the cell until Esteban is far away."

"Mother," Esteban said. "Do not ask this of Teresa. It is not right."

When Cata Valeria stepped toward me, I wondered if she was going to attempt to seize the gun. I was not certain I could stop her if that was her intention. Halting just short of where I stood, she said, "Then go to Benito Juarez. Ask him to pardon your brother. It is within his power to spare Esteban's life."

I looked at Esteban. "Have you petitioned the president for a pardon?"

"Yes. As did Jeanne and Mother."

"What did he say?"

"He said he must abide by the decision of the court."

Since it was the position he had taken in the case of Maximilian, I was not surprised.

"He will listen to you," Cata Valeria said. "He is in your debt."

"In my debt?"

"We know what you did," she said angrily. "If not for you Esteban would not be here, condemned to die like a common criminal! Maximilian would be alive. We know about your visit with General Grant! How could you do that to your own brother?"

I stepped away from the cell and looked at Jeanne. "Please. May I visit with my brother alone. It will be for only a few minutes, and you can return."

She nodded and led both Max and Cata Valeria outside.

Before the door closed, Cata Valeria shouted, "Go to Benito Juarez! Save your brother's life. You must do it! Beg him for your brother's life!"

I put my hands through the bars to Esteban. He held them tightly and looked into my eyes. Smiling, he said, "I'm afraid she has been quite a nuisance. She has been to see Benito Juarez dozens of time. She has gotten on her knees and begged him to pardon me."

"He does not want her to get on her knees."

"I know, Teresa. President Juarez came to see me to explain why he cannot pardon me. He is a good man. I know that now. I wish I had known it before. I—"

Esteban stopped because his voice was wavering. Tears came to his eyes, and I touched my lips to his face to comfort him.

"Oh, Teresa," he whispered. "I am so sorry! Nothing happened the way we planned. So many people have died. And now, Maxl is dead. How did he die, Teresa? Was he brave?"

"He died with dignity. He forgave and asked to be forgiven."

"Poor Maxl. I should have been at his side. I wish we could have died together."

"Cata Valeria was right, Esteban. I bear responsibility for what happened. I went to see General Grant in Washington City. I urged him to send his soldiers to the Rio Grande and to provide weapons and gunpowder to the Juaristas."

"You did what you had to do."

"I wish you could have known Sam Grant, Esteban. He and our grandmother were very close when he came to the Rio Grande during the war. She was like a second mother to him."

"Abuela," he said and lowered his head. "If not for me, she would still be alive."

"She loved you, Esteban. You know she loved you."

He looked at me and smiled. "I've been thinking a lot about when we were children. I remember Abuela and Abuelo. They did love us, didn't they?"

"Yes."

His smile broadened. "I've been thinking about Old Chief. There was nobody like Old Chief. It is too bad he never became President of the United States."

"He would have made a good president."

I did not want to leave, but Jeanne and little Max were outside. They should be the ones with whom Esteban would spend the last hours of his life. It was heart-wrenching to pull my hands away from his and look into my brother's eyes for what I knew would be the last time. I kissed him and walked quickly to the door and into the office.

Jeanne embraced me before leading little Max back to see his father. Cata Valeria lingered behind, and I waited for her to say what she must.

"You can save your brother's life, Teresa. Benito Juarez will listen to you. Go to him."

I stood in the office and watched her return to the cellblock ahead of the guard who locked the door behind her.

We left the jail and walked back to our house. I went to a chair by the window and stared into the darkness of the night. Jorge brought me a cup of warmed milk, but I did not think my stomach would tolerate even that.

Finally, I turned to my husband and asked, "Should I go to Don Benito? Should I petition him to pardon Esteban?"

"That is something you will have to decide, Teresa." He looked out the window. "There is a light in Don Benito's house. He has not yet retired for the night."

"He would not pardon Maximilian. Many people from all over the world wrote to him and asked that he pardon Maximilian, but he would not do it."

"Benito Juarez believes in the law, Teresa. When the law is based upon the principles of liberty and equality, it must be obeyed. No person can be above the law."

"What right do I have to ask President Juarez to go against what he believes? I know he does not wish for Esteban to die anymore than I do. He does not want anyone to die."

I rose from the chair and paced the floor of the little room containing so many things given to us by the people we had left behind in Texas. There were many items we had yet to unpack because the government would soon be transferred to Mexico City, and we would have to move again.

"Jorge, I need to walk. I feel as though I cannot breathe."

"Do you wish for me to go with you?"

"I think it is best if I am alone for awhile. I must decide what to do."

Before leaving the house, I unstrapped the gunbelt and placed it on the little desk we both used to write our correspondence. I wanted nothing more to do with guns or weapons of any kind. We lived on the edge of town, and I followed a dirt pathway past a dairy goat farm where the animals had long since entered their sheds for the night. The farmer's dogs came out to greet me. I clapped my hands to send them back to the house so they would not follow me up the trail their masters used each day to herd the goats to pasture on the hill. It was dark; but as long as I followed the soft dirt path, I knew there were no obstacles to block my way.

Further up the hill, there were outcrops of stone and thorn bushes; and so it became necessary to be more careful. I was wearing straw sandals which did not offer much protection for my feet. Eventually, I came to the top of the hill which was flat like a plateau and supported islands of junipers and thick red sage. Out of breath from the climb, I found a clearing and sat down.

Looking across the broad expanse of land stretching miles to the south, I noticed faint flickers of light on the horizon. At first I was startled because it reminded me of the flashes made by cannons fired at night. I jumped to my feet, horrified by the thought that soldiers in one of the Imperial Armies had reassembled to launch a new assault on the Juaristas. Miramon and Mejia were dead, but there were always younger officers to take the place of fallen leaders. It occurred to me that the French may have returned. Carlotta may have been successful in her bid to get Louis Bonaparte to reverse his decision to abandon his plan for a North American empire.

I relaxed as I recognized the low rumbling noise was not artillery, but thunder. A great storm was building in the south. There was even the faint aroma of rain which would be welcome in the parched land around San Luis Potosi. I sat back down and tried to collect my thoughts.

Closing my eyes, I tried to clear my head of the image of the way Esteban had looked at me in the jail. He wanted me to do something to prevent his life from being ended. He was looking to his sister to help him stay alive. I was his only hope. But I would not do it. I would not go to Benito Juarez and ask him to pardon my brother. And why not? Were legalities and abstract principles more important to me than my brother's life? Or did I not go to the president because I believed Esteban should be punished? He had committed a crime, a very great crime. Many people had lost their lives because of what he had done. What Esteban said was right: if not for him, my grandmother would be alive. Lebe Seru and Jorge's grandparents would be alive.

Slowly, I got to my feet and stood at the edge of a steep cliff on the east side of the hill. How many years had the American Civil War been extended because the French arranged for cotton from the southern states to be exported through the Mexican ports? Sam Grant had said it. The guns and gunpowder the French allowed to be sold to the Confederate Armies had cost thousands of lives that would not have had to be sacrificed if Louis Bonaparte had not placed Maximilian von Hapsburg on the throne of a Mexican Empire. Was it my anger over these things that made me refuse to even attempt to save Esteban's life? Was I seeking retribution in the form of my brother's life?

As I watched the storm to the south grow larger, I became aware that I was not alone on the hill. Someone was behind me. Turning quickly, I put my hand where my pistol would have been when I saw a figure in the darkness.

The person drew closer, and I recognized who it was.

"Cata Valeria," I whispered.

My mother came closer.

"You followed me."

"I did not know you were here, Teresa. I needed to get away for awhile. Jeanne and Max should have time alone with Esteban."

Her attire was inappropriate to climbing a dirt trail to the top of a rocky hill. Her ivory colored dress was made of silk.

Looking to the south, she said, "A storm is coming."

"Yes. The wind is beginning to increase."

For a moment, Cata Valeria stared at the flashes of light on the horizon and then, her voice soft and low, said:

> *Be still, deadening north wind.*
> *South wind come, you that waken love.*
> *Breathe through my garden,*
> *and let its fragrance flow;*
> *and the Beloved will feed amid the flowers.*

She tilted her head at my puzzlement. "You do not remember?"

"No."

"They are words from a poem by San Juan de la Cruz. When you were small, we would go to the seashore to collect shells. If the breeze was strong, you would cry. Your father would hold your hand and recite those words to you. It made you smile."

"Yes," I said. "Galveston Bay. I remember."

Cata Valeria studied my face as if she had never seen me before. "You have grown into a beautiful woman, Teresa. You remind me very much of Carmen. You favor her."

"Esteban told you what happened to your mother?"

"Yes," she said and looked again to the south. "It did not surprise me. Nothing, absolutely nothing, would deter Carmen from her cause. You are like her that way. Her cause was everything. It was more important than me. After I was born, she left me with her father and ran away to fight for her cause. She died for her cause. She was probably very happy in the way she died."

Though her anger had abated, her voice was edged with bitterness. I understood something about Cata Valeria that I had never grasped before. "You resented Carmen for leaving you with her father."

She looked at me. "No, Teresa. I did not resent being left with Don Esteban. I had a very good life. I wanted for nothing, and my grandfather loved me. He was a good and kind man. If I had never come to Texas, I would not even have known my mother. She never once came to see me in all those years."

"She did not wish to put you in danger. She was a follower of Miguel Hidalgo. She stayed away from you to protect you."

"That is what she said."

"You are angry at Carmen, even now. You have always been angry with her, and your anger at her somehow became anger at me. Even when we lived in Houston Town, I sensed your anger at me, the same as with my grandmother."

"How could I be angry with you? You were just a little girl."

I was a little girl, but now I was a woman; and I was looking at my mother for the first time through the eyes of a woman. "You were angry with Carmen, and your anger affected how you treated me. You were always distant and cold. You were not that way with Esteban."

"Perhaps you are right, Teresa. I was angry with Carmen."

"Why?"

She folded her arms against her body. "Carmen and my father fought on the side of the Republicans in Texas. They were with those who made a rebellion against Santa Anna. If that had not happened, your father would never have had to come to Texas. He was an officer in Santa Anna's army. I followed him with you and Esteban, because I could not bear to be separated from him. We had to stay in Texas because we had helped my parents. We could not go home. Santa Anna would not allow it.

"And then Texas took your father from me. That dreadful disease. If we had never gone to Texas, he would have lived. He might be alive today. It was not enough that Carmen left me for her cause. I did not care. But it was her cause that took your father's life. And I loved your father."

She had never spoken to me of these things, and I was moved. "I suppose I can understand why you resented Carmen, but why would you be angry at me?"

"You were so much like Carmen, Teresa, even as a little girl. You had such an indomitable will. I would tell you to stay home, but you would disobey and run off to be with that bizarre man. And when we went to Austria, you refused to come. You promised you would come. Carmen said she would bring you. Both of you promised me. But you did not. By then Carmen had fashioned you into a perfect copy of herself. You both stayed to fight for Carmen's cause which, I suppose, became your cause. You did not think of me. You did not consider what I wanted."

"Do you not think I wanted my daughter with me in Austria? I wanted to give you things and make your life good. I did not want my daughter to be in Texas living in the forest like some wild animal. I knew what Carmen was doing, and I knew what could happen to you. Not a day of my life has passed that I have not thought of how my father was killed. Do you think I wanted what happened to my father to happen to you?"

"Your father was brave."

"I know my father was brave, but that did not make it any easier for me. I loved my father. I did not want what happened to him to happen to my children. Is that so very wrong?"

The flashes in the southern sky were becoming much brighter, and the thunder was louder. I watched the storm as I considered my mother's words. She was speaking from the heart, and I thought I understood what she was telling me.

When I again looked at Cata Valeria, I saw that she was no longer watching me. Her gaze was fixed behind me, and there was fear in her eyes. The intensity of her expression was such, I hesitated to look at what caused her distress.

Turning, I saw a small woman standing some twenty feet behind me.

My mother drew back. Concerned she might fall over the cliff, I rushed to take her arm. She was trembling.

"What is wrong? Who is that woman?"

Cata Valeria looked at me and then back at the woman who was coming toward us. I saw the deep scar across her forehead. And I saw the blue cape she held tightly against the brisk wind. It was the same woman who had taken my pendant at Galveston Bay so many years ago. It was the woman who had given my brother the broth the night he had been hurt.

"Mother, who is she?"

At first, Cata Valeria could not speak. Finally, she whispered, "It is . . . It is Doña Lupe."

The woman had stopped several yards from where we stood. Her face could be seen clearly only when the lightning flashed. I watched as my mother walked slowly toward Doña Lupe. She knelt before the small woman and bowed her head. Doña Lupe spoke, but I could not hear what she said. She placed something in Cata Valeria's hands.

"Mother," I asked when she returned to me, "what is it? What did she give you?"

For a moment, Cata Valeria looked into my eyes, and then she reached up quickly and secured a cord around my neck. Looking down, I saw that it was the jade pendant. It was the carving of the head of Chimalma above the Toltec Cross.

"It is yours," I said. "She gave it to you."

Cata Valeria placed a finger to my lips. "It is for you, Teresa."

"It is the one you gave me when I was a baby?"

"No," she said. "I never gave this pendant to you, Teresa. Carmen gave it to me when I was born. I wore it until your father died. I no longer wanted it after that, and I returned it to my mother. I guess you do not remember, but she gave it to you. Carmen gave it to you. But now, I have given it to you. That is what Doña Lupe wanted me to do."

I looked at where the small woman had been standing, but she was no longer there. Thinking she had gone down the hill, I started after her; but Cata Valeria took my arm. "Let her go, Teresa. Do not try to follow her. Not now. Stay with me."

Turning, I embraced my mother.

"Teresa," she whispered, "I love you."

"I love you, Mother."

The wind began to blow harder, and drops of rain started to fall. Taking my mother's hand, I led her down the trail and back to our house. Because I was shielding my eyes with my hand, I did not at first see Jorge outside beside our carriage, which had been harnessed to a team of four horses. He called my name.

"Jorge!" I shouted above the noise of the wind. "What are you doing? Why are the animals in the rain?"

He wrapped both of his arms around me and held me tightly. Looking over his shoulder, I saw my brother in the carriage. He was with Jeanne and Max.

"Jorge, what is happening?"

"Don Benito has released Esteban to my custody."

I saw Josefa with three saddled horses. "But the sentence, Jorge? What of the sentence?"

"I am taking your brother to Texas. Let us hurry. We will stay ahead of the storm if we leave now."

"Jorge. Did Don Benito pardon Esteban?"

"No, Teresa. He did not. I have assumed responsibility for Esteban."

"If you take Esteban to Texas, Jorge, we shall never be able to return to Mexico."

"That is right. We can never return."

Jorge lifted me to the back of one of the horses. He and his aunt rode the other two. Esteban helped our mother into the carriage, took the reins and followed us out of San Luis Potosi.

Our friends in Texas were happy we had come home. For a season, we lived on the north bank of the Rio Grande but then moved to a farm on the Guadalupe River east of San Antonio, where Esau and Tom Blue built a hotel and a restaurant. Alma and I supplied them with vegetables and eggs and milk from our farm. Binu Seru took care of our farm animals as well as the mules and oxen Ralph, Josefa and my brother used to pull their freight wagons between San Antonio and Houston. Binu Seru also attended the school that Jorge opened for young men and women who wished to study the arts and sciences. My nephew attended Jorge's school, and his mother taught languages there.

Our first child was a girl. We named her Maria del Carmen. It was only when Cata Valeria returned with Jacob that I placed Carmencita in my mother's arms and tied the leather cord holding the jade pendant around her neck. She grasped the stone tightly in her little fist and smiled. Looking down into those dark eyes, I could see my grandmother. I could see my grandfather. I saw Jorge's grandparents. But I also saw Lebe Seru. I saw all those who had given their lives so that others could live in freedom. I saw their love. As my daughter opened her hand to gaze at the stone carving, I knew she would honor the memory of all these people; and I knew she would always be protected.